Éilís Ní Dhuibhne

the shelter of neighbours

BLACKSTAFF PRESS

BELFAST

ACKNOWLEDGEMENTS

Versions of the following stories have been previously published:

'It is a miracle', *Arrows in Flight: Short Stories from a New Ireland*, ed. Caroline Walsh (London: Townhouse/Scribner's, 2002); 'The moon shines clear, the horseman's near', *Phoenix Book of Irish Short Stories*, ed. David Marcus (London: Phoenix, 2005); 'A literary lunch', *Faber Book of Irish Short Stories*, ed. David Marcus (London: Faber and Faber, 2007); 'The man who had no story' and 'Sugar Loaf', in *Éilís Ní Dhuibhne: Perspectives*, ed. Rebecca Pelan (Dublin: Arlen House, 2009); 'Trespasses', *Best European Fiction 2011*, ed. Aleksandar Hemon (Champaign/London: Dalkey Archive Press, 2010), 'The Yeats', *John McGahern Yearbook*, volume 4 (Galway: National University of Ireland, Galway, 2011).

First published in April 2012 by
Blackstaff Press
4c Sydenham Business Park
Belfast BT3 9LE
with the assistance of
The Arts Council of Northern Ireland

Reprinted November 2012

Typeset by CJWT Solutions, St Helens, England
Printed in Great Britain by the MPG Books Group

A CIP catalogue record for this book
is available from the British Library

ISBN 978-0-85640-886-1

www.blackstaffpress.com
www.blackstaffpress.com/ebooks

For Olaf
and Nadezhda

Contents

The man who had no story

Needless to say, it's bucketing down like, like I don't know what. Like rocks from an Icelandic volcano, or like rain from an Irish sky. Which is after all what it is. The Irish summer monsoon, just as wet and blinding as the Irish winter monsoon, or the Irish spring monsoon, or the Irish autumn monsoon. Even in sunshine (and when did we last experience that?) the M50 has been as easy to navigate as the seventh circle of hell all this blighted year. For most of it you have to drive at sixty kilometres an hour, steering on a narrow track between rows of red and white cones, a good few knocked over and rolling around, doing their best to trick you into crashing into something and causing mayhem and painful death. You'd be a lot safer and probably a lot quicker going through town. But you never know, and at least it's all moving along now, at this in-between time. Four o'clock. Sunday. Not many people leave town so late, and the great return from down the country has not yet started.

Finn O'Keefe is going down the country for his holidays.

Gráinne, his wife, is in the summer house they've rented for July and half of August, at a high enough price, down there in the south. They 'moved down' – he liked saying that, even to himself – three weeks ago. The plan was that they would relax, go for walks in the green hills and swims in the bracing ocean, eat good little things bought in the local town. He was going to write. He's a teacher – so is she. He writes in the summer, is the theory, and Gráinne chills. But it hasn't worked. Not after the first few days, when he wound down by reading a travel book about Tuscany called *Bella Tuscany*, which was so good that he started writing a similar sort of thing except about the south-west of Ireland. 'Bella Kerry' – a working title. Obviously. He got right into it, and when you thought about it, the place had plenty in common with Tuscany. The sweet smell of the clover, the wildflowers all over the place. Cute little shops and restaurants in the town. The farmers' market. It hadn't rained the first few days, so that had encouraged the comparison. They'd been able to go for long walks up the hill at the back of the house – stunning with gorse and heather, purple and yellow, exactly the same colours as the Wexford football jersey, as he noted in his writer's notebook, in case the simile would come in handy. (How could it? Who cared that the mountain where Finn was on holiday reminded him of the Wexford strip? His writer's notebook was full of such useless items.) Those first days, they let the waves and the wind do their work. Of cleaning out their cobwebbed heads. Their sticky, tacky, tired-out hearts.

Then the troubles started. First, the rain. Then Gráinne's back acted up. After all the housework before they left home – she had to do it, nobody lifted a finger apart from her, all that – and the long drive. A whole day in the medical centre – a country medical centre, local colour, characters. OK. OK. He wrote about it in his 'Bella Kerry' book – you could include some bad stuff in that sort of book, as long as it had a bit of eccentricity, and as long as you kept it to a minimum. One flat tyre, say, to ten examples of rural bliss. One bad back to ten gastronomic orgasms: food was the fuel of the genre.

Next thing, their son, Mattie, who is minding the house in Dublin, which to him means putting out food for the cat when the thought strikes him – it could be every two days – phoned. The cat's sick. Doesn't eat anything. Doesn't even move. *Quelle surprise!*

But Gráinne worried. So back to town they went, the two of them. Three days running to the vet with the sick cat – Pangur Bán, she is called, the most common cat name in Ireland, thanks to that quirky monk who wrote about his cat in Old Irish high on a mountain in Austria in the eighth century or something. Everyone's favourite poem. Pangur, apparently – their Pangur, the real cat, born in the twentieth century but living still in this one, a two-century cat – may have Aids, or cancer, or both. She definitely has a heart condition and there's something wrong with her kidneys. And she's dehydrated. Hard to explain that, said the vet, giving Finn a suspicious look. It was Finn's guess that Pangur hadn't been given a drink of water or milk or anything at all in approximately ten days. But he didn't reveal this to the vet, who disapproved of him. As if it was his fault the cat was sick. Which of course it was, in a way. Maybe the owners of ageing cats should not go off down the country to chase words. Or go anywhere, to do anything.

The vet ran tests, cleaned out Pangur's system with a twenty-four-hour drip, administered a few injections, all of which Pangur hated. Then he prescribed antibiotics and heart pills, and advised, in that solemn, slow voice of his, that they would have to consider things and make a decision. Meaning, Finn supposed, it was soon to be curtains for Pangur. Seven hundred euros later and now they should consider putting her down. Shouldn't the vet have mentioned that before?

Anyway, after all the medication, Pangur looked not too bad. So Gráinne decided they should bring her back with them, down the country. 'Mattie loves Pangur; she's his cat.' Yes. Indeed. He had brought her home one day when he was ten and she was four weeks old, a little cute white kitten with bright blue eyes – he had fair hair then, too, falling like flax into his eyes, also blue, sparkling like the sea in sunshine – thirteen years ago. Finn and Gráinne had never wanted a cat. Or any pet. 'But I don't think he looks after her properly. It's not fair to expect that of him. She needs a lot of attention and he's got his own life.' Mattie is busy, reading Nietzsche, playing the guitar, and watching television, not necessarily in that order, from midday when he gets up until 1 a.m. when he hits the sack after his long strenuous days sitting on the sofa.

Pangur isn't keen on long journeys. (Or short journeys. She howls her head off even on the five-minute drive to the vet.) But she came to Kerry, in her cage, on the back seat of the car. After four hours, she stopped howling and dozed off – you couldn't say she slept, as such. It was more that she collapsed into a state of semi-consciousness, like a prisoner whose body just can't take any more torture. They made lots of stops to encourage her to drink a drop of water, nibble some 'treats'. She refused every time, but Gráinne kept on trying.

To Finn's amazement, Pangur survived the trip and began to recover – the change of scene seemed to do her good. Being away from home worked for her the way it's supposed to work for a human, though often doesn't. This cheered them both up no end. For once they'd done the right thing, by the cat. Instead of killing her, as suggested by the vet, they'd taken her down the country for a holiday, and she got better.

Then, no sooner was Pangur settled in, eating a mouthful of treats and a tiny can of gourmet cat-food a day, than Mattie was on the phone again. He never phoned when things were OK, so Finn smelt a rat as soon as he overheard Gráinne talking to him. Mattie always talked to her first; even if Finn answered the phone, he'd ask for his mother.

A mouse. Mattie had seen one, in the conservatory, eating from the cat dish. A dish of cat-food that had been left out even though there wasn't a cat in the house. It made Finn want to puke, thinking about it. And – troubles don't come singly – the fridge had stopped working.

They'd have to go back to Dublin, obviously, to deal with the mouse and the fridge. But somebody had to stay and mind Pangur. It wouldn't be fair to put her through the ordeal of the journey again. Or Gráinne, with her back.

Finn had spent a whole week in Dublin, and now he's on the road south for the third time in a few weeks. Maybe his break can start at last. July is nearly over. Before you know it, it will be September. Can he write 'Bella Kerry' in four weeks? He wonders how long the woman who wrote *Bella Tuscany* spent doing hers, Frances something – he likes her style; he must google her sometime, see what she looks like. He envisages her as laughing, with shining fair hair. Tall and slender – she mentions, on page fifty, that she has 'long rabbit feet'. A gazelle, undoubtedly.

The Red Cow roundabout. It's in transition from being a

roundabout to being a cloverleaf junction and is essentially a twenty-first-century torture chamber – last time he took the wrong lane, he found himself at the toll bridge having to pay to cross over, do a U-turn, then pay to get back, losing forty minutes and four euro as punishment for his mistake. But it's a bit easier this time; they've put up a signpost. Soon enough he's escaped to the N7. From then on, it should be plain sailing down across Ireland. And apart from some thunderstorms – Laois has transmogrified into the fifth circle of hell – this turns out to be right.

'Bella Kerry'. It's easy to do. But he has to write something else. Not a rip-off of *Bella Tuscany*, which, he knows quite well, is a waste of time and will never get finished. Basically, writing it is an excuse for not writing something else. This happens more and more, he finds. Something else is what he's always writing, never whatever it is he's supposed to be doing. Which is, at the minute, a short story. A short story that will make his name. Again. Or even a short story that he knows in his heart is a good short story, no matter what anyone else thinks.

He used to write them when he was younger. He even published a collection once, ages ago. Retrospectively, it seems to him he wrote those stories effortlessly. Some autobiographical, about things that happened to him – mainly women ditching him, him ditching women. (This was before he was married, of course.) Made-up ones about people he saw on the bus or the train, mainly about women ditching them, or them ditching women – these imagined lives bore a close resemblance to his own.

But now he can't think of anything to write about. He never thought much of his talent but, looking back, he admires his younger self, the self who had the wit, the imagination, the energy, to write any kind of story, even a bad one. How on earth did he do it?

He hasn't the foggiest idea.

He hasn't the foggiest idea, although he is a teacher of creative writing. He tells other people how to do it and encourages them. It always surprises him that they can write anything, and he's even more surprised that plenty of it is good. And how they can write, all those kids! He just tosses them an idea, a topic, an opening line (a trigger, he calls it; he's getting tired of that 'creative writing' word but hasn't come up with a satisfactory alternative), and off they go. Writing for all they're worth. Trouble is, he can't give himself a trigger. Well, that's not true, of course he can – he knows hundreds, literally, enough to get him through a ten-year course with the same class, although no course actually lasts longer than ten weeks. But none of those triggers fires anything, shoots anything – whatever triggers do. None of them hits the target. Because his imagination is dead. Dead as a fox on the motorway (he's passed three of them, flattened like eggs in the pan, poor buggers). He used to have loads of imagination. It was his hallmark. But it's gone, like the colour in his hair, and the other things he had when he was younger. Such as? *Joie de vivre.* Passion. Bright dreams.

There's a story he heard. On the radio. There used to be storytellers in the place they are staying, that deep, green valley on the edge of the ocean, but not any more, that he knows of. It was a recording of a storyteller who used to live down the road from his rented cottage, in the same townland, which is Baile na hAbha, the town by the river. 'The Man Who Had No Story'. That was the name of the story and that's what it was about. The man – let's say his name was Dermot O'Keefe, from Baile na hAbha – was looked down upon by the people. Everyone was expected to have at least one story they could entertain their neighbours with. Good storytellers knew a few hundred, the professor guy who was commenting on this story said. But Dermot hadn't even one. He was hoping for a free night's lodging but he couldn't sing for his supper, as it were. And it just wouldn't do. The man was thrown out of the house in disgrace.

'Go to the well and fetch a bucket of water,' the woman of the house said crankily. 'You'd better do something for your keep.'

And at the well poor old crestfallen Dermot came across some fairies. And the fairies lifted him up in a blast of wind and swept him through the sky. East and west and north and south they carried him. And he landed in front of a big house. And in the house a wake was going on. As soon as he stepped inside the door, a very nice-looking girl with curly black hair asked Dermot to sit beside her. Which he did. Gladly.

And the man of the house said: 'We need a bit of music. Somebody go and find the fiddler.'

The beautiful girl said: 'No need. The best fiddler in Ireland is sitting here beside me. Dermot O'Keefe from Baile na hAbha.'

Dermot was gobsmacked. 'Who, me? Sure, I've never played a tune in my life,' he said.

But lo and behold there was a fiddle in one of his hands and a bow in the other, and the next thing, he was playing the most beautiful music anyone had ever heard.

And then, later, the man said: 'Somebody go and get the priest to say Mass, because we want to get the corpse out of the house before daybreak.'

'No need,' said the curly-haired girl. 'Isn't the best priest in Ireland right here beside me?'

Dermot. Up he stood and said Mass, and all the prayers afterwards, as if he'd been doing it every day of his life.

Then four men took the coffin on their shoulders to carry it to the graveyard. There were three very short men and one very tall man. And the coffin was wobbling all over the place.

'Somebody call the doctor!' said the man of the house. 'So he can shorten the legs of this long fellow, and make the coffin even.'

'Isn't the best doctor in Ireland here at hand!' said the lovely girl. 'Dermot O'Keefe from Baile na hAbha.'

And – to his own surprise – Dermot performed the amputation like some millionaire surgeon in the Blackrock Clinic. And off they all went to the graveyard. But just before they reached it, a big blast of wind came and swept Dermot off his feet. And he was blown east and blown west and north and south. And when he was finished being blown all over the place, down he fell at the well, where he had gone to fetch the water. The bucket was full to the brim with sparkling clean water. He picked it up and brought it into the house.

'Well now, Dermot,' said the woman of the house. 'Can you tell us a story?'

'I can,' said Dermot, pleased with himself. 'Indeed. I am the man who has a story to tell. You'll never believe what's after happening to me ...'

'This tale seems to tell us that if you just let things happen to you, you can make a story out of them,' says the professor.

God, these guys! thinks Finn. So patronising. As if that isn't obvious to anyone.

'Basically the story is saying, get a life, then tell your story.'

'Yes,' says the interviewer. 'And get confidence in yourself, so you can make things up? Play the fiddle, even if you never learnt.'

'It's saying that, too,' agrees the learned one thoughtfully.

Because how can you play the fiddle if you haven't learnt, is probably what he's thinking. Every eejit knows it's out of the question. Anyone can have a go at hacking off a leg, for sure, but nobody without the gift can squeeze a tune out of a violin.

But the professor says, 'Yes, Dermot has never played the fiddle, and yet he can play a good tune, when requested.'

'And he has never amputated a person's leg,' says the interviewer. There's a critical edge creeping into his voice, a hint of a sneer. 'That's a bit weird, isn't it? How did your man feel, minus a chunk of his legs? I mean, he's not even a corpse, he's alive as you and me and, *whap*, off with half his leg! Nothing about anaesthetic.' The interviewer chuckles and so does the professor. Both sound uneasy.

'Of course, the fairies have given him the gift,' says the professor.

'The gift of being a surgeon?' asks the interviewer, in a dangerous, neutral tone.

'The gift of imagination,' says the professor emphatically. 'Imagination,' he repeats. 'What they are telling Dermot is that it doesn't matter if he's a fiddler or a priest or a doctor, he can make believe that he is. In a story. He can make it all up.'

'That's it, I suppose,' says the interviewer. He cheers up. 'It's just fiction! A pack of lies. Blame the fairies for it, folks!' He's nearly singing, the interviewer. 'And now we'll go east and go west and east again – to a commercial break.'

Get a life. And use your imagination. It's the sort of thing

Finn tells his own students. In fact, he could give them this story, as a sort of insight into the history of story in Ireland – they might like that. As for him, well, he's had as much life, interesting life, as he's ever going to get, and he doesn't believe in the fairies. In the old days, the storytelling days, they were always there. To frighten ordinary, decent people. And to give the gift of music, or story, or song, to the other ones. To the artists in the community.

The mouse was, as Finn had suspected, a rat. 'And they usually aren't alone, my friend,' said the rat-man. He kept addressing Finn as 'my friend', which was nice – the kind of thing he might mention in 'Bella Kerry', although the rat and the rat-catcher were in a suburb of Dublin – the pest control company was, in fact, just around the corner from Finn's house, a thing he had never known before, and which he did not find reassuring, even if it was convenient. He could shift everything down the country, though, for the purposes of the story. The rat-man put plastic bags of bright red poison down various holes. The skirting boards were full of little holes, which Finn had never noticed before. The rat-man promised to come back in a week and do another round of poison. 'We'll get them, my friend,' he said. He was a small wiry man, with a sharp face and smooth, iron-grey hair. An intelligent, cheerful manner. He reminded Finn of some character from Chaucer. The Pardoner? 'They're everywhere. You're never more than six yards from a rat. See you later, my friend,' said the man. Three hundred euro for the basic job. About an hour's work. But who'd want do it? He was a hero, the rat-man, all things considered. These people were the real heroes.

Finn could be a hero, too. Especially since he wanted to escape from town and get back to the country and to his writing. He'd help the Pardoner. He'd back up the bags of poison with traps.

Rat-traps: big versions of mousetraps. Like the holes in the skirting, he'd never seen them before, but there they were, in Woodie's. Down in the garden section, next to the weedkiller.

Before going to bed, he set two of them near the fridge, where the rat came out, he was pretty sure.

Ten minutes later, Mattie came up.

'The mouse is in the trap,' he said, in a thick voice. His blue eyes had darkened since childhood. The colour had not changed, but the light had. They didn't sparkle any more. It was not a thing Finn had noticed before, but he saw it now, and wondered, as he went downstairs, when that had happened.

Death had been instantaneous, Finn guessed – though he didn't care one way or another. Broken neck. Long brown body. Surprised expression in the eyes. He picked up the rat, in its trap, with a plastic bag wrapped around his hand, and dumped the whole thing in the wheelie bin. To his surprise, he felt suddenly queasy, as if he might vomit. But he gritted his teeth and set another trap before going back to bed. He was going to get them.

Three rats in two days.

And he could hear them eating the rat-man's poison.

By the third rat, he still felt sick after disposing of them. But by then he was feeling sorry for them, too. Their little pointy faces looked so shocked in the trap – a vicious machine. They just came up from their home under the floorboards for a bite to eat. And snap. Guillotined. He was beginning to know the rats now – their habits, their points of ingress. They'd been under his house for quite a while, was his guess, and they'd eaten lots of things. Mostly cat-food, but other stuff, too. They loved plastic. He cleaned out the cupboard under the sink, one of those cupboards that gets left, uncleaned, for years and years, and found heaps of shredded plastic bags in at the back, behind the old tins of shoe polish and dried-up window-cleaner. They were also very fond of electric wires – that's what had happened to the fridge. The cable to the dishwasher was well gnawed, too, but was holding out for the minute – apparently they preferred the poison to electric cables. Poor things. They'd probably watched their nearest relatives, their mother and dad, their brothers, getting electrocuted. Death Row in the O'Keefe kitchen.

Finn stayed in Dublin for a week. A whole week out of his precious 'month in the country', his writing summer. The Pardoner had made a return visit and pronounced himself well pleased. He'd come back in another fortnight. Finn arranged with Mattie, who was sickened at the thought of dead rats

(Mattie was a vegetarian, and a sort of Zen Buddhist), to let the rat-man in, and only to call him, Finn, back to town if it were absolutely essential. He'd tried to start a conversation with Mattie a few times in the course of the week; he'd seldom been alone in the house with him before. But nothing doing. Mattie got that stony look in his eye and left the room whenever his father tried to talk to him.

Six hours later and he's back in the cottage.

Gráinne is sitting in front of the fire in one chair, Pangur in the other.

Pangur miaows when Finn comes in, which is more than Gráinne does. She doesn't even look at him.

Finn sighs.

Pangur is thin. Now that he's been away for a week he sees her with clear eyes. He sees that she's not really getting that much better, even here, in the country. He's been deluding himself.

Also he sees that there's no dinner on the table. He'd been imagining. A nice bit of marinated lamb. Mint sauce. A bottle of Chianti. Candles. Gráinne had had no car, of course. She could have got the bus, though – there's one on Fridays, bringing the old folk into town to collect their pensions. Anyone can use it if they pay the fare.

'You look tired', is what she says, in an accusing voice, when she finally looks at him.

That means, you don't look sexy. You look old.

Of course I'm bloody tired, he thinks. I've spent a week catching rats instead of writing my story. I've driven two hundred and forty miles across Ireland in the rain.

He says nothing.

'Rats,' she says with a sigh.

And then it blows up.

A full-scale row.

His selfishness. The rats. The way he never cooks or cleans anything. His fathering. He's bad at it, that's why Mattie is the way he is, which is too closed in, too involved with his own hobbies, just like his father. His stupid writing. His diary. She'd snooped, she'd read it when he was away. Fantasies about Frances in Tuscany. When he never had sex with her (her choice, but of course she conveniently left out bits of the story in this version, the quarrelling version).

It's over.

She wants out.

And on and on.

The rows.

They have them periodically – every few weeks, over a stretch of time. Then months might go by. Half a year, more. They have a spot of rowing, it finishes, they struggle on. He believes marriage is like that for a lot of people. But of course how would he know? And does that make it right?

Frances and her second husband in *Bella Tuscany* never seem to have a row. They have candlelit dinners, long walks, holidays. Outings with friends. He wonders what it was like with her first husband. How could a marriage to someone as lovely and charming and pleasant as Frances come to an end?

'I want some peace and happiness while there is still time.'

That's Gráinne.

He's heard the words a hundred times before. He's even said them himself, once or twice, and thought them much more often. Some peace and happiness. How wonderful it would be, how wonderful. But would there be peace and happiness if they split up? He can't imagine life without Gráinne. He could hardly say he loves her, not in the old sense, the erotic sense. Eros and Agape. Maybe Agape, hardly any Eros – infatuation, being in love, lasts for eighteen months, he's read somewhere. It's over before you even marry, apparently. Still, he missed Gráinne when he was in Dublin catching the rats. Trying to talk to his silent son. *Is fearr an troid ná an t-uaigneas*, he heard on the radio another day. The fighting is better than the loneliness. They'd a proverb for every situation, the old folks. Finn wonders who made them up in the first place, and if anyone does that any more. If he was making one, it would be this: Life is a matter of balance. But they have one for that, too. You've to take the good with the bad. Only the very young, like Mattie, believe it should be all good and that, if not, it's not worth living. But Mattie's wrong. A balance is as good as it gets.

He thinks he should kiss Gráinne, now, here in the dark kitchen. That would, he is ninety-five per cent sure, calm her down, put a stop to the row. But he's afraid to. She's still really angry. So instead he says, 'I am very tired', which is perfectly true. 'I'm going to get some sleep.' And off he trundles to bed.

His laptop is on the table in the window, its blue light still on. On standby, which is what he hopes Mattie is on – someday in a year or two he'll switch on and talk again, stop being a Buddhist and climb off the sofa and back into ordinary life. He looks at the laptop, and out the window at the dark, blue-black sky, milky with stars. He considers writing a few lines, but he's too tired. Tomorrow he'll sit down. He'll stare out the window at the green island and the green ocean and start telling his story.

He gets into bed. The sheets are cool, the room fresh and uncluttered. It's a nice cottage, this place they've rented for their summer in the country. But when he closes his eyes, he's back in the messy Dublin kitchen. And the rat is there, in the big trap beside the fridge. A puzzled look in its eyes – death surprised it. Its long rat body, long tail, sticking out behind. Mattie is standing silently by the kitchen door, looking at the rat. His eyes are as sad as sad can be.

Nausea grips Finn. His stomach heaves with that queasiness he got when he tossed the dead rats into the dustbin. Even as he lies flat on his back between the fresh, cool sheets in the room that looks out on the dark beauty of sea and sky and stars. He is filled with terror.

He makes a supreme effort. He pushes the rat out of his mind. Because everyone knows what dreaming about rats means.

Near Exit 13, which is where the Dundrum shopping centre is, on one side, and the Dublin Mountains, on the other, he saw from the corner of his eye this thing: a bank of wildflowers. Long, golden grass. Buttercups splattered through them, brilliant yellow. And a profusion of poppies. So scarlet, so scarlet. At that very moment the sun broke through the massed grey clouds and drenched the wildflowers of July in its warm summer light. The rock of the mountains appeared on his left then – the very heart of the mountain, which they must have blasted away to make the road. He passed the bank of flowers – you weren't allowed to stop – but tucked the picture away, stored it safely, to take out when he wanted to. Next up was the sign that appeared like magic at odd intervals along the motorway and that always lifted his spirits: 'In Case of Breakdown, Await Rescue'. The only road sign that does not try to frighten you, or nag you and make you feel guilty. The road sign that made him remember his mother, who died two years ago, whom he still missed, especially when he was leaving home to go on a journey.

And then – because the motorway was still slicing through the mountain – came the yellow sign with a picture of a deer on it. A black deer, springing carelessly into the bright air.

A deer rampant. Young and lovely. Full of energy and full of joy.

A literary lunch

The board was gathering in a bistro on the banks of the Liffey. 'We deserve a decent lunch!' Alan, the chairman, declared cheerfully. He was a cheerful man. His eyes were kind, and encouraged those around him to feel secure. People who liked him said he was charismatic.

The board was happy. Their tedious meeting was over and the bistro was much more expensive than the hotel to which Alan usually brought them, with its alarming starched tablecloths and fantails of melon. He was giving them a treat because it was a Saturday. They had sacrificed a whole three hours of the weekend for the good of the organisation they served. The reputation of the bistro, which was called Gabriel's, was excellent and anyone could tell from its understated style that the food would be good, and the wine, too, even before they looked at the menu – John Dory, oysters, fried herrings, sausage and mash. Truffles. A menu listing truffles just under sausage and mash promises much. We can cook and we are ironic as well, it proclaims. Put your elbows on the table, have a good time.

Emphasising the unpretentiously luxurious tone of Gabriel's was a mural on the wall, depicting a modern version of the Last Supper, a mural of typical Dubliners eating at a long refectory table.

Alan loved this mural, a clever, post-modern, but delightfully accessible, work of art. It raised the cultural tone of the bistro, if it needed raising, which it didn't really, since it was also located next door to the house on Usher's Island where James Joyce's aunts had lived, and which he used as the setting for his most celebrated story, 'The Dead'. In short, of all the innumerable restaurants boasting literary associations in town, Gabriel's had the most irrefutable credentials. You simply could not eat in a more artistic place.

The funny thing about the Last Supper was that everyone was sitting at one side of the table, very conveniently, for painters and photographers. It was as if they had anticipated all the attention that would soon be coming their way. And Gabriel's had, in its clever, ironic way, set up one table in exactly the same manner, so that everyone seated at it faced in the same direction, getting a good view of the picture and also of the rest of the restaurant. It was great. Nobody was stuck facing the wall. You could see if anyone of any importance was among the clientele – and usually there were one or two stars, at least. You could see what they were wearing and what they were eating and drinking, although you had to guess what they were talking about, which made it even more interesting, in a funny sort of way. More interactive. It was like watching a silent movie without subtitles.

A problem with the arrangement was that people at one end of the Last Supper table had no chance at all of talking to those at the other end. But this, too, could be a distinct advantage, if the seating arrangements were intelligently handled. On this sort of outing, Alan always made sure that they were.

At the right end of the table he had placed his good old friends, Simon and Paul. (Joe had not come, as per usual. He was the real literary expert on the board, having won the Booker Prize, but he never attended meetings. Too full of himself. Still, they could use his name on the stationery.) Alan himself sat in the middle, where he could keep an eye on everyone. On his left-hand side were Mary, Jane and Pam. The women liked to stick together.

Alan, Simon and Paul ordered oysters and truffles and pâté de foie gras for starters. Mary, Jane and Pam ordered one soup of the day and two nothings. This was not owing to the gender division. Mary and Jane were long past caring about their figures, at least when out on a free lunch, and Pam was new and eager to try everything being a member of a board offered, even John Dory, which she had ordered for her main course. Their abstemiousness was due to the breakdown in communications caused by the seating arrangements. The ladies had believed that nobody was getting a starter, because Alan had muttered, 'I don't think I'll have a starter', and then changed his mind and ordered the pâté de foie gras when they were chatting among themselves about a new production of *A Doll's House*, which was just showing at the Abbey. Mary had been to the opening, as she was careful to emphasise; she was giving it the thumbs down. Nora had been manic and the sound effects were appalling. The slam of the door that was supposed to reverberate down through a hundred years of drama couldn't even be heard in the second row of the stalls. That was the Abbey for you, of course. Such dreadful acoustics, the place has to be shut down. Pam and Jane nodded eagerly; Pam thought the Abbey was quite nice but she knew if she admitted that in public, everyone would think she was a total loser who had probably failed her Leaving. Neither Pam nor Jane had seen *A Doll's House* but they had read a review by Fintan O'Toole, so they knew everything they needed to know. He hadn't liked the production, either, and had decided that the original play was not much good, anyway. *Farvel*, Ibsen!

In the middle of this conversation Pam's mobile phone began to play 'Waltzing Matilda' at volume level five. Alan gave her a reproving glance. If she had to leave her mobile phone on, she could at least have picked a tune by Shostakovich or Stravinksy. He himself had a few bars by a young Irish composer on his phone, ever mindful of his duty to the promotion of the national culture. 'Terribly sorry!' Pam slipped the phone into her bag, but not before she had glanced at the screen to find out who was calling. 'I forgot to switch it off.' Which was rather odd, Mary thought, since Pam had placed the phone on the table, in front of her nose, the minute she had come into the restaurant. It had sat there under the water jug, looking like a tiny pistol in its little leather holster.

In the heel of the hunt all this distraction meant that they neglected to eavesdrop on the men while they were placing their orders, so that they would get a rough idea of how extravagant they could be. How annoying it was now to see Simon slurping down his oysters, with lemon and black pepper, and Paul digging into his truffles, while they had nothing but *A Doll's House* and one soup of the day to amuse themselves with.

And a glass of white wine. Paul, who was a great expert, had ordered that. A Sauvignon Blanc, the vineyard of Dubois Père et Fils, 2002. 'As nice a Sauvignon as I have tried in years,' he said, as he munched a truffle and sipped thoughtfully. 'Two thousand and two was a good year for everything in France, but this is exceptional.'

The ladies strained to hear what he was saying, much more interested in wine than drama. Mary, who had been so exercised a moment ago about Ibsen at the Abbey, seemed to have forgotten all about both. She was now taking notes, jotting down Paul's views. He was better, much better, than the people who do the columns in the paper, she commented excitedly as she scribbled. No commercial agenda – well, that they knew of. You never quite knew what anyone's agenda was, that was the trouble. Paul was apparently on the board because of his knowledge of books, and Simon, because of his knowledge of the legal world, and Joe, because he was famous. Mary, Jane and Pam were there because they were women. Mary was already on twenty boards and had had to call a halt, since her entire life was absorbed by meetings and lunches, receptions and launches. Luckily, she had married sensibly and did not have to work. Jane sat on ten boards and Pam had been nominated two months ago. This was her first lunch with any board, ever. She was a writer. Everyone wondered what somebody like her was doing here. It was generally agreed that she must know someone.

One person she knew was Francie Briody. He was also having lunch, in a coffee shop called the Breadbasket, a cold little kip of a place across the river. They served filled baguettes and sandwiches as well as coffee and he was lunching on a tuna submarine with corn and coleslaw. Francie was a writer, like Pam, although she wrote so-called literary women's fiction, chick lit for PhDs, and was successful. Francie wrote literary fiction for anybody who cared to read it, which was nobody. For as long as he could remember he had been a writer whom nobody read. And he was already fifty years of age. He had written three novels and about a hundred short stories, and other bits and bobs. Success of a kind had been his lot in life, but not of a kind to enable him to earn a decent living, or to eat anything other than tuna submarines, or to get him a seat on an arts organisation board. He had had one novel published, to mixed reviews; he had won a prize at Listowel Writers' Week for a short story fifteen years ago. Six of his short stories had been nominated for prizes – the Devon Cream Story Competition, the Blackstaff Young Authors, the William Carleton Omagh May Festival, among others. But he still had to work part-time in a public house, and he had failed to publish his last three books.

Nobody was interested in a writer past the age of thirty. It was all the young ones they wanted these days, and women, preferably young women with lots of shining hair and sweet photogenic faces. Pam. She wasn't that young any more, and not all that photogenic, but she'd got her foot in the door in time, when women and the Irish were all the rage, no matter what they looked like. Or wrote like.

He'd never been a woman – he had considered a pseudonym but he'd let that moment pass. And now he'd missed the boat. The love affair of the London houses and the German houses and the Italian and the Japanese with Irish literature was over. So everyone said. Once Seamus Heaney got the Nobel, the interest abated. Enough's enough. On to the next country. Bosnia or Latvia or God knows what. Slovenia.

Francie's latest novel, a heteroglossial, polyphonic, post-modern examination of post-modern Celtic Tiger Ireland, with special insights into political corruption and globalisation, beautifully written in darkly masculinist ironic prose with shadows of *l'écriture féminine*, which was precisely and exactly what Fintan O'Toole swore that the Irish public and Irish literature was crying out for, had been rejected by every London house, big and small, that his agent could think of, and by the five Irish publishers who would dream of touching a literary novel as well, and also, Francie did not like to think of this, by the other thirty Irish publishers who believed chick lit was the modern Irish answer to James Joyce. Yes yes yes yes. The delicate chiffon scarf was flung over her auburn curls. Yes.

Yeah well.

He'd show the philistine fatso bastards.

He pushed a bit of slippery yellow corn back into his sub. Extremely messy form of nourishment, it was astonishing that it had caught on, especially as the subs were slimy and slippery themselves.

Not like the home-made loaves served in Gabriel's on the south bank of the Liffey. Alan was nibbling a round of freshly baked, soft as silk, crispy as Paris on a fine winter's day roll, to counteract the richness of the pâté, which was sitting slightly uneasily on his stomach.

'We did a good job,' he was saying to Pam, who liked to talk shop, being new.

'I'd always be so worried that we picked the wrong people,' she said in her charming, girlish voice.

She had nice blond hair but this did not make up for her idealism and her general lack of experience. Alan wished his main course would come quickly. Venison with lingonberry jus and basil mash.

'You'd be surprised but that very seldom happens,' he said.

'Judgements are so subjective vis-à-vis literature,' she said with a frown, remembering a bad review she'd received seven and a half years ago.

Alan suppressed a sigh. She was a real pain.

'There is almost always complete consensus on decisions,' he said. 'It's surprising, but the cream always rises. I … we … are never wrong.' His magical eyes twinkled.

Consensus? Pam frowned into her Sauvignon Blanc. A short discussion of the applicants for the bursaries, in which people nudged ambiguities around the table like footballers dribbling a ball, when all they want is the blessed trumpeting of the final whistle. They waited for Alan's pronouncement. If that was consensus, she was Emily Dickinson. As soon as Alan said, 'I think this is brilliant writing' or 'Rubbish, absolute rubbish', there was a scuffle of voices vying with each other to be the first to agree with the great man.

'Rubbish, absolute rubbish.' That was what he had said about Francie. 'He's persistent, I'll give him that.' Alan had allowed himself a smile, which he very occasionally permitted himself at the expense of minor writers. The board guffawed loudly. Pam wouldn't tell Francie that. He would kill himself. He was at the end of his tether. But she would break the sad news over the phone in the loo, as she had promised. No bursary. Again.

'I don't know,' she persisted, ignoring Alan's brush-off. 'I feel so responsible somehow. All that effort and talent, and so little money to go around …' Her voice trailed off. She could not find the words to finish the sentence, because she was drunk as an egg after two glasses. No breakfast, the meeting had started at nine.

Stupid bitch, thought Alan, although he smiled cheerily. Defiant. Questioning. Well, we know how to deal with them. Woman or no woman, she would never sit on another board. This was her first and her last supper. 'I feel so responsible somehow.' Who did she think she was?

'This is a 2001 Bordeaux from a vineyard run by an Australian ex-pat just outside Bruges, that's the Bruges near Bordeaux of course, not Bruges-la-Morte in little Catholic Belgium.'

Paul's voice had risen several decibels and Simon was getting a bit rambunctious. They were well into the second bottle of the Sauvignon and had ordered two bottles of the Bordeaux, priced, Alan noticed, at eighty-five euro a pop. The lunch was going to cost about a thousand euro.

'Your venison, sir?'

At last.

He turned away from Pam and speared the juicy game. The grub of kings.

Francie made his king-size tuna submarine last a long time. It would have lasted, anyway, since the filling kept spilling out onto the table and it took ages to gather it up and replace it in the roll. He glanced at the plain round clock over the fridge. They'd been in there for two hours. How long would it be?

Fifteen years.

Since his first application.

Fifty.

His twelfth.

His twelfth time trying to get a bursary to write full-time.

It would be the makings of him. It would mean he could give up serving alcohol to fools for a whole year. He would write a new novel, the novel that would win the prizes and show the begrudgers. Impress Eileen Battersby. Impress Emer O'Kelly. Impress, maybe, Fintan Fucking O'Toole. And the boost to his morale would be so fantastic ... but once again that Alan King, who had been running literary Ireland since he made his Confirmation probably, would shaft him. He knew.

Pam phoned him from the loo on her mobile. She had tried her best but there was no way. They had really loved his work, she said. There was just not enough money to go round. She was so sorry, so sorry ...

Yeah right.

Alan was the one who made the decisions. Pam had told him so herself. 'They do exactly what he says,' she said. 'It's amazing. I never knew how power worked. Nobody ever disagrees with him.'

Nobody who gets to sit on the same committees and eats the same lunches, anyway. As long as he was chair, Francie would not get a bursary. He would not get a travel grant. He would not get a production grant. He would not get a trip to China or Paris or even the University of Eastern Connecticut. He would not get a free trip to Drumshambo in the County Leitrim for the Arsehole of Ireland Literature and Donkey Racing Weekend.

Alan King ruled the world.

The pen is stronger than the sword, Francie had learned in school. Was it Patrick Pearse who said that or some classical guy? Cicero or somebody. That's how old Francie was, they were still doing Patrick Pearse when he was in primary. He was pre-revisionism and he still hadn't got a bursary in literature, let alone got onto Aosdána, which gave some lousy writers like Pam a meal ticket for life. The pen is stronger. Good old Paddy Ó Piarsaigh. But he changed his mind, apparently. Francie looked at the Four Courts through the corner window of the Breadbasket. Who had been in that in 1916? He couldn't remember. Had anyone? Eamonn Ceannt or Seán Mac Diarmada or somebody nobody could remember. Burnt down the place in the end, all the history of Ireland in it. IRA of their day. That was later, the Civil War. He had written about that, too. He had written about everything. Even about Alan. He had written a whole novel about him, and six short stories, but they were hardly going to find their mark if they never got published, and they were not going to get published if he did not get a bursary and some recognition from the establishment, and he was not going to get any recognition while Alan was running every literary and cultural organisation on the island ...

At last. The evening was falling in when the board members tripped and staggered out of Gabriel's, into the light and shade, the sparkle and darkness, that was Usher's Quay. Jane and Mary had of course left much earlier, anxious to get to the supermarkets before they closed.

But Pam, to the extreme annoyance of everyone, had lingered on, drinking the Bordeaux with the best of them. They had been irritated at first but had then passed into another stage. The sexual one. Inevitable as Australian Chardonnay at a book launch. They had stopped blathering on about wine and had begun to reminisce about encounters with ladies of the night in exotic locations. Paul claimed, in a high voice that had Alan looking around the restaurant in alarm, to have been seduced by a whore in a hotel in Moscow, who had bought him a vodka and insisted on accompanying him to his room, clad only in a coat of real wolfskin. Fantasy land. That eejit Pam was so shot herself she didn't seem to care what they said. Her mascara was slipping down her face and her blond hair was manky, as if she had sweated too much. It was high time she got a taxi. He'd shove her into one as soon as he got them out. He couldn't leave them here, they'd drink the board dry, and if they were unlucky, some journalist would happen upon them. He stopped for a second. Publicity was something they were always seeking and hardly ever got. But no, this would do them no good at all. There is such a thing as bad press, in spite of what he said at meetings.

He paid the bill. There were long faces, of course. You'd think he was crucifying them, instead of having treated them to a lunch that had cost, including the large gratuity he was expected to fork out, one thousand two hundred euro of Lottery money. Oh well, better than racehorses, he always said, looking at the Last Supper. Was it Leonardo or Michelangelo had painted the original? He was so exhausted he couldn't remember. He took no nonsense from the boyos, though, and asked the waiter to put them into their coats no matter how they protested.

Pam had excused herself at the last minute, taking him aback.

'Don't wait for me,' she had said. She could still speak coherently. 'I'll be grand, I'll get a taxi. I'll put it on the account.'

She gave him a peck on the cheek – that's how drunk she was – and ran out the door, pulling her mobile out of her bag as she did so.

Not such a twit as all that. 'I'll put it on the account.' He almost admired her for a second.

With the help of the waiter, he got the other pair of beauties bundled out to the pavement.

Their taxi had not yet arrived.

He deposited Simon and Paul on a bench placed outside for the benefit of smokers and moved to the curb, the better to see.

Traffic moved freely along the quay. It was not as busy as usual. A quiet evening. The river was a blending delight of black and silver and mermaid green. Alan was not entirely without aesthetic sensibility. The sweet smell of hops floated along the water from the brewery. He'd always loved that, the heavy, cloying smell of it, like something you'd give a two-year-old to drink. Like hot jam tarts. In the distance he could just see the black trees of the Phoenix Park. Sunset. Peaches and molten gold, Dublin stretched against it. The north side could be lovely at times like this. When it was getting dark. The Wellington monument rose, a black silhouette, into the heavens, a lasting tribute to the power and glory of great men.

It was the last thing Alan saw.

He didn't even hear the shot explode like a backfiring lorry in the hum of the evening city.

Francie's aim was perfect. It was amazing that a writer who

could not change a plug or bore a hole in a wall with a Black & Decker drill at point-blank range could shoot so straight across the expanse of the river. Well, he had trained. Practice makes perfect, they said, at the creative writing workshops. Be persistent, never lose your focus. He had not written a hundred short stories for nothing and a short story is an arrow in flight towards its target. They were always saying that. *Aim, write, fire.* And if there's a gun on the table in act one, it has to go off in act three, that's another thing they said.

But, laughed Francie, as he wrapped his pistol in a Tesco Bag for Life, in real life what eejit would put a gun on the table in act one? In real life a gun is kept well out of sight and it goes off in any act it likes. In real life there is no foreshadowing.

That's the difference, he thought, as he let the bag slide over the river wall. That's the difference between life and art. He watched the bag sink into the black lovely depths of Anna Livia Plurabelle. Patrick Pearse gave up on the *peann* in the end. When push came to shove, he took to the *lámh láidir.*

He walked down towards O'Connell Bridge, taking out his mobile. Good old Pam. He owed her. 'For each man kills the thing he loves,' he texted her, pleased to have remembered the line. 'By each let this be heard. Some do it with a bitter look, some with a flattering word. The coward does it with a kiss; the brave man with a gun.' That wasn't right. *Word* didn't rhyme with *gun.* 'Some do it with a bitter look, some with a flattering pun.' Didn't really make sense. What rhymes with *gun?* Lots of words. *Fun, nun. Bun.* 'Some do it with a bitter pint, some with a sticky bun,' he texted in. 'Cheers! I'll buy you a bagel sometime.' He sent the message and tucked his phone into his pocket. Anger sharpened the wit, he had noticed that before. His best stories had always been inspired by the lust for revenge. He could feel a good one coming on … maybe he shouldn't have bothered killing Alan.

He was getting into a bad mood again. He stared disconsolately at the dancing river. The water was far from transparent, but presumably the Murder Investigation Squad could find things in it. They knew it had layers and layers of meaning, just like the prose he wrote. Readers were too lazy to deconstruct properly but policeman were probably pretty assiduous when it came to interpreting and analysing the murky layers of the

Liffey. Would that Bag for Life protect his fingerprints, DNA evidence? He didn't know. The modern writer has to do plenty of research. God is in the details. He did his best but he had a tendency to leave some books unread, some websites unvisited. Writing a story, or murdering a man, was such a complex task. You were bound to slip up somewhere.

Perfectionism is fatal, they said. Give yourself permission to err. Don't listen to the inner censor.

He had reached O'Connell Street and, hey, there was the 46A waiting for him. A good sign. They'd probably let him have a laptop in prison, he thought optimistically, as he hopped on the bus. They'd probably make him writer-in-residence. That's if they ever found the gun.

Illumination

I was spending the summer at an artists' retreat in the hills on the west coast of America. The house where I lived was a brown wooden building, sheltered by a grove of pine trees, where bobcats had their den. My room was large and plain and comfortable, with a wooden ceiling, a desk, an easy chair, and a wide bed, covered by a blue patchwork quilt. A small balcony faced east to the rising sun, and in the mornings I sat there. Hummingbirds, like large insects, stood in the air near my head, making their sound, which is more like a whirr than a hum. Rabbits, looking like pictures cut from a children's pop-up book, nibbled at the grass in the garden below, where agapanthus, Shasta daisies and orange nasturtiums bloomed. And climbing up the wooden wall to the balcony railing was a rambling rose bearing small pink blossoms that had no smell. All around me were layer upon layer of undulating hills, smooth and rounded, their long grasses the colour of pottery left too long in the kiln. Here and there among the dry hills were dark green stains, cool and inviting as oases. That was the forest. Redwoods, exotic pines, oak and arbutus, which here is called the madrone.

At night the coyotes barked, and the bobcats screamed, and it was said that a mountain lion roamed in the hills and sometimes came down to the house where the artists lived and worked. But no one had seen it for a long time. During the day, one saw only rabbits, and hummingbirds, and flowers. In the forest, hiding among the trunks of the redwoods, furrowed deeply like sticks of chocolate flake, small deer would run, startled by the walker, and bound along the woodland trails as if on springs.

In the mornings I wrote, sitting by the window, and I spent an hour sitting outside on the balcony, beside the pink and scentless roses, catching the sun before it moved around to the south and the west sides of the house. I wrote a novel, doggedly, without hope or despair, trusting that sometime the work would find itself, although my experience told me that with novels this does not always happen. In the afternoons I walked in the hills or in the woods, and in the evenings I read.

There was a good library in the house, warmly coloured, with dark wooden shelves, and a few thousand books, many left there by previous residents. The collection of biographies was particularly good and after a while I understood that the original owner of the house had been married to a biographer – her own works formed part of the collection, but there were many other lives there, captured between two covers. The lives of Isak Dinesen, of George Eliot, of Anne Sexton, Sylvia Plath, Franz Kafka. I read some swiftly. (Anne Sexton, whose life was not edifying; Sylvia Plath, whose story we all know too well already.) The other great writers had led longer and more varied lives, though all in their different ways were very strange. In the end, Isak Dinesen, or Karen Blixen, the lion huntress of Copenhagen, with her hooked aristocratic nose and intolerable snobberies, her incurable syphilis, tragic love affairs and ridiculous fantasies, seemed the most balanced and normal. Such biographies make me wonder if an ordinary, sane person, lacking any stunning eccentricity, could be a writer at all.

I was not alone in this wooden house. There were, during my stay, two others in it. A Chinese man of a very sweet disposition, a painter of abstract pictures. Li had a studio in another building at some remove from the house, and went there in the mornings to make his paintings, which consisted of beautiful, kaleidoscopic images built of thousands of minute coloured segments. They suggested fairgrounds, roller coasters, childhood, golden memories broken down into a million fragments. When he spoke about them, it was in a stream of associations – he might mention macaroni, Taormina, the sea, Paris, Plato, Frida Kahlo, Ingmar Bergman, rice pudding, Shakespeare, Woody Allen, Avedon, strawberry ice cream, all in one long, intricate sentence. At first I tried to keep up with his train of thought but soon I abandoned it, realising that I could not go into that mysterious labyrinth and follow the thread to its meaning.

Also, there was a woman from Germany, Frederike, a composer who spoke very little. She spent the whole day and most of the evening in her studio, playing the piano, creating music, which, I think, represented alienation and disconnection, the absence of harmony characterising our world. Its randomness. There were many long pauses in her music and Li told me that one of her compositions consisted only of fifteen minutes of silence, fenced between two single notes.

When he was not talking about his work, Li talked about food, in which he was very interested. He was an excellent cook and made delectable meals for the three of us every evening – not just Chinese, but Indian, French, American. He would go into the kitchen at six o'clock and by seven thirty an array of dishes would be laid out on the counter, ready to be eaten. Salads of chicory and baby tomatoes and feta cheese, home-made breads, spicy curries, grilled fish or meat. Sauces of indescribable deliciousness, tart and sweet. We shared a bottle of white wine every evening, but he drank just a small glass.

When our meal was over, Frederike would go back to her studio and I would retire to the library and read the stories of Karen Blixen, Anton Chekhov, William Trevor: the old masters. I knew I should pay attention to more gritty contemporary writers but once I had started on the clear sentences and meandering thoughts of Chekhov, the flowing fantasies of Blixen, once I had been transported on one night to the idyllic summer woodlands of a Russian dacha, painted in Chekhov's watercolour, and on the next to the cool slopes of the Ngong Hills, embroidered like regal tapestries, fabulous fantasies that sometimes succeeded in shaking the heart, I could not revert to the urban jangle of irony, menace and gruesome murder, which is the stock in trade of contemporary fiction. It would have been like moving from Beethoven's Fifth Symphony to one of Frederike's pieces, with its jabs of sound, its long silences, its love of dissonance.

The truth was, my life was not dissonant, but whole and fulfilling while I was here in the golden, sun-washed hills, with the Pacific Ocean beating on a distant shore, with the merry hummingbirds and the sombre redwood trees, the dark library and the bright meals. But it lacked what I had thought I would find here. Brilliant insights into life and literature. Answers. I had none to offer myself but I had hoped to sit at the feet of philosophers, listen to discussions that Plato might have organised, symposia where the dialogue itself led to the solution of the problem, or to some great discovery. All my life I had been waiting for some answer to come to me, from the conversation of others, or from a book, or from the clouds themselves, or the sunlight on the ocean. And as yet this had not happened.

My housemates did not like to walk in the woods, or in the hills, or anywhere. Frederike preferred to do gymnastics, and Li was afraid of mountain lions. The chances of being attacked by a lion are one thousand times less than of being struck by lightning. Li knew this – it was written out in our guidebook – but he still did not want to take the risk. It would be such a painful and messy way to die – although possibly, I said, possibly not as painful or messy as being killed in a car crash. But so terrifying, he said. We could both easily imagine the moment when the victim sees the face of the lion, those ferocious tawny eyes, the huge teeth bared within inches of one's flesh. We could hear the deep growl, the deadly scream, and feel the bottomless fear they would arouse, which would be much worse than the pain, than death itself. The long, golden grass that grew abundantly on the slopes surrounding us, the scrubby green bushes and the dense redwood thickets, provided miles of hiding places for the canny lion. Li could imagine them, everywhere.

'To him I am a mouse,' he said. 'Have you seen a cat take a mouse? I do not want to be treated in that way.'

I thought it would be worse. More violent and bloody, and noisier. But maybe compared to the terror the mouse feels it would be the same. That is one of the many things I should know, as a writer, but cannot: how it feels to be a mouse, at the gate of the cat's mouth.

But anyway, I did not believe so much in the lion, and I walked on my own, in the afternoons, between three and five o'clock. Then the sun was still warm, which I liked, but my day's work was done. I had two favourite walks – one up the golden hills to the top, from where I could gaze down over the hills that rippled out to the coastline – in its habitual shroud of mist, there was always, from the high vantage point, a strip of white foam visible, like a trimming of white fur on a winter hood, on the far-off beach. My other walk led into the depth of the woods, through colonnades of the ridged redwood trunks, ferny groves, a babbling creek. I would see snakes, occasionally hear the menacing jingle of the diamond-patterned terror. Deer. Red-tailed hawks and the beautiful, harsh-voiced blue jay. But never the mountain lion.

About a week into my stay at the lodge I followed a new trail. In a clearing in the wood – known as the picnic grounds, although nobody ever picnicked there – I noticed a gate that I had not before observed. This was not surprising, because the gate was constructed of logs, old and clothed with that pale green moss that hangs on the oak trees, a strange, dry, lacy green that looked like something that would grow on an ancient coffin, or like the cobweb veil of a skeleton.

The gate opened easily and I found myself on another track through the woods. I decided I would walk on it for ten minutes to see if it led anywhere of interest, then turn back – I did not want to get lost. Mobile phones did not work here, and my companions would never find me if I failed to return to the house. Perhaps in a day or two Li would phone for help, but the woods, I knew without experiencing them, would be another world once darkness fell, a world where the coyote and the bobcats ruled, and the mountain lion. As I lay in my bed I heard the noises of the night – barks and howls and hoots and screams. It was comforting to lie tucked up under the patchwork quilt, watching the moon gleam coldly over the branch of the fir tree outside my window, and listen to the nocturnal symphony. But I did not want to be a member of the orchestra that produced it, or to hear it at closer range.

The trail went slightly downhill through the forest for about half a kilometre, through an avenue of tall redwoods, sentries to the gravel drive. I glanced at my watch. Eleven minutes had passed; something rustled in the leaves, and there was a quick scurrying sound in the undergrowth. I considered turning back, but I went on.

In front of me was a wide clearing. Nestling in the back, stretched out like a sleeping dog, was a white house, low and long. Behind it and around it, a sheltering half-moon of tall, dark trees. A colonnaded porch ran all along the front of the house, and a stretch of lawn, where Shasta daisies and agapanthus grew, just as around our house. But this lawn was much bigger and so green and soft it looked like emerald silk, not grass. At one side was a swimming pool, open to the sun. Someone was swimming and on the side of the pool were two women, one reclining on a lounger and one sitting at a poolside table.

I went over to them, realising that I seemed like an intruder. As I came closer they both stared at me. The woman at the table was middle aged, dressed in a white blouse and beige skirt, and the other was young, wearing a spotted bikini, brown and yellow. They did not look frightened.

'I strayed off the trail,' I said. 'I'm sorry.'

I introduced myself, and told them I was staying at the artists' lodge, that I was a writer of fiction, and walked every day in the woods and hills for exercise and inspiration. The latter was not true, because the woods never inspired me, although I liked them well enough.

'Sit down. Have some lemonade, you must be thirsty.'

The older woman's voice was kindness itself. Her face was heart-shaped, like the chocolates you get in boxes made for lovers on Valentine's Day, and the irises of her slightly slanted eyes were of an unusual hazel colour, bright and penetrating. She wore gold-framed spectacles, and her tawny hair was swept off her face and caught in a big tail at the back of her neck. She had exceptionally neat ears, which I noticed because they were studded with minute black earrings. Her name was Ramalina.

The younger woman's name was Isabel, and I assumed her to be Ramalina's daughter. The person swimming in the pool, who had not stopped swimming, was her son, she told me: Marcus.

Isabel wrapped herself in a yellow silk robe, and sat at the table while I drank my lemonade. She was beautiful, with long, black hair, eyes of a similar colour to her mother's, but rounder and with more penetrating pupils. Her skin was smooth and honey-coloured, and her lips thick and rather pale.

They lived here, the three of them, all year round, although this was an area mostly inhabited only during the summer.

'We have an apartment in the city,' Ramalina said, 'but we only go there for the Christmas shopping. We just seem to like it better here.'

'What about you?' I asked Isabel.

'Oh, I stay here, too.'

'You don't go to college?'

'No.' She did not offer a further explanation.

I felt clumsy, as if I had been rude to ask such questions, although they had asked me a few themselves, and in most company such enquiries would have been no more than polite, meaningless words.

The swimmer climbed out of the pool and, dripping, came up and shook my hand.

'Marcus,' he said. 'How are you?' As if I were an invited guest.

He was older than Isabel – brown and very slim, he looked at least thirty to me, or even older. He had reddish hair, like his mother, but of a darker shade. It was cut very short, in a sporty style, and this made his ears look exceptionally large, by contrast with hers. His feet, I noticed, were small and small-toed, for such a tall man.

'Got to go up to the house,' he said. 'But call by again. Come to dinner.'

'Oh yes, please do, my dear,' said Ramalina.

I muttered something about not wanting to intrude but she pressed me, and her invitation seemed to me so heartfelt, so warm, so motherly, that I accepted it. I would come to dinner the next night.

Li had not heard of them.

'Lots of rich people have houses in this neighbourhood,' he said. 'It's probably some family from the city, on holiday here.'

'They live year round. The girl doesn't even go to college.'

'I'll ask around.' He stirred the pan, full of chopped vegetables and herbs and emitting an intoxicating smell. 'I'll ask Kim.'

Kim was the director of the programme, who called to see us twice a week and brought provisions from the town.

The following evening I headed towards the trail at about six o'clock. The sun was still warm on my bare arms, but the countryside was changing gear. The hummingbirds had gone to wherever hummingbirds go – their nests, presumably. One or two sudden flashes of blue indicated that some jays were still about, and their sharp squawks occasionally darted from the branches. The rabbits were out in force, eating the grass as if they were starving, and in our garden two small deer chomped doggedly at a hydrangea shrub, systematically denuding it of all its flowers and leaves.

The forest was cold and shadowy. Every moment the undergrowth rustled and the branches whispered. White owls hooted; animals cried. The walk to the picnic ground took an eternity. I considered turning back, and I do not know why I did not. Because I had promised to come to dinner? It was not that – Isabel and Ramalina and Marcus would wait, perhaps. Soon they would realise something had happened, and they would dine, shrugging. Perhaps they had already forgotten that they had invited me. That was very likely. The invitation had been warm, but abrupt, perhaps whimsical. No doubt Ramalina was always issuing such invitations, knowing that many of them would never be taken up.

It was not fear of disappointing them that kept my feet on that forest path; it was my own fear. I did not want to give in to cowardice. On and on I went, my heart in my mouth, the primeval screams of the forest in my ears. We have always feared the forest, I told myself, for it holds in its heart the wild creations of our nightmares, the flipside of our daylight selves, the threat of unimaginable madnesses. Our instinct is to overcome that threat and that fear, to tame or kill it. Karen Blixen, walking around her manor house at the foot of the Ngong Hills, did not worry about prowling leopards. Even when she did not have her gun, she did not fear them. So why would I run in terror from a harmless forest, where a lion had probably not attacked a human being in hundreds of years, not since these valleys were the preserve of some indigenous tribe whose very name was forgotten.

Finally, I reached the house. And although it was still light, the shadows cast by the trees made the roof dark, and in its windows lights fluttered. No one was on the lawn or the porch or by the pool, which had that lonely, tearful look swimming pools get at night, when the revels of the day are over. I walked up the wooden steps to the front door. It was half open, so I knocked and then stepped in.

The hall was dappled with puddles of coloured light, deep red, ochre, flowing through a stained-glass window on the landing above. A table made of polished applewood leaned against the panelled wall, and on it, a glass vase filled with fat, pink roses, whose fragrance filled the room. Through an open door the sound of piano music filtered. I followed it and there in the drawing room Ramalina and Isabel sat in the French window, listening while Marcus played. I did not recognise the piece and it was mesmerising, and his playing seemed as good as that of the most professional pianists.

As soon as I entered the room Ramalina stood up and came to greet me with a warm embrace. Isabel did not get up from her rattan chair, but she smiled and said hello, and her smile seemed full of genuine welcome. Marcus stopped playing and turned to grin at me.

'It's so great that you could make it!' Ramalina said.

She was wearing a white blouse again, a high-necked, Victorian one, and a long skirt of old gold silk which almost swept the floor. Isabel's black hair was piled on her head, and she was wearing a black cocktail dress, short and girlish, showing off her long, tanned legs. It looked good on her. Since I'd been walking in the woods, where snakes and ticks abounded, I was in my jeans and hiking boots. I had put on one of my nicer tops, in honour of the occasion, but I felt clumsy and rough around the edges, like a workman who finds himself in the drawing room to collect his wages after repairing the plumbing. Even Marcus was wearing a white shirt, and pale chinos, looking every inch the lord of the manor at rest.

Ramalina sensed my unease, with her natural tact and thoughtfulness, and offered me some house slippers, which I accepted. I thought they would be the big, flat, shapeless, fit-all-sizes slippers that some people have in a basket at their front door, but they were not. Silently, with a downcast look, Isabel handed me a pair of red moccasins, beautifully embroidered.

I slipped them on.

'They fit!' I said.

'Yes, I thought this would be your size,' said Ramalina, and she smiled.

Isabel and Marcus at that moment exchanged the most fleeting of glances, and for the only time that evening I felt a prick of unease, although my feet had never felt so comfortable.

We ate immediately, in a dining room at the other side of the hall, a room of perfect proportions, beautiful furniture. On the wall hung a painting of a woman reading a letter, her face, circled by a white linen hood, the pale porcelain of the pictures by Vermeer. So quiet she was, so absorbed in her reading, a reading that had happened hundreds of years ago and was still happening, here. Although the back of the white page was all the artist let us see, a hint of a red seal, there was no other clue to the content except the gentleness of her eyelids. Beside her stood another woman, with a grey bucket under her oxter, exactly like a bucket I had at home. She also held a letter, or perhaps an envelope, in her free hand. A small dog looked on, as often in a Chekhov story.

'What is it called?' I asked.

'*The Letter*,' Ramalina answered. 'It's anonymous.'

'Dutch?' I ventured, although I am often wrong about these things.

'Yes. From the golden age of Dutch painting.'

I nodded, pretending to know when that was, not sure about the dates. Seventeenth century, probably. That is a century that I always feel is out of reach. That rich stillness of the uncluttered interiors. The durability of the clothes – ermine, velvet, linen. The strange porcelain complexions, skin the colour of bone. The eighteenth century I can grasp – we have the houses, and the sense of humour is familiar. The nineteenth seems like yesterday, and the Middle Ages like my schooldays. But the seventeenth is another country and this reader of letters, this bearer of buckets, belonged there. In their clarity, quite foreign.

The table was laid with silver and white linen napkins, two silver vases of lily of the valley, my favourite flower, decanters of white wine and red wine and iced water. Food waited on the sideboard in crockery bowls – salads, rice, vegetables, spiced chicken and lamb rolls. Fresh home-made bread, herbal, was beside it. The food was warm and seemed to have been placed on the sideboard just moments before we entered the dining room, but there was no evidence of other people in the house, no cook or servant. Nor were they referred to. The food must have been prepared in advance, by Ramalina, I thought, but she did not claim credit for it. In a way it seemed to have appeared without agency, although this could not have been the case. Of course, it was delicious, and the wine was smooth and lovely, from a local vineyard.

We talked about the area and the artists' centre where I was staying, about what I was working on – a novel. (I was told once to always give that answer to the question 'What are you working on?' and I always do. It is what people want to hear.) They asked me about my life at home and I told them what I wanted to reveal. That I taught literature sometimes, and lived in a house in the country, and would publish my novel next year if I finished it. I did not tell them I was married, or that I had two children, aged fifteen and seventeen, who wondered why I had left them for the summer, again, or that last year I had spent two months in a psychiatric hospital, recovering from depression. And they did not ask any prying questions, but accepted what I told them as if it were the only thing in the world they wanted to hear and accepted it as if it were the complete truth.

When dinner was over, Ramalina and Isabel cleared the table and told me to sit in the front room with Marcus, and relax with a liqueur or a cup of coffee. Although Ramalina delivered this instruction in her usual warm and soft purr, it was an order; I would have liked to help with the washing up – I would have liked to have seen the kitchen – but I followed Marcus back to the drawing room, where a small log fire was now burning in the grate. Darkness had fallen; the big windows were black pools; branches and shrubs shuddered against them. The owl was hooting, a siren of loneliness, and in the distance an animal growled. Marcus went around and pulled silk curtains across the windows, shutting out the wilderness. He poured coffee and drinks and we sat by the fire and talked.

He told me about his music. He played the piano and the saxophone and the organ, and composed for all three. Sometimes he left the house and performed at concert halls in the city and all across the country, and he had been to Germany and England and France and Sweden and other places far away.

'But I prefer to compose here; here, I work best. I can't create music anywhere else. The walls of the house inspire me.'

He laughed at his own pomposity, but it was clear that he was speaking the truth.

Now that we were alone together, I could see that he was forty, at least. Could he be Isabel's brother? Ramalina's son? She looked about fifty, too young to have mothered this man. But she had introduced him as her son.

In this room, sipping the Cointreau, smelling the roses and the pine wood in the fire, it seemed vulgar and inquisitive to ask such questions, even in one's own head. The atmosphere was so harmonious, so perfect, why try to disturb it with requests for facts and information? Anyway, Li was going to make those enquiries. Back at the lodge, inquisitiveness would not be out of place. It would be natural there, in that world of rougher edges, less fine sensibilities.

Ramalina and Isabel spent a long time clearing up after dinner, an hour at least, which passed easily in Marcus's company. He told me that music was the most important thing in the world, and he was happy with his compositions so far, but he knew his best work was yet to come.

'I don't know exactly what it will be,' he said. 'But I'll know it when I make it. And it will be very new and very beautiful, which is saying a lot, in the context of contemporary classical music.'

We discussed, then, interesting questions that had been bothering me for many months. I wondered if it was possible to make new fiction, by which I meant, find a new template, a new mould, and also a new subject, and still create something that was, to use his word, beautiful. Post-modernism had failed, I said to him. The idea of the fragmented universe, mirrored in the fractured novel or work of art, was interesting, valid at the level of thought, but it had failed artistically because a fractured narrative is not enjoyable – it just does not work. But what is the point of continuing to write using the pre-modern template? And what subject can the new novel deal with? Traditionally, the stories were about the conflict between the desire of the individual and the rules of the society. But does that sort of society exist, in our world, the Western world, the only one we can honestly or usefully write about? Divorce is not a social disaster; homosexuality is legal and accepted. Nobody is forced to marry for money or to please their parents. There are taboos, but not so many, and there must be a limit to the number of explorations of paedophilia or psychopathic crime that the world can endure. So one is left to write only what has been written – in a slightly different way – a million times already.

Marcus believed that in the perfect setting, by which he meant this house, his mother's house, the answer to this problem could be revealed, but he did not explain how.

'You talk as if the place were magical,' I said.

'Yes,' he said. 'It is the right atmosphere for the creation of great art. But still I will have to work, and try to make that good art myself.'

This led, naturally, to the questions: What is music for? What is writing for? What is life for? But before we could discuss these things the washing-up was finished and Ramalina and Isabel returned, padding so silently into the room that I wondered if they had been in a corner, listening to us, unobserved, for some time. The conversation moved off in a different direction.

When I looked at my watch, it was midnight.

Seeing my glance, Ramalina said, 'Why don't you stay here and go back in the morning?'

'I would rather go home,' I said, almost involuntarily.

I did not like the idea of the track through the woods, the hoot of the night owl, the distant rumble of hidden animals. But I felt the strongest resistance to staying in this house. I never liked overnighting anywhere, abruptly, in this way, so my resistance was automatic.

'Can I call a taxi?'

'You can call, but it won't come,' Marcus said. 'They never come out here, they get lost, and if they do promise to come, it costs not a small fortune but a large fortune.'

In his drawl, this sounded funny, for half a second.

There was a pause, during which they all waited for me to do the reasonable, civilised thing, and change my mind. But I did not speak.

Eventually, Ramalina said, in a voice that was more chirpy and sharp than usual, 'Marcus will drive you home.'

He'd drunk half a bottle of wine and two Cointreaus, but I said, 'Thank you. Sorry to put you to this trouble.'

A four-wheel drive, which I had not previously seen, was parked in front of the porch. We got in and drove through the forest, along a track, also new to me. Marcus did not speak and neither did I. The car rattled occasionally against the bumpy road but otherwise the silence was dense and complete; it was like being at the bottom of the ocean.

Far from being soothed by this, I was terrified. My heart froze and I waited for some terrible shock: the lion would appear now; I knew it in my blood. In the beam of the headlights the amber eyes would shine and the great mouth open and the roar shatter the quiet of the night.

But no lion roared. No coyotes, or racoons, or bobcats. Not even an owl hooted.

'Good night.'

The door clicked, and I realised I'd been locked into the jeep.

'See you soon!'

The drive had taken about five minutes.

I was relieved to enter the safe ordinariness of the lodge, with its smell of herbs and garlic, its comfortable old sofas and shelves of well-thumbed books. Relieved. Also subtly disappointed.

Li had discovered something about the family. They were called the Klarstads. They had lived in the house in the forest, Moss Lodge, for fifty years. Ramalina's husband's family had built the place as a holiday home; he had died fifteen years ago and since then she had lived there all the year round. It was known that Marcus was some sort of musician but he had the reputation of being a recluse; he gave no interviews and disliked being televised while performing, and he had not performed locally. Kim had not heard of the daughter, Isabel, but that was probably just an oversight: she was not known for anything, and did not leave home, so who would know about her?

'They're OK. They probably just need a bit of company,' Li said.

I called in in the early afternoon a few days later. The scene was exactly as it had been on my first visit. I walked down the drive between the fir trees, and sighed with pleasure when the low white house came into view. Isabel reclined and Ramalina sat by the pool, and Marcus swam languidly in the cool water.

The fragrance from the roses was stronger than before, something I attributed to the heat of the day. Even here, in this paradise, where the climate is temperate and invariably perfect, it was slightly too hot, while the rest of the nation sweltered in a terrible heat wave.

'Hello! Great to see you!' Ramalina called, as I approached the poolside.

Isabel smiled and nodded, but as usual said little.

I could hear Marcus's body plashing in the water, a sound as natural as the whirring of the hummingbird or the shiver of the breeze in the leaves.

Ramalina offered me tea, and cucumber sandwiches, in some sort of misguided deference to my native tastes. Isabel, who had put on her yellow silk robe soon after I appeared, glided across the lawn and brought this snack from the house on wicker tray. We talked about 'my day'.

'How was your day?' Ramalina's manner was as poised as that of a television presenter, it now seemed to me. She smiled and I felt penetrated by the look in her slanted, golden eyes; she was as controlled as if she were reading her questions from a monitor.

'Did you go to finishing school?' I asked rudely.

Isabel raised her eyebrows – an exceptional show of emotion for her – and there was a loud *whoosh* in the pool as Marcus pulled himself out of the water.

'Why yes, I did,' said Ramalina, with her wide smile. 'How clever of you to guess. As a matter of fact, when I was nineteen, I spent a year in a finishing school in Lausanne.'

'I didn't know they still existed,' I said.

'They existed then!' she laughed. 'It was a wonderful year. I met so many interesting people from all over the world, and I saw so much of Europe. We travelled extensively, on the train, to Paris and Rome and Trieste and London and Copenhagen.

41

Yes, it was a truly magical year for me.'

'When was that?' I asked.

'Oh, long ago,' she said, and smiled her rejection of the question.

'Did you visit Dublin?' I asked.

'No, alas,' she said, smiling. 'And I would so love to visit your beautiful city. I feel as if I had been there, I have heard and read so much about it.'

Marcus came then, and we talked about *Ulysses* and *Dubliners*, while he dried off in the sunshine. Ramalina and Isabel left the pool and went into the house. He asked me to stay for dinner but I refused, and then said I would come the next evening, if I could get a lift home.

And every day or two for weeks I visited their house in the woods, and had tea or lemonade or dinner, and a pleasant, easy conversation with Ramalina about my day and my work and what I was reading, and a long, intense conversation with Marcus about literature and life.

Every day I believed I was on the brink of finding out something wonderful, something radically important about the meaning of life and the meaning of fiction. I felt, as I walked through the redwood forest, through the whispering glades, the shifting pools of sunlight dappling through the long, trailing branches, the promising ferns, that today an amazing truth would be revealed, a moment of illumination would come, and that it would provide me with the answer I was seeking, the breakthrough I longed for, and needed.

I was not thinking of the kind of epiphany we talked of all the time, as we sat by the log fire after the dinners Isabel had cooked (for it was she who did all the work in the house). Not the Joycean moment of epiphany, where some ordinary Joe Bloggs realises that life is often sad, that we are mortal and lose the people we love, that loss must be tolerated, that compromise is the name of the game. I did not want one of those epiphanies that really just confirmed the truths that most sensible people know anyway, instinctively, and do not make much of a fuss about.

Nor yet did I hope for some big revelation about the nature of the universe. God exists. God does not exist. We will end. We will live on in some other form; our spirit will migrate to some other being; there is an afterlife; there is not an afterlife. The world will survive; the world will end; love matters; the world is beautiful and that is why we go on, and at the same time everything we know is doomed to extinction.

Maybe that last line was close to it, but it was not what I was looking for, not only that.

Some answer about writing is what I wanted. What is it for? Not just to entertain people with stories about other people very like themselves. It must have some more profound and important purpose, surely, even in the context of our knowledge of our imminent extinction, perhaps especially in that context.

Every day I felt I was on the brink. That the next day my brain, my self, would fill with light; that something wonderful would happen.

My period of residence in the lodge was drawing to an end. I had not said this, specifically, to the Klarstads. But they knew, as they knew most things.

'Stay on with us,' said Ramalina, with her most persuasive smile.

'Yes, do,' said Marcus. 'You can live here for as long as you like. It's easy to write here. You know that already.'

'Yes, I know that,' I said.

We were by the swimming pool, where they always were in the afternoons. Isabel was not there. In fact, I had not seen her for a few days, but since I seldom talked to her I had not liked to enquire where she was. I knew such an enquiry would not be welcome, and would be met with a blank stare.

Ramalina and Marcus showed me the room I would have if I stayed – at the end of the house, with a long window opening to a balcony, facing the rising sun, and another window to the south, directly onto the garden, with its oleanders and wisteria, and the branches of the redwoods like the drooping arms of ballerinas right behind. I loved my plain room in the lodge but this room was just as tranquil and at the same time much more beautiful. I could not imagine, I could not design, I could not conceive of a room that more perfectly matched my taste, my requirements. Indeed, when I stepped inside, I felt I had been

43

there many, many times before, and I knew it was a room I had dreamt of, in the dreams I often have of houses and castles, about which I wander, from room to room, in search of the perfect one.

'You'll write well here,' said Marcus.

He pulled me aside, and whispered, as his warm arm caressed my neck and an electric bolt of pleasure ran through my body. 'You'll make a breakthrough here. Here, you will be enlightened.'

And, as if in response, outside the window the lawn sprinkler went on, shooting a delicate fountain of raindrops into the air, and the sunlight caught them and transformed them to a rainbow, dancing there in a myriad diamond droplets outside the window of my dreamed-of room.

We went back to the drawing room, where Marcus played a new piece on the piano, and never had he played so well, and nothing he had composed was as moving and harmonious, and at the same time unlike any music that had ever been composed before on this earth. The sun dappled the polished floor and the rugs shone like soft jewels from some bazaar of the *Thousand and One Nights*, when the Orient was the land of magic and mystery beyond all imagining. The glass bowl of pink roses scented the air with a promise as tantalising, and true, as that of the music. They said, here is the answer you have been waiting for. Tomorrow you will learn what you were born to know.

And then we had dinner, the most delicious dinner yet. We served ourselves from the bowls and dishes on the sideboard, and I dared to ask where Isabel was.

Ramalina's yellowish eyes sparkled at my question, but her voice was as soft as a cat's fur when she answered.

'She's indisposed.'

I knew from the way she flicked her golden braid that I would learn nothing further.

Well.

There is only one ending, as you who read stories know.

The next day I woke later than usual, and when I opened my eyes, something had changed. The sun was not shining, and the hummingbird was not whirring, and a grey fog filled the valley and blotted out the hills and the trees and the skyline.

Li said, 'Kim is picking me up at ten to go to the airport. What time is your flight?'

'One o'clock.'

'It won't take more than forty minutes to get down there. You should be OK. What time is your connection?'

'It's at 11 p.m.'

'So you'll land at what time?' Li always said 'what time?' Never 'when?'

'Six o'clock tomorrow morning.'

That is when the flights come in, to Ireland, after the Atlantic crossing.

And as I said it I could see the west coast of Ireland as you see it from the plane at dawn, moist and green as lime jelly, and I could see, as well, the grey rain on the runway at Dublin, and I could feel the cold grey air on my skin, even as we sat and ate granola at the sun-bleached table. And I knew I would go back to the fogbound, beloved island, and struggle on towards an answer, like a woman who has stepped on the stray sod, and will wander around in one field for the rest of her life.

Taboo

Berry pulled my skirt and pleaded in a mock-sweet voice: 'Time for my story!' I was washing the dishes after tea – or supper, as they called it here. Her parents, Morgan and Warren Roley, had gone out for a walk by the lake. So they said.

I turned with a wet plate in my hand and let a few suds drip onto the top of her head, accidentally on purpose.

'Just give me two minutes, sweetie pie!'

'Now!' She didn't exactly stamp her foot, but she positioned it in readiness for stamping. Berry could throw the mother and father of a tantrum at the drop of a popsicle. Well, to be fair to her, it was past her bedtime. She was tired – according to the philosophy of the Roley school of child-rearing, this would excuse anything up to and including murder. 'Hansel and Gretel! Hansel and Gretel! Hansel and Gretel!'

She made me tell the same story every night. We had half a dozen new endings, some that involved the eating of the children by the witch, some the eating of the witch by the children. Berry (Beryl the Peril, I called her in my letters home) was bloodthirsty. Cannibalism enthralled her. More to the point, it sent her to sleep. To my knowledge, she was not troubled by nightmares.

I grabbed her middle finger and scrutinised it.

'Darn and double darn!' Morgan said that when she was

46

cross. It sounded absolutely ridiculous, but I had enough sense not to use the curses we had at home, even when she wasn't around to hear them. 'This little girl is still much too skinny!' I glanced meaningfully at the cooker. 'My sweet little child, you must eat lots and lots and lots of candy, so you'll grow big and juicy and fat … oops, I mean, big and strong!' And I gave my version of a witch's chuckle. *Hargh Hargh Hargh.* A bit like a donkey's braying. (Do they bray? Or do they neigh? What's the difference?)

Berry was five years old, sweet as a biscuit, with blueberry eyes and skin like maple syrup. I was her au pair. Just for the summer. I'd come over after the Leaving to take the job, which a teacher at home had fixed up for me. The first six weeks I spent at the Roleys' gingerbread house in Morristown, New Jersey, minding Berry while her parents were at work. Now it was August and we were on holiday, at a lake somewhere in Upper New York State. Lake Elizabeth. It was very nice: a long sliver of blue water with enormous rocky mountains as a background and black spiky trees all around the edges, like eyelashes. It wasn't like anywhere I'd ever been or even heard tell of. Morgan just called it 'Lake Elizabeth', and once or twice Warren referred to it as a resort. 'Resort' meant somewhere like Kilkee, to me, or Ballybunion. Blackpool. Seaside towns, real places. This was more like a boarding school, or monastery, even if its only purpose was pleasure. (It had its own little white chapel, mind you, discreetly tucked away in the woods.) There was a big house like a hotel down by the canoe harbour, where we ate sometimes, fabulous feeds of chowder and crab bakes. Pancakes and waffles and maple syrup. You could stay in this big house if you wanted to, but we lived in a log cabin. That was considered a cut above the hotel, to my surprise. I'd never stayed in a hotel; I would have loved to try it. But the cabins cost more, apparently.

I got along well with the Roleys, or as well as it's possible to get along with people whose servant you are, even if the au-pair label lifted my job out of the absolute mud; I told myself again and again that I wasn't really a maid or a servant. I was a student, or soon would be. After this summer I'd be starting college, I'd be studying anthropology and English, I'd be a free person. But even though I knew this, and believed that being a student was an occupation that carried plenty of dignity with it, plenty of *class*, and even though I made sure everyone knew that I was a student doing a holiday job, not some Irish lowlife immigrant, it was impossible to convince myself of this. That is a most peculiar thing: after less than week with the Roleys, I started to feel like a slavey in a James Joyce short story or one of those maids in frilly white caps in *Upstairs, Downstairs*. I stopped reading the books I had brought with me: Margaret Mead's *Coming of Age in Samoa*, and Claude Lévi-Strauss's *Tristes Tropiques*. Nietzsche's *Thus Spoke Zarathustra* (a long shot, anyway). Instead, I started browsing through Morgan's *Cosmopolitans* and *Vogues*, and began to eye hungrily the paperbacks she'd stocked up with for the holidays and which so far she hadn't opened.

Morgan wasn't the one to dispel my low self-esteem. She was a medical doctor, and anthropology students probably weren't much higher up the social scale than hired help, as far as she was concerned. The day after we moved up to Lake Elizabeth, she asked me what my father did for a living. I considered redeploying him there and then – he was a plumber, but I could say, 'He's a chemist', for how would she know, ever, one way or the other? But I didn't have the guts to lie.

'Eoow!' she said, with a little smile. 'Interesting!'

Before this conversation I had only babysat, but after it, I was asked to do some little chores – wash the clothes and put them in the dryer, and clean up the kitchen. Vacuum. Morgan didn't even ask 'Do you mind?' She just said, 'Ew! Rosemary! Um could you just um vacuum the bedrooms, and maybe the living room? They've gotten so dusty I can hardly breathe!' And she wafted her hand in front of her nose like Lady Bracknell when she hears about the handbag. I was to do the dusting and the rest of the housework when the Roleys were down at the lake swimming, or playing in the woods. But I was happy enough to be left alone in the cabin, even if it meant doing chores.

Anyway, I'd get through the hoovering or whatever it was I was supposed to do as fast as I could – which was pretty fast – and then I'd sit on the porch and delve into Morgan's holiday reading. As well as women's magazines, they had the *New Yorker* and *Time Magazine*. And her books were brand new ones, just out – Marilyn French's *The Women's Room* and

Alice Munro's *The Beggar Maid*. I started with Marilyn French because it was a novel, which I always liked better than short stories because you can get right into a novel and live in it, sort of, whereas a short story is, I don't know, sort of in and out before you've really got used to it. Lost in it, which is what I wanted then, when I was reading. I pulled a deck chair out of the shade, where the Roleys usually sat. They hated the sun and were always trying to escape from it, but I sat where the sun was strongest, because more than anything I wanted to get a tan that would make me look more American, make me smooth and suave. Like them. I ignored the fact that my lines would never be right: I had a potato face and a blob of black curls like a crop of blackberries on top of my head. Everything about me was round. That was my problem. I was a racoon, whereas the Roleys were racehorses: fine-boned, narrow, their brown limbs like sticks of cinnamon.

Out on the porch I pulled up my skirt – Morgan liked me to wear a skirt, more maidy – so the sun could get at my blancmange legs, and I started reading, letting the sun and the breeze from the lake wash over me. I loved that, the feel of the warm air on my skin. It set things stirring, deep inside me, vague but powerful feelings and longings that I couldn't identify. Before I came here, to America, the name I put on all those yearnings was just that: America. But here I was, with as much America as anyone would ever want, and the yearnings hadn't gone away. Now they seemed to be a hunger for warm breezes, for silky water, for happiness, which was still just out of reach, just around the corner. If only I knew what it was.

So I was sitting there, my legs in the air, engrossed in an article on how to examine your genitalia with the aid of a hand mirror – it was absolutely disgusting – when Trish and Chip found me. I pushed the magazine under a cushion and pretended to be reading the novel, but she saw, all right.

They were neighbours, from the next cabin. Morgan knew them – their father was a big shot from somewhere near Morristown. They'd brought Berry for a walk once or twice.

'Oops! Beg pardon!' he said. He was already on the porch.

'We dropped by to say hello to Berry,' she said, in a raspy, dry voice, much more confident than his.

'Oh,' I said. 'She's not here. They're all out. They're down at the lake swimming. They usually go swimming at this time, before their lunch.'

I had a tendency to tell people much more than they needed to know. I was pretty sure this pair were up to no good, that they'd come to snoop around, maybe even to steal something, but all the same, I was deferring to them. It wasn't that they *looked* super-rich or anything. They dressed like most of the teenagers at Lake Elizabeth, in shorts and T-shirts. Flip-flops. She was stocky, almost fat, not one of the svelte, smooth-skinned model types. She looked rather Irish, actually, although she wasn't. He was averagely tall, with curly, reddish hair, and fair skin. Intense blue eyes, the same as Berry's. Navy blue. Even so, I didn't think he was especially handsome. Most of the young men around here were like gods, and he looked more ordinary, like a nice-enough-looking Irish boy, not like a basketball player from somewhere off the Garden State Turnpike or Route Nine Oh One. (I loved the names they had on their roads: they made them sound so important.)

'Who are you?' she asked peremptorily. She'd no manners. And she should have known who I was because she'd been introduced to me once, down in the restaurant.

'Rosemary.' I felt the heat of the day pressing in on me suddenly.

'Hm,' she said, with an enigmatic pursing of her lips that was almost a sneer.

'Uh, I'm Chip,' Chip said hurriedly. 'Chip Johnson. And this is my sister, Trish.'

I pretended not to know. It struck me that they looked more like boyfriend and girlfriend than brother and sister. Although who'd have wanted Trish as a girlfriend?

'What're ya reading?' Chip pointed at the book.

I told him.

Trish's eyebrows shot up. 'I've heard of that.'

Most of the women I'd met over here spoke in hilly lines, their voices rising and falling, then rising like a ski slope at the end of the line, open and hopeful. Trish's sentences were downhill all the way, and when she finished one, it was shut and locked up for good.

She picked up the book without asking if she could and riffled through the pages.

Probably to cover his embarrassment, Chip asked me if I'd like to go canoeing with them sometime.

Trish stopped snooping in my book the minute he said this and looked as cross as a bobcat. I said I'd love to go out in a canoe, which was the truth.

In the books I'd had at home, on the sofa in our kitchen in Dublin I'd read of children who messed about in boats, who rode horses, who ice-skated, and who did a myriad other things which were off limits so completely for me that I never dreamt of asking my mother if I could do them, even though I longed to. Actually, we didn't know anybody who went out in a boat, or rode a horse.

Here at the lake they did all that stuff. Canoeing was just one of the dozens of desirable activities on offer, free to guests at the resort. Free to me. There was a harbour where all the silver canoes were lined up: they were long, with those nice turned-up pointy ends, like the shoes the prince wears in pantomimes. Smooth as silver herrings, they glided along the lakewater and it had not even crossed my mind that I could actually go out in one. But now that Chip had planted the notion in my head, I thought of it all the time. Plus, I was picking up courage from *The Women's Room*, seeing myself as an exploited female, although that I was exploited mainly by Morgan somewhat messed up the theory. Still, I asked my oppressor if I could have an hour or two to go to the canoes some afternoon when she was swimming with Berry. I'd never had the chance to do it before, I added, to strengthen my case.

'Don't you have canoes in Ireland?' It sounded like an anthropological question. She was genuinely curious about the customs of my tribe.

'No,' I said, although we did, naturally. I had seen them at Seapoint when I went to swim there in the summer. And on the Liffey, racing down past Islandbridge.

'Well ...' She looked at Warren, puzzled, and he shrugged. 'If you get through your chores, I guess it's OK.'

'Oh thank you!' I was amazingly happy. To be given an hour off out of twenty-four. How lucky I was!

The next afternoon I called over to Chip's cabin, which was identical to ours. He was on the porch, in the swing chair, reading. He looked up when he heard me coming up the steps.

I said hi and he looked at me in a confused way for a few seconds before he remembered.

'Oh yeah! Canoeing, right?'

'If that suits you,' I said, in my meek hired-girl voice.

'Sure!' He got up slowly, and the chair creaked. 'Give me a minute while I get my stuff.'

He was back in five minutes, in shorts and a vest, carrying a towel.

I wondered where Trish was.

'Um,' he hesitated and then said, 'Shopping with the folks, I think.'

My timing couldn't have been better, then.

When I remember that time, what I see is a photograph – although I haven't got a photograph of this or any of the experiences I had with Chip, since I couldn't afford a camera. He had one, of course, but he never took snaps of me. The photo in my head shows the two of us in the long silver-coloured canoe, out on the glimmering blue lake, with the bottle green trees and sombre mountains in the background. It's a lovely picture – you can't see the struggle I had to manage the paddle, Chip's disbelief that I was making such a bags of it. Or my fear that the canoe would overturn and that I'd have to clamber back onto it out of the deep water and would fail and drown. Because, as with many things that I yearned for, especially sporty things, canoeing was much harder and much less enjoyable than I'd anticipated.

Chip was a good teacher. He repeated the same instructions over and over again, as a mother names her child, without showing the exasperation he must have felt. His patience, his ability to suspend disbelief and to have faith in the pupil, were qualities that must have stood to him later.

They stood to me then. In a few days I was good in the canoe. We were able to move far out into the lake – there was a barrier of red buoys preventing us, but Chip just lifted the rope and we slid under. I would have liked to stay close to shore, but he wanted to go right out to the opposite side. Luckily that was impossible in the stolen hour I would have at my disposal.

I didn't fall in love with him during the first few days. I fell in love with the lake itself and with the canoe, and the paddle, and my developing skill in propelling the long, elegant craft through the ice-clean water. Then, about a week after the first canoeing, I woke up in the early morning and Chip's image was in my mind, and I felt a lightening of spirit, a miraculous change of perspective, as if my mind had been lit up and was now casting a bright, rosy light on everything. I knew I would see him sometime that day. That was all I wanted, and the rest of the day – six hours – was a preparation for that meeting. Time didn't drag, it was transformed by the knowledge that Chip existed, and that at three o'clock, when Morgan and Berry and Warren were at the beach, I would be on the water, heading out into the lake with him.

Trish never came with us, although Chip always invited her.

'I've got stuff to do,' she'd huff, giving me a look for which the best and only adjective is a simple one: dirty. 'I'll go down later when you two are finished.'

She'd toss her head and flounce off into the woods, a book under her oxter. Some people have a special talent for making others feel bad, and Trish had this gift in abundance.

On the seventh day I put my hand on Chip's when we were out in the lake, where nobody could see, especially not Trish – unless she spied on us with binoculars from some hidey-hole in the woods. That, oddly, was the first time I noticed something funny about his hand – he had only three fingers on the left one. The long finger was missing – it had been cut off, I never found out exactly how – when he was six years old.

He put down his paddle and we kissed. As well as we could, which is not very well in a canoe. The next day we didn't go out into the middle of the lake, but paddled along the shoreline until we came to a sheltered cove, where we pulled in, lay on the beach, and embraced. Kissing and pressing – I wasn't going to go further; you didn't, then, when you were seventeen, even in America. I'd stopped going to Mass (you couldn't, anyway, at Lake Elizabeth). I was definitely losing my faith, but nevertheless I felt the spying eye of the Blessed Virgin on me at certain crucial junctures. It's hard to get rid of that person, even when you know she doesn't exist.

The thing is, time flies when you're kissing someone you're

in love with. You kiss and then you look at your watch and three hours have passed, three hours that felt like three minutes. When I got back to the cabin, Morgan was already there, fuming. Berry had refused to go to bed, since I wasn't there to tell her the bedtime story. She'd become so upset they had to give her a sedative. And they – herself and Warren – had wanted to go out to dinner – they'd made friends with another couple the same age as themselves, and now they wanted to go out every night and have fun down at the café in the big house, drinking fruit punch and coke. (There was no alcohol at Lake Elizabeth, it was the big taboo, which didn't strike me as in any way unusual at the time, since I had taken the pledge when I made my Confirmation and had never drunk myself.)

I said I was sorry and tried to look it, but her annoyance had no effect on my mood. She could do nothing to dishearten me. Nobody could. I was buoyed up by love. My heart is a canoe, I said to myself, a silver canoe sailing through the silver sky.

Morgan noticed.

'OK!' she said. 'I get it. But don't be late again – OK? Or no more canoeing.'

'Canoeing!' I overheard them talking about me. Warren laughed in his not very nice way. 'Is that what she calls it?'

'Oh well, nothing will come of it,' said Morgan. 'How could it?'

'Chip is dumb,' said Warren. 'He's dumber than he looks.'

My eyes filled with tears. Of rage. It was not on account of the insult to Chip; it was on account of the insult to me.

There was no more canoeing, anyway.

The day after our landing on the beach Trish became seriously ill.

Poison ivy.

She'd stumbled into a patch of it while walking in the woods and was covered in a horrible rash.

They were always going on about poison ivy at Lake Elizabeth, but so far nobody had ever been stung. I'd begun to wonder if it really existed.

'It's not just a rash. That's bad enough, but Trish is allergic to it,' Chip's mother explained, when I went over at three o'clock as usual. His mother was like Chip, not Trish. 'Her throat has swollen. She can hardly breathe, poor old thing!' Chip and their father had driven to the hospital with Trish. 'I'm just hoping they'll let her back.'

They didn't. She had to be kept in. Two days later, the Johnsons cut short their holiday and left the resort.

We exchanged addresses and I wrote a few letters to Chip. But he didn't reply, to my surprise – and sorrow – and, after nearly two months of anguish, as debilitating as any physical fever, during which I read Yeats's poems about unrequited love and waited every morning and afternoon for the postman, willing him to bring the longed-for letter, I fell out of love more abruptly than I had glided into it.

This transition occurred the day I started college. The journey to college was not the adventure it is for some – it just involved catching the number 10 bus at the corner of the road where I'd always lived, and getting off it twenty minutes later at the university stop. But it was a momentous event. As I got off that bus and walked up the long, windswept avenue past the football grounds to the brand new college, I knew – I believed – that neither I nor anyone else in my family would ever be a hired girl again. The building had been designed in the most modern brutalist style by a young architect who had just defected from Poland and whose grey concrete theatres and white classrooms held for me the promise of freedom, knowledge and unimaginable wisdom.

The conference on 'The Concept of Taboo in Primitive and Contemporary Society' in San Francisco was one of those enormous ones, with up to four concurrent sessions running for most of the time, and one plenary at the end of every day. There were a thousand people in attendance, anthropologists from all over the world. I gave my paper ('The Persistence of Endogamy in a Suburban Community') on the first day. Since I had never visited San Francisco before and could only stay for one extra day when the proceedings were over, I escaped more than once to have a look around the city – I wandered along Mission, and took my chances on Haight, the old centre of the hippy culture which had been such a magical influence on my growing up, part of the promise my college days had contained.

Chip was giving a plenary. I didn't recognise his name, because, of course, it was not 'Chip', but something quite different: Hamilton. He had never told me that Chip was just a nickname, and I was so bewildered by America in the days of my au-pairdom that I had not known that 'Chip' often was just that. His surname seemed different to me, too – Mills. Surely it had been Thompson? Or Johnson? I'd written him three or four letters – I'd written his name on envelopes – but perhaps I was mistaken. That had all happened thirty years ago or more. Professor Hamilton Mills, he was now, anyway. He spoke with the suave assurance, elegance and humour that marked all the most successful academics; words rolled mellifluously from his mouth in long, perfectly shaped sentences, not a hum or haw anywhere, and his vocabulary was enviably rich. He was never at a loss, for one second, for the *mot propre*, as I often was, although I had been lecturing now for years. And yet he was undoubtedly Chip. The same stocky figure, the intense blue eyes, the shock of hair – which was grey now, but the shape of which had not changed.

The lecture was illuminating and entertaining and the round of applause exceptionally hearty. Afterwards, people milled around the eminent scholar, congratulating him, touching the hem of his garment (the regulation linen jacket, the male anthropologist's summer garb). There were no questions – he was far too important to answer questions.

I did not get close to him in the lecture hall.

But later, at the reception, in a great open space in the hotel, which looked out on the bay towards Alcatraz and the Golden Gate Bridge, I approached him, as he stood, wineglass in hand, freed for a moment from the swarm of sycophants which clustered around him, abuzz with praise and opinions.

I had prepared my speech in advance.

Hello, Professor Mills, I would smile gently. I am sure you don't remember me, but I met you a very long time ago when you were on holiday at Lake Elizabeth. You taught me to canoe.

That would be sufficient, I felt, to bring back all the memories.

No need to mention love, or the day on the beach, or poison ivy.

I glided through the room and by some miracle the crowds thinned as I moved, so that I bumped into no one, but sailed a straight course from the door to the verandah, where he stood with the bay and the bridge and the islands, all that magical panorama, in the background.

As I drew near, a woman joined him.

A stocky woman, with a mop of thick white hair, and a sensible outfit that made no concession to pleasure or fashion, or even the formality of the occasion: she was wearing a loosely cut navy blue pants suit, flat shoes. Her face had a scrubbed look. She was not at all the kind of woman one would expect Chip – Professor Mills – to have as a wife or a partner.

And of course she was not his wife. As I came up to them and began my spiel, her expression changed from one of indifference to one that was familiar to me: exasperation. Her pale blue eyes swept me up and down, taking in my red shoes and my black cocktail dress, my round, painted face, and dismissing them with the contempt I recognised only too well.

She said something to him, in her dry raspy voice, which had not changed one iota.

I finished my speech, to which he had listened with attention.

'I'm delighted to meet you,' he said. 'But no, I think you must be mistaken. I was never on holiday at Lake Elizabeth.' He shook his head in mock sadness. 'I can't even canoe.'

His companion – Trish, for sure – pursed her pale lips and regarded me smugly. She was drinking iced water with a slice of lemon in it.

He turned to her. 'Allow me to introduce my wife, Patti,' he said.

She smiled her cold triumphant smile and extended her hand.

'I'm so sorry,' I said. 'My memory plays such tricks on me these days. Thanks for a really inspiring lecture.' I turned to his wife and smiled. '"Taboos of the New Age". It's a subject I'm very interested in. It's an area where anthropology can teach us a lot about contemporary people.'

'Yes,' she said, in a voice like cold, rusty iron, which could cut you dead with one syllable.

The cocktail party was sparkling and went on for a few hours. I lingered, chatting to many people, keeping an eye on Professor Mills, keeping track of his movements. But in the end I gave up. I gave up whatever I was hoping for. I allowed some sliver of desire to slide away from me into the gathering mist of the Pacific night.

As I was collecting my jacket and bag from the cloakroom, he came out. He didn't say anything but he took my hand in his and pressed it.

Bliss ran through me then, sharply, as if I had received an injection of some euphoric drug.

He smiled, pressed my hand again. I felt his fingers and looked. The long finger on the left hand. Missing.

Odd that he hadn't replaced it. Can it be that fingers are irreplaceable, even today, unlike, say, kidneys, or livers, or even hearts? There are still some parts of the human anatomy which, once gone, are gone for good. Eyes, probably. Fingers.

I was wondering about this as Chip retreated.

Since then I have never seen him.

I check the Internet occasionally, just to see if he is still alive. Which, so far, he is.

The Yeats

Olivia had had her eye on the stoves for some time. There were four of them on display in the new hardware shop on the edge of the town – a vast place, with a big bathroom department full of Victorian tubs and Roman tiles, and a garden centre overflowing with ornamental plants and terracotta pots of every shape and size. The shop was owned by Murphy's, which had served the town for a century from a cramped premises on Main Street. The new branch had been designed to cater to the needs of the affluent community, which wanted hot tubs, landscaped gardens and big gas barbecues.

But almost as soon as the new shop opened all the things it was designed to cater to – wealth, optimism, sunny days – stopped. Suddenly the country, which had been so rich, descended into poverty, like a hiker who had been striding blithely along, his rucksack of goodies on his back, singing, *tra-la tra-la*, stumbling without warning into an ancient well. Aeons deep, dark as outer space. The glass doors of Murphy's wonderful shop slid open for the first time just as the world began its rapid slide into recession.

Nobody wanted barbecues, or Greek goddesses, or even roses, any more.

Energy-saving devices were what they wanted now. Anything that would save money (and – by the way – the planet).

Murphy's got the stoves during the winter. There was a big cream one, a replica of the Aga Olivia remembered from her childhood home, into which her mother would pour cindery coke from a brass scuttle several times a day. She wouldn't want one of those. And there were smaller black ones, simpler and more decorative devices, which you would use instead of an open fire. They were eighty per cent efficient, according to the sexy architect on the TV programme about doing up your house, whereas an open fire was twenty per cent efficient.

The stoves looked nice and cottagey. They were named after Irish writers: the Beckett was the smallest, the Yeats was the middle one, and the Joyce was the biggest (it could heat twelve radiators).

'Most people go for the Yeats,' Joe McCarthy told her. 'That's probably the one you'll be needing.'

Joe had been in the shop in town for as long as Olivia could remember. A wiry man, with sallow, leathery skin, bright brown eyes, he looked as if he should have been a jockey or a lion tamer, rather than a shop assistant. On Main Street, he used to be on the counter where they had the nails and screws, where the men went. But sometimes he'd be on the cash register, too, and Olivia had often bought a few cups and saucers or a potted geranium from him. They never spoke about anything other than hardware, but there was a spark there all the same and she was always pleased to see him prancing around the shop on his bow legs. Out here in the new place he was in charge of everything. At least, he was the one you had to ask for advice. They had young people on the cash registers, who didn't know anything. 'Joe McCarthy is the one you need to talk to,' they would say, if you asked about the stoves, or electric cables, or paint. 'He's on his lunch now but he'll be back at two. Unless he went on the late lunch. Did he, do you know, Emma?'

Alex was against the stove. He liked the open fire and he didn't like change. But it was chilly in the house this summer. The sun never shone. The fire looked lovely, flickering away, but it gave no heat to speak of. It seemed sinful to have the central heating on all the time, oil being the price it was, and the global supply of fossil fuels running out.

On St Swithin's Day, Olivia took the plunge.

For weeks fog had enveloped the valley. When you went for a walk, up the hill, you could hardly see your hand in front of you. An occasional sheep loomed out of the mist, eerie-looking in its long, shaggy coat, like a prehistoric animal. The sheep were lethargic in the fog, hardly bothering to move away, instead standing with lowered heads, looking as if they'd once had a dream of attacking you with their weird twisted horns, but hadn't got the energy. After a few days of this fog, Olivia, too, felt half-dead, gliding around like a ghost in the clouds.

But then the sun came out and the whole countryside – the bay and the ocean and the island and the mountains and the fields and the sky – were revealed like a great painted set on a stage, as the mist rolled back like a curtain. Her heart leaped. For forty days, she hoped – she knew it was a silly superstition – they would have days like this. Half-foggy and half-sunny. Fifty per cent better than it had been.

The day the fog lifted, she decided to buy the stove.

The chimneypiece in the house was its principal feature. It was a nice enough house in many other ways – wooden beams on the ceilings lent it a cosy air, and wide, long windows opening directly onto the field meant that the barrier between indoors and outdoors was minimal. You could sit in the kitchen and believe you were sitting in the field, like a cow in the long, waving grass.

All very nice indeed. But the chimneypiece was the most special thing.

'It was the builder's pride and joy,' Alex had told her several times over the years, when he was telling the story of the house, the only new rectory built in Ireland in about two hundred years. Its construction, which had become a family myth, was often recounted. The adventure, the misadventures. It had been one of the first new houses in the coastal parish, which was now full of them. For everyone, the experience had been novel and exciting: for the architect, from Finland; for the builder, from the next village. Most of all for Alex's first wife, Lyndsey, from the other side of the ocean, who was a person with an exquisite flair for choosing just the right thing. The beauty of the house was thanks to her.

At first, when Olivia married Alex, she had felt this as a burden. The mark of his former wife on the house was indelible. Olivia wanted to sell it and buy an old farmhouse and do it up with the money (that was the fashion now; the new places were looked down upon).

Alex wouldn't dream of it. 'Why? This house suits me perfectly.'

And gradually Olivia had accepted his way of thinking. Now she often felt grateful to the first wife. It was as if she had made Olivia a gift of the house, along with her husband.

The design for the chimneypiece called for plain grey cut stone. But the builder ignored that. He and Lyndsey went to all the beaches and collected all the different kinds of stone you get around here. It couldn't happen now. You weren't allowed to take stone from the beaches these days, and their chimneypiece was nothing less than a rare monument to local geology. Red lava, green aeolian sandstone, grey siltstone. All the rocks that you found in the hills and the cliffs and scattered along the battered shoreline had been looted and were represented right here in the living room.

And in the centre, a big fireplace, where turf had burned for the past forty years, flickering and dancing and casting shadows on the walls.

'And most of the heat going up the chimney,' said Olivia.

'I've never felt cold,' said Alex. He spoke with some bewilderment. He was the sort of man who lived inside his head and who seemed to pay no attention to his surroundings. Then occasionally, he would make some surprising remark, indicating that he did, in fact, notice ordinary things just like anyone else.

'That's because of the central heating. But we can't go on burning oil,' said Olivia. 'It's running out. And it's three times the price it was two years ago.'

'But we're away a lot of the time in the winter,' Alex said.

(Olivia's brother lent them his apartment in Alicante for January every year. The minister from the next parish – eighty miles away – drove over on Sundays to do the service.)

Olivia stared at him, hard. 'I just want to try this. OK?'

Alex shrugged. 'OK,' he said. But he looked sad.

'You never want anything to change,' she said accusingly.

'I know,' said Alex, with a tiny laugh. 'It's true. I don't.'

They ring from Murphy's first thing in the morning before she has woken up. Her mobile trills loudly, vibrating on the bedside locker.

'Where exactly are ye living?'

She gives them the complicated country directions. 'Turn left at Alice's B & B. Drive up the hill. You pass the old Church of Ireland where the road bends. There's a white farm gate. A red station wagon parked outside.'

She didn't expect them to deliver it so soon. Down she runs, all excited, in her dressing gown, to clean out the hearth.

Last night they'd lit the fire. She'd built it up with the new Eco logs, which burned bright but very fast as they watched a new art-house film on DVD. Alex's son, Andrew, who is literary, had lent it to them because he knows Olivia shares his taste in movies. (She and Alex have no children; he already had two sons, now grown up, when his wife was murdered, stabbed to death by an insane neighbour on the small, almost private, beach below the house, where she liked to skinny dip in the hot summers they used to have then.) Alex hadn't liked the movie. It was too modern for his taste, confusingly plotless. She'd poured them both a glass of wine, towards the end, to reward him for having stuck it out. And although it was almost midnight, she'd thrown a few sods of turf on the fire. Real turf, bockety, with bits of straw stuck to the sods. The faint peaty smell had floated into the room.

'This is the last fire,' he said.

She reached over and patted him on the knee. 'The stove will really look quite nice,' she said. 'And it will be so much more efficient.'

Now she tries to envisage what it will look like, sitting there, a squat, black, cast-iron stove, blocking the cave where the fire used to be. She can't actually imagine it in place. And how efficient will it really be?

She runs upstairs, takes off her dressing gown and pyjamas and puts on her jeans and jumper. Through the window she can see the truck making its way along the road by the coast. Red, with an ad for lawnmowers on one side and the name of the shop, Murphy Ltd, on the other. She is just tightening her belt when the knock comes to the door.

A man in a blue overall stands on the step, one of the big, thickset men who don't talk much, whom you get in these parts, alongside the quick, fiery type, like Joe in the shop.

'Murphy's, sor,' he says.

That is a peculiarity. Some people here call everyone, man and woman, 'sor'. When she first came across this, just after she and Alex married and she came to live in the rectory, she wondered if they were mistaking her for a man. Alarmed, she let her hair grow and did away with the country-look clothes. After a few years, she noticed that 'sor' wasn't gender specific, necessarily, and she started wearing her wax coat and big boots again. Alex never seemed to notice what she wore, one way or the other.

'Where do you want it put?'

She points to the pride and joy of the house, and then follows him outside. The enormous truck is parked out on the road. Perched on its back, all alone, is a small brown cardboard box.

'I won't be able to get the truck through that!' He looks accusingly at their gate.

Olivia wonders why they use such a big truck to deliver a small object, but she knows better than to ask.

'I'll have to swing it over. It's very heavy.'

She nods. The man is kind, sorry that everything has to be so awkward and that circumstances conspire against efficiency. It is an attitude she's accustomed to. After much foostering around, he hooks the cardboard box to a crane, swings it over the gate, and begins to lower it onto a trolley he's wheeled into the garden.

The name of the stove is printed on the box in red block letters: YEATS. Olivia watches it swinging in the bright air. She has to dodge out of its way as it swings close to her – she doesn't want to be killed by a cast iron Yeats. A seagull sitting on the roof of the house cocks his head and observes what is going on with great interest.

'Sixty per cent efficient,' the man says, as he pushes the Yeats into the house. 'The fire is only forty per cent. Most of the heat goes up the chimney.'

Different from what the architect on the television said. Twenty per cent of a difference. And what does it mean, anyway, twenty per cent heat, forty per cent? Olivia feels a pang of doubt.

But soon the Yeats is in place and the cave where the fire used to burn can be seen no more. Although, as Olivia explained to Alex, the grate will still be there, behind the stove. They can go back to the fire if they don't like the new arrangement, is what she was implying. But watching the man installing the flue, with much fiddling and the application of bags of cement, she knows going back will not be easy. It never is.

'There are two things that are good for man,' Alex says, when he emerges from his study some hours later. He has stayed in there, working on an article for the archaeological and historical journal, for as long as he could before facing the Yeats.

Olivia has read the instructions and lit a small fire in the stove. Already she is getting used to it. Already, she tells herself, it looks as if it has always been there. She pecks him on the cheek before he can complete the sentence – she knows he's suffering, but what can she do? – and leads him outside. The sky has clouded somewhat and the fields are now a muted, quiet green. Just a few weeks ago, at midsummer, everything was saturated with colour. Sapphire. Emerald. Purple. Gold. Now you see a gentle fading, the inexorable move towards autumn. The foxgloves, which people here call lady fingers, are almost gone, and the early purple orchids. The montbretia, which will come out soon, like sharp orange flames, and stay in the ditches until the blackberries ripen, have not yet blossomed, although they are gathering, relentlessly, in the damp air, like ears of corn.

Alex is older. Older than Olivia. Older than most people in the parish now. He looks young for his age, people sometimes take him for sixty-seven, not the age he is. Seventy-seven. He has been in this parish for forty-five years, and would retire if there was anyone to take his place. When he first came to the valley, to the old house that his wife replaced with this one, there was no running water, no electricity, only oil lamps. The women in the valley baked bread in pot ovens, which hung from black iron cranes over the fire on the open hearth, roasted potatoes and lobsters and crab claws in the embers. The men told long stories about ghosts and the fairies, gathered around the same firesides, until the early hours of the morning. And Alex collected a lot of those stories on his tape recorder, and transcribed them, slowly, painstakingly, for hours and days and years, in the study where he spends most of his time. (He stopped collecting stories after Lyndsey's death. Although they never found the murderer, everyone knew who did it. The son of the best storyteller. He moved to England two days after the funeral, which everyone in the valley, all the Catholics as well as the C of I's, attended.)

Now all those people have died, too. The place is full of ghosts. Walking around, Olivia sees dead people regularly – that is, she sees someone and thinks she knows them, then, with a start, remembers that they're gone. But Alex has survived, to write the articles for the historical journal, to preach his friendly, wise sermons on Sundays to the congregation of a dozen (on good days). He does this even though his own belief has been veering towards atheism for many years.

'Two things are good for man,' Alex says.

Olivia knows what he is going to say. He knows reams of poetry off by heart, is always quoting something. She waits. But he doesn't finish the line. Instead, he sighs again deeply. Olivia finishes it for him. 'The heat of the sun, and the fire on the hearth.' Those are the two things that are good for man, according to an Icelandic poet, writing in the Middle Ages. She says the lines, and squeezes Alex's hand, and thinks it's just a stove, for God's sake. But she doesn't say that.

They stand and look at their small field, and at the bungalows below, and the foaming ocean. It is the middle of July. You have to keep reminding yourself of that. There is still some hope that some sort of a summer will come. Winter is a long way off.

It is a miracle

It is the last weekend before the schools reopen. Let's call it the feast of the First Harvest. Everyone is celebrating, with wine and schnapps and shellfish, with paper hats and Chinese lanterns. But what good is any of that if you have no children? And no friends.

'We should have thrown a party,' Sara says to Thomas, her partner. Thomas smiles and says cheerfully, 'We are throwing a party. At each other.' He picks up his wine glass and pretends to toss it to Sara. She raises hers and says, 'Cheers', not for the first time this evening.

Thomas is wearing a baggy yellow T-shirt printed with a photograph of a moose and the words 'Cheer up! Everything will be OK!' A few years ago the company that insures his car gave their customers badges and T-shirts and caps decorated with this silly mantra. Thomas wears the T-shirt whenever he's in festive mood, and at many other times as well.

'Two's company!' He pats Sara on the bottom. He has hung Chinese lanterns on the porch and has put on an Abba CD in the living room. He forgot to the get paper hats.

'Yes,' Sara says wanly. Sometimes she finds Thomas's proverbs and maxims comforting, wise and profound. At other times, they annoy her to death with their unbelievable predictability. Thomas is not unaware of the range of her reactions but he loves his clichés far too much to abandon even a single one. On the contrary, he is constantly adding to his collection, savouring particularly trite specimens.

He squeezes her arm and chuckles.

She pushes his hand away. 'I'm going for a swim,' she says.

'What, now?' Thomas is taken aback. It's almost nine o'clock and he's just about to cook the crayfish.

'Just a quick dip.' Sara is pleased. It's not easy to dent Thomas's complacency. 'My last evening here!'

She slips down the path to the lake before he can stop her. Not that he would. Not that he would dream of it. He looks after her for a few seconds, bemused and as hurt as he ever can be, and then he finishes setting the table for dinner.

The mosquitoes bite. They are mustered in smudged clouds over the reeds, ready to stab as soon as she approaches the water's edge. But Sara takes off her old robe, hangs it on its hook at the edge of the dock, and lets them do their worst. She's well sprayed with insect repellent, so that only the bravest, most relentless, monsters succeed in puncturing her skin. Still, they hover around her, as always at this time of evening, making her itchy, until she slides from the wooden steps into the soft, cold water and swims away from the shore.

She swims out into the lake, keeping her head above the water so that she does not lose a second of the sunset – the sky behind the dark fringe of trees on the western shore is a lovely orangey colour. It looks edible, like a dark chocolate filled with sweet cream. She'd love to eat it or grasp it or somehow hold onto it, but as she swims towards it the colour melts away and vanishes much faster than you'd think it could.

The lamps are already lit in some of the lakeside cottages, and on many docks summer torches flicker. She can hear feathery music floating across the water from someone's garden, its source sheltered by reeds, by trees. All around the lake, the parties are starting.

Her movements are lazy as the evening, and the water laps against her skin. A small fish jumps, plopping close to her with a quick, quiet flip, a surprisingly comforting sound. She feels a kinship with the fish; she feels a kinship with the water itself, and with the colours and the rhythms and the sounds of the evening. Only when the sun vanishes behind the black spiky rim of the forest, and the moon – full – takes its place in the dark blue sky, does she turn and swim back to the shore, faster than she had swum out.

Their torch is lit on the porch when she returns, and she can see candles flickering on the table there. The flames keep the mosquitoes at bay.

'We can eat whenever you're ready,' Thomas says, as she passes into the house, wrapped tightly in her robe. He is happy again and has decided to forgive and forget, as usual. It's going to be OK.

'I won't be a minute.' Sara pats his head. Swimming always lifts her spirits and she knows he likes having his hair ruffled.

She flip-flops into the bedroom and pulls on loose cotton trousers and a muslin shirt with long sleeves. Her wet hair she pulls out of its band and brushes quickly, then ties back up again, in a tight, mean little black knot on top of her head. In the small mirror she looks worn and old, although her body feels rejuvenated after the swim. How she feels is not necessarily how she looks any more.

They sit on the wooden porch, overlooking the unkempt garden and the long, narrow strip of white flowers and long grass and reeds that stretches down to the lake. Ten o'clock and it is quite dark, just the flicker of lights on the docks and the ripple of moonlight on the black water relieve the heavy velvet autumn dark. The music is louder now, and occasional bars of laughter come floating across the lake, like silver canoes of joy.

But the bulging red eyes of the crayfish stare accusingly at her over the edge of the white dish. She eats them purposefully. Little Turkish crayfish, frozen until an hour ago, they consist mainly of shell; you have to bulk out the fish with bread and butter and salad, and wash it down with plenty of white wine, to make a meal of it. Their music – it's still Abba, 'Dancing Queen' – plays at a low volume in the background. The mosquitoes buzz around but don't descend onto the table; the Chinese lanterns grin, yellow and blue and red, from above.

Sara eats and drinks, and thinks that although the food is good and the setting lovely, although she likes sitting here with Thomas, she feels she would just as soon be reading, or watching television, as being here, pretending to have a party. And she knows he feels exactly the same. But it's the harvest festival and they are obliged to celebrate it just like everyone else. As the level of the wine decreases, their mood lifts; they feel better, they talk more. By the time they have drunk two bottles and the moon has moved around to the side of the house, they feel they really have had a party, as good a party as anyone could wish for. Then they tumble happily into their separate beds.

Thomas is a writer; every Christmas, without fail, a new work appears and sells about five thousand copies, after which it disappears without trace. In addition to the royalties, he gets a grant from the Writers' Union, which supplements his income, and as a result, he is reasonably well-off. How he can find topics for so many books – most of them novels – is a mystery to Sara, since he has difficulty in coming up with new topics of conversation, at least with her. They have been together for ten years and have grown so alike that people sometimes ask if they are brother and sister.

Sara works in a library. She has been working in a library, the same library, for fifteen years, ever since she arrived in this country. Initially, the work was very challenging: she had to master the language, and she had to take a course at the university, for two years, which she managed to do while working thirty hours a week in a supermarket, stacking shelves. The transition from supermarket to library was gratifying, was wonderful, when it came. She does not stack shelves in the library. She doesn't even catalogue books; that's all done centrally these days. Her days are spent talking to the customers, the readers, about books, and other things. Many of the readers are old people who want to tell her about their grown-up children or their illnesses, to hint at the condition of their routine bodily functions or to discuss their plans for the important calendar festivals, such as Christmas or Midsummer or the Harvest Moon.

Sara's library encourages this sort of thing. It is furnished with sofas and easy chairs, and a pot of coffee is always at the ready, so some old folks spend a good part of their day with her, drinking coffee and chatting. Her function is as much social worker as librarian. But there is, of course, more to it than that. She checks books in and out; she decides what to display on the 'New Books' rack; and she organises things: lectures, book clubs, storytelling sessions. Readings by popular writers – or not so popular writers who happen to be local.

It was in this way that she met Thomas, who came to read from his latest novel before Christmas one year. Only about five people came to the reading. So afterwards, Sara treated him to a glass of sherry and home-made marzipan biscuits, even though she would have preferred to go home. He talked to her about his life. He had just come back to town from his summer cottage on the lake, where he had been the only resident at this time of year. The lake was frozen, the garden snowed up, and the house heated by a huge log fire.

This all sounded very romantic to Sara. She pictured sitting by the fire, with the flames flickering like friends and casting interesting shadows on the walls. In her picture, she was reading and listening to classical music. There were candles, and mulled wine, and Christmas was in the air. Thomas was not actually in this scene but, then, she hardly knew him at the time.

A week after the reading fiasco, he telephoned her, and they ended up spending Christmas Eve together. Sara could not return to her own family, since they did not celebrate this feast, and she had no plans of her own. Neither had Thomas. The reason was, he had been divorced less than a year – news that surprised Sara, who could not picture him married. His parents were dead and he did not feel like inflicting himself on his sister and her family, just because he no longer had a wife (the sister had invited him).

He treated Sara to pickled herring and meatballs and cold beer, in his flat, which was full of books and smelt musty. No decorations. Not a tree, or even a card. No fire. But one large window overlooked the river. The trees on its banks were festooned with lights, which glittered like stars against the black sky. Sara munched her meatballs and thought of the cottage by the lake.

The relationship prospered. Now she and Thomas have a house on the outskirts of the town, perched on a rock among pine trees, and a view of a lake from the kitchen window: this country is full of lakes. You can't get away from them. Everywhere you go, there is a lake, glittering like a knowing eye at you from among the rocks and the dark trees.

She still works in the library, spending much of her time there, while Thomas sits in his own library at home, typing up his novels.

Sara feels her heart sink when she drives out of the cottage garden and honks goodbye to Thomas, who stands beside the flagpole, flapping a big white handkerchief in big childish waves. Now that she is leaving, a gush of love overwhelms her. Both he and his cottage, which is ramshackle, like an abandoned magpie nest in its untidy cluster of trees, grab at her heart. Sadly, she makes her way along the narrow dirt track that connects the lakeside to the main road, sneaking hungry looks at the neat summer houses, all with lacy white facing boards and fancy porches, baskets of nasturtiums and late roses. They're sweet, but she hasn't felt particularly drawn to them during the past month, as she cycled along in her shorts and T-shirt, inwardly contemptuous of the whole place, its ritualistic certainties, its bourgeois safeness. Everyone rushes down here the day before Midsummer's Day, like migratory birds, or clockwork toys controlled by some remote authority. They stay for at least a month if they're workers, for three if they're pensioners, which a lot of them are. But what do they do once they get here? Go for a walk or a cycle. Some of them swim. There are occasional gatherings, which you'd hardly call parties: coffee and seven kinds of cake in the afternoon; sometimes someone has a birthday and then there's wine and smoked salmon, seven kinds of salad. They like to count things, and measure: their lives are measured in walks and cycles; summer succeeds summer, they come to the cottage in June, they return to the city in August, they come to the cottage in June. Then one summer they're too old to drive and they stay in the city for the summer. And then – very soon after this, because what is the point of living if you can't go to the summer house? – they die.

So what's wrong with that? she's thinking now, as she leaves it all. The petunias and the fresh paint, the woodland walks? Now it all seems like the very pinnacle of civilisation. Peaceful and harmonious, warm and luminous, it is heaven on earth. She can't stand the idea of going back to the bustle of the city. It is still summer, but autumn will descend very soon. Quick like a curtain it will fall and the iron-cold fogs of November will put a lid on the year and usher in the snow.

Lucky Thomas, whose work allows him to milk every last drop of summer, to stay here in the country, walking in the woods and swimming in the lake. At night he will light his candles and listen to the lap of water on the shore and the buzz of the mosquitoes. All for another month, at least.

If he loved her, wouldn't he sacrifice that and come home with her? Now?

She's there, home, by mid-afternoon, and she is opening the windows to let the fresh air into the living room when Lisa, her friend at work, telephones and asks if she can call around.

'Yes,' says Sara. 'Of course.'

It's an unusual request. Normally she chats with Lisa only at work – at coffee breaks, sometimes during lunch time in a café. They don't visit each other's houses. In fact, unarranged visits by anyone are rare in these suburbs.

Lisa's life is dominated by her two children, who are in their early twenties. They are students and whenever Sara has met them they have been taciturn, sulky even. But Lisa adores them and spends most of her life rushing around looking after them, although that is not how she sees it herself. 'I've got to hit the supermarket,' she cries, as she dashes out of work five minutes early. Or 'There's a mountain of washing to be done!' More often than not, she is rushing home so she can give one of the children a lift somewhere. An unpaid chauffeur, that's what she is. She doesn't mind. Even though she claims to be feminist and liberated and assertive, she admits to being an unpaid chauffeur, an unpaid cook, an unpaid washerwoman and unpaid charwoman, as well as a badly paid librarian. 'How long can it go on for?' she asks good-humouredly. 'I thought I'd be pursuing my hobbies as soon as they got to be fifteen! I thought I'd be doing the round-the-world tour, and writing a novel!' But it's pretty clear to Sara that Lisa has no real wish to do hobbies. She thrives on all this rushing around, juggling, hard work. She enjoys grumbling about the children, and Anders, her husband, or ex-husband – he left, or was turfed out, years ago. They got a legal divorce but never quite separated. 'He never darkens my bed!' Lisa says, waving her hands in the air to underline her words. He never darkens her bed but he darkens her kitchen door almost every day, and eats dinner with his ex-family five days out of seven.

Such arrangements are not common, but from her chats in the library, Sara knows that odd arrangements are on the increase. Separated couples do not make the clean break that was de rigueur in the past. Now it is all right to re-create a domestic limbo, to bring the new partners home to the old partners, to realign the family players into a formation that looks like a *ménage à trois*, or *à quatre*, or *à dix*. High drama is out of fashion. Nobody screams, 'Betrayal!' They regroup, grinning and murmuring, 'Think of the children!'

Lisa is short and roundly built. She keeps her fair hair tied in a bun on the top of her head and, of course, she has a fringe. Surprised blue eyes. Face pink as a cupcake. She doesn't have a new partner, as far as Sara knows. But she could have; she's attractive enough, in mind and body.

Lisa looks calm and relaxed when she arrives. She bounces into the cool, dim hall.

'Welcome back!' she laughs. 'Was it good?'

'Very good,' says Sara.

The sun is still shining, so they go to sit at the back of the house, on a terrace overlooking the suburban valley. Sara's house is built on the side of a steep enough hill, one of many houses scattered among the trees. All the gardens are nature gardens: patches of hillside. They aren't separated by fences, but everyone knows exactly where their boundary is, and they never step over it.

They drink a glass of champagne, which seems appropriate for such a sunny, glowing afternoon, and suits Lisa's clothes. She is dressed in a very summery, girlish outfit: a long, flowery cotton skirt, a pink top with lace around the neckline. Also, a straw hat with a floppy brim and a small white daisy in its pink band. She is tanned, and she has lost weight since Sara last saw her, about six weeks ago. Her whole appearance suggests that she has good news, and the hat hints at what the good news involves: love.

'I got married,' Lisa says. She smiles and raises her glass.

Sara's face does not drop but her response is slower than it might be. She forgets to raise her glass as she stares past Lisa's hat at a blue hydrangea down at the end of the garden and takes a few seconds to let this information sink in.

'Congratulations!' She jumps up, all smiles, and kisses Lisa on the cheek, which smells of Chanel No. 5, not a perfume Lisa ever wore before. (She used to smell of washing powder and sweat.) 'That's wonderful!' She sits down again and gulps some wine. 'Who is …' How do you best put it? The lucky man? 'Who … em … is it?'

It occurs to her that it could just be her former husband. Remarrying your ex is an event that occurs among the children of the old library users; three or four of her regular readers have experienced this over the past few years (they, the old mothers, don't get invited to the second weddings, which are very low key). But would remarrying Anders call for such a physical transformation? The perfume, perhaps. But would marrying your ex call for a hat, with a flower in the brim? Probably not. Anders would think that hat was silly.

'He's someone I met on holiday,' says Lisa. 'You remember, Kirsten and I went to Turkey?' Kirsten is the younger daughter; she's doing media studies, like most people's younger daughters. 'To a resort on the Black Sea. Well, she made friends with some young folk at the hotel and I was left to my own devices most of the time.' That would be Kirsten all right. 'Pottering around the bazaar, sitting on the beach in solitary splendour. Well, I often had to eat alone! You know how it can be for single ladies!' She giggles gleefully, no longer one of them.

'Oh yes.' Sara sees, incongruously, a boiled sausage in a nest of sauerkraut. 'I know, all right.'

Lisa pauses and looks at her, smelling a story. But she is too eager to tell her own to delve.

'I was sitting outside a restaurant, eating lunch, happy as a clam. It doesn't bother me to be alone, especially during the day.'

Sara laughs.

'I mean, eating during the day. Eating dinner at night in a hotel is different. I don't like being alone for that. You know what I mean.'

Sara nods.

'Anyway, there I was, sun and wine, sardines and bread. This man came up to my table and asked if he could join me. The tables were otherwise full. Cheeky devil, I thought, but for some reason, possibly wine-induced, I said yes. Anyway, one thing led to another and now I'm married. To someone I picked up in a restaurant. It's unbelievable.'

The only unbelievable part of the story is that he married her, Sara thinks. Suddenly she remembers a woman she knew when she lived in London, before she came here. Sara was teaching then, and this woman was a fellow teacher, one of the single ladies who seemed to be so numerous back then – now she knows that they seemed numerous in schools and hospitals and libraries because they were the only women who had jobs. The married ones were all at home, glad to be there and smug about it, too, as she recalls, since marriage was still considered a victory for a young woman, her passport to economic security and a good life, an escape from the schools and the offices.

This woman – whose name was Bridget – began to joke about having married the school gardener, who was called (incredibly) Paddy. Maybe the conjunction of the names planted the idea in her head? Bridget described the wedding in great detail: what she wore (an off-the-shoulder cream silk dress, a cream hat with a silvery veil and mauve flowers), what he wore, what they ate (roast lamb with mint sauce, sherry trifle or strawberries and cream for dessert). The honeymoon was in Tenerife and they had put a deposit on a dinky little house in Wimbledon.

The story went on for weeks, becoming more elaborate, and more embarrassing for everyone in the staffroom. Their main concern was Paddy, that he should not get wind of it – it wasn't likely, since he never came to the staffroom, having a shed in the grounds, where he stored his tools and drank his tea. But it turned out that Bridget was the person they should have been worried about. One day she didn't come to work. She'd taken an overdose of sleeping pills. At the funeral they shrugged and said they'd never suspected that she was depressed, she always smiled so much and loved a joke. She drank, of course, some added, as if that explained a lot.

So did Lisa. Maybe she is making it all up.

'He's called Tacumsin,' she is saying. 'He's divorced and is a lawyer.'

Sara wants more specific details. She asks where the wedding took place.

'In the registry office in this city,' says Lisa, seeing her game. 'The marriage is as valid as boiled potatoes.'

'So, has he moved in with you?' Sara feels more concerned, not less.

'No,' says Lisa. 'I'm going to move in with him. In Istanbul.'

What about your job and your precious children? Sara needs to know. Not to mention your friends, your country, your home? And that now-you-see-him-now-you-don't ex-husband of yours?

'It's ME-time!' Lisa closes her eyes and smiles in the direction of the sky, where the sun is beginning to sink into the velvety trees. She opens them wide and speaks quickly. 'I've already handed in my notice to the library, so there's no need to worry about that. The kids will stay in the house here; I don't need to sell it and they can look after themselves, really.'

So. Tacumsin is not a con man, after your house and salary, and access to the best social welfare system in Europe?

'He's rich,' Lisa says. 'Isn't it lucky? He's got a big apartment in Istanbul and a summer place by the sea. His former wife took their house, which is a kind of palace.'

'Have you seen the apartment?' Sara doesn't have to ask about the palace.

'I've seen the summer apartment,' Lisa says. 'Sara, don't be so suspicious! He's bona fide. He loves me! I know it's hard to believe.'

Sara murmurs something, which Lisa doesn't pay any attention to.

'I'm a big girl, I can look after myself,' she says. She gives Sara a big kiss on the lips and hugs her. 'Look, you come and see the apartment for yourself. And meet Tacumsin. Come around Christmas, do a bit of shopping. How about it?'

'That would be lovely,' says Sara, with as much enthusiasm as she can muster.

'I am so happy,' says Lisa, and she laughs aloud, a laugh of pleasure and triumph. Or bliss.

Sara doesn't ask what age this man is, or what he looks like or what he's like in bed. But the last she can guess.

In the spring of this year, Sara went alone to a strange restaurant. This was in a city in the south, in another country, where she attended a conference on the digitisation of library records. For the past two years, digitisation of library records has been the main topic at all the library conferences. Sara doesn't find it very enthralling as a subject. (Why can't they just copy the books, instead of talking about it as if it were rocket science?) But she goes to the conferences because she likes the free trips to nice cities. She goes to three or four a year, and has seen most of the capitals of Europe, and a few others, in this way, at the expense of the nation. She always stays on for a few days after each conference to look around. This she was doing on the occasion in question, keeping to her room in an old hotel in the centre of the old town. The hotel was described as 'charming' on the Internet, which seemed to mean there was old furniture in the bedrooms – one baroque chair in a dusty shade of pink in hers; the head of the library had a grand piano in his, apparently, and a four-poster bed. There were faded old prints on the walls. Also, the hotel had literary associations: in the lobby hung a portrait of a famous writer who liked to stay there: Franz Kafka.

Some of the other librarians had stayed on after the conference, too, and were visiting a Nazi concentration camp at Mauthausen, near Linz, about an hour's journey from the city. Sara decided to forego the experience. She wasn't attracted to concentration camps, as tourist destinations, and this wasn't one of the well-known ones. She'd never heard of it, in fact. So she spent her free morning tramping around the museums and art galleries. These were many and magnificent and had been built by the emperors to store the collections they had taken from other countries, sometimes looting, sometimes buying (at cheap prices). She had seen the feather headdress with which Cortez had been presented by a great Mexican king. And, more oddly, a reconstructed house from Greenland. It was part of the Inuit collection. Just a little wooden house, not an igloo, probably something made from a pre-fab in a packet and put up by some Greenlander in the 1950s or thereabouts. It was of Scandinavian design, a bit like the summer houses around Thomas's lake, or a bit like their garden sheds. Just one room, with a range and a few sticks of furniture, some pictures of Christian saints, the kind you see in Ireland.

Thomas wrote a historical novel about it, Greenland, about a Norse settlement that had died out in the Middle Ages, nobody knows why. Sara had visited the site of the settlement with him. Brattahlid; now it has an Inuit name but she and Thomas called it by the Old Norse one, which is easier to remember. At Brattahlid people live in concrete apartment blocks, which look as if they were built by some Soviet apparatchik who'd strayed over from Siberia. But there had been a village with a little shop, so maybe there were some small houses, too. Thomas had been very excited by the place, and she had become infected by that. She'd read all about the old settlement, and the new settlement, too. She could have written a book about it herself, by the end of the visit. But she didn't. She has always believed she could write a novel, if she wanted to; she watches Thomas doing it, it looks easy enough, easier than lots of things. But she has never bothered. Why should she? There are enough books in the world – thousands, that nobody ever reads, in the library where she works.

She hadn't thought about the Inuit for years. The sight of that little house, so humble and simple, in this museum, transformed from basic cabin to work of art by virtue of a change of venue, was deeply moving. Her interest in the people of that bleak, icy country revived.

But not for long. As is the way with such moments of inspiration, in museums, her profound feelings were replaced by more mundane considerations the second she stepped out the door. Lunch. She wanted to eat some local dish – her colleagues had eaten at an Italian restaurant, a Greek trattoria, a French bistro, but hadn't tried the native cuisine. Maybe with good reason – the city is famed for its cakes, not its dinners. But there was an old-fashioned, stodgy-looking restaurant near the museum, and she decided to try that, now that she was alone.

When she stepped inside, she knew she had made a mistake. It was a dark, cluttered room. Thick curtains shut out daylight and the place looked smoky, even though nobody was smoking. The tables were covered with heavy green cloth, the walls panelled with dark wood. It looked more like a pub than a restaurant, but it was crammed with people eating. Waiters ran around frantically, balancing trays and plates heaped with food. Sara decided to leave, to go back to the Italian place in the hotel. But before she could escape, a waiter came and insisted he could find her a table. He asked her to sit on a sofa near the reception desk and she felt obliged to obey him. Five minutes went by. Eventually, another waiter came and smiled as he pushed Sara towards a table. It wasn't empty. Would she mind? She would, but she agreed, anyway, and next thing found herself seated opposite a man who was eating some sort of stew, not presented with any attempt at style. She buried her head in the menu and ordered what looked like the most local dish; the menu was handwritten and the writing wasn't very legible, apart from which she only understood some of the words. She also ordered a glass of wine – the man had one.

He gave her a friendly smile. That is where she made her first mistake: she returned it.

He looked like the kind of food she was looking for: local and authentic. Black hair, skin like polished copper. His shirt was snow white, with billowing sleeves, framed in a waistcoat of black boiled wool, or felt, which was the most typical cloth of the country. Sara could only see him from the waist up, so unfortunately could not take note of his trousers: probably not made of leather, probably perfectly ordinary black trousers, or jeans, although knee breeches would have complemented the folksy look of the waistcoat. He was like a woodcutter in a fairytale; he reminded her of Red Riding Hood's father. This country was rich in fairytales, forests and wild animals, abandoned children. Looking at him, sipping his glass of white wine, you could see where those characters had come from.

But he turned out to be foreign, like her, not authentic at all. Of course, a real local would never wear a waistcoat like that, off the stage, an outfit redolent of peasants and opera and folk dances, which probably real peasants had never worn. (They'd never have managed to get the shirts white enough, would they? Without extra strong detergent and top-of-the-range washing machines. Peasants washing in wooden peasant tubs, by peasant mountain streams.) He came from Italy; he had come up for the weekend.

Italy. Sara is no racist. But she knows what Italian men can be like when they come across a single woman; she'd been to Italy more than once. She smiled tightly, she tightened the muscles in her legs, she crossed her arms across her breasts, squashing them.

He didn't notice. He often came to this city, he was telling her, as if she'd asked. He loved it here.

'And how about you?' he asked. What was she doing?

Sara made up a story. She said she was attending a conference of writers; that she was a writer of detective novels. In the nick of time, she prevented herself from saying she was going to give a reading later on that afternoon – he might want to come and hear her. So she said she had a meeting in half an hour and had just slipped out for a quick bite to eat.

He nodded and she could tell he didn't believe her.

Her glass of wine came and he looked at it slowly. If you drink wine, they assume you're up for anything; it gives some sort of message, like red trainers (though what message, precisely, they give, she isn't sure – she just knows it's safest to avoid wearing them). Hump him, she thought, taking a large gulp. It was cold and dry and fruity, and there was about half a pint of it in her glass. They served wine as if it was lemonade here.

Her food arrived.

An enormous boiled sausage, pink and fleshy, draped itself over a mountain of pickled cabbage. They both stared at it, speechless. Obscene. Grotesque. Pornographic. These were a few of the adjectives it triggered, in Sara's mind. He returned to his stew, which had looked repulsive but now moved down several notches on the disgust register – his bowl of brown mess was positively prim by comparison with Sara's plate. She glanced around at the nearby tables to see if everyone was staring at her lunch in shock. But no, most heads were bent over their own plates, most mouths were masticating energetically. And she saw that most of the food looked nearly as disturbing as hers. The tables were crowded with oversized sausages, shanks of bloody lamb, robust bony ribs. A big grey fish with its head still on stared wildly up from the silver plate where it waited to be eaten, like a witch waiting for the torch to light the faggots.

No attempt had been made to disguise the food, to make meat look like chocolate buttons or vegetables like garden flowers. It all looked like what it was, which was something you might give to a not very fussy cat.

Sara sliced a bit off her sausage and told the woodcutter that she was married. She isn't married, since Thomas doesn't approve of it (any more – he has one wife already, anyway). But, what matter, she might as well be. The woodcutter was married, too, he is quick to assure her. And, better than that, he has a daughter aged twenty and a son aged twenty-two. To cap these impeccable credentials, he mentioned that he was a medical doctor; he named the city where he lived, in northern Italy – a serious, respectable, working city, not an operatic set of a place, a tourist postcard, not Venice or Florence. He went on and on, entertaining her with the details of his autobiography in broken but exceedingly fluent English. (Can it be both broken and fluent? Ungrammatical, she means. Lack of grammar seldom stops anyone who knows enough words to tell their story.) She began to dig into her sausage. It tasted much better than it looked. It tasted great, in fact, and so did the cabbage. Sara launched a serious assault on both. She realised that she hadn't had any real vegetables for days – just the odd lettuce leaf, or half tomato sculpted to the shape of a red star, decorations rather than food. Now she really appreciates this cabbage patch on a plate, which this interesting restaurant had provided her with. Her body was screaming for iron and, needless to say, she was constipated, as she always was, at conferences.

The woodcutter ordered a bottle of wine, for both of them. Sara shook her head; he was going much too far. But he wouldn't take no for an answer. The waiter colluded with him, filling her glass against her wishes. Of course, once it was there, she drank it. Who cares? she thought. I'm practically an alcoholic, anyway, and here I am in a restaurant that looks like an opium den, surrounded by fifty people stuffing themselves with schnitzel and strudel.

The waiter smiled triumphantly whenever he passed their table, keeping an eye on the wineglasses, planning to refill them the second it was needed. He looked pleased with himself, smug in the knowledge that he had brought two lonely people together, got a little *je ne sais quoi* started in his section of the restaurant. Maybe he was some sort of matchmaker, on the side?

Mr Riding Hood was separated from his wife. Sara presumed this was true. On the other hand, if you're chatting up a woman, presumably you don't tell her you are happily married. She was beginning to find it difficult to grasp exactly what he was saying. His English deteriorated as the meal continued and the level in the wine bottle sank. That's how it is as often as not when you're speaking a foreign language. It's great for the first five or ten minutes and then you get tired and it's downhill all the way. He knew no German and Sara had only a few words of Italian, so English it had to be. He stumbled now when he came to a preposition; he tripped over certain phonemes and floundered in tenses. But the words kept coming, a jumble of episodes and characters and feelings. She let herself drift away. She hadn't asked him to talk to her, why should she exert herself? His voice, and the German sounds all around her, the clatter of cutlery and china, floated into her ears like a bizarre concerto, played by characters clustered in some quirky corner of a painting by Brueghel. She closed her eyes momentarily, to let the music blend.

When she opened them, the waiter was removing her plate – empty. She ordered coffee.

His wife threw him out. It wasn't clear if this had happened yesterday or at some other time in the distant past. He was now reduced to one tense, the present. 'I try to love her, and I love life,' he was saying. Or, actually, 'Wine, life, I love. Women!' He mentioned Homer and added that he was reading the *Odyssey* at the moment. Sara presumed he said this to impress her, thinking she was the kind of person who would appreciate an *Odyssey* reader. She had read it once but didn't remember most of it. Circe, he was thinking of, perhaps. Penelope at home, weaving and waiting. The subtext was that he had been unfaithful to his wife, who did not wait but who tossed him out, and now he was here trying to get over it, flirting with strangers whom he encountered. Adventure.

'Oh dear,' said Sara. He looked woebegone. She started to comfort him, in case the story was true, and he had been recently thrown out of home. 'Can't you phone her?'

'I phone. I write letters. I write my daughter a long letter saying I am sorry, I love her ...'

Then he revealed Exhibit A. The letter. It was long, several pages long. So it was true. True that he had been writing a letter, anyway. She took a good look at it. Handwriting on pale blue paper, certainly a personal letter, not something he had written to the tax commissioners or somebody.

'It's going to be OK.' She remembered the words on Thomas's T-shirts. 'Everything will be OK. Your daughter is twenty. She knows you love her.'

He looked puzzled, and then stared into Sara's eyes – he was very skilled at eye contact. It was not clear to Sara that he understood exactly what her words meant, but he understood that there was something new in the air over the table: the soft air of goodwill replaced the sharp scepticism that had filled the space between them before.

'My daughter I love,' he said, and she suppressed the urge to correct the word order. Wouldn't it be as easy to say 'I love my daughter'? But, on the other hand, why should he?

'And she loves you,' she said gently.

It was undoubtedly true. Their fathers they usually love, daughters, and he looked like a nice one. Sara began to wish he was her father. That would have made her Red Riding Hood, but no matter. Her own father had been more like the wolf. But he was dead, she didn't have to worry about him any more.

'You think?'

He was sincere now, and vulnerable. Sara could appreciate how beautiful he was. He could have anyone. She imagined his wife: one of those polished marble women, smooth as moonlight – beige cashmere, fine leather boots, chunks of gold here and there. One of the Paolas or Claudias you see gliding along the street in Florence or Rome, looking like visitors from another, more finished, planet than ours. Why would the husband of a woman like that flirt with a woman like Sara? She was never any beauty, and now she's fat. Or fattish. At best she must look like a woman of substance, togged out in her conference gear: the black suit, diamond earrings, good leather bag. She probably looked … mature. And sometimes a man finds that appealing – especially just after he's been kicked out by a woman who does not look mature, who looks like a sophisticated princess. At times like that, a man likes a woman who does not remind him of his daughter. Sara wasn't old enough to be his mother; he was older than her, in fact. (He'd told her his age – there wasn't much he hadn't told her at this stage.)

Sara was draining her coffee.

A surprising thing happened.

The woodcutter started to cry.

Sara was startled. Very. So, of course, she again grasped at her usual philosophical resource in times of acute need: Thomas's T-shirt. 'Everything will be OK!' She read the useful slogan off the picture of his yellow chest – in her mind – doing a simultaneous translation as she uttered the timeless, consoling words. Then she paraphrased them in a few different ways. 'Everything will be all right. Don't worry, it's going to be fine.'

But he went on crying. Tears poured down his lovely bronze cheeks, plopping into his wineglass, where they splashed, *plip!*, raindrops falling into a pond.

She reached across the table and ruffled his hair. It was very soft and not as thick as it looked from her side of the table. She repeated the mantra: 'Everything will be OK!' She gave it another good ruffle. 'Just telephone your daughter. She will understand. And you will see her on Monday.'

He began to dry his eyes with his table napkin. 'I'm sorry,' he said. 'I do not know why ...'

Words failed him and a few more tears fell into the glass.

'It's fine,' said Sara. 'A good cry does you a power of good.'

Her mother used to say that, back in Dunroon, when Sara was a child. She had not heard the phrase in about thirty years.

The woodcutter smiled and dried his eyes. He poured more wine for both of them – he'd somehow ordered a second bottle when she wasn't looking, the sneaky devil. But now she didn't even make a token protest.

'It is a miracle.' He was quite composed now, his old self and more.

Sara just drank her wine.

'In all this huge city, I meet you.' He looked at her with admiration.

'Well,' said Sara modestly. She didn't know what to say.

'How many people in this city?'

She hadn't a clue. But he did.

'About two million,' he said. 'One million, two million.' So he didn't really know. But, lots. 'And I sit here and you come here and you are the one person in this city of two million people I can talk to! Yes, it is a miracle!'

He threw up his hands to emphasise the wonder of it all. She smiled in spite of herself. She had been called various quite nice things in her life, but never before described as a miracle. It was nice. Very nice.

His English had picked up again. The crying had empowered it, as it does – it gave him an injection of renewed linguistic vigour. And other vigour.

He pushed his card into her hand.

'Please meet me for a glass of champagne later,' he said. He mentioned a wine bar which she had heard of, because it was famous. 'That is what we drink here, for an apéritif.'

'I'll be at the conference,' said Sara. 'I can't really meet you.'

He ignored her.

'Six o'clock,' he said. 'Just a nice glass of champagne.'

Sara laughed.

'I won't be there!' she said, getting up and leaving the table.

He was laughing, too. Either he didn't hear her, or he didn't believe her, or he didn't care one way or the other. All of these possibilities existed.

They told her at the desk that he had paid for her lunch, and she had to put up with that. She didn't want to go back to protest. She wanted to get out of the restaurant as fast as she could, and back to her hotel, and she didn't want him to follow her and find out where the hotel was. As soon as the thick door closed behind her she ran as fast as her legs would carry her and did not stop until she was in the lobby of her own hotel, under the portrait of Kafka. Even there, the receptionist smiled in a knowing way and she felt mistrustful of him and of the entire staff of the hotel.

And from then on everyone in the city seemed to look at her in an odd way. She got knowing glances when she was sitting alone in one of the coffee houses, drinking a tiny cup of coffee and eating rich cake and cream. Women, perched at tiny delicate tables, would look at her and then at one another, and smile, as if sharing a joke, or a secret. It happened when she was walking around the cathedral square, a tourist among many. One of the natives – you could tell them, they often wore little green hunting caps, with a feather in the brim – stared questioningly at her. It could hardly be the colour of her skin, she thought – they had plenty of dark-skinned women here. Was there something about her clothes?

They knew something about her that she did not know herself.

So it seemed. So she was glad to get away, after one more day of it, glad to get home, or to the place she now called home.

In the place she now calls home, in that city, there is a famous amusement park, prettily spread over the slopes of a gentle hill. You can go there even if you don't want to go on the rides, just to walk around, to listen to the fairground music, to eat in one of the many restaurants. To enjoy the special fairground atmosphere, which is different from any other mood, in its combination of smells and music and laughs. The smell of summer grass. The screams of blissful terror. The warm sun on your skin.

Sara has not been there for years. But now, after the champagne, Lisa gets a whim; she wants to visit the fairground to celebrate her marriage; she wants to have fun in the sense this city understands it. And she wants to go immediately, because in a few days she will be leaving to join her husband and she seems to suspect that she may not return for a long time. She wants to go to the fair, tonight.

The Teacup. The Flume. Grandfather's Motor Car.

They're the easy ones.

The Ghost Hotel. The Hangover. Mount Everest.

They stroll through the fair. It's dark but still warm. The coloured lights twinkle and the tinkling music sparkles in the air. There aren't many people around; tomorrow the schools open, and so do many workplaces. Half the population will be back to work after the long summer holiday. It feels like the height of summer, but this is the night when people are gearing up for winter. Going to bed early, packing their bags and lunch boxes, like squirrels are packing their dens with nuts against what's ahead.

Sara and Lisa sit in a Teacup, on a merry-go-round that moves at about a kilometre an hour. It's usually patronised by toddlers, and the occasional granny. Tonight Sara and Lisa are the only passengers. The boy who collects the money doesn't bat an eyelid as he takes their cash and starts the machine. They revolve slowly and don't talk because the music is so loud. Sara is bemused, but Lisa smiles and looks around at everything, as if she is memorising what she sees.

'Let's try Mount Everest', is what she says, the minute they get out of the Teacup.

The roller coaster. A kilometre of track, swooping and looping and soaring high above the fairground. From its cars people scream in a mixture of delight and terror. Little faces far away, mouths open and eyes closed, being shuttled up and down the steep track, looping the loop, turned upside down for seconds at a time. Little faces with closed eyes and screaming mouths belonging to people who are eighteen years old, max.

Could even they enjoy it?

Sara has never gone on even the easy roller coaster, the Mountain Train, which is cushioned by trees and shrubs and pretends to be a precipitous version of a country railway.

She is disbelieving.

'Let's!' says Lisa. 'Just once in our lives.'

She persuades her.

How?

Sara has never once in her life wanted to go on any roller coaster. She has visited this amusement park often, with Thomas, with visitors from Ireland. Her nephew from Dublin went on Mount Everest – he was thirteen at the time. He came off, trembling and white as a ghost, weakly protesting that 'It was cool'. Sara hadn't been able to watch while he was on the thing.

And now she finds herself standing in the queue – long, since this is the most spectacular, the most scary, the most popular ride. She is handing over a lot of money to the girl in the ticket office, a brusque and impatient individual who, when Sara hesitates as she clambers into the car, tells her to hurry up, in a cross voice. Sara is fastening her harness, listening to Lisa say, 'I always wanted to do this but this is my first time.'

Slowly the car climbs up the first track, a few metres at a time, as other customers embark. By then they are close to the top of the first loop, and although they have inched their way up, Sara is already frightened. She can't bring herself to look at the ground, about thirty metres beneath. She flies half a dozen times a year, she has climbed mountains ten times higher than this roller coaster, she is perfectly safe, strapped into a little steel car on a machine that has been tested and double tested by health and safety inspectors in this country, probably the safest country on the planet. She tells herself this, and other things: you have to do it once, you have to take the risk, it will do you good. But she feels more terrified than she has ever ever felt.

Abba sings. 'Dancing Queen'. She can just hear it, mixed with the laughter, the shouts.

Once she was attacked by an Alsatian dog as she walked in the country, back in Ireland. He pulled her around by her coat-tails for a minute or perhaps an hour – when you are frightened, you move to a different clock, or to a timeless state, as close as you get to experiencing infinity. Eventually, the dog bit her neatly on the calf and ran away.

While he had been assaulting her, she had thought of people ripped apart by dogs in Nazi concentration camps, and she had waited for the dog to bite her eyes or her cheeks or any part of her body. But, like a Christian confronted by a lion in the circus, she had not lost her head. Far from it. Her mind worked hard, on a strategy for escape; and she was still working on that when the dog bit her – harmlessly, it hardly even hurt.

This is a thousand times worse.

She is strapped in. There is no point in planning an escape because she cannot get out. The machine, the person who operates it, is in control. All she can do is repeat to herself that hundreds of people go through this every day. Everything is going to be OK, everything is going to be OK.

But even Thomas's mantra does not console her.

A whistle sounds. Her blood curdles and the pace quickens. It is still slow as they mount the crest of the first hill but then they hurtle down the other side at a speed that makes her want to die. Then they race up the next slope. She glances at Lisa, who is smiling, just as she smiled in the Teacup. Is it a fixed grimace? Is she pretending?

Down they go, like a stone falling over the side of a cliff into the churning sea.

*

Oh God, oh God! I say. I don't believe in God. My family converted to the Church of Ireland soon after they came to Ireland from Lithuania and I am an atheist. This is ridiculous, I say, soon it will be over and you'll be glad that you did it. It tests your courage – which is lacking. When you get off, you won't worry about anything ever again – maybe that's why people do it. They ascend Mount Everest, strapped into a steel box, to put everything else in perspective? Words fail me.

I can't open my eyes but I can't close my ears and everyone is screaming. As we hurtle up slopes and are flung back down, the air is rent with bloodcurdling screams. Screaming must make it easier. I try to scream but I can't. Words fail me, screams fail me.

Now we're looping the loop.

I am the dancing queen.

We are upside down, we are defying gravity, my hair is hanging down over my face. And now I scream, I scream Lisa screams we all scream. Make it stop God make it stop.

It stops.

The machine stops.

The timbre of the screaming changes from one of pretend terror to a real scream of fright. Because the machine stopped in mid-flight. Every car is frozen exactly where it happens to be, on the slope, on the crest, on the loop.

Sara and Lisa are upside down on the inside of the loop. The harnesses are secure and the car locks to the track by a magnetic force, so they don't fall to their deaths. But they are upside down and the blood is going to their heads.

'Hey? What's happening?'

They can still talk.

'It's broken down,' says Sara calmly. It is not nice being stuck upside down on a roller coaster, but it is marginally better than being in motion. Her prayer has been answered. 'I'm sure they'll fix it soon,' she says consolingly. She notices that Lisa's hat has disappeared. It obviously fell off when they looped the loop.

Abba have stopped singing. In fact, a hush has descended on

the entire amusement park and up here in the air Sara feels enclosed in a silence as comforting and mysterious as the silence of the seabed.

She begins to get a headache.

A voice booms out and says that the roller coaster has stalled due to a mechanical fault. The fault will be fixed as soon as possible. There is no danger, do not panic. We apologise, we apologise.

'It's like an announcement on a train,' Lisa says.

'Except we're upside down. How can we not panic?'

'We're not quite upside down,' Lisa points out. It is true. They are slightly left of centre on the inside of the loop.

'I'm more upside down than I ever was before in my life.' Sara makes a face. 'I don't like it. I'm starting to feel sick.'

More announcements.

They can't fix the fault. The air rescue service has been called, the fire brigade. Help is at hand, be patient.

Do not panic.

Do not panic.

'Why don't they send an angel around with free drinks?' says Lisa. She looks different, upside down, with her hair floating in the air – her hair looks more plentiful and thicker, and with her pink cheeks, she looks younger than her upright self.

'Do I look different, this way round?' Sara asks.

'Ten years younger,' says Lisa. 'It suits you.'

'Hm,' says Sara. 'I must do it more often. I must practise walking around on my hands.'

Sara is sick and dizzy but she is not in the least bit frightened.

On his way back to Italy, the woodcutter planned to visit the Nazi concentration camp.

'Why?' asked Sara.

It was where her colleagues at the conference had gone, and she had wanted to ask them the same question. It had irritated her, although she did not understand why, that they were all so eager to go to the concentration camp. Hitler had lived in

91

this city for years as a young man, and, although it was a city alive with music and art, with psychology and culture, with architecture and every aspect of civilisation, it was this one fact, this aberration, that obsessed the librarians. They went to the Jewish Museum, they had to go the concentration camp, they were prejudiced against the citizens in a visceral way. 'They look like woodland animals, in those little hats,' a woman from the children's library in Birmingham had said. 'Their fur coats, their little noses.'

You would think the English had an unblemished history, free from guilt.

'It's good to get close to the concentration camp,' said the woodcutter, or words to that effect. 'It is good to feel it in the heart. You read about it, it is different. You do not feel until you go. To the place.'

'I suppose so,' nodded Sara. Thinking, voyeurism. Vulgar. Like visiting those medieval torture museums that have sprung up all over the place, in any town with any pretensions to a medieval origin. Tourists like to visit them, too, to gawk at the rack and the thumbscrews between their morning swim and their cappuccino on the terrace. They contemplate, not the sins of the politicians or the religious zealots, but the pain of the martyrs. Misery likes bedfellows. Misery likes greater misery. Tasting terrible pain in the safe confines of a museum puts personal suffering into perspective. It's all relative. Healthy people make these comparisons all the time, weighing a divorce against execution in the gas chambers, chronic arthritis against the Iron Maiden. 'Musha, it could be worse,' Sara's mother had said. Often. That's why the woodcutter is going to Mauthausen now, the weekend after his wife has turfed him out. He's going to contemplate something worse than being dumped by a donna in cashmere.

Naturally, Sara kept all these thoughts to herself.

'Also,' said the woodcutter, 'I am a Jew. My family was hidden in a convent during the war. An Irish priest helped them – Father O'Flaherty, I think. Have you heard of him?'

'No,' said Sara.

'Some of them were sheltered in Italy. But some of them went to Mauthausen.'

'Did any of them survive?' Sara was feeling sick.

He shook his head and said neutrally, 'Mauthausen was a Level Three camp. Nobody survived.'

When she met Thomas in the library, he had read from a thriller, an excerpt about a woman who is strangled and then tied to a kitchen chair, in a sitting-up position. When the detective arrives, he thinks the woman is alive, in her kitchen, reading the paper or something. Sara found it hard to envisage. Wouldn't she have looked dead, somehow, even after a few days, even if the job of tying her to the chair had been skilfully done? Life departed so rapidly from everything, once dead. How would a detective not see death in the back of a head? In an arm or a leg? The details were ignored in the novel and Thomas made the scene sound convincing enough.

Thomas read the grisly passage in a low key, ironic tone, and went on to read even more graphic horror scenes. The five old ladies who constituted his entire audience listened with polite attention, and smiled and clapped their hands when he had finished. Then they lined up to get books signed and to thank Thomas for coming to the library. He was friendly and grateful. 'Thank you,' he said. 'Thanks for coming. Thank you for listening.'

What Sara knew about Thomas when he phoned to ask her to dinner was that he had written some nasty, and apparently not very popular books, mostly about murdered women.

The amusement park management brings everyone to the hospital for a check-up, then sends them home in taxis. It's after midnight by the time Sara reaches home. She sees the message light flashing on her phone. There is no message, but she guesses Thomas has been calling, wondering where she is. He never leaves messages. She telephones the cottage. No reply. She leaves a message summarising what happened.

Then she writes an email to Ernesto, which is the woodcutter's name.

> *Dear Ernesto,*
> *You may remember me? I am the woman who had lunch with*
> *you in Vienna last March. You told me about your divorce. I*
> *have been thinking about you and wondering how you are.*

She deletes 'wondering how you are', which is a bit Hiberno-English and would confuse him. She replaces it with a full stop and 'I wanted to say hello. How are you?' Then she continues.

> *Thanks for everything. The lunch and the conversation. It was*
> *a miracle.*
> *I am sorry I did not meet you in the wine bar. But please write*
> *to me. Please tell me about Mauthausen.*
> *My family is Jewish, too. Was. Until a generation ago. I forgot*
> *to mention that, when we were talking.*
> *All the best,*
> *Sara Feldman*

She puts the letter in her draft folder, as she has been advised to do with emails. Leave them, reread them before launching them into the ether.

Then she writes another email, to Thomas, telling him about her misadventure on the roller coaster, and Lisa's marriage, and the trip back from the cottage. She tells him the house has not been burgled, the grass is not too long, the asters and the goldsturm have come out in the garden. She says everything is OK.

This email she sends immediately. The rule about keeping it for a day does not apply to things you write to your partner or loved one. You can tell them anything.

Trespasses

Just as the bin lorry turns the corner and drives out of the estate Clara reaches the footpath. Now her rubbish will be festering in her bin for a month because she's going abroad the day after tomorrow and she doesn't feel brave enough to ask her neighbour, Martha, to take it out next week. Martha has already offered to look after Bran, Clara's dog. Martha adores Bran, and is delighted to take care of him, but you can't push your luck. So the bin will be there for her when she comes back. Stinking the place out.

C'est la fucking vie.

She drags the bin back through the house with a certain ease – it's heavy, and there's a step to negotiate, but Clara's arms are as strong as a weightlifter's. You wouldn't think it to look at her, a petite woman, with a certain smart quality to her, even when dressed, as now, in a faded dressing gown, spattered with raindrops. (She was in bed when she heard the drone of the bin lorry.) Clara would look chic in a sack, some of her friends say. The thing is, she looks a bit like what she is: a beautician. And it's her job that explains her physical strength, too – she paints nails and puts on make-up, but quite a lot of her day is spent removing hair from women's skin. You need to be strong, as well as dexterous and determined, to rip off the waxed paper so swiftly that the client doesn't realise what's happening. Zapping upper lips and chins with the laser beam all day long develops the muscles of the upper arms, too, although it's not heavy work in itself.

She puts coffee in the coffee machine as soon as she's stowed the bin, and lets it filter away while she's getting dressed. There's a hectic day ahead, even though she's closed her salon, as she calls the 'shomera' in the back garden where she sees her clients. Before you go on a trip, even a short one, there's always a load of things to do. Maybe if you were better organised, it would be different, but Clara is not organised – she tends to put things on the long finger, to throw an important letter on the kitchen table and say, 'I'll file it away later'. As a result, she spends half her life looking for mislaid items. Today, when she has plenty else on her plate, she has to dash off to her accountant with the P60s and the other tax stuff. All those horrible forms with the anaemic-looking red print. Halloween's coming up. Tax time.

The rain doesn't stop. It's still bucketing down as she makes a dash for the car. Everything looks awful in this weather. The suburbs of south Dublin (and this is supposed to be the good part) are bleak with cement gardens and grey pebble-dashed walls. If there's anything Clara can't stand, it's pebble dash. Those hard little nubbles, like pimples, make her shiver. She longs to plane them down to a creamy smoothness.

But they don't bother her today. Nothing can really dent her happiness because in a few days' time she will have left this place behind her and be with her son, Eoin, in San Francisco. He's been there for two years, working in a hotel. He can't come home because he's one of the undocumented. Clara has not seen him in all that time. She didn't realise how much – how very much – she missed him until she was filling in the form online for her air ticket. Then, as she keyed in her credit card number, she started crying and she didn't stop for twelve hours.

But that was ages ago. In two days she'll be with Eoin and therefore everything makes her happy. She is playing 'San Francisco' on the CD player – she's been playing it for about two months, nonstop. There's a Bewley's porter cake in a tin with shamrocks on the lid lying on the passenger seat, ready to go into her case the day after tomorrow – Eoin's favourite cake. Everything is wonderful.

Even this boring suburb that she's driving through. It looks as if all the roads and houses fell out of the sky and just happened to land on these unremarkable fields, miles from anywhere that makes sense. Miles from the city and miles from the mountains and miles from the river and the sea. Such places look haphazard and bleak when you're passing through them, but Clara knows when you live in them, they have a meaning. When you live in them, they can be as lovely as any medieval village with its castle and churches and narrow, cobbled lanes. She knows this because she lives in a similar place herself, less than a mile away.

If you're going to San Francisco
Be sure to wear some flowers in your hair.

Watermill Grove. That's where the accountant lives, in a semi-detached house with pebble-dashed walls and a picture window looking out directly on another semi-detached house with pebble-dashed walls and a picture window. His office is around the back in a wooden shed. There must have been a watermill here at some stage, although you'd never guess it now. And there must have been a river, or a stream, which has been long buried under houses and tarmac. Maybe it's under this very road, under Watermill Grove, but who's to know? She parks her car in the first free spot she sees, which, as luck would have it, is just opposite the accountant's house. *You're gonna meet some gentle people there.* She turns off the motor and grabs the big brown envelope. Off she dashes across the road.

The accountant is not in the office.

But his wife is. His wife is a woman with soft creamy skin and a big warm smile. She is padded and comfortable-looking in a baby pink jumper made of cashmere or some smooth wool. A fawn skirt.

'Michael had a bypass operation two weeks ago,' she says cheerfully. Michael is the accountant.

'What!' Clara says. What will happen to her tax returns now? She gives the office a furtive glance. It has a reassuringly worked-in look: papers are stacked in wire trays and a few letters are scattered on the desk. And there's a work smell: coffee and computer and sweat. 'That's terrible! How is he?'

'He's fine.' The wife smiles. 'He made a really fast recovery.'

'Oh, good, good,' says Clara. Only four days to the deadline.

After that they'll start shovelling on the fines. Heart surgery will be no excuse. 'I'm really shocked. I didn't know.'

'He didn't know himself until three weeks ago,' the woman says, and she laughs proudly.

'Really? Didn't he have pains ...' Clara fiddles with her brown envelope. 'Angina or whatever?'

The accountant's wife shakes her head. 'Not a thing. No pain. Apparently when the blockage is on the left side, you feel nothing. If it's on the right, you get shortness of breath and chest pains and so on.'

'You get a warning?' Clara nods, interested. Her mother, who died two years ago, a month after Eoin went to America, used to have angina. She had pains on the right side. She got a warning. But she didn't get a bypass because she was on the Medical Card, so she got some pills and then she died. Eoin couldn't get back for the funeral. If he'd come home, they'd never have let him in again.

'But on the left, not a thing. No warning. I never knew about any of this until now,' the woman laughs.

'No,' says Clara. 'You only learn all the complicated details when something happens.'

'He wants me to take files in to him already!' the woman says, pleased. 'Can't wait to get at them!'

'Oh don't, it's much too early for that,' says Clara. She hands over the brown envelope. He'll be able to do her returns, sitting up in bed, on a laptop. Pass the time for him. 'He should rest.'

'Don't worry,' says the woman, still smiling. 'Most of them are done. It's only a few of the stragglers that are left. I can do them myself; they're the little ones.'

'A woman's work is never done!' Clara laughs. It's so great not to be made to feel guilty, even though she is ridiculously late. She's always ridiculously late.

The woman sighs contentedly. 'If there's a problem, I'll give you a ring.'

While Clara was in the accountant's shed the sun came out. Now golden light washes the houses, so they glow softly in their frames of autumn shrubs and trees. In the driveway of one of them, just beside where Clara parked her car, an old man and woman are working. The woman is raking leaves and he's putting them into a wheelbarrow and wheeling them around to the back of the house. Light mounds of golden foliage are lined up along the sides of their drive, like a range of tidy little mountains. It's a pleasant sight. *There's a whole generation with a new explanation, people in motion.* Clara smiles at the woman and is about to say, 'Isn't it a lovely day?'

The woman looks up from her sweeping.

Venomous.

That's the only word to describe the expression on her face.

'Are you the person who blocked my driveway?' she hisses.

Clara glances at her car – a twenty-year-old Mercedes-Benz, the only luxury – near luxury – she allows herself. It's parked very close to the edge of the gateway. She hadn't paid much attention to how she was parking because she was so glad to be getting the tax papers out of her hair.

'Oh gosh, I'm really sorry!' she says, in dismay. 'I didn't notice I was so close to your drive.' She smiles then and adds, 'But not to worry, I'm off now, anyway!'

The woman is not placated. Instead, her face grows angrier.

'You parked illegally,' she hisses. 'You broke the law. Do you always park like that?'

'What?' Clara is puzzled. 'I'm sorry!'

She looks carefully at the woman. Elderly. Her clothes are verging on the shabby: grey pants and an anorak in a drab shade of yellow old women often wear. The clothes are ordinary but her face is not. It is contorted with rage, like the face of a witch. Clara wonders if she suffers from some mental disturbance.

'It was only for a few minutes!' she says, and shrugs, dredging her keys up from the chaotic depths of her handbag.

The old woman snarls. 'It was not a few minutes! It was not a few minutes! You broke the law. Are you always breaking the law?'

Are you always breaking the law?

Clara inhales deeply. She feels like a child, in her tight jeans and purple leather jacket, her high boots. She feels like a child, although in fact she is probably not that much younger than this angry old woman.

'You broke the law,' the woman says again. 'I couldn't get into my drive.'

Clara glances at the car parked behind hers and assumes several things without thinking too deeply about them. One of those assumptions is that the car behind hers, a red Yaris, is the woman's. She must have arrived when Clara was in with the accountant's wife and had to park on the road, instead of on her driveway. But would that be so irritating that you'd eat the face off a complete stranger? Not being able to get into your drive is not quite the same as not being able to get out of it.

'You're overreacting,' says Clara, frowning. She glances at the house. It has a name, carved on a piece of fake wood: Assisi, and a number: 134. Probably holy statues all over the place inside. She shakes her head.

She should go now, before she says things she'll regret. One part of her is urging her to leave. But some emotion boiling up inside stops her doing that. She's getting drawn in.

'You're crazy.' She can't stop the words.

'And you're a criminal!' The woman's voice rises to a real scream.

Then Clara makes a supreme effort, suppresses her annoyance, and climbs into her car.

She has to retreat down Watermill Grove, do a U-turn and come back up, to get out onto the main road. As she drives back towards the corner she sees that a small crowd has gathered at the old woman's gate. There's a young woman, with a pram, and the old man, his face as angry as his wife's. The old woman is pointing at Clara and the others are looking at her accusingly. There's something unreal about the group. It looks choreographed, like a scene from an opera or a ballet.

The old man beckons Clara over, crooking his finger and gesturing menacingly. With his big hooked nose, he's the evil count. He could be wearing a black cloak and three-cornered hat, shiny pointy-toed boots. But his clothes are as ordinary as his wife's. It's the eyes that belong to the other dimension, as they splutter and sparkle with rage. The two old people glare at her. The house and driveway are like a backdrop on a stage. The faces are like masks, not like real faces, which change expression in response to what people say. She wonders, seriously, if this is some sort of reality TV hoax. But Watermill Grove isn't the sort of place where they do reality TV hoaxes. It's too far from town. It's too boring. It's too real.

Clara could decide to ignore him and drive away from this farce. She's calmer than she was; she's distanced herself. Discretion is the better part of valour, that she knows. But something holds her, some dark spell. She stops the car. The evil count stalks up to her and she rolls down the window.

'Show me your driving licence,' he barks.

'What?' She wasn't expecting this.

'Do you have a driving licence?'

'Of course I have a driving licence,' Clara says.

'I'd like to see it,' he snarls.

Naturally, Clara hasn't a clue where it is. 'I'm not showing it to you,' she says.

'In that case, I'm going to report you to the police.'

She laughs in surprise. 'OK,' she says, with an elaborate shrug. 'Go right ahead. Report me to the police!'

Now he's taken aback.

'Go on,' she says, encouraged. 'Report me! Report me to the police!'

'I will,' he says uncertainly. 'I will. I will.'

Repetition is the name of the game.

He ambles off across the road and into his house.

The young woman moves away down the road, her head bent towards the contents of the pram. The old woman picks up her rake and begins to work at the leaves. The scene is beginning to lose momentum; it's time to draw the curtain. But the old man hasn't made his final exit. He returns with an old envelope and pencil and makes an elaborate show of taking down the registration number of Clara's car. He gives a last grunt, scowls at her and returns to his garden.

Clara's mobile phone rings.

Eoin.

'Hi, Ma.' He sounds as if he's next to her in the car. 'Just checking that everything's on track.'

'Yes, sweetie,' she says, glancing out the window, which is open. 'Everything's on track.' Her heart is thumping. There's a shake in her right knee. 'I'm just leaving in the tax returns, you know, with the accountant.' The old woman's head is bent over the leaves, her rake is raking. The old man is gathering up the heaps of leaves and putting them into a green bucket. He clamps them down with his foot, to compress them, squeeze more in. 'Someone is reporting me to the guards, for illegal parking. Some crazy people.' She says this very loudly, hoping they'll hear.

'Oh.' Eoin sounds alarmed. 'Don't worry, Mom. Don't mind them. Just drive away. OK?'

'OK.'

The old man looks over at Clara and spits in her direction. The glob of spittle lands far from her, on the footpath outside his gate. He picks up the bucket and shuffles into the house with it, stooping under the weight of leaves.

Eoin says, 'Promise me you'll drive away as soon as I ring off.'

'Yes, yes,' says Clara.

There's a pause.

'Have you sent in your ESTA form to Immigration?'

'Yes, yes,' she says again. 'I did that weeks ago.' All those stupid questions. Do you suffer from a contagious disease? Are you a drug addict? Have you ever been convicted of an offence by the police? Offense. Felony. That's not a word Clara ever uses. It's not a word used in Ireland. 'I did it. I got an email back. That's all OK.'

'OK.' There's a pause and he adds, 'Ma, wear something ordinary, for the flight. You know what I mean?'

She smiles.

'Just makes it easier at Immigration.' He sounds sheepish.

'I'm not a complete eejit,' she says. The last time she saw Eoin his hair, red, was down to his waist, and he was wearing a T-shirt that said 'FCUK'. 'Don't worry. I'll put my hair in a nice little bun.' Her hair is partly purple and partly blond at the moment, but she'd already planned to dye out the purple bit before travelling. 'I've got a nice black suit all ready. I'll look like a plain-clothes nun.'

'That's the spirit,' he says.

She can see his grin but wonders if he's cut his hair? It's curly. It's beautiful. He looks like a poet.

'See you on Friday then, 9.30 p.m.? Twenty-one thirty, right?'

'Right! Twenty-one thirty,' says Clara. 'What time is it over there now?'

She always asks this, even though she knows perfectly well that it's nine hours behind; in her head she has one of those clocks you see behind the reception desk in hotels. Hers gives the San Francisco time, so she knows what Eoin is likely to be doing at any hour of the day or night. She asks just to prolong the conversation. But he's already rung off.

Clara breathes deeply, turns the key in the ignition and drives off. She stops at a garage and fills the tank; she'll drive to the airport because she has to be there at cockcrow. Filling the tank cools her down, in spite of the latest hike in the price of petrol. One hundred and forty-six euro a litre today, and the Merc guzzles the gas.

> *All across the nation*
> *Such a strange vibration*
> *People in purple …*

She flicks off the CD player and goes over to the radio.

There's a report of a court case on the news. John O'Hara, a farmer in the midlands, died after being assaulted by Dan and Robert Ryan, his neighbours. John O'Hara's heifer strayed into Robert Ryan's field and John went after the cow to make her come back to his own field, her own field. A row broke out about property and trespassing and the men fought. John O'Hara sustained head injuries and died almost a year later, never having come out of hospital. The question was, was it murder or manslaughter or neither? The jury would have to decide. The men were forty years old and this happened in 2008, although it sounded like the plot of a play you couldn't put on because it is so dated and old-fashioned.

When Clara comes home to Dunroon Crescent after the encounter with the people on Watermill Grove, she sits down at the old blue table in her kitchen, which is filled with stuff she's collected from skips and second-hand furniture auctions, and writes a letter to them. The letter says, 'I have never encountered two old people whose faces were so uglified by anger.' It adds that she has reported them to the police.

She tears that letter up and writes another one.

The second letter says that she had not blocked their driveway, that their behaviour was antisocial and that they were a public nuisance. She adds that they would be hearing from her solicitor.

That one gets torn up, too.

Then she thinks she could shame them by using a bit of reverse psychology. She gets a thank-you card and signs it with a false version of her name – Ellie Murphy is the pseudonym she selects – puts it in an envelope, and addresses it to The Residents, Assisi, 134 Watermill Grove.

But she doesn't post that, either.

Clara has plenty to do – she should be packing, making lists, preparing for the long journey she must soon make the day after tomorrow. Buying a month's supply of food for Bran. But instead, she sits and writes letters to two cranky old people whose name she doesn't even know.

She can't get them out of her head.

At six o'clock, when it's dark, she gives Bran his evening meal and he settles down for his long night sleep in front of the stove. Clara takes the thank-you card and the porter cake she bought for Eoin – she can get another one tomorrow, or even at the airport, although it'll cost more there. She drives back to Watermill Grove, parks around the corner and walks to number 134, Assisi.

A small blue Micra is parked in the driveway – even in the dark she can see it is a very bright blue. That wasn't on the road this morning. It's such a screaming shade of blue, she couldn't have missed it. She wonders where their own car is, the red one. No sign of it. Then she wonders if they have a car at all. The Micra looks like the kind of car a grown-up daughter living at home, a schoolteacher or a civil servant, might have.

The curtains are drawn and there is no light at the front of the house, so she guesses they are in the kitchen, eating their evening meal. Their tea. Rashers and sausages, sliced pan. Something like that. She walks quietly up to the door and leaves the card and the fruit cake, in its bright tin, in the porch. A pot of geraniums catches her eye. Through the glass in the front door she sees a crack of light down the hall. She imagines she hears the sound of voices. The old woman's, she thinks, and a younger voice. The daughter's? Maybe it's just the news on TV. Almost without thinking what she's doing, she roots in the flowerpot. Her fingers find a keyring, buried just half an inch below the surface. Just what they're always warning you not to do. Two keys – the Yale and the long one for the safety lock.

She opens the hall door.

Inside, exactly what you'd expect the old farts to have. A crucifix on the wall, a horrible paper with a pattern of some sort of sharp, unnatural-looking grasses, like swords, all over the walls. The yellow anorak is hanging on one of those old walnut hall stands. It's cold in here. They are too poor or too mean to keep the heating on. It's a house in a time warp; it reminds Clara of the house she grew up in, forty years ago.

A door at the end of the hall opens and the old witch comes out. She is still wearing the gardening trousers. But she has an apron on – a surprisingly nice apron, white with pink flowers and frills. A present from someone, obviously. It's one of those aprons with a huge pocket all across the skirt and the old woman is carrying something, clothes pegs perhaps, in this pocket.

'What?' Her face falls, falls as if it is an egg that has been hit with a fork and smashed. All the sharp, cross features collapse into a puddle of wrinkles and shock.

'It's me,' Clara says. She's shy now, subdued by this old woman, just as she was this morning. Feeling silly, she holds out the fruit cake, proffering it: the peace offering.

The old woman lifts her hand. But she does not take the cake. No. She dips her hand into that big pocket on her apron and pulls out a knife.

Now it's Clara who gasps, 'What?'

The witch lunges and stabs her chest.

Ineffectually, of course. It's quite a good quality knife she's got there, with a sharp point, and she does manage to make a tiny dent in Clara's leather jacket. But there's no way she could injure Clara, given her feebleness and the thickness of the purple leather, and Clara's agile dance to the side.

It's quite a good quality knife she has in her hand. And when that knife is in Clara's deft, strong hand, it easily slices into the old woman's scrawny throat – it slices into the bulging blue veins as easily as it would into the white flesh of an apple.

Blood spurts out. A red puddle spreads over the brown floor.

Clara is already out the door, down the path. She's in her car, driving down Watermill Grove, before the old woman has realised what has happened, before she has a chance to die.

In the morning when Clara crossed the road from the accountant's house, what she had thought was this: that they looked like figures in a soothing pastoral painting, with a title such as *The Reapers*, or *The Gleaners*. So rhythmical were their movements, so accustomed were they to working together. Like a couple working together making hay, or footing turf, or gathering seaweed, on a golden morning in a blessed landscape in the west of the country, miles and miles and miles away from this cold suburb, which looks as if all its roads and houses fell out of the sky and just happened to land on these unremarkable fields, miles from anywhere that makes sense. Miles from the city and miles from the mountains and miles from the river. Miles and miles from the silver sea.

The shelter of neighbours

W hen Martha wakes up in the middle of the night, she stays right where she is, in bed, and waits for sleep to return and rescue her from her worries – which it invariably does, although often not till about half an hour before it's time to get up. During that half-hour, sleep is as sweet as cut grass. On this night in September she has spent more than an hour brooding over something her neighbour, Mitzy, said to her. Something about how public servants are parasites, ruining the country. It's over a week since Mitzy said that. It's a common, a banal, opinion; every time you turn on the radio someone is dissing public servants and blaming them for the economic downturn. But it annoyed Martha and it's still on her mind, coming between her and her night's sleep. None of her usual tricks works – visualising a peaceful rural scene – a lake, a green field, some fluffy sheep – or imagining that her body is being sponged down from the toes to the crown of the head with warm water. So she tries a new strategy. She gets up. She gets up to make herself a cup of tea. An article about insomnia in the Sunday newspaper – today's, or yesterday's now – recommended this. Anything is better than lying there, the article, which was in the 'Life' section, said. Martha agrees. Even though the last thing she feels like, at 4.20 a.m. – she glances at the time on her the clock – is a cup of tea, a drink she never much cared for.

107

Seamus, Martha's husband, is snoring away. His neat body is a low wave in the pale duvet; a cap of glossy grey-black hair peeps over the top like the head of a seal who has got stuck in a net. Seamus is one of those lucky sods who fall asleep as soon as their heads hit the pillow, and never opens an eye till morning. The snoring – and the tossing and turning, the sleep-shouting (at pupils, or colleagues, or maybe at her) – is one of the reasons for Martha's insomnia. She could move to another room but she knows he'd hate that, so she's hasn't suggested it. Yet.

Yawning – and how can she yawn when she's wide awake? – she pads over to the window and opens it. A breath of air comes into the room and kisses her face like a friendly animal. She hears a bird singing, clear as a star. The front garden is ghostly in its pale coat of dew but there's a rosy stripe in the navy blue sky over the houses on the other side of the street: Dunroon Crescent is edging into daylight. At this in-between time a deep harmony settles over the road. Everything looks perfect: the white houses, the clipped gardens behind their tight hedges. Maybe it would be better if people stayed in bed, sleeping? It's when they wake up that all the hassle starts.

She thinks these thoughts and notices the sliver of rosy sun and the velvet hush and the eerie grass. But the main thing Martha notices is that the O'Keefes have their green bottle bin out. Finn is always quick off the mark with the bins. And of course he gets through plenty of wine; he could keep the bottle recycling crowd in business all on his own.

Lucky she got up.

She goes downstairs and puts on the kettle, then hobbles out the back to get the bin. Clara Byrne's dog, Bran, one of life's great opportunists, tries to get in as soon as she opens the kitchen door. He seems to live on Martha's patio, waiting for the main chance. 'Shoo, Bran,' she says. Usually she lets him in – sometimes she has to ask Clara, who is a beautician and works from home in a shed in her back garden, to look after her cat, Fluff, when they're are away, so Martha gives Bran a lot of leeway. (And food. Fluff's leftovers. Fluff is a Norwegian Mountain Cat, a cat with a capital C, a fusspot.) But today she kicks Bran, not all that gently, in his scruffy behind, and down the garden he shoots like a bullet into the shadows, yelping. Unbelievable the speed of him, and he fifteen years old if he's a day. Martha can't be bothered working that out in dog years at this hour of the morning. You don't have to do the sums to know that Bran's ancient.

Just as she's pushing her bin through the gateway, someone comes around the corner of the road. Martha feels a cold bite of fear. She can't see the man's face. But there are young men in hoodies around this neighbourhood – they live in Lourdes Gardens, the Corporation housing estate at the other side of the railway line – who frighten her even when she meets them in broad daylight. Those eyes they have – defeated and aggressive at the same time, eyes that tell you they'd think nothing of scratching *your* eyes out if you so much as looked at them sideways. It's not their fault they're so sad and angry. But it's not hers either and she'd rather steer well clear of them. She'd move to another, more secure, neighbourhood if it weren't for Seamus. She'd like to try living in the middle of the city – but Seamus won't hear tell of it. He loves Dunroon, a *rus in urbe*, between the mountains and the sea (they're two of his reasons for loving it; he can come up with quite a list, if pushed; he's good at rationalising his whims and desires). Seamus feels strongly about the house and has told her, if she moves, she moves alone. Also, that she can move when he's dead – as if she needs to be told that.

The man sees Martha seconds after he turns the corner and he stops dead in his tracks. Just stands there on the footpath. Frozen. Why? What is he afraid of? A short, tubby, middle-aged woman in her nightdress? She's hardly reached the path and the bin is over the dish of the gateway but she leaves it exactly where it is, half in and half out, and takes to her heels. Like the hammers of hell, she sprints across the garden and in through the side door.

They call it a side door but it's not a door. It's a wrought-iron gate, with a complicated pattern of twisted black leaves and shoots and branches, some of them rusting. As soon as she closes it she peers out through the wrought iron. The person is walking right past her house now – she can see him over the escallonia hedge. And it isn't a man at all. It's just a girl. Or woman, really. It's just Siobhán Moriarty from next door. Mitzy's daughter.

Siobhán is skinny as a sweeping brush, and nearly six feet

tall – the height she gets from her father, Eugene, who is the biggest man in the parish. She has herself all wrapped up in a big anorak or coat or something, so in the half-light she looks like a man. Still, Martha has known her since she was five years old – Siobhán must be over thirty but she's living at home at the moment, between jobs or relationships or flats or something.

Martha shakes her head and smiles at her own foolishness. How did she not recognise Siobhán's walk? Siobhán has that gait all the girls have these days when they're out on the town, dressed up (or down, because they go out in their underwear, it looks like). They mince along on their spindly high heels like blackbirds after a worm in the grass. Siobhán is more like a young heron as she picks her way along Dunroon Crescent. She must have come home on the Nitelink, or a taxi – does the Nitelink run this late? She could have waved, then Martha wouldn't have felt scared. But Siobhán had been startled, too – the old and the young don't normally meet on the road at four thirty in the morning on Dunroon Crescent.

The kettle is well boiled when Martha gets back into the kitchen and she has to switch it on again. She makes her cup of tea, and sits at the black granite counter in their new extension and drinks it – then she goes back to bed and, yes, she manages to fall asleep, as usual, exactly one hour before the alarm rings and another week starts.

The Moriartys have been Martha's neighbours for ages. They were already living on the road when she and Seamus moved in. Eugene wasn't the friendliest then. He had a way of examining Martha with a shifty look in his sharp green eyes – the eyes of a pet fox. It was as if he suspected she was capable of doing something abrupt and untoward – taking a swipe at him or something. He didn't know what to make of her, he told her later, when they got to know each other better. She wasn't – she isn't – warm and chatty like most of the women on the road, and didn't take care of her appearance, like Mitzy. Martha was surprised to hear this, since it seemed to her that she took plenty of care – it's just a different appearance from that of the other wives on the road. More casual and, in those days, hippyish:

maxi skirts, flat sandals, and she wore her mop of curly hair parted in the middle and tumbling down any old way over her shoulders – no hairdresser got within a hairdryer's roar of Martha in those days. Mitzy, however, always looks as if she's just stepped out of a salon; she's as smart as the president of Ireland even when she's, say, driving up to the shop for a bottle of milk; but she's a dote, inside and out.

Mitzy called on Martha the day after they moved in with a loaf of bread. 'It's an American custom,' she said. Martha thought for some time that Mitzy was from America. It would have explained something about her – her confidence, her teeth – even though she spoke in her own polished version of the local drawl. 'We got used to it when we were in Boston.' Eugene had worked in an international bank in the US for two years, before he got his job as something significant in health insurance over here. (He's an actuary, able to work out when people are going to die. Though when Martha once asked him to reveal the fateful date to her, he laughed and said, 'If only!') 'Welcome to Dunroon Crescent,' Mitzy smiled and gave a little mock bow. Martha said nothing. For a few seconds her mind turned to sponge as she stared at Mitzy: her thick fringe of auburn hair, her cream polo neck, her small golden earrings. Mascara, grey eye-shadow. Against the backdrop of the neglected garden, all scutch and dandelions and thistles, she looked like a princess who had strayed into a pigsty. Then Martha felt the heat of the bread through the white linen tea cloth and she inhaled its smell – as nutty and yeasty and calming as a mother's love. It restored her. 'Would you come in for a cup of tea?' she asked, even though she hadn't the time, and Mitzy said yes, even though she hadn't time either – Siobhán and Conor were due to be collected from school; Mitzy's mother was with Lauren, but couldn't be relied upon to watch her for long – not many people could, Lauren was a real monkey. But Mitzy always accepted invitations to tea, knowing that a refusal can be hurtful.

'Excuse the mess,' Martha said, delighted that Mitzy had agreed to come in, that she already was making friends after just one day in her new home. 'A mess' did not go halfway towards describing the house. That implies untidiness, unopened boxes, furniture in the wrong places. It doesn't indicate that there was a huge damp patch on the hall ceiling, that the lamps in the living room had been pulled off the wall, leaving exposed wires, that the lino had been ripped off half the kitchen floor, leaving depressing patches of grey concrete here and there, like puddles of rain. Seamus had insisted that the house, which was not too far from where he worked, was in walk-in condition because it had central heating, unlike lots of the older, more picturesque ones he had decided against. But apart from the heating, which didn't work properly anyway, it had nothing. It was a shell. Martha planned to move out after a few years and get a house she liked herself.

They sat at the table – Martha's first table, made of shiny beige Formica imitating wood – and drank instant coffee out of china cups painted with roses, which Martha's mother had given her when she and Seamus bought the house. Mitzy, who took in the state of the house and of Martha in one discreet glance, gave her some useful information about the neighbourhood: after Mass on Sunday is a good place to meet people; you can play tennis by the hour at the club, you don't need to be a member; and the Protestant school is the best by far, but you need to put your child's name down the minute it is conceived.

Martha shook her head and laughed. She assumed she would never have a baby, because her periods were light and irregular. Seamus wasn't desperately interested in getting a child, since he already had one, a son, Shane, who lived with his mother. And on top of all this, they weren't married, since there was no divorce. But, in fact, she was already pregnant as this conversation was taking place, although she didn't realise it for another six weeks. Then she went to the doctor because she believed she was suffering from travel sickness. She was working, then as now, in an office in the city – the Department of Justice – fifteen miles away. She commuted by train, the old brown diesel train that ran along the coast of Dublin before the DART came on track, in 1984, and changed life for the better. It stopped at Dunroon station at 8.15 a.m. If she missed it, the next one was at one o'clock. She came home again on the five fifteen – there was another evening train at six and that was it. Because it ran so seldom, the train was always crammed. People were squeezed into every crevice – even the accordion-pleated corridors were packed with bodies. You had closer physical contact with strangers on that train than you had with any other human being, ever, apart from your spouse or lover. Everyone on the train had the same fantasy, as, glued together into one writhing snake of human flesh, they lurched from the suburbs into the city. And it wasn't an erotic daydream. The fantasy was about Jews on the trains going to the concentration camps. Everyone knew the association was absurd. Martha, too. But she couldn't stop it popping into her head as she endured the nightmare, morning and evening, those first months of her life with Seamus. They must have felt like she did. Sick as dogs. Sick as dogs, and trapped, and unable to move one inch.

'Good news,' the doctor said. She had a chirpy English accent. Martha was speaking to her on a public telephone in the entrance hall of the Four Courts, beside a statue of a flabby naked woman with a broken nose, holding a tiny weighing scales in her right hand. Martha knew what good news meant. But she stalled as she took it in and said, 'What do you mean?' She'd only been living with Seamus for three months. They didn't have a sofa for the front room, or a proper double bed, just two singles shoved together, one lower than the other.

'You're pregnant,' said the doctor, getting impatient.

Martha wanted to put the child's name down for Mulberry Primary School, the Protestant school that Mitzy had recommended.

'Jesus Christ!' said Seamus. 'He's not even born. He doesn't have a name.' He thought for a second and added, 'He mightn't be a boy.'

'The school is co-ed,' said Martha. That was a word still in currency at that time. 'Luke, if he's a boy; Lucy, if he's a girl.'

They didn't have the scans then that let you know the sex of the baby. You just had to wait the whole nine months and find out what it was when it was born.

'What's wrong with the local national school?' Seamus started to light his pipe, which he was soon going to have to give up, for the sake of the baby, although he didn't realise it. 'St Bernadette's.'

'It's too rough,' said Martha. Mitzy had said the children from Dunroon Crescent who'd been democratic and tried it – it was in the middle of Lourdes Gardens – got beaten up by the other kids every day of their lives. And they got bad results in their

Leaving later on because their primary education had been so traumatic.

'Crap,' said Seamus, shaking his head disbelievingly.

He taught in a rough school himself. He ran one, in fact: he was a headmaster. Before he opened his school in the mornings he drove around to the houses of three or four of the worst cases, honked his horn and waited for them to come out and get into the car. He drove around, resenting the price of the petrol – it had gone up to nearly two punts a gallon. But if he didn't drive around and round them up, they would never attend. Seamus's ambition was to get fifty per cent of his ruffians into good secondary schools and half of them on into third level, an ambition that he eventually fulfilled, almost.

Seamus didn't want his child to attend his own school, though not because it was the roughest school in the country – which, Martha was pretty sure, it was – but because he just didn't want a conflict of interest. But he was down on snobbishness of all kinds and especially snobbishness where education was concerned. That business of sending your child to a Protestant school got his goat. (He was an atheist, something which of course he, as a schoolteacher, had to keep quiet about. His separation they could just about stomach, as long as he kept quiet about it. He was a Catholic atheist.)

Martha didn't argue further. Two weeks later she took a morning off work – in those days it was like a sparkling gem of a present to herself, one free morning – and walked to the school.

It was surrounded by a high grey wall and spreading chestnut trees. A gravel drive led from a simple white gate up to the front door. The stones crunched under her feet, and twice she trod on a shining chestnut, which split like an apple under her shoe. The oldest part of the school was built of rough cut stone, with a slate roof, and the weathered plaque over the door said: MULBERRY SCHOOL 1890. The new bits had flat roofs and windows with red wooden frames. On one side were two tennis courts and on the other a playground with an old swing and a wooden seesaw. Children were playing in the playground when Martha arrived. Children were actually chanting 'SeeSaw Margery Daw' and 'Red Rover, Red Rover, I call Sarah over!' Their voices rose into the clear autumn air and to Martha the old rhymes sounded like the songs of angels.

It turned out that you couldn't put down the name of a child who had not been born, or even of a child who had been, until he or she was three. Mitzy had been wrong about that, or maybe just exaggerating for the sake of effect, the way good storytellers do. 'Contact us on the day of the third birthday,' the secretary said. She smiled at Martha, who looked very young that day, in her new denim maternity dungarees, her snow-white jumper. Martha's hair tended to frizz, but pregnancy had tamed it to a wavy mane. The hormones had a similarly beneficial effect on her skin. There was none of the patchy redness that plagued her; even her freckles had vanished. 'Don't worry,' the secretary said kindly. Her own severely bobbed white hair was held back with a pink plastic slide and this plastic slide made Martha's eyes fill with tears and her mouth with the unmistakable comforting taste of rich tea biscuits. She knew Mulberry School was just what she wanted for the child in her belly.

Over the years, Martha did not get to know the neighbours as well as she might have. That was largely owing to her personality – the words people used about her were 'reserved', if they were nice people, like Mitzy, and 'a cold fish', if they had sharper tongues, which Linda Talbot, for instance, had. But she put it down to something else entirely: to logistics, to timetables. She was a worker, away from home for ten hours a day, in the Department, where she was a Higher Executive Officer in the Prisons Division (she was moved to Family Law when it expanded and got very busy in 1997 after divorce came in). Mitzy and most of the other women on Dunroon Crescent were full-time mums, apart from Audrey Bailey, who was single and eccentric, and taught in Mulberry Manor, and Clara, who spent her day in her shed, removing unwanted hair and giving facials. (No planning permission, a bone of contention with some, but they didn't report her because they felt sorry for her. Single mum.) That's because most of them were about ten years older than Martha. At the time Martha was doing the Leaving they were busy getting married and starting their grown-up lives. By the time she had graduated from college they had had their first babies. It wasn't that they had not gone to college themselves. Some were well educated. Mitzy, for instance, had a degree in science, and Linda had studied Latin and Greek in Trinity, though you'd never think it. Audrey of course had a BA in English and something else. German? But as far as Martha could see, they'd never felt either ambition or pressure to have long-term jobs, or careers, as she and her friends called their work, whatever it was.

In the ten years that separated Martha from Mitzy all those rules had changed. Whereas before, you had to stay at home and look after your children, now you were supposed to go to work and find a childminder for them. Whereas before, you changed your name to your husband's, now you were expected to keep your own – perhaps, after a while, adding his to it, which resulted in a lot of double-barrelled names and people wondering where it would all end. In three generations, would all surnames have sixteen components? Molly Maguire-Murphy-Sweeney-Byrne-O'Connor?

Mitzy and her peers would have felt guilty, and their husbands, too, if they had jobs. 'He has her out working', was a phrase you might have heard about a man whose wife was a schoolteacher, say. As if he were exploiting her. It was almost as bad as beating her up when you had too much drink taken. But for Martha and her friends it was the exact opposite. They would have felt guilty if they'd stayed at home. It wasn't just that that seemed old-fashioned, and a betrayal of the fight for equality, which it did. But if they decided not to keep their jobs, people would have thought they were lazy. Their own husbands would have thought that, and their mothers-in-law. In some cases – not so many – their own mothers would have.

When Martha and Seamus moved to Dunroon in the eighties, Conor Moriarty was eight and Siobhán was five and Lauren was two. Five looked old, to Martha, for a child, when her baby was not yet born. She would see Conor and Siobhán walking to school when she was on her way to catch the train. They were both tall and athletic, and to Martha they looked very independent, able to go to school on their own, while her baby was still rocking around in a puddle of fluid inside her body. And she was rocking inside the train, still feeling sick.

The train. Work. Sleep. The train. Work. Sleep.

Martha saw the sense of working, and she often said she liked her job. She knew that life had changed for the better, for women, and would as soon have given back the new entitlements to equality and jobs as she would have handed in her voting card. But at the same time she was consumed with envy of Mitzy, and the other Dunroon Crescent women. She envied them their freedom. She envied them their time. She envied them their chance to work on their houses and gardens and their hobbies, and, after a while, to be with the children.

She wanted to go to their coffee mornings. Not that they had formal coffee mornings, as such, they're an American thing or a figment of novelists' imaginations. But some of the women occasionally got together, little groups of them, or couples. There were best-friend partnerships, just like in school. All this friendship, chatting, laughing, went on during the day when the men and the children were out of the way. When they came home, there would be no time for such frivolity. Then the women of Dunroon Crescent would go back into their kitchens and look after their families.

On Dunroon Crescent, Martha was like a man or a child, heading off in the morning and coming home on the train at night. So it took a long time to get to know the neighbours. And if you spend too long getting to know people, you never become close friends. The moment when people can change an acquaintanceship into a friendship comes soon enough in the chronology of a relationship, and if you don't seize that moment, it won't, as a rule, come again. Time is a factor, and timing. Lots of people know this instinctively, even when they're very young. But Martha didn't and she let various opportunities pass.

It was even harder when the children came. Then her life was so busy she never had time to be with the neighbours, at all, at all. She rushed through her days, from early morning to late at night. There was hardly time to sleep, in those days, when she had no trouble at all doing it, when she, too, became unconscious the second her head hit the pillow.

When she had lived on Dunroon Crescent for more than sixteen years, Martha started to cut down on work. She and Seamus had got married as soon as the divorce legislation came through.

Being married gave her a sense of security, oddly enough. Also, their mortgage was nearly paid. Interest rates had dropped and salaries had gone up and Martha and Seamus had more money than they needed. For the first time they were never in the red. It was the era of the Celtic Tiger – that is how Martha experienced it, at first: the debt to the bank diminished, then vanished, without her doing anything about it. Later, the affluence affected her in other ways. More holidays. Their holidays used to be down the country, in the west of Ireland. They'd rent a damp bungalow near some windswept beach, or, less often, they would drive around the country – 'getting to know our own country', they called it – and stay in B & Bs, also bungalows, though with more expensive, frillier curtains and bedspreads than the rented places. Now they began to use hotels. Cheap hotels at first. Soon Martha became a connoisseur. In particular, she had high demands where bathrooms were concerned, and bathrooms were what changed most, she noticed, during the time of the prosperity, every year becoming bigger and more and more beautiful, until in the end they were the most palatial and ornate rooms in the entire land, nicer than any other part of the house or hotel – like the tombs of the Pharaohs (whose mosaics and carvings they often emulated).

But the best thing about the healthy economy was that it created thousands of jobs, and that conferred a new sense of freedom. Being employed was no longer a privilege – there was more than enough work to go around for the first time ever, it seemed. Nobody wanted to work in the Public Service any more; the big money was to be made elsewhere. So the Public Service enticed people in with better pay and better conditions. Flexitime, career breaks, parental leave, term-time leave – all these inducements became available. Management was bending over backwards to make life easier for parents – by which was meant, mothers, although they pretended it was for fathers, too. In the Four Courts, women were doing four days, three days; one young woman in Family Law was doing a one-day week. (She had twins; the crèche would have cost more than her salary, even though they gave her a ten per cent reduction on the second twin. And of course she lived in one of the new housing estates in Portarlington, sixty miles away from Dublin, and had to get up at six in the morning on the days she worked.)

After nearly eighteen years of full-time work, Martha decided to give herself a break and try the three-day week. So she was at home on Fridays and Mondays. She had time for herself – which she interpreted as time for the house and the garden, for Seamus and Robbie (a giant of a boy aged fourteen who needed mothering as much as he needed a broken leg). And for the neighbours.

But things had changed for the women on Dunroon Crescent. Now that Martha had time to befriend them, her neighbours were all out working. Women who had seemed destined for a life devoted to children and housework and tennis and gardening, who had indeed seemed to disdain any other kind of life, were going back into teaching, they were taking up jobs as receptionists and bankers, and in computers. Ingrid Stafford was in college, getting a law degree – there was a lot of work in conveyancing because the property market was so strong.

Even Mitzy had a career of her own.

She had started when Lauren went to secondary. She didn't want to apply for a job. 'I don't think anyone would take on an old hag like me,' she said, caressing her fingers, which were long and nimble, white as marble. She was in her early fifties.

Martha nodded. Anyone over fifty *was* ancient then, as far as she was concerned.

'I'm going to buy an old house and do it up,' Mitzy said.

'That makes sense,' said Martha, although it didn't really. 'You have a flair for decoration.'

Mitzy agreed: it was obvious. Her house was perfectly, effortlessly, beautiful.

'But will you make money on it?' Martha wondered. She had heard that doing up your house was something you did only for yourself. You couldn't expect anyone to pay extra for a house just because it looked nice inside.

'I think so,' said Mitzy. 'I think people will pay more for a house that is really nice and ready to walk into than for somewhere that needs a lot of work.'

She bought an old Edwardian house for fifty thousand pounds. This was at the end of 1996. The owner of that house had been trying to sell it for more than a year. The place was a dump, inside and out. Mitzy got the worst of the structural problems attended to, and did a big redecoration job herself – she could paint and hang wallpaper and bore holes in the wall for hanging things. The garden was a wilderness but she trimmed and tamed it in no time, popped in a few flowering shrubs and geraniums in pots. In November the following year she sold it for three hundred and fifty thousand pounds. And then she bought two small Corporation houses in Harold's Cross. They tripled in value by the time she sold them nine months later. By 2000, Mitzy was a millionaire twice over, and set to get richer.

Even though Mitzy was busier than she ever had been, Martha got to know her much better after she went part-time herself. Mitzy was busy but she worked from home – she set up an office in one of the bedrooms. They had six, so there was room for it. As the first decade of the new millennium moved on she worked less. The restoration of houses she left to others, and she bought and sold less and less, anyway – it cost so much to buy property, even a run-down shack, that the business was not as lucrative as it had been at the start of the decade. She and Martha had lunch together on Fridays, and on these occasions they talked about their families mostly, and the neighbourhood, and their houses. But also about themselves.

Because Mitzy was so cheerful, good-looking, elegantly turned out, Martha had always assumed she came from a well-to-do background. But this was not the case. Mitzy (she had been called Patricia, even Patsy, as a child) was not even from the city. She had been born on a farm. Twenty acres, six cows. 'Yes, I was up before school, feeding chickens!' It was hard to imagine. Not because of her posh accent, or her clothes. But there was something about her face that looked quintessentially urban – classical, absolutely regular, with a tiny nose and large, slightly hooded eyes. She always looked made up, even when she wasn't. When Martha heard that Mitzy had been brought up on a farm, the image that popped into her head was of *Green Acres*. Who was the star in that? Eva Gabor? *New York is where I'd rather stay*, that was the line in the theme song, *I get allergic smelling hay.*

'I loved it,' she said. 'Mucking about. There was a great sense of purpose to it. And you belonged not just to your family, but to a community. Everyone knew everyone. And looked out for them. *Ar scáth a chéile a mhaireann na daoine.*' She quoted the well-known proverb in Irish, about neighbours depending on one another.

Martha nodded, surprised because she had never heard Mitzy say a word of Irish before. They were at either side of the long, stripped pine table Mitzy had in her enormous kitchen – new. Like almost everyone on the crescent, Mitzy had built an extension, even though her house was already huge. Behind her was a pale yellow Aga, and an old dresser filled with painted jugs and plates – all the most well-known potters in the country were represented on it. She'd replicated the country style here on Dunroon Crescent, although everyone knew no real country kitchen had ever looked like this.

'It's so different now for the kids in the suburbs,' Mitzy said. 'I pity them.'

'But they have an easier life.' Martha was thinking of the swimming clubs, the piano lessons, the designer tracksuits. Now it looked as though they would have their choice of careers, too – that they would not be forced to take whatever job they got, and stick to it for life, lest they don't get a second chance, which was what she had done.

'I'm not so sure about that,' Mitzy said.

That's when she told Martha about Siobhán, who wasn't a kid, anyway.

She had tried to kill herself a few months ago.

'Overdose,' Mitzy said. 'She took all the pills she could find in the house and swallowed them.'

'Why did she do it?'

'Broken heart. She was living with Mark for four years. He seemed so nice!'

Martha remembered him, although to her all young men look pretty much the same.

'Some tart from Poland got her mitts on him!'

'These things happen,' Martha said, remembering, with a sour twist in her stomach, her own history.

Mitzy laughed – harshly, for her, like a magpie squawking – and shook her head. 'That was just the immediate cause. But there's something deeper. She was carted off to the hospital, of course, to be detoxed, and they insisted on sending her to John of God's.'

The psychiatric hospital. Martha tried to look deeply shocked and sad – the fact was she had heard some of this already, though in disjointed scraps, from other neighbours.

'She was there for three months.'

'But she's OK now?'

Mitzi shrugged. 'She's back at work. I don't think she'll ever be OK. She'll never get over it.'

But you have to, Martha thought. Everyone has to get over things like that.

That conversation with Mitzy took place about a month ago. Martha is listening to the eight o'clock news. Seamus has already left for school; he goes off just after seven. She's exhausted, after being up during the night. She puts Fluff out for her morning pee and sees Bran slinking around the fuchsia bushes. He hates her now, after that kick – well, he'll get over it. In the end, most people and animals get over everything, if you give them time.

Martha's dopey as she drinks her coffee and eats her All-Bran. There's the usual dispiriting news about the downturn in the economy. The leader of the small businessmen's association is interviewed and calls, it must be for the hundredth time, for a reduction in the number of public servants and for more cuts to their pay. He has convinced the journalists and the public that public servants caused the financial crisis.

Martha thinks those people are the Nazis. They're looking for a scapegoat. And for a while, until the hand of blame is pointed elsewhere, she and Seamus, the public servants, are it. It's astonishing how easy it is to influence public opinion, and how easy it is for public opinion to influence the politicians. You plant an idea and keep watering it on the airwaves, and very soon a myth is transmogrified into a fact.

This is the very thing Mitzy and she fell out about last week.

Mitzy is feeling the pinch. She has four properties on her books now that she can't sell, or even let, and she lost money in some sort of investment shares she has – not the kind the government is protecting, obviously.

'We'll be all right,' Mitzy said. It was Friday, one of their Friday lunches. This one was in Mitzy's house. 'But we've taken a hit.' She shook her head sadly and pursed her lips, but she didn't disclose details.

They were in the conservatory at the back of the house, overlooking the pool Mitzy had put in a few years back. The water in the pool glistened under the autumn sunshine; Mitzy's lemon trees, in tubs behind the glass, were in flower – they flowered at the strangest times – and their intoxicating scent filled the air. Martha could inhale that perfume as if it were opium – this must be against the law, she said sometimes, as she sniffed greedily. The white wine sparkled in the shining glasses. They were eating smoked salmon terrine and Caesar salad, and the soft smoked Wexford cheese they loved that you could only get at the farmer's market in Glendalough. (Dunroon Crescent women drove down especially, on Sundays, to buy it.) A year and a half into the downturn and their lunches hadn't changed. Or their clothes or their holidays. As yet nothing in their lives had changed, although they were hearing every day that the country was in recession and that disaster was on the horizon.

That's when Mitzy took a swipe at the public servants.

'They're bleeding the economy dry,' she said, waving her pale hands in the air, and repeating what you could hear on the radio any time you turned it on.

Then she told a little story.

'A friend of Siobhán's was working in some department last year,' she said. 'Education, I think. I'm not sure. And in November, some of them said, "We haven't taken our sick leave yet!" And they took two weeks off, before the Christmas holidays!'

Mitzy shook her head in disgust. Her fringe was silver now, but it was as thick and shining as ever.

Martha's innards boiled; her stomach felt like a pot of poisoned stew on a high flame, ready to erupt.

She looked out the window, instead of into Mitzy's eyes. There was a congress of starlings in the garden. Hundreds of them were sitting in the big sycamore trees, looking like black plums on the branches, gathering for that thing they do. A murmuration?

'I'm a public servant.' Martha kept the lid on. As she always did. Almost always. 'And so is Seamus.'

Mitzy was confused, but not for long. Mitzy was never confused for long.

'I don't mean you,' she said quickly. She laughed. Her earrings danced. They were silver now, to match her hair, and her white linen blouse. 'I don't think of you in that light. I meant ...' She paused. 'I meant, you know ... the mandarins who sit in offices all day drinking tea at the taxpayers' expense.'

Martha nodded and ate a bit of salmon. She could never think of the right thing to say when a friend insulted her. The smart retort always occurred to her long after the conversation was over, when it was too late.

And – when it was too late – Martha remembered that she'd heard that rumour before – the story about the sick leave. She'd heard it from her own mother about thirty years ago. Now it was doing the rounds again. When it was too late, Martha remembered that no civil servant is allowed more than two days' sick leave at a stretch, without a doctor's certificate. And the Public Service year doesn't end in December, anyway, but in March, so there'd be no reason to use up any kind of leave in November. When it was too late, Martha realised that Mitzy's story was just one of those urban myths. But you never cop on to the urban myths until it's too late, that's the way they work.

She finished the terrine and the wine, although she couldn't stomach the cheese. She watched the starlings lift off the sycamore tree in one giant black flock and then vanish into thin air. How do they do that? So abruptly and so thoroughly. Where do they go?

She has not spoken to Mitzy since that day. If Mitzy is in her front garden when Martha comes out of her house, Martha withdraws and waits till she has gone, even if it means being late for work. And she didn't invite her to lunch last Friday. Now Mitzy has got the message. When she spots Martha, she makes herself scarce.

Morning Ireland.

'A report has just come in about a body found in the south suburbs this morning.'

Martha, filling the kettle, turns off the tap to listen properly.

'The woman is believed to be in her late twenties and her body was discovered by a man walking his dog in shrubbery near the railway track in Ashfield. The woman, who sustained multiple stab wounds, has not yet been identified. The state pathologist is on her way to the scene. It is believed that she was killed in the early hours of the morning.'

Later it is revealed that the dead woman is Katia Michalska, aged twenty-five. She had been at a party in town but left alone. It was thought that she had walked home and been attacked when she was within two hundred yards of her own house, which was in Ashfield Park, the next suburb to Dunroon.

On Dunroon Crescent, it's generally assumed that somebody from Lourdes Gardens murdered the Polish woman. Those thugs were bound to murder someone, sooner or later. There's a rumour that Katia was mixed up with a fellow over there, and that she was into drugs.

'She was no better than she should be,' Mitzy said. In the excitement of it all she has forgotten that she and Martha have fallen out and aren't on speaking terms. They're talking over the garden wall. 'Not that that excuses anything. Poor creature!'

According to Robbie, Katia was involved with Siobhán's ex, Mark.

Mitzy didn't seem to be aware of that.

Hmm.

Over the next few days the Gardaí call to every house in the neighbourhood.

'We're doing a routine check,' one of the two Gardaí says. They are in Martha's sitting room. Seamus and she have to give an account of their movements on the night of the murder. Sunday night. Robbie has already been questioned – they talked to the young folk first, naturally.

Seamus does most of the talking. They'd gone to bed at 11 p.m. on that Sunday night. Robbie was in bed, too, because he had to get up for college in the morning.

'Didn't you wake up at some stage?' Seamus puts this question to Martha.

The guard has only asked a few things, and it's clear that he doesn't expect anything to come of this interview. He gives Martha an interested look.

'I suffer from insomnia sometimes,' Martha says to him. 'I woke up in the middle of the night.'

She sees Siobhán, walking down the road, wrapped up in that enormous coat. It hadn't been cold. And young people hate coats even when it is. Mostly they wear tiny jackets in the middle of winter. Or no jackets at all.

She hears Mitzy, sitting at her table overlooking the swimming pool, saying, 'They're bleeding the economy dry.'

'I got up and made a cup of tea, and I drank it. I heard a bird singing and I went to the window to look out.'

The bird must have been a blackbird. She can still hear its song – one line, repeated over and over again. She can't write music but she knows the bird had three or four notes and the line sounded like words. *Help you me, help you me, help you me.*

'You looked out the window? What time would that have been?' The Garda's face has come alive, or as alive as a guard's face ever comes.

'It was twenty past four. I looked at the alarm clock. Then I put out the bin.'

The two Gardaí look at one another and you could smell the tension in the room as if it were a gas.

Martha never put Luke's name down for Mulberry School, or any other school, because he died when he was two and a half years old. He was ill for almost a year before that – he had leukaemia. Many children recover from leukaemia and for most of that year Martha and Seamus and the doctor clung to the hope that he would be one of those, that he would pass through this nightmare and come out at the other side, delicate obviously, but alive. Alive. Alive. The thing you want most in the world, when all is said and done: your child, alive.

Martha wanted to stay with him all the time in hospital, but she couldn't. It was impossible to get time off work. There were no career breaks. You could get only one month's compassionate leave. When Martha explained the situation to the Personnel Officer, that person – a woman – made her feel that she was a malingerer, trying to cheat the system. She made her feel that she was the typical new type of public servant, the working mother, who now wanted the system to bend over backwards to grant her favours and privileges, which no public servant had ever had before, because until a few years ago there were no mothers, no married women, messing things up. They'd been obliged to resign on marriage; now there was all this change, this chaos. Married women. Maternity leave. Mothers demanding endless favours, causing headaches for the entire system and especially for the Personnel sections. This Personnel Officer was not going to give in to Martha, the very first mother to work in her section in the Department of Justice, and, the Personnel Officer hoped, the last.

'She seems to hate me,' Martha said to Mitzy. Cried to Mitzy. She couldn't bear it. Luke was so tiny, and sick, and she wanted to be with him from morning till night.

'Wouldn't you give up work?' Mitzy asked.

No, said Martha. She wouldn't. If she gave up her job, she knew she would never get another one. Seamus was older than her. If he died, and she didn't have a job, she wouldn't be able to pay the mortgage, she wouldn't be able to support Luke.

So Mitzy came to the rescue. She often sat in the hospital with Luke all day, when Martha was at work. Frequently, Siobhán, who was just six then, sat with her. They did that for eight months. In the end, Martha, although she got no time off officially, was told by her immediate boss, who had four children himself, that she should just take as much time as she needed, they would not report her to Personnel. She could make it up when Luke got better.

Her boss told her this around the time that it was becoming clear to him and to most people that Luke was not going to recover. But that was not something Martha accepted until Luke was dead and buried and she was expecting again.

Mitzy had a hand in that, too. Martha thought she would not have any more children after Luke.

'You must.' Mitzy had been quite firm about this and her conviction cheered Martha up and calmed her.

'I don't think we can,' Martha said, wondering. Something had happened to Seamus. He wasn't interested. He wasn't able.

'These days, that shouldn't be such a problem,' Mitzy, who

had more cop on than anyone Martha knew, said. 'You'll be able to get around that.'

The Garda repeats his question.

'Did you see anything from the window? Did you see anyone?'

Martha – and Seamus, and the other Garda – look at the window, as if they might see someone now. At that moment the street lamps go on, illuminating the hedge and the footpath. The evenings are closing in earlier and earlier. It's the twenty-first of September, the start of the dark nights, and – as it happens – Martha's birthday. Her fifty-first. They will celebrate later, with a special dinner and a bottle of her favourite wine.

She shakes her head slowly. 'I noticed that I'd forgotten to put out the bottle bin.'

Seamus gives a start. He doesn't like it when he forgets to do his chores. The Garda waits.

'So I put it out.'

'That must have been about four thirty?'

'Yes. It must have been.'

Seamus looks at her and bites his thumb, a habit he developed after he gave up smoking, all those years ago. Martha meets his eye.

'But you saw nobody?' the Garda went on.

Martha is sitting on her hands. She looks at the faces of the three men, all staring at her.

Waiting.

She lets them wait. She's in no hurry.

The shortcut through IKEA

In her fifth queue of the morning, the one at the traffic lights at the exit from the airport, Ingrid Stafford, middle-aged Swedish immigrant in mystical, mythical Ireland, realises something, which is this: today belongs to her. Her husband, Tim, is right now taking off his shoes and belt at the security check in the airport and will spend the next seven hours or so safely locked into a tube of steel crossing the Atlantic. The kids are at college (they are aged nineteen and twenty-one but still live at home, in the strange Irish way, and can justifiably be called 'kids'; they certainly act the part). She has a day off – a rare treat, since the solicitor's office in which she has been working since she got her law degree, just a few years ago, is literally run off its feet. They specialise in conveyancing, and people are buying property – houses and apartments – with frenzied enthusiasm, as if the skill of building was about to be lost forever, tomorrow or the day after. Not much chance of that, to judge by the cranes that stretch across the horizon like the arms of benevolent giants, reaching out to embrace the Irish nation, with a paternal, irresistible, if steely, hug.

Today Ingrid could do anything. She could have a cultural day, visit all the art galleries in Dublin, or go to Newgrange, Monasterboice, the archaeological treasures of north Dublin (like many southsiders she only crosses the river to go to the

129

Abbey Theatre or the airport). She could spend the day watching films in the Irish Film Institute – she is always missing something good that is on there. She could go to the zoo. Who would know? Or take the ferry to Wales and have lunch in Holyhead.

She fills the tank at the filling station near the exit. Petrol has just gone over a euro a litre; a year or so ago she wondered if it would ever go over a euro, which looked like a kind of rubicon. But of course it has, its rise is relentless and inevitable. And it is still cheaper here than up north. As she watches the clock on the pump rush through the euros – at least the two windows match now, litres and euros neck and neck as they spin to thirty, forty – she realises that is why she is tanking up now, because the North is where she is going to spend the day.

She does not tell herself what she is going to do. Not yet. But she knows it is unlikely to be cultural. Not up there in the North.

She met Tim in the north. In Uppsala, her home town in Sweden. Uppsala is one of those cities that is more of a passage than a destination. It is full of people in transit. Students in transit through college, and old people in transit from work to death. Not so many people spend their ordinary working lives there, but of course some have to, as in all such places. Her father had a job in the civil service and her mother in a school. Tim was over from Ireland on some sort of scholarship for a year; he studied botany. Ingrid was doing English. The chances of their paths crossing were one in a thousand. Or one in ten thousand, who knows? Anyway. Slight.

But they did cross, in the waiting room of the hospital. She had sprained her ankle skating, and so had Tim. This was December 1982, when the rivers still froze in winter, and the snow still fell reliably in Sweden. 'That's a bit of a coincidence,' said Tim. He had noticed that she was good-looking, before finding a pretext to speak – he was adept at that sort of thing.

Ingrid had broken up with her boyfriend, Tomas, six months previously, at the start of term. Or he had broken up with her; he had met someone else during the summer holidays, on a dig in Gotland – archaeology was his subject. This had broken Ingrid's heart, which was not a thing she had ever anticipated happening to her; in fact, it was not something she believed could happen to anyone, until she saw Tomas walking across a street, hand in hand with another girl – that girl had been wearing a skirt identical to the one Ingrid had worn all summer, a gathered denim skirt, to below the knee, which somehow made Ingrid want to scream and tear her hair out right there on the street beside Ofvandahls Konditori (the skirt was from a chain store, so it was not much of a coincidence). Since that day she had been crying for weeks, months, and had considered killing herself as she sat at her desk, hoping the telephone would ring, and trying to type her essays about Jane Austen's comic style or Shakespeare's tragic heroines. Many methods had occurred to her. For instance, jumping into the river at a deep part with stones in her pocket. But she had not done that, or taken a lot of pills – she had dismissed slitting her wrists in the bath, she knew she would never do that, it sounded so horrible. And she was not practical, it would be hard to do it right. Ditto hanging. What do you tie the rope to? *Clickety-clack*, the keys of the typewriter sang out, mocking her, while the phone maintained a cruel silence.

The river was frozen and she had been persuaded to go skating by her mother, who was constantly trying to find diversions for her. She fell on the ice first time out – she was not concentrating. Three months, recovery should take, one of her friends told her. From the broken heart, that is – the ankle would heal faster. The friends had theories about heartbreak: it turned out that everyone knew about this condition. It was like some sort of familiar, though not everyday, disease – not like a cold, more like shingles, say. You never notice that such an illness exists, but if you get it yourself, you quickly meet dozens of people who have had it. Ingrid's friends swapped stories about their broken hearts the way people exchange anecdotes about their stay in hospital, or what happened when they got tonsillitis. And they had various suggestions about cures, too. Getting drunk was one, though not very effective. Time was the other most common suggestion for healing: a month for every year of the relationship was the theory. It was more than six months now and she still suffered. She wondered who came up with these theories. Were they scientifically proven? Had anyone done a survey?

Tim might know, since he was a sort of scientist. But she did not ask him, or tell him much about Tomas. She could have. He was – is – very kind. She did not think he would find her sad story very interesting, and she did not think he would even understand it. Heartbreak. He loved her, very much, but in a practical way. The way a tree might love another tree, and cross-fertilise it. Botanically, without undue emotion.

It takes about two and a half hours to drive from Dublin Airport to Belfast City Airport. That is where she is off to. She admits it, when she crosses the Boyne over the new bridge, those tons and tons of gleaming silver steel flung over the narrow enough river at Drogheda. It is a day in a million. And how is she going to use it?

Going to IKEA.

The new store that opened in Belfast a few months ago to cater to the voracious appetite of the Irish for furniture, new kitchens, the latest kind of sofa. The only IKEA on the island of Ireland so far, although they have been trying to get a branch in Dublin. The planners are holding them up, with a million and one excuses – no doubt the local furniture stores are pressurising, maybe bribing, the county council to keep the big foreign invader at bay for as long as possible.

But over the runway of Belfast City Airport the Swedish flag flies high! Nobody flies flags in the South, though up here in the North they are addicted to them. Even today she has seen Union Jacks in some estates, tricolours in others, as she drove along the A1. Seeing the flag of Sweden over Belfast City Airport makes her laugh and brings a lump to her throat at the same time. Direct rule from Stockholm might be a pretty good answer to the Ulster question.

Her feeling about this shop is also ambivalent, but it neither makes her laugh nor cry. She does not know what to make of it. It is much bigger than the one she knows in Uppsala: an enormous, brash, blue and yellow block, shamelessly ugly, without windows or any softness, like a blue and yellow prison colonising a bit of Northern Ireland. IKEA Maze.

She makes her way through the showroom. The sofas, the kitchens, the bedrooms. Lots of things have Swedish names. The Karlstad, the Ektorp. Her father came from Karlstad – a square town, plain as ryebread, with a huge river running through it. The sofa is bright orange, not a Karlstad colour, but it has, she fancies, the same boxy, down-to-earth shape as that town. She begins to think about her father's family home, a fairytale house with high gables, shingled roof, a garden full of flowers and fruit trees.

It is not just Swedish place names that IKEA uses. Many items are labelled in both English and Swedish. Sax/scissors, gardin/curtain, agga/runner. Taken in by it all, Ingrid finds herself speaking Swedish to one of the assistants, who looks bemused. Ingrid laughs at herself and repeats her question in English.

Although she does not really buy anything, in the sense of a kitchen or a sofa (she would like to; she would like to buy everything in the shop), her trolley is full when she comes to the checkout. Full of rubbish. Then just outside the big checkout area is the food store, where she stocks up on pickled herring, tins of biscuits, Swedish mustard, and other things, the things she takes great pains to acquire every Christmas from Sweden, so that they can celebrate the feast in authentic Swedish style in Dublin. So now she will not have to make her November trip home, an extravagance she introduced to her life when Ryanair started a direct Dublin–Stockholm flight a few years ago. But lingonberries and ginger snaps seem less important if all you have to do is drive for two hours up the M1 to buy them. Probably, the ease of access will make them less tasty, too.

If they want a Swedish Christmas this year, they will have to go to Sweden. But how could they? Her parents are dead; her brother is busy with his own family. She has not seen him for three years – just after their mother died. She could not turn up, uninvited, and ask to spend Christmas with him. She still thinks of Sweden as home. But since her mother died, she has nowhere to stay over there.

She brings her trolley load of things back to the car, then returns to the canteen to have lunch. It is three o'clock – she has managed to spend four hours walking around the store. The canteen is thronged with people. The chirpy Belfast accents are counterpointed by the flat intonation of Dubliners, middle-aged women slagging each other about the shopping trip. 'Wouldn't it be awful if you came all this way and went home with nothing?' 'Look at me lovely toilet seat!' 'I ordered the fish and chips.'

Ingrid goes for the meatballs. You can buy either ten, or fifteen, or twenty, depending on how hungry you are. It is very fair. She goes for the ten.

'Will ye have the jam with them?' The waiter has a thin, handsome face, which she thinks typical of young Belfast men. They look like young Swedish men. The narrow skulls and noses, not the round heads you get in the south of Ireland.

'Yes,' says Ingrid, and he spoons on some lingon jelly. *Sylt*. And the creamy gravy.

'A few chips?' he asks encouragingly.

'Yes, well, a few,' she says.

He heaps the plate with so many chips that they spill over the edge.

The food is quite good, especially the gravy and jam – the meatballs are so overcooked that they have developed a hard skin, like little leather footballs. Maybe that is because she is so late, or else it is the Belfast way with meatballs. She is very hungry – she was up at 6 a.m. or so, and has been driving or walking constantly since then. She should have taken the twenty. The sauce and the combination of gravy and jelly and meat taste good: a blend of tastes that takes her back. They had this dinner on Wednesdays when she was a child. The berries collected by themselves in the forest during the summer, everything home-made – better than this, but not that much better, all things considered. The hours of work that went into one simple meal – not that the berry-picking was work, as such, at least not for the first half-hour. They would go on for about four hours, though – her mother made about fifty pots of lingon preserves at a time, and the children were expected to supply the berries. That is how it was at home, over there in Sweden.

She drinks her water but does not finish the meatballs. A small Ryanair plane speeds down the runway and takes off into the clustering grey clouds. The hill on the far side of the airport has darkened to a deep black purple. The chatter of the other diners is louder than before – a huge choir, in which she has no part, is raised in a harmony of many varieties of English in a crescendo around her. She is the only person sitting alone at a table in the canteen. The only silent one, with nobody to talk to.

She would have nobody to talk to in Swedish even if she had somebody with her. Tim never learnt – even back then, they gave botany lectures in English. And the children have not picked it up, which is her fault. She had thought it sentimental to speak Swedish to them, not thinking that she might have enjoyed having her own language around her occasionally, that it would have been a little personal luxury. Not thinking that she would miss it. Which she does. Especially here in this weird shop, where the language is just out of reach, like a stranger rushing away down the street, or a ghost passing, a shimmer of mist flitting across the garden.

Suddenly she feels sick and overwhelmed with a need to get out of here, to get back to her car and home to Dunroon Crescent. She cannot finish her meal. Stacks her tray on a trolley and gets out of the canteen as fast as she can.

But when she reaches the foot of the stairs, there is no exit. She asks a staff member where it is.

'You have to go through the showrooms again,' he says, slightly apologetic. She has done something wrong. You are supposed to eat before you pay for your goods, then leave the premises for good. That is the system. You are not supposed to go out and come back again. 'But there are shortcuts,' he says. 'Just follow the signs saying "Shortcuts". You won't have to go through everything again.'

He is a big Belfast man, about six foot four. A sort of bouncer, maybe, making sure that people like Ingrid do not break the rules.

The shortcut signs work up to a point but she finds herself retracing her steps for much of the way, going past the sofas and the kitchens and the home offices, and all the rest, at a brisk pace. And now everything looks different. What was cheering and delightful in the morning, looks dusty, tawdry, in the evening. The Ektorp and the Karlstad and the Jenny Lind chair – which she had loved earlier, wanted to bring home with her – have lost the vitality that made it possible to envisage them in her own house, part of its personality, part of the furniture. They look flimsy now, insubstantial, like stage props, or like furniture in a folk museum. Second time round, all the life has drained out of them.

She is trying to find her way out of the bathroom section when Tomas appears.

She knows it is him, even though she has not seen him for thirty-odd years. She hides behind a shower enclosure and looks at him.

He has not put on weight, which means that you can assess the effect of the years on him accurately – there is no distortion apart from the one. The same frame, the same features, but aged, like a tree in winter. No flaming autumn for the human race. Tomas's hair is grey and white, a bit thinner than back then but still present and correct. Nothing disastrous has happened to his face. The skin is redder, or darker; it has the thickish, leathery look men's skin gets – the opposite of the translucent, baggy thing that happens to women. (Hers has not started doing that, not yet. Maybe under the eyes. When she looks in the mirror, she sees the same face she saw thirty years ago.) He has glasses, fine gold-rimmed ones. That is new. She has glasses, too, just for reading, and she is wearing them now, because she cannot read the labels without them.

He obviously works here – he is wearing a work suit and has one of those green plastic clipboards that managers in shops carry under their arms.

He loved archaeology, his dream was to excavate something in Greece, she cannot remember what.

Oh well. Archaeology. One of those luxury subjects that does not necessarily lead to a career. Though he was good, he believed in himself and the subject. He was determined to make it.

They should talk. But now the exhaustion of the long day overcomes her, and she cannot act. Does she really want to hear about his shattered dreams – or remind him of them? – because, like hers, they will not have shattered in some big, brilliant crash. That is not what happens. The dreams slowly fizzle out, drip by drip, so that you hardly notice until … now. What were her own dreams? Apart from him?

Another thing that she feels, rather than thinks. She is not looking her best. Her hair is a mess. And she wore clothes she does not like much, in the rush of getting up and out this morning. The linen skirt with the uneven hem does nothing for her, or the white T-shirt that has gone greyish in the wash.

To escape for a moment, gain time, she slips into one of the display bathrooms and pretends to be fascinated by the taps on the bath.

Tomas passes this bathroom and looks right in through the fake door.

He sees Ingrid. She turns her head and they stare at one another across a funky square toilet bowl.

She decides at that moment. She is going to speak to him. Of course she is. He was the love of her life.

Then her mobile rings, loud in the little space, playing the Nokia tune.

Tim. He has landed in Boston. He's waiting at the carousel for his luggage – his last queue of the day, he hopes, because somebody is coming to collect him and drive him into town.

She hears these details as if they were messages from another planet, referring to someone she has never known.

While she is on the mobile, Tomas nods politely, the way you would nod at someone you half-recognise but cannot put a name to, and walks away before she has the conversation. When she emerges from the bathroom, he has disappeared.

They sat on a bench by the river at the end of April. The riverbank was filled with the home-made rafts that students had constructed for the madcap race down the rapids, which would take place on Walpurgis Night, the last of April. Igloos, wigwams, flying saucers, polar bears – all kinds of things had been constructed from plywood and stuck onto the flimsy rafts. Toadstools. Shoes. The river flowed sweetly, the ducks bobbed on the water, unconcerned about the mayhem that would erupt in a day's time. Tomas put his arm around her shoulder, and pulled her close to him. It was the first time this had happened to her, ever, the first time ever her body had felt the warm embrace of a man she was in love with. Joy shot through her from head to toe. The river, the silly boats, the ducks, the red bridge, the yellow houses on the other side, leaped into life, as if someone had plugged them into a high voltage stream of energy. The world was switched on.

She had long fair hair, pale skin, a shy but hopeful look in her eyes. The person on the bench, wrapped in the arm of Tomas.

She looked a completely different person from the Ingrid who is now unlocking her car, driving out the slip road, heading back to Dublin. Looked. Was.

She wonders, as she drives past the Mountains of Mourne, in the sunlight that has emerged now as the day is drawing to an end, if he could find her address, her contact details, by tracing her credit card. Probably they are not supposed to do that. But probably it is possible. It is possible. He saw her. He could trace her, if he felt like it. It is very easy to track people down, anywhere in the world, these days.

The hills in the distance shine with that luminous, mellow green shade they get in the evening light. Impossibly beautiful and melancholy. Shadowy.

What would it have been like? Her other life.

She could have had more than one other life. Any of us could. We make choices, readily enough, thoughtlessly enough, at a time when we have choices to make. Before we know it, we are stuck with the consequences of one or two of them. Forever. Ingrid is thinking about the life she gave up, without really realising what she was doing. About her birthright. Her life in Sweden.

She drives along very fast. Towards the South, towards Dunroon Crescent, where she has lived for much more than half her life. Getting home as fast as ever she can to the people she loves.

But.

How she longs to go back.

The Sugar Loaf

Then the woman on the weather forecast says: 'Try to get out and enjoy the good weather tomorrow.' She gives a big, motherly smile and points at the little suns that are dotted all over the map. Tonight she is wearing a velvet jacket: a deep mellow plum colour. And earrings. She must be going on to something after the news – Audrey imagines her at a party, holding a crystal glass of champagne, chatting to elegant people near a roaring log fire. Or maybe eating dinner in some cosy restaurant, the candlelight flickering, the forgiving light making everyone look beautiful.

This woman has been doing the weather for ages. She has always smiled brightly, even when telling the nation to expect more unsettled weather, issuing gale and flood warnings. But she has never before said, get out and enjoy it. Not that Audrey, who has hardly ever in her life missed the nine o'clock news followed by the weather, can recall.

It seems right to take her advice.

It's October. The summer was dreadful. In two weeks the clocks will go back, at the same time as the leaves fall thick and heavy from the trees, which are now in their autumn beauty.

*

139

Sunday morning. Honey-coloured sunlight pours into the front room. Get out and enjoy it, the advice rings in her ears, like a command from a kindly tyrant. But Audrey can't, not yet. There is far too much to do. She has to prepare her classes for tomorrow. Audrey has been teaching English in Mulberry Manor for thirty-three years but she still always has to prepare every day. She can never find her notes. Her mother used to raise her eyebrows at her.

'If you spent a few days tidying up, you'd save yourself a lot of time in the long run,' she'd say.

'Ah, will you stop annoying me!' Audrey would respond. 'If I had time to tidy up, I'd tidy up, but when would I get the time?'

Her mother had no answer to that. But she set her mouth in a straight line like a one-inch zip. That was how she expressed disapproval, or dismay, or despair.

The truth was, Audrey really was very, very busy. Preparing, correcting copybooks. Exams. And she had her busy social life. She did salsa dancing. Drama. Belonged to a choir, although she wasn't much of a singer. She had her piano lessons, too, at least until the teacher said she was moving to another country and could no longer take private pupils. Audrey had asked if she could recommend another teacher, but no, she could not.

She drinks her coffee – she can't face the day without a few strong mugs, although the doctor has told her she'd be less anxious if she cut it out altogether, but that's easy for him to say, and she's sceptical about that coffee taboo. Fashions change so often, in health, as in everything else. It's not so long ago that doctors were sticking disgusting leeches to sick people and bleeding them to death. Doctors differ and patients die, she says to herself, as she drinks her third mug. She's sitting on the only chair in the kitchen that is not piled with newspapers, letters, schoolbooks, essays or exams by pupils, some still in Mulberry Manor and some long gone. Long graduated from university. Two are dead, but their compositions still survive in the archive of Audrey's kitchen. Audrey never likes to throw anything out. When she was alive, her mother occasionally insisted on doing a blitz, clearing at least one room in the house so they'd have somewhere to sit in comfort, or to place a guest. Not that they often had a guest, apart from Ben, Audrey's brother, who lives in England and used to come home to Dunroon Crescent about once a year. (You'd think England was the far side of the moon.) As Audrey's mother got older, she wasn't able to do much herself, and no amount of her sulks could get Audrey to tidy up. She just never had the time. That was the long and short of it.

She goes to her desk, still wearing her dressing gown. It's fluffy turquoise with a big brown stain on the side. It doesn't look very attractive but nobody sees her, so what matter? She knows the brown stain is just hair dye. Iced Chocolate. It's a good dye, her hair is always shiny and natural-looking – if young, shiny hair is the definition of natural – for at least a week. After that, it turns the dead black of ink. Or black clay. Her hair was always her crowning glory, the one beautiful thing she had, so she doesn't want to let it go grey before she has to. Iced Chocolate is the answer. It's close to her real colour, that is, the colour she had until she was about forty-two or -three, which is when it started to fade. (She doesn't know what its real colour is now, because it's always covered with Iced Chocolate.) The hairdresser might give a more lasting shine but it would cost ten times as much as the home stuff. A hundred euro for highlights and blow dry. You can buy six fluffy dressing gowns for a hundred euro. In Penney's. Which begs the question, how much do the women who make the dressing gowns get? Audrey asks this question sometimes, usually of some class in school. But it doesn't stop her buying all her dressing gowns, and most of her other clothes, too, in Penney's. She can't really be expected to solve all the problems of the world on her own. She's busy enough solving all the problems of Mulberry Manor.

Tomorrow they'll be doing John McGahern, *Amongst Women*. It's a hard enough novel even for sixth years but they'll have to make the most of it. She'll ask them which characters they find most interesting. And they'll say Rose or Maggie, Sheila or Michael. They'll all pick a different one. That's what she likes about the novel, that everyone has their own favourite character. Hers is Luke, the son who runs away and stays away. He's intriguing because he is never in the book. And she admires his guts. Anyone can run away, but it takes real courage to stay there.

*

141

The sun is around at the back of the house by the time she's even got herself dressed. Hot enough to sit out. The garden looks great in this forgiving light. Nasturtiums climb over everything – the fence, the hedge, the trees, the lawn. They're even creeping over the yard and into the drain, they're incorrigible, they'd grow anywhere, even in a sewer! The yellow dahlias, too, are exuberant. They are a special tough kind of dahlia, those, which would survive anywhere. Some of them are pushing up the slabs on the patio, so strong are they, and growing through them – the nasturtiums are doing their best to strangle them, but good for the yellow dahlias, they're holding out. So are the nerines, which her mother planted the spring before she died. Their bubble-gum pink is a pleasant shock in the autumn palate of dark reds and yellows. Bulbs, they are, which are great in a garden, they just look after themselves. Like weeds, which is what most of the garden is covered with – but weeds is just another name for wildflowers. Audrey's garden, once her mother's pride and joy, has been transformed to a nature reserve. Not appreciated by the neighbours, but beloved of hedgehogs, urban foxes, insects of all kinds. And mice and rats (they have a nice nest in the old compost heap, lovely and warm).

She could easily spend the day here. Enjoying the weather and maybe going so far as to do a bit of gardening. Even for a nature reserve, it's getting overgrown. The nettles at the back of the garden make it difficult to get to the big bin tucked away behind the shed, where she throws the empty bottles. Her mother had plenty of time to look after the garden and she went on doing that till she had her heart attack. Audrey could get someone in, but why would she? They rip you off and what do you get for it?

The Sugar Loaf she can see from the front garden. It rises from a nest of green hills, the Dublin Mountains and the Wicklow Mountains, a dramatic peak that looks like a volcano, although it has never been a volcano, she knows, from listening to *Mooney Goes Wild on One* on the radio. (She used to listen a lot to the radio, before she mislaid it. It must have got thrown out by mistake. Or else it is buried under papers somewhere in the kitchen.) Audrey has seen the mountain almost every day for fifty years, ever since they came from a house in the inner city to live in Dunroon, on the outskirts, when she was four and Ben was two. They moved out of town because their father had got a promotion and that's what people who were doing well did in those days. They said goodbye to the old Victorian terraces and colonised the new white estates built on the fields and farms all around the edge of the city. Audrey can remember the excitement of all that, how pleased she and Ben and her mother were with the big windows, the bright rooms filled with light. The enormous, bare garden.

During that fifty years – her life – she has driven close to the Sugar Loaf dozens of times and seen people walking up the road that winds to its summit. But she has never climbed it. Not even when she was a child. When she and Ben were kids, their parents brought them out on a drive almost every Sunday. They'd drive to some field or beach. Then they'd eat tomato sandwiches and sweet biscuits, drink sugary orange juice, in the back of the car or sitting on a rug spread on the ground at the side of it. There was a flask of hot tea for Mammy and Daddy. They called that a picnic. When it was over, they'd turn around and drive back home. They never climbed a mountain or went for a hike or anything like that. They never even went for a swim in the summer because Daddy had a thing about water. (His grandfather, a policeman in the country, had drowned – he had been pushed into the sea by a smuggler he was apprehending. This happened when Daddy was four years old, in 1918. Daddy's earliest memory was of seeing somebody empty the water out of his grandfather's rubber boots. He'd never forgotten it.)

Audrey had revived the Sunday drives when Daddy died ten years ago. She did it to give her mother a change of scene, at the weekends, and to ease the tension that could arise when they were both cooped up together in the house for too long. Of course, they'd never climbed the Sugar Loaf. Her mother couldn't have, at that stage. She was old, she had a weak heart, and arthritis, and various other complaints (as she called them, although she never actually complained but bore her pains in silence).

*

It is almost three o'clock by the time Audrey gets away. She doesn't know where the day has gone to. She has managed to get dressed but she has not managed to finish her preparations for tomorrow's classes. She's slower than usual today. When she opened the McGahern novel, her heart sank and her head swam. She couldn't engage with Maggie and Moran and Rose and all of them. All she could see was 6C sitting in their desks, like flowers in a bed of weeds, eager to get space and light, eager to escape from school and get started on life. Their big, kohled eyes full of contempt for people like Audrey, locked in the school forever.

She drives out to the main road and stops at the little garage on the Bray Road, where she has filled her tank for the past thirty-odd years. He's the only garage left around here now, anyway; the other three sold up, as sites for apartments, over the past year or two. If she doesn't fill here, she has to drive to Bray. Here's usually a cent cheaper than the Bray garage, she's noticed. One hundred and fifteen cents here, that means it's one hundred and sixteen in Bray – she'll try to look when she's passing.

As soon as she passes the Dunroon shopping centre, the Sugar Loaf disappears from view. After about ten minutes' driving, it occurs to her that she doesn't actually know where it is. Not in the way you need to know where a mountain is in order to climb it. Audrey often does this – sets off in her car, sure she knows the way to some place, only to realise en route that she has no more than a general clue as to its whereabouts. She has to ask at the filling station outside Bray (where the petrol is actually one hundred and seventeen cents a litre!). The young fellow is Chinese and has never heard of the Sugar Loaf. Or so he says. Can't be bothered telling her the way, probably, is more like it.

Of course, she knows the mountain can't be far away; otherwise she wouldn't see it from her front garden. She drives along, glancing to the right all the time, to see if she can spot it over the cars and trucks that roar along the motorway. Eyes off the road, she swerves out of her lane twice. A driver honks at her, and another gives her that sign with his fingers that means 'Fuck Off!' Obviously, someone with road rage syndrome. The Sugar Loaf remains elusive.

At Kilmacanogue, on a hunch, she turns right towards Glendalough. Then she does a sensible thing, the sensible thing she should have done at home before she set out. She decides to consult a map.

Parking outside a bungalow, in a little lay-by, she searches for the map of Ireland. There are ten of them at least in the car, on the front seat and in the glove compartment and on the back seat, mixed up with some other things made of paper, and some not (there's an apple butt on the seat, and a packet of chicken liver pâté she bought two years ago). She picks up the cleanest map and looks at it. Yes, she seems to be headed in the right direction. In fact, if she is reading the map correctly (she's not all that good at reading maps), she could be halfway up the Sugar Loaf already. According to the map, this road she's on is on the side of the mountain. She looks out. The bungalow is an ordinary one, with a tiled roof and a little tarred patch of yard in front, two green wheelie bins and an old fridge at the side. Behind it is a slope covered with heather and furze. That could be a mountainside all right.

There is a tiny little thin blue line off this road, and the spot called Sugar Loaf on the map seems to be somewhere between this road that she is actually on, and that little thin one. The L1031.

To her surprise she finds the L1031 without difficulty.

It's nearly as narrow as the line on the map. Just a track, really. There is nothing to indicate that the Sugar Loaf is on it. You'd think there would be a sign at least, but no. They expect you to be divinely inspired as usual. Sugar Loaf. She goes along, anyway. She has no choice once she starts – turning back wouldn't be easy on this narrow track. It runs through flat fields, with sheep in some of them and cows in others, and a bog. That must be Calary Bog. She always liked that name. She doesn't know why.

She hasn't gone far along the narrow track when she sees cars. Something is happening – some country event. There are lots of cars, parked along the side of the road, which is wide enough for two only. Families stand around their boots, eating sandwiches and drinking tea. It must be a point-to-point, Audrey thinks. She's not quite sure what a point-to-point is. But all these people look as if they're waiting to see horses, or dogs, hunting

145

some animal across the bog. They don't look as if they came to the side of this narrow road just to eat their sandwiches and then go home. To Audrey, other families have always seemed purposeful, in control of their lives, their Sunday afternoons.

She drives carefully along the free side of the road. After half a mile or so, there's a gap in the line of cars. And suddenly, out of the blue, the mountain appears. That familiar sandy peak. The Sugar Loaf – unless there is some other mountain around here. The Little Sugar Loaf? Or that one with the name that sounds like 'Juice'? Funny name for a mountain. Though it sort of goes with Sugar Loaf.

Whatever it is, the peak is close to the road, and not high. I'll be up that and down again in less than half an hour, Audrey thinks, as she starts to plod across the springy turf. The sun shines in a clear sky, but she's wrapped up in her warm green cardigan, and she put on her green parka, too. Just in case the temperature is lower at the top. (On Mount Etna, where she was in the summer, there was snow.) The landscape is exhilarating – the hill, fields with cattle and sheep, spread behind. Hundreds of people are walking up and down the hill. Half of Dublin is here. On its crest there's a line of things that looks like burned spruce trees. Or crucifixes.

She overtakes a family: a mother and father, with two small children in tow.

'Are we there yet?' the little boy says, whining.

They have hardly left the carpark. He looks to be about three, so he may not know it's a cliché. Though children are so precocious now, it's possible that he does and is being ironic.

'Not yet,' his mother says patiently.

His father looks at the boy in exasperation. 'We're going up there,' he says, and points to the peak. 'See where those people are? Up there.' He points at the crucifixes and utters the words with slow, exaggerated patience.

'All the way up there?' the boys whines. 'Will you give me a carry?'

'That'll be fun for you!' says Audrey, smiling at the father. 'He's no light bundle!'

The father nods, but doesn't say anything. The little boy looks alarmed. He runs back to his mother and takes her hand. The mother gives Audrey a sharp, questioning glance.

She hurries on.

A big group of girls, long-haired, mostly blond, clad in light summery clothes, blocks the path. They stand right across it, so Audrey can't pass. One of them, dressed all in white, comes tentatively towards her, holding out a camera.

'Yes, yes, of course!' says Audrey, without waiting to be asked. Relieved, although she knew nobody could attack her, here, with half of Dublin to witness it.

The white girl goes back and stands with her crowd.

'Smelly Sausages!' says Audrey, and the girls smile, but they don't laugh. So she says it again and takes another one. They don't laugh this time, either.

'I should take one more,' Audrey says to the white girl. 'I didn't hear a click.'

'I did,' says the girl, with the trace of a German accent.

'Sure I'm half-deaf,' says Audrey, and waits for them to laugh. But they don't. They give a little smile and look away.

It takes her an hour to reach the foot of the final peak. It's further away than it looks. She's sweating by the time she gets there – it's much too hot for the cardigan and the parka. The parka she takes off – she doesn't feel like removing the cardigan; then she'd just have to carry it. Most people are in their T-shirts. She looks up at the peak – a mound of rocks. Scree. Grey stones tumbling down the slope – that's what the sugar is. The peak, which looks like the point of a needle from her garden, is about twenty square metres in circumference, at least. It's a little platform at the top of the stony scree.

Audrey feels just a tiny bit light-headed, and also a bit queasy. Altitude sickness? The mountain is five hundred metres high – she noticed this when she was looking at the map – but maybe some people can get altitude sickness at that height? She wonders if the Twin Towers were five hundred metres high. Probably about that. You wouldn't get altitude sickness at the top of a building that you worked in every day, even one that a plane could crash into and destroy. It must be her heart.

She sits down to takes a rest.

Maybe she shouldn't go up any further.

The view from here is good, anyway. The cars are a necklace of black diamonds strung gently around the foot of the mountain. There is Powerscourt, nestling in its dark woods. The big hotel at Kilternan in a patchwork of fields. Her landscape, where she has lived for most of her life. It's lovely, she thinks, gratefully. Of course, she's always known that.

Someone sits beside her. An older woman – older than Audrey.

'Stay here and we'll be down soon,' says someone. She is a comfortable-looking person, in a tracksuit. She settles the woman, who is clearly her mother, into a fold-up chair.

'I'll be grand,' says the older woman. 'It's lovely here. Take your time, enjoy the view from the top.'

The younger woman kisses the older woman and starts to climb the mountain. She has two children, a boy and a girl, who also kiss the older woman and shout: 'Bye-bye, Granny, bye-bye, see you in a while!'

Last year, Audrey and her mother had been down there at Powerscourt one Sunday afternoon. An overcast day, it was not looking its best. But her mother had loved it.

'You go and walk for as long as you like,' she said to Audrey. 'I'll sit here and wait, I'm grand.'

She sat on an iron seat in the garden, looking down at the steps, the statues, the fountain. The flowers. The Sugar Loaf, soaring over the garden, as if built for it as a suitable backdrop.

Audrey had walked dutifully through the gardens, looked at a few unusual trees with labels on them, tripped across the tiny bridge in the Japanese gardens. The things everyone does at Powerscourt. But the grey day depressed her. In the pets' graveyard she was overwhelmed with loneliness. A sense of being totally lost, abandoned, although there were people all around. Within ten minutes she was back with her mother.

'I'd love a cup of coffee,' her mother had said.

She seldom asked Audrey for anything. She loved having cups of coffee in cafés but knew Audrey didn't share her taste for this form of amusement and usually refrained from asking. This day was different, for some reason. She hadn't been out of the house for weeks, and she was overjoyed to see something different from the four walls of the messy sitting room. She was overjoyed to see the gardens and the fountain and the great house. To see the Sugar Loaf soaring over all that.

'OK,' said Audrey gruffly.

They went into the café. Of course it was packed, as Audrey knew it would be. Everyone in stuffing themselves, escaping from the nasty weather. She put her mother at a table in the corner – lucky to find one – and queued for coffee and cakes.

For about twenty minutes. That's how long it took to get two coffees and one slice of chocolate meringue gateau and cream.

By the time she got back to her mother, Audrey was as cross as a bear. She snapped and snapped. But her mother didn't mind. She was used to Audrey's snapping. She no longer heard it – like someone who lives beside a railway track and doesn't hear the trains roaring by every five minutes. She sipped her coffee and ate her chocolate meringue gateau slowly, with great enjoyment. She was happy. Anyone could see it. She glowed. In love with the fields and the flowers and sky. In love, yes, with the chocolate cake.

Audrey didn't hear her own snapping, either. While she was doing it, snapping away and drinking her coffee, she was thinking, it's great to see her having such a good time. I must bring her on a holiday somewhere before the end of the summer. Wales, say. Somewhere that would be easy to get to, but a different country. They could go over on the ferry, bring the car. Go up to the top of Mount Snowdon on the Mountain Railway and drink coffee up there, look down over Wales. And Ireland. They say you can see Ireland on a clear day from the top of Snowdon.

Her mother had been finding the summer long and gloomy. The garden was out of bounds most of the time, because of the rain. She had to sit in the house, listening to Audrey snapping at her, eating sandwiches for dinner more often than not – Audrey didn't bother cooking much since Daddy died. The sandwiches weren't bad. Ham and cheese, smoked salmon. Crisps on the side and often a bit of salad from a bag. Audrey had her wine to wash it all down, which seemed to make a difference. But her mother didn't like wine. So she had nothing but tea to flavour the sandwiches. It got monotonous.

Audrey didn't bring her on a holiday. Because a very strange thing happened last summer. A man in the choir, Brendan, asked Audrey out, and then he asked her to go on a holiday with him, to Sicily. Brendan was fat and had big, sticking-out ears. Still, he was nice enough. Audrey didn't want to go – she couldn't leave her mother for so long. But it was her mother who insisted. She phoned Ben and persuaded him to come over to stay for the week Audrey would be away. Audrey was sure everything would go pear-shaped, in Ben's incompetent hands. But when she came home, the two of them, Ben and Mammy, were sitting in front of a blazing log fire in the front room, which he had cleaned up, listening to nice music, and looking as happy as larks.

The hotel in Sicily was great. Five star, with a lovely pool surrounded by mature palms, and a view of Mount Etna, conveniently erupting. The food was good, although the wine was a bit expensive, and of course they drank a lot of it. On the second day, after settling in, they went up to the volcano in a bus. Audrey loved that, even though Brendan shivered when he got out of the bus, and instead of climbing upwards with the other tourists, they had to head for the café to have a cappuccino, then get the bus back down again. But it was great even halfway up – you could see for miles around, the gorgeous coastline, the deep green interior.

After that day, things started to go downhill. Brendan became far too fond of getting massages from the Chinese girls who worked the beaches. They were pests, you couldn't get a minute's peace from them. As soon as you settled into your lounger one of them was over, with her straw hat and little simpering smile, whispering, 'Massage, massage?'

'Go away, go away!' Audrey had said to them, swatting at them with her towel, as if they were flies.

Brendan had laughed at her. At first. Then Audrey started refusing to go to the beach, saying she preferred the pool, anyway. She told him the story about her grandfather and the boots. So he had to put up with it – he couldn't force her and he wouldn't go to the beach alone. But it annoyed him. When they came home, he never contacted her. He stopped attending choir practice.

That was at the end of August. Her mother had a heart attack on the first of September, the first day of school, and a month later, she died. The Sunday in Powerscourt, it turned out, was her last day out. Ever.

She used to come here as a girl. Audrey's mother. She had often talked about that. With her best friend, Myrtle, who worked with her in a grocer's shop, she would cycle out to Enniskerry on Sundays. They would go to the Powerscourt Waterfall, and stand under it, getting splashed all over with the water that cascaded down the side of the cliff. Then they'd have tea in a café in the village, if they had a shilling to spare. Myrtle and Audrey's mother, in their gabardine coats and headscarves, laughed a great deal. There was a black-and-white snapshot of them on the mantelpiece, them and their bicycles with the waterfall behind, laughing their heads off. This was in the 1940s because by 1950 they were both married and no longer worked in the shop or cycled out to the country on their bikes. This place had been on her mother's map, all her life. Just as it is on Audrey's. The place you could go to on a Sunday for a drive or a walk or a climb or a cycle.

Audrey looks up at the top of the mountain. The things that looked like trees or crosses from below are just people, standing on the crest. Happy to have got up there. Now she knows that is where she has to go.

She says goodbye to the granny, who doesn't answer because she has fallen asleep.

You have to clamber up the rocky slope. It's steep. But Audrey finds this bit easy. She used to love climbing frames when she was small. There was a good one in the park in Dunroon, beside the graveyard. 'You're my little monkey, you're my little monkey,' Daddy used to say. He used to bring her there to get her out of her mother's hair sometimes. 'My monkey,' he would say, catching her from the top of the frame and swinging her, swinging her, in the crisp bright air, so her skirt flew out in the wind and she screamed with delight.

There's a constant stream of people going up and coming down the rock face. They all use the same track. You have to move out of the way all the time to let someone coming down pass.

She is about a third of the way up, her eyes fixed on the rock face in front of her, when someone bumps into her and nearly knocks her down.

A man.

He apologises, then stares at her. He is long-legged, dressed all in black, like a spider. Dark grey hair. The kind of face that is called distinguished in a man. There is something familiar about him. He must be somebody's father, someone she has met at a Parent–Teacher meeting. They usually recognise her, although she can't possibly be expected to remember all their names and faces.

'It's you,' he says abruptly. This is not a thing the students' fathers say to her.

As soon as he speaks she recognises the voice. She takes a good look at him, as he stands there on the uneven rocks, with the sky all blue behind him. His grey hair turns black before her eyes. His young face emerges from his old face, where it is buried, to be discovered by those who know how to find it.

Pádraig. She was 'going with him' (that's what you did then, you went with a person) from the 10th March 1972, which is when she met him at a dance in college, till the 15th June 1974, when he went elsewhere. To America, just for the summer. She was to go, too, and if she had, she might still be with him. Going with him, to wherever people who stay together go in the end. But at the last minute she got cold feet. Her mother was encouraging, but her father had reservations. The US. Anything could happen there. What if Pádraig abandoned her? What would she do then? 'Ara, couldn't she just catch the plane and come home?' said her mother. 'And he won't abandon her, what would he do that for?'

The religion thing was never mentioned. But it was there, nevertheless, unvoiced, like a huge mountain hidden in fog. (They didn't know – how would you? – that when the fog cleared, the mountain would have disappeared, melted away like sugar in water.)

In the end she didn't go to America. She just couldn't face being away from home, from her mother and father and the house she had lived in for such a long time. She wasn't ready to leave.

During the first weeks, Pádraig wrote letters and postcards.

There was no question of telephone calls from America in those days. After a month, the letters stopped coming. And she never heard from him again.

'Yes,' she says now. So she is still recognisable. She wishes, how she wishes, that she looked smarter. She hasn't even bothered to comb her hair. The green cardigan is about twenty years old. The sleeves are black with coal dust, from emptying the ashes, something she noticed yesterday but she wore it, anyway. And the trousers are work trousers, not sporty-looking, not feminine. (She remembers that Pádraig had preferred skirts on girls.) Her hair is a rat's nest. If she'd even stuck a scarf on to cover it up. But how could she have known that half of Dublin would have the same idea as herself? Would heed the weather woman's advice to get out and enjoy the good day? She hadn't thought she'd meet anyone at all on the mountain. Still less this man whom she hasn't bumped into since June 1974.

'How are you?' he asks, in a calmer, kinder tone.

His voice had always calmed her down, made her feel all right. He was the only person who could do that for her. Ever. She had loved him much more than her father or her mother or her brother or anyone she met in later life (two other men, including Brendan). The realisation, which should have come to her that summer all those long years ago, is like a light going on in her brain. A light that makes her feel very sick and very well at exactly the same time.

'I'm grand', is what she says.

'We should meet sometime in more comfortable circum-stances,' he says, smiling. 'Can I give you a call?'

'That would be nice,' she says. 'I'm in the phone book.'

'Under your own name?'

She admits it.

'Yes, my own name. Bailey, Audrey.'

'I can remember that!' he says, grinning. He looks up at the top of the mountain. 'Well, don't let me keep you from your climb. This last bit is hard but it's worth it.'

'I'm sure it is,' she says.

After forty years, he doesn't want to keep her from her climb.

She wants to scream, stay, stay. She wants to grab him by the black anorak and keep him here on the side of the scree.

Already he has started to go down the slope, facing away from her this time. Even though there are several people trying to get past her, she stands for a full minute watching him retreat. The back of his head. His trim body in its black jeans and anorak. A woman is coming towards her now, down the sugary slope. Something tells her this is Padráig's wife. Younger than him. And good-looking. Lots of women who are not good-looking have husbands. But not husbands like him, successful and presentable and talkative. They always get pretty wives and if you're not pretty, you just won't do.

Audrey never said this to herself before. It's simple when you realise it.

Someone should tell the girls at school.

Or maybe they know that. They know so much. And so much has changed. Nobody cares whether you're Catholic or Protestant. Nobody cares whether you're married or single, either. (The girls paint their eyes, though, and diet, and care dreadfully about clothes. So they do care about something, although it's not quite clear what, or why.)

Audrey reaches the top. And there are the twelve German girls, in their light, white blouses, their long hair blowing in the wind. They are standing on the crest of the Sugar Loaf in a circle. They must have passed her by when she was taking her rest on the ridge beneath.

Last Friday she had 4C for English, last class of the week. It's never easy. They get so giggly and so damned silly. But she knows how to deal with them. Mountains of work if they dare to step out of line, she threatens them with. Not that they bother doing it, that's the trouble. She has to send them to the Principal then. And the Principal is getting fed up with her, but what can she do? it's not her fault. She was late for class on Friday, she'd stayed too long with 1B. They've been in the school for less than two months, so they haven't learnt to be brats. She was nearly ten minutes late. The door was closed and there was the usual cacophony of noise inside the room. Bracing herself, she opened it.

Jessica Black was sitting on the teacher's desk. She was draped in a big red coat, which looked just like Audrey's coat, however she'd managed to get her hands on it. Her hair was pulled back into a bun and she had painted a big black moustache on her face.

'Girls, girls, girls! Quiet please, girls. You're so bold,' she said.

'Please, Miss Bailey, where does your big black moustache come from?' Rebecca Murphy said. 'Can we shave it off for you?'

'No,' said Jessica Black. 'If you did that, I wouldn't be the ugliest woman in the school, would I? Now, open your novel, girls. I hope everyone has read Chapter Five?'

There are clouds in the distance, over Enniskerry and Powerscourt. A few swathes of rain, like cobwebs hanging in the valley. But they won't make it here. The woman on the weather promised. All sun and no rain. Those veils of rain will evaporate before they reach this mountain.

She takes off her green cardigan.

The German girls are dancing now on the crest of the mountain, in a ring, their white blouses fluttering, their hair floating on the wind. She knows she should go and offer to take a photo of them now that they are at the top of the mountain. Before and after. If she were a different sort of person, she would do that. It would be easy. It would be a kind and friendly act.

But she doesn't.

She sits down on the heather.

In the clean air the laughter of the German girls sounds like a nice nocturne by Chopin or John Field. It is the very sound of human delight. On her bare arms, on her bare face, the sun is warm and sweet, like the breath of someone you love dearly.

Below, the cars glide noiselessly along the N11 like toys. Then the sea. Bobbing sailboats, and the big white ferry slowly making its way eastwards. Pale blue, dark blue, azure. On the horizon a bumpy grey line, and a triangular peak rising out of the bumps.

It could be some sort of cloud formation. But she knows it's not. It's Wales, and the triangle is Mount Snowdon. They say you can see it, on a really clear day, from the top of the Sugar Loaf. She had always heard that, but she had never really believed it. Who would credit that you can actually see another country from the island of Ireland, which always seems so far away from the rest of the world?

The moon shines clear,
the horseman's here

The house is a holiday house, one of dozens dotting the landscape around here, each one perched in its own scrap of field, overlooking its own septic tank. Polly can see the chunks of thick white pipe sticking up from hers, her tank for the moment. The pipes are the main feature of the field, or garden, or patch of lawn, or whatever it might be called, which surrounds the house. The other feature is the well, a concrete block with black pipes emerging from it and snaking across the grass to a hole in the wall of the kitchen.

Polly had lived at home in this valley until she was almost eighteen. Her father was a teacher in the village school, and her mother a stay-at-home mother. She baked, milked cows, scrubbed the house, and was very particular about her religious duties, although not, thought Polly (not called Polly then, but Póilín), very seriously religious. Anyway, she made fun of the ladies who became *ex officio* keepers of the church, arranging the altar flowers and pandering to the priest and his every need, although she must have known that such women were found everywhere, were essential to the efficient running of the parish. Without them, there would certainly have been no flowers, no choirs, no special ceremonies on local feast days. Without them, the priest would have provided the bare necessities – Mass on Sunday, confession once a week, no frills. 'My New Curate', Polly's mother called the local women who provided all that decorative trimming of song and flowers and extra special prayers. However, she would never have missed Mass herself on Sunday; wearing a showy hat and white gloves, she and Polly sat with Polly's father in the first pew. This was the time when men and women sat on different sides of the church, but Polly's mother protested; she sat on the men's side. It was not a blow for gender equality but quite the opposite. She sat there to proclaim her superiority to all the other women, in their headscarves and dark old coats, or their trousers and anoraks. In the parish, she felt like royalty, and Mass was the appropriate context in which to give public expression to this attitude.

The family observed other essential religious formalities, some seemingly private in themselves but linked by invisible threads to the social and cultural web that enmeshed everybody. For instance, they said the rosary every night after tea, praying for the souls of the departed dead and also for living souls to whom they were closely related or who had power and prestige. They prayed for their cousins, the Lynches and O'Sullivans, in Cork and Tipperary, and for Eamon and Bean de Valera, and they prayed for the Taoiseach, and they prayed for the Archbishop of Dublin and the Bishop of their diocese. They prayed for the Inspectors of Education, who would descend on the school once a year and ask the pupils insultingly silly questions, and for the county football team. It seemed to Polly that this praying strengthened their connections to these people; it seemed to her that she had some role when the county won the All-Ireland final in Croke Park. She might have been a cheerleader, not that she knew the word then. She was a silent supporter speeding her team to victory, and she had a hand, too, in the running of the country. Then sometime in the late sixties, the rosary stopped. It seemed as if all Irish families reached some communal decision overnight, or as if someone in a position of authority had issued an edict and all the Catholics of Ireland obeyed it. Could there have been some telepathic referendum? Anyway, it stopped.

Polly's mother was different from the other mothers in the valley. Polly would have found it difficult to pinpoint in what this difference resided, but, if pushed to select one word, would have said 'old-fashioned'. Her mother did not like to wear make-up; indeed, she never even owned a lipstick. Her clothes were slightly out of date – excessively elegant white lace blouses and long skirts – when other, younger mothers had slacks with straps under the insteps and tight polo-neck jumpers. She never wore trousers, even though a lot of her work was out of doors with the cattle and in her garden. At night she liked to do embroidery, executing tiny white flowers on white table runners, broderie anglaise, although she called it Mountmellick lace.

Polly's mother was snobbish. She was not a native of the valley, but of a big town, where her family had been leading lights in the Irish language movement. It was thanks to this that she had come to the valley to learn its dialect, and there met Polly's father. Now she lived in a simple way, but she still considered herself and her family a wide cut above most of her neighbours, and this sense of difference coloured every single aspect of her life. That was probably why she did not wear lipstick or mascara, or slacks, and it is definitely why she did not go to bingo on Thursdays with all the other women. Polly accepted her mother's self-assessment, and believed that she was more ladylike, more refined, more valuable, than other people's mothers, although she often felt more comfortable in those other people's kitchens than she did in her own.

The view is sublime. That's what Polly was told all the time she was growing up. That she lived in the most beautiful place in Ireland was drummed into her, along with tables and catechism and alphabet. She believed it as certainly as she believed that God made the world, or that Ireland ununited could never be at peace, or that Gaelic was the one true language of Ireland and eventually would be spoken by every Irish citizen. In fact, she probably believed in the beauty of the place more profoundly than in any of those other tenets of the local faith. It seemed verifiable. The crashing waves, the grey cliffs, the purple mountains; did these not, in their awesome wild grandeur, constitute perfect beauty? But even then she felt drawn to nature in its more intimate manifestations: a tern breaking the surface of the sea, a seal poking its shiny nose above the black water, hares boxing among the rushes at Easter. The little flowers that bloomed from May to November in a relentless routine of colours. Primroses, violets, orchids. Saxifrage, the colour of bloodshot eyes. Eyebright, selfheal. But she was not enjoined to admire such details. They were taken for granted, like the hidden natural resources, the still unpolluted wells, the little farms that kept the valley humming in tune with the seasons. Somehow she deduced that all of this minor nature was commonplace, perhaps occurred in places that were not the most beautiful place in Ireland, perhaps in places not in Ireland at all.

There are no flowers in the fields now, because it is December. Rushes sprout like porcupines among the tussocks, and the rusty tendrils of montbretia spread themselves here and there in limp abandon. Otherwise nothing. What a month to choose for a dramatic return! Polly turns from the window and decides to light a fire, the traditional antidote to the gloom outside. When the briquettes are blazing in the grate and she is sitting in front of it, with a glass of red wine in her fist, she feels happier. Unlike its garden, the house is attractive, designed according to some international template for country cottages, with wooden roof beams, rough white walls, a slate floor. The fire makes it perfectly cosy.

When she was twelve, Polly went to secondary school in the nearby town, travelling by bus every morning and evening. The bus was a new idea; until recently anyone who could afford to go to secondary school from this area would have had to board, and Polly's mother wanted her to go away, as she had, to a convent in the middle of Ireland, where she would learn to recognise how superior she was to her neighbours. But her father opposed this; he wished to encourage his pupils to avail themselves of the new educational opportunities. Polly had to set an example. She had to use the free bus. Her mother agreed reluctantly. If she had had the faintest idea of what went on in the bus, her resistance would have been stauncher. It was much more vulgar than a bingo hall. It was worse than the pub, to which her mother never went; it was as bad as the disco that was held in a hotel outside the town on Saturday nights. Boys on the bus teased, cursed and swore. Girls huddled in the girls' section and either pretended not to pay any attention to the barrage of insults and mock endearments that was constantly fired at them from the boys' section, or they encouraged the boys, subtly, by glancing at them in a knowing, sly way, or overtly, by joining in and giving as good as they got. 'Give us a kiss.' 'Have you got your Aunt Fanny?' 'Fancy a carrot? Try this on for size.'

There were two kinds of girl on the bus: slags and swots. The slags wore thick beige make-up over their acne, and had long spiky eyelashes, a sort of badge of slagdom for all the world to see. Their hair was usually artificially coloured or streaked, or looked as if it was, although one might wonder why this should be, since they were aged between twelve and eighteen. But maybe they coloured their hair as they coloured their eyes, just to show the world who they were, just to show that they were defiantly, proudly sexual, just to show that they were not like the swots. The swots wore no make-up, and their hair was usually left severely alone and tied back from their faces with bands or ribbons. Or it was short, although that became more and more unusual as the sixties dragged to a close. The swots sat together at the front of the bus, quietly chatting among themselves about teachers and homework, and ignoring what was going on around them. The slags chewed gum ostentatiously, with the slow, long chews slags specialised in, and cast their sidelong, odalisque looks at the boys. The looks were also slow, slowness being one of the chief slag characteristics. What's the rush, their sauntering swagger seemed to say arrogantly. Time belonged to them and they had lots of it.

Sometimes a boy and a slag, who were going together, tried to share a seat and hug and kiss en route, but this was not allowed by the bus driver. Girls and boys were not supposed to sit together. The bus driver was a man aged about sixty, Micky the Bus, who, though old, was sharp as a razor. He tolerated almost everything, except sitting together and canoodling. If he caught a couple breaking his one rule, he threw them off the bus. It was against the rules of the Department of Education, but that didn't bother Micky. He knew, quite rightly, that the Department would never find out what he had done. He knew that his word was law on this bus. This was before the days of litigation and before the days when children or teenagers were aware that they had any rights at all. Nobody would have dreamed of questioning Micky's absolute authority on his own bus, not even the beigest, blondest slag.

Once in town, boys and girls separated, going to their gender-specific schools – girls to the nuns and boys to the Christian Brothers. They never really understood what went on in the different schools, and this mystery about how the other half actually spent their day added spice to their lives. Polly, long before she was interested in any specific boy, felt it when they got out of the bus at the bank and the blue-clad boys all walked off in one direction, gaining dignity when revealed to their full height, their long, thin, blue and grey bodies moving purposefully up the hill to the grey castellated structure that looked like a fortress or a prison. She found them interesting then, and intriguing, as they disappeared into the secrets of their days.

There was a loneliness about going in the other direction, with the flock of girls in brown skirts and blazers, to a place as ordinary as a bowl of cornflakes. Polly felt that where she was going lacked importance, although, as soon as she got there, everything that transpired seemed important enough, and challenging. She was a good student.

A good student. She had to be, to satisfy her mother and father. And it was not easy to keep it up. Not because she was not clever, or interested in her work, but because her friends did not approve of her academic achievement. Polly was in danger of going too far, which would have pleased her parents but outraged the girls in her class. So when she found herself speeding up – finding that she could enjoy reading history, or botany, derive a pleasure from learning and understanding, which was true satisfaction, not just the fulfilment of an urge to please some adult – she sensed some sort of danger. She held back. It was not so hard to do, and involved nothing more onerous than not reading as much as she was supposed to, half-doing her homework instead of doing it properly. Doing well was easy, it was a habit she could see her way into clearly, as if doing well were a clean, shining river, down which she could sail effortlessly once she had caught the wind. But not doing well was even easier. All she had to do was fail to hoist her sail, slide along under the work instead of gliding on top of it. She espoused the mediocrity that was what girls in that school, at that time, aspired to, even the best of them: her friends Katherine and Eileen, both of whom had been her closest friends since she was four years old and to whom she was bound by ties of eternal loyalty.

Polly has a week to spend in Ireland, and during that time she is going to face the devil. She has read somewhere that in everyone's life are seven devils, and only when you meet them and overcome your fear of them can you find your guardian angel. (It was a novel about Chile, which she read in Danish: devils, angels, saints and sinners have lead roles in Chilean folk belief, according to this novel.) Her mother. That is one of her devils, the one she is going to meet and talk to, regale with the story of her life, Polly's version. Until Polly tells this story to her mother, she will be unfree, ununited, unwhole. She is not acting under psychiatric instructions. She does not need a psychiatrist to tell her this elemental truth. There is unfinished business between herself and her mother, between herself and this valley, and time is running out.

But there are distractions. She takes time settling in. She has to find her bearings. She has to find the shops. It is easy to fill the time with routine tasks when you are in a strange place, even if it was once a place called home. The first days she spends trying to heat the house, and organise the water supply. The water is cloudy, white like lemon squash, full of clay or lime or something worse, and the central heating does not function. Men in caps come and mutter darkly in Irish to one another and hammer at the pipes, and Polly has to be at home to let them in.

Then it is desirable to explore her old haunts. She goes for a long walk to the hill at the back of the cottage. A road winding up past other bungalows, a few with grey smoke trailing up from their chimneys and most seeming empty, closed up like her house had been. After the last bungalow, a gate and then heather, sheep, sky for a mile, until you come on something

163

surprising: a cobbled hilltop in the middle of nowhere. It is not the usual place for a school, exposed and far from where anyone lived. A film set, that is what it is. Polly remembers suddenly, a chink opening like a trapdoor in her head. There it is, something she has not thought about in thirty years: the commotion when the film had been made in the valley, the trucks trundling up the hill, the star-spotting, the jobs for extras. Everyone had been an extra. Katherine and Eileen had been schoolgirls in the classroom scenes. All the other people had been villagers, or men drinking beer from funny tin mugs in the pub, or country folk at the market. Even the animals got parts: Eileen's mother had hired out her hens for a pound apiece per day. But Polly had not participated. Her mother would not allow it, disapproving as she did of the film, which, although the word was not used, focused on a passionate adulterous affair, conducted in a range of scenic Irish settings. How Polly's mother discovered this was a mystery. Nobody else knew what the film was about. It was impossible for the extras to follow its plot, such being the nature of filming. But Polly's mother had her sources. And unlike most of her neighbours, she did not need whatever extra money she could lay her hands on. She did not need to prostitute herself or her daughter to Hollywood. The film had been a disappointing experience, an experience of total exclusion for Polly. No wonder she had forgotten all about it.

Polly kicks the film-set cobbles with her walking boot, and continues to the crest of the hill. The sun is shining, low and strong, but the joy has gone out of the day. She can feel night falling already, the afternoon is sinking into the silvery grey dusk although it is only four o'clock. The sheep bleat on the bare hillside. Polly feels a huge yearning for her home in Copenhagen; she longs to be there. In her old house, with the bustle of the city ten minutes away on the electric train, the opera at a moment's notice, a glass of wine in a warm pub, with the lovely Danish Christmas decorations up, the sense of a simple tradition of paper hearts and straw goats and tiny flickering candles everywhere, in every window, on every table. Copenhagen celebrates light in the deep midwinter, glows with optimism and hope.

Back in the house, she pulls the tweedy curtains to shut out the bleakness and throws a few sods of turf on the fire, then phones Lia, one of her friends, and tells her how she is feeling.

Lia says, 'Come home if you want to', which is what Polly knew she would say.

And Polly says, inevitably, 'I don't really want to. Not yet.'

'You don't have to do any of this if you don't feel like it, you know,' Lia goes on. 'And you are allowed to change your mind.'

'I know, I know. I will in a day or two if I decide that,' says Polly, laughing.

This is the sort of conversation she always has with Lia, long, meandering sentences full of pauses, and words like 'feel' and 'decide' and 'maybe', phrases like 'well, wait and see' or 'it'll probably be OK'. They are so different from the conversations that Polly has with Karl, which are to the point, conducted in short, complete sentences, verging on the terse. He is practical and decisive, and it has taken him a long time to understand Polly's meandering, ever-changing mind.

Paddy Mullins sat with the rough element on the bus, smoking hand-rolled cigarettes and slagging people. A lot of the time these boys were laughing as they pushed one another and exchanged insults. 'Done your sums, Smelly?' 'Yes, Fat-arse, but I'm not showing them to you.' 'Surprised you had time. Seeing as how you were cleaning the pigsty again most of the night.' 'Shut up, Fat-arse, don't pick on him 'cos his daddy's a farmer.' 'Farmer? Tax dodger.' The language of the bus was English, although the language of home and of school was Irish, and some of the children, especially those from Polly's valley, did not know English very well. But they had to speak it, anyway; English was trendy, the language of pop singers and films, the universal language of teenagers. Only the most prim or the most childish, the most excluded, would persist with Irish in this context. The slags had a name for people like that. Ireeshians. Polly knew the rule of the bus and spoke English on it, but she was called an Ireeshian, anyway, because her father was a teacher and her mother was a snob and generally disliked.

She was also called 'Lick'. All teachers' children were called

'Lick-arse'; 'Lick' was its derivative, used by the girls, who eschewed strong language. Farmers' children were given the epithet 'Smelly'. Paddy was called 'Mackerel' because his father was a fisherman. He answered to the name, and gave as good as he got in these bouts of slagging, most of the time. But there were occasions when for no discernible reason he would fall out of the teasing loop. He would fall silent, and stare into space, thoughtful, enigmatic. Most of the boys did that. They had quiet moments, moments when they seemed to withdraw from the hullabaloo of a schoolboy's life and think deeply about something for five whole minutes at a time. What were they thinking when they did this? Polly did not know. But she would have liked to have found out, although as yet she had no inkling of how she could do this. Inside a boy's head was as impenetrable as inside a boys' school, somewhere she assumed she could simply never go.

Paddy would sit on his bus seat, gazing ahead of him, not necessarily out the window. Gazing at nothing. Then anyone could get a look at him. Not that he was anything special. Indeed, until this week Polly had considered that, whereas the girls on the bus all looked different, the boys all looked alike. There were smaller ones and taller ones, of course, with one unfortunate individual at either extreme. And there were a few fair-haired ones, with pale complexions and gentle manners – they tended to be short-sighted and wore glasses – who were not rough boys but good boys, and who sat near the girls, consulting their books or more often chatting to girls. Their fair, feminine looks seemed to give them an advantage when it came to making friends with girls, as if they were less threatening in their less blatant masculinity. And of course they were not as aggressive as the bulk of the boys, that band of brown-haired barbarians, who exuded maleness like a herd of bullocks and could not sit still. Dark, large-boned, stubble-chinned, too big for almost all the spaces they were obliged to inhabit, too big for the bus or the school, for the houses they lived in, these were boys whose true element was not a classroom or a school bus, but the high seas, or a meadow or a bog on the side of the mountain. A battlefield. Most of them were good footballers. Their school won the All-Ireland schools championship nearly every year.

Paddy was on the team but was the keeper, a position regarded with mockery by the girls and the fair-haired boys, although his team mates appeared to respect it well enough. Polly was accumulating information about him, almost without knowing what she was doing. He was a keeper, he was good at maths and chemistry, he was planning to be a scientist. He had once danced with a girl from the next parish for a whole summer but the relationship had fizzled out. He had been to Dublin many times with the team but never went on holiday anywhere. His father was a fisherman; they did not own even a small farm, just a house and a field, and he lived about ten miles from Polly's home – he had not gone to her primary school, and she did not know his family. They did not speak Irish in his house. There was some anomaly about his mother. Like Polly's, she was not from the district. Some people said she was English.

School finished at three thirty and at four o'clock the bus collected pupils from both schools and ferried them home. So that meant almost half an hour in the town if you were very efficient about leaving your class. Usually this half-hour was spent looking in the shops, or getting chips if you were lucky enough to have a shilling. People with a boyfriend or girlfriend found other ways to use the time – walking hand in hand on the pier, or chatting in the town park.

Paddy and Polly bumped into each other at the corner of the main street, one day in May. This was about a month after she had begun to look at him. By now she knew the contours of his head, the line of his eyebrows, the set of his shoulders, better than she knew her own. But she did not know how he felt about her, although Eileen had said once, in her most serious tone, 'I think Paddy Mullins likes you.' So now Polly muttered hello, and averted her eyes, preparing to move quickly on. Even as she let his face slide from her view, to be replaced with a view of the pavement, she felt angry and frustrated, because she knew he would not have the same *savoir faire* to initiate any sort of conversation; one of the svelte, fair boys could do that, but not Paddy, one of the bullocks, the goalkeeper. He would not be able to talk, even if he wanted to as much as she did. Also, she knew in that second that he did want to. His surprise, his pleasure, when they met like that, told her everything she needed to know.

She was wrong about his *savoir faire*.

'Póilín,' he was saying. She stepped back and looked at him, astonished at her good luck, their good luck, that he was able to say the necessary words. 'I'm going down to look at the boats. Do you want to come?'

It was as if he had been doing this sort of thing all his life.

They got through the town as quickly as they could, and then strolled down the pier. The sea was choppy, but a choppy dark blue trimmed with snowy white, and the sun was shining on the fishing fleet, on the clustering red and blue and white boats: the *Star of the Sea* and the *Mary Elizabeth*, the *Ballyheigue Maiden* and the *Silver Mermaid*. The air was full of energy.

'That's the one I go out on.' He pointed at the *Silver Mermaid*. It was a large white fishing smack with lobster pots on deck, and heaps of green seine nets piled on the pier in front of it.

'Do you go out often?' She could not think of anything more original to say.

'Weekends when they're out and I don't have a match.' He smiled. His smile was stunning; it lit up the day and gave his face a sweet expression that it didn't normally have. Usually he looked rather worried, as if he were carrying some burden.

'Do you like it out there?' Polly realised that although she saw fishermen around every day, she hadn't a clue what they experienced, out in those boats in the middle of the night, hauling in fish, which disappeared into the new fish plant down the street. She could see it now, a grey block on the edge of the harbour and, in front, the bay with the low hills on the other side, and the blue bar in the middle distance, beyond the great ocean. 'What's it like?' Out there, she meant, on the sea.

'OK.' He looked out, then at the *Silver Mermaid*, then out again. He reflected and seemed to come to a decision to say more. Possibly he had never described the experience before. 'It's dark, and usually cold, and usually wet as well. We let down the nets over the side, five or six of us. Then we wait. That's the best part, waiting, gripping the net, wondering what happens next. Sometimes we talk or someone sings or we all sing. But usually we're just quiet. Standing there, waiting, in the night.' He paused and Polly wondered if she should say something, contribute some question or comment. But she could not think of anything. 'When we haul in the nets, there are all kinds of fishes in them. Lots we have to throw back. Catfish, dogfish, cuttlefish. The cuttlefish are interesting. They have big brains, for fish. Once, I kept one in a jar.'

'For a pet?'

'No. To dissect in the lab.'

'Did you?'

'I didn't use enough alcohol and it rotted. It exploded. Very smelly!' He held his nose and laughed. Polly laughed too, looking at the sea, trying to imagine the smell of exploded cuttlefish. In a minute Paddy said, 'It's time to get the bus.'

It was a glorious May, as it often could be in that part of the world. Long, sunny days, some so warm you would feel like swimming, although the water would still be freezing. Swallows were flying high over the meadows, and larks twittered constantly, tiny dots so far away that they could have been daytime stars. Polly's mother was busy in her garden, one of the very few gardens in the valley. She raised bedding plants from seed in trays, which all through March and April had been placed under the windows of the house. Now she was raking beds, planting out nasturtiums and antirrhinums and sweet william, nicotiana, stocks. She was feeding her long rows of lettuce and onion, carrot and parsnip, her beds of herbs.

When Polly came home from school, at five o'clock, her mother would still be in the garden, her gardening apron over her summer dress, her red rubber gloves sticking out of the pocket. She would greet Polly with, 'You could get an hour in before tea!' Meaning, an hour of study. Then she could get three or four hours in after tea. Polly was doing the Leaving Cert in a month's time, in June, and her mother expected her to do well. What she meant by 'well' was quite specific. Polly would win a scholarship, a medal proclaiming her to be the best student in the county. At least that.

Polly had studied hard in secret for the last few months. To Eileen and Katherine she said, 'I'm hopeless. I'm way behind!' But at home she realised she was way ahead, and it astonished her that progress was actually possible, even now, even after her years of calculated dawdling: that by concentrated attention, careful effort, an improvement was discernible even to her, even without the endorsement of good marks or teachers' comments. She had never felt so in control of her work before.

The change in her relationship with Paddy did not alter this. After the walk on the pier, she knew something had happened to her. She had thought about Paddy quite a lot before, but in an idle, controlled way: she could daydream about him at will, when she had nothing better to do, almost as if he were a book she could open when her day's work was done, and close again as soon as more urgent considerations beckoned. Now she found herself filled with a glow of emotion no matter where she was or what she was doing; a pleasurable excitement shimmered not far under the surface of every single thing she was doing, bubbled in her veins, as if her blood had been injected with some lightening, fizzy substance, as if the air she breathed were transformed. *Light, bubble, crystal.* These were the words for what was happening to her. Walking on air, people said. And she felt light as air, translucent as one of the new green leaves in the hedges. Since the whole of nature seemed to share in this lightness and newness, the fresh-looking waves and the new crop of grass, the tiny bright leaves on the brown fuchsia bushes, she felt that she was part of the world around her, the world of nature, as she had never felt before. She could have been a leaf, or a blade of grass, or even a calf or a bird or a lamb. Even a fish, swirling in the cold blue ocean.

She worked as hard as before. But sometimes she could not keep herself seated. Her physical energy got the better of her, rushed through her like an electric shock and forced her to abandon her sedentary ways and go for a long run along the lanes. Her mother watched these bouts with some foreboding, but said, 'I suppose you need some exercise.' Often she added, 'As long as it doesn't interfere too much.' Polly smiled. She smiled at everyone now, even her mother, and could not care less what anyone said to her. She transcended it all. She was superior, blessed, different, special, and none of the trivial irritants of life had the slightest influence on her.

The Leaving would be fine. She knew it. There was less than a month to go. If she did not open a book from now till the exam, she would probably still do very well.

Paddy and she met every day after school. They walked on the pier or they walked on the streets. Within days, the entire school population within a thirty-mile radius knew they were 'going together'. That meant it was a matter of a few more days till the adults got wind of it; some blabbing girl would be sure to mention it to her mother. But it did not mean that Polly's parents would find out, unless some malicious person, some mischief-maker, decided that they should. In this community all normal adults would know that the last thing that Polly's parents wanted was that their daughter should be a having a relationship with a boy, especially a boy like Paddy. All normal parents would protect Polly and Paddy, and leave her parents, who were not popular, in the dark.

This is what happened.

After about a week of walking around in a state of increasing physical excitement, Paddy steered Polly to the town park, the known courting spot for schoolchildren. It was a walled park, secreted in the middle of the town, behind rows of houses and shops on all sides, and had a sheltered, enclosed atmosphere, very unusual in this place of exposed bare coasts, windy hills. Also, it was full of high trees, sycamores and elms and flowering cherries; the sheltering town allowed them to thrive here, whereas in the valley where Polly lived hardly a single tree would grow. They sat under an elm in the corner of the park and kissed, their first long kiss, so longed for that it stunned both of them. Paddy apparently had not kissed the girl he had been connected with the previous summer – Polly did not think he could have, because his experience of this seemed to match hers so exactly. That is, he was surprised by the powerfulness of the experience, by the delight it gave him, and at the same time it seemed the most natural thing in the world. He and she kissed as if they had never done anything else. You had to learn how to do almost everything else, even the most basic physical functions, but sex, apparently, you did not have to learn. Your body knew precisely what to do, without having a single lesson. At least, if you were like Polly and Paddy.

They had missed the school bus.

Every single child on that bus would know precisely why they had missed it.

Polly was OK. She had a phone in the house, and her father had a car. She telephoned from the kiosk on the square; for once the old phone was not out of order. She told her father she had been delayed in the science lab, finishing an experiment, and he came to pick her up. Paddy had to set out on foot, hoping he would manage to hitch a lift.

From then on they had to be careful about time.

The Leaving started. Polly sat in the school hall, at a brown desk, and read the pink examination papers. Nothing in them was a surprise; the traps they had been told to watch for had not been set, as far as she could see. The predictability of the whole examination had been the most surprising thing, and it was also vaguely disappointing. She had been given dire warnings. You must read the entire course. You never know what will come up. But when it came to the crunch, you did know. She felt cheated.

Paddy did not. In the boys' school, the examination technique was more refined. They knew exactly how much they had to do, and did not do a jot more. After every paper, Paddy was able to calculate exactly what marks he had got – A in Irish, C in English, A in chemistry. Polly breathed deeply, superstitious. How could he be so sure? Wasn't he tempting fate? The results were, according to her way of thinking, as mysterious and unforeseeable as any aspect of the future. That there was a direct link between the work she had done and the results she was afraid to believe now, although she must have believed it when she was studying. She wanted the exam to be a lottery. That was the attitude of the girls in the girls' school, whereas the boys regarded it as something much less like a game of bingo and much more like a field to be ploughed. Such a sense of control was essential for schoolboys, whose main ambition and duty was to win football matches. Pretending the Leaving was some mystical rite of passage, a mysterious test of intellectual prowess, was a luxury they could not afford.

Polly never found out if Paddy's calculations were correct, but she won the lottery. Straight A's. Three separate scholarships. Money flung at her from the county council, the Department of Education, the university. Her mother must have been so pleased. But no, she was not. She could not have cared less.

Her mother is sitting in front of the television watching a soap, when Polly comes into the room. She has not bothered to get up, but the door is open. It is still safe to leave the door on the latch, then, in this place. Polly walks in and says, 'Hello! Hello!' There is no response whatsoever. Her mother continues to watch TV and does not even turn around.

She tries again. 'Hello,' Polly says. 'It's me, Polly.' She speaks Irish; although she has not spoken it in thirty years, as soon as she set foot in the valley it emerged from her mouth automatically. She repeats her greeting and calls herself Póilín, which does seem unnatural.

Nothing happens. So Polly goes and puts her hand on her mother's shoulder. Her mother turns. She does not seem at all surprised. Her poise has not deserted her. She smiles, so that her whole face lights up. She reaches towards Polly and Polly prepares for an embrace. But it does not come. Instead, her mother shakes her hand. She shakes hands and Polly feels a sudden giggle rising in her throat. The gesture seems so ridiculous. Her mother's hand, though, is very warm and Polly remembers that they were always like that; to feel those on your hand, on your forehead, had always been an intense comfort and a pleasure.

'Póilín!' she says. 'Póilín!'

She is deaf. Suddenly Polly realises this. She is deaf and apparently her sight is poor also; thick glasses occlude her eyes.

'I decided to come back,' Polly says slowly, looking closely at her mother. She has aged terribly. Of course. Her hair is white and sparse, she is wearing those horrible goggle-like glasses, her face is wrinkled with deep, shadowy ridges, the kind black-and-white photographers love, like the cracks of a river delta. But when she smiles, her face is still recognisably her face, whatever the essence of it was – its sweetness, its primness – has not changed. That same expression of polite surprise, the head tilted in a manner both coquettish and disapproving, the same poise. The same superiority.

The surroundings have not changed at all, in one sense, and in another, the house looks totally unfamiliar.

Polly had regarded their bungalow, which was the very first bungalow in this valley, as an extension of her mother, elegant and superior, better than any other house for miles around. But now she sees it is shoddy and lacks any vestige of style, as the old, derided houses do not. The floor is covered with green linoleum, with brown-grey patches in front of the range and near the door. The cupboards are painted cream; the table her mother is sitting at is red Formica. There is a kitchen cabinet, also cream, with red trimmings, against the wall. Nothing has been changed. Outside, the garden is overgrown with shrubs – ginger-coloured fuchsia and olearia block out the light in the kitchen. The grass is not knee high but it looks rough and unweeded. A solitary, crazy bramble taps against the window pane.

'Your father is dead,' her mother says.

'I know.' Polly has to talk, although talk will mean nothing to her mother. Can she lip-read? Probably not, with those glasses. 'I heard.'

'And I'm deaf,' her mother says, without rancour. 'In case you didn't notice. I can't hear a thing you're saying. Are you speaking Irish? It's all the same to me what you speak.'

After the examinations, as June was drawing to a close, there was licence. Released from school, work, examinations, young people were given leeway to enjoy life. They were, for a while, expected to act their age, to explode with fun and vitality and youthfulness, by sharp contrast with what had been expected of them just weeks ago. The rules changed completely; studious, quiet types were out of fashion now and the correct thing to be was wild and exuberant. Polly's mother loosened the reins.

'Enjoy yourself!' she said. Her mother was weeding vegetable beds, hunting slugs from the lettuce, freeing the cabbage and parsley and onions from choking bindweed. 'Have a good time!'

It was, Polly knew, an order. Well, she would obey it, though not in the way her mother imagined.

An advantage of summer was that there was a bus twice a day, linking the valley to the town. In the new dispensation, Polly was able to take this bus every day, and could spend hours away from home. All her mother required to know was when she would return (on the last bus – there was not much choice about this). Occasionally, Polly mentioned that she was going swimming with her friends, and occasionally she was.

Most of the time she spent with Paddy. He was going to work in the fish factory, but had postponed this for two weeks. He was fishing at this time, for salmon, but usually the fishing expeditions took place during the night, leaving him free to be with Polly during the day.

They avoided the town as much as possible. There was still about their relationship a furtive air, since Polly had not told her parents about it, and as it progressed it seemed increasingly impossible to imagine confiding in them. It was no longer just her belief that her parents regarded all boys as out of bounds, indeed seemed to believe that any sort of relationship between the sexes was essentially wrong, and, what was worse, in extremely bad taste. It was not just that Paddy was everything her mother would abhor: English-speaking, poor, a fisherman, a member of a family which had turned its back on every value that she held dear. It was more that the nature of her relationship with Paddy had become, literally, unspeakable. Polly could not describe it in any words she knew, in any language, and her connection with her mother was, it seemed to her, only by means of words, the formulae Polly selected from her rich store of clichés to dish out, sparingly, to keep her mother at bay.

She got off the bus in the main street, outside the pub that served as a bus stop. Everyone got off there, and usually there were several neighbours to be nodded to, as well as some tourists – young people from Dublin or America, usually, backpackers with long, floating, hippy clothes, long curtains of hair, flowers in their hair. (Polly's dress was beginning to be modelled on what they wore, although she could not obtain the right things here, and in these hot days she wore a purple scarf tied over the top of her head and under her hair at the back.) She walked down towards the central part of town, just like everyone else, and usually bought some bread and cheese, and cans of minerals, at a small grocery before continuing to the end of town and turning up the road that led to the hills. This was a narrow road, winding between a few farmhouses and a few bungalows, then rising until it passed through the mountain range far above the town. The road was always busy with tourist cars passing, and that was why Paddy and Polly went there. When she met Paddy, they hitched a lift. All cars were going to the mountain pass. There was a carpark there, with a viewing point, where all visitors stopped and looked at the valley on the other side of the gap, and took photographs. Local people hardly ever visited this place.

At the viewing park, Paddy and Polly said goodbye to whoever had given them the lift – a German woman travelling with her son, joking and eating chocolates; a lonely man from Boston who had come to Ireland to play golf – and said they were going for a walk. The visitors usually smiled indulgently and waved goodbye, and Polly could see that they did what she could not imagine anyone in the valley doing – they approved of her and Paddy; they were looking at them and thinking, this is a handsome young couple, authentic Irish folk, in love, how delightful. She knew these people from America and England and Germany viewed her and Paddy as components in the landscape, partly, like the sheep, and also as ambassadors from the universal land of youth, the land of love.

At the top of the hill, they turned and walked back in the direction of their own town, the direction from which they had just come. They turned off the road and down a turf track. Within seconds, the trail of cars vanished, and they were in a wilderness. Nothing but the rough heather, the clumps of bracken, sheep bleating all around them.

They lay in the heather and kissed and pressed their bodies together. 'With my body I thee worship,' Polly said to him, tracing the line of his profile with her finger. Where had she heard those lines? 'They are in the wedding service,' she said, because she had read this in a novel.

'Are they? I never heard them,' he said. He had not been to many weddings and neither had she, and it was years later that she had discovered he was right, nobody said that, not in Catholic weddings. It was the English service, the Church of England, and when Polly realised that if you married in Ireland, which she never did, you did not mention anyone's body, she felt acutely let down, and bitter, and thought it was typical. How could she have imagined her mother uttering such a line? In Irish? Or in English or Latin? In the Catholic Church, as it happened, all you had to say at a wedding was 'I do'. The priest said everything else, speaking on your behalf.

She loved his body. The dark brown hair, thick and spiky – spiky with salt. The salty taste of his brown skin. His deep grey eyes, which reminded her of the sea as well, of the stillness, as she imagined it, the calm of the fish, although when Paddy encountered fish they were anything but calm. She liked the dark hairs sprouting on his arms, thick like a bear's, and later she found those hairs on his legs and elsewhere. She loved his wide, generous mouth. It seemed she could not tire of exploring this body, even though it was one body, a tiny thing on the mountainside. It was a world, it was a continent, as John Donne said, in some poems she had found in the library. 'You are a continent,' she said, again tracing the line of his profile. Hill, rock, river. 'You are a map of the world.' He liked that better than the line from the wedding service.

They talked endlessly about themselves. She told him about her family, covering up the worst aspects but letting him understand that they would find him surprising when they finally had to meet him. He understood that, he was used to being disapproved of, especially by schoolteachers and people of that kind. The priest. His father was a native, a speaker of the language, but his mother was from a suburb of Dublin, not a very posh one, and that was the trouble. Not only did she speak English, she spoke it with a working-class Dublin accent. Paddy had a touch of this himself. She went to bingo religiously, and she went to the pub on Sundays with her husband, something that shocked even Polly. Her mother would have preferred to die, she was quite sure of that, than enter a public house.

'What does she look like? Your mother?'

He had difficulty describing her. 'Her name is Muriel. She has black hair.'

'Short or long?'

'Kind of shoulder length. And she's about five five. Thin.'

'What sort of clothes does she wear?'

Paddy laughed: 'What is this? Is my mother wanted for some crime? Not speaking Irish?'

'No, sorry.' Polly kissed him and caressed his hair.

He said, in her arms, 'I don't know what sort of clothes she wears. Normal women's clothes. Jeans and jumpers mostly. She has shorts, actually, for this weather.'

Shorts. Polly imagined a short, fat woman with dyed jet-black hair, red lips, white legs bulging from red shorts. She imagined her with a cigarette dangling from her lips and with gold earrings, a sort of gypsy. She did not know where this picture came from.

The next time Polly comes, which is just the next day, she does not bother ringing the doorbell, but just walks into the kitchen, not making much noise. She wants to have a good look today before she lets her mother know she is here. She explores the parlour, goes back and has a look at the bedrooms. It is all like the kitchen, plain, 1970s style, nothing cute or old or cute and new, like the house Polly is staying in. It seems like her parents gave up on interior decorating, on their aim to be the best in the valley, a long, long time ago. A big photo of Polly is on the piano in the sitting room. Polly when she was twelve and making her Confirmation, in a pink tweed suit and a white straw-boater.

When she slips into the kitchen, her mother is in her chair in front of the television, talking. There is nobody else there, just herself, but she is engaged in a long monologue. Polly stands just inside the door and listens. It takes her a while to get accustomed to the flow of words, which seem to pour out of her mother's voice in a stream, not monotonous but unbroken, fluent as a river.

This is what she does all day.

She tells stories.

Today it is a story about a boy and a girl. The boy is called William, but the girl does not seem to have had a name, oddly enough.

> She was rich and beautiful, however, a landlord's daughter. Lots of rich young men came courting her but she wouldn't have any of them. And one day a poor farmer's son came and wasn't he the one she fancied? She'd have nobody but him. Well now, her father was none too pleased about this turn of events, as you can well imagine, and what did he do but send his daughter away, away to her uncle's house, so that she would have no more to do with the poor young man.
>
> She went, and was far from happy with her fate. And while she was there, the poor young man, William, pined away and

died. But she heard nothing, nobody bothered to let her know. And she stayed on at her uncle's for months. A year went by. And a marriage was arranged for her with another young man, more suitable than William. And she was going to bed one night a few days before the wedding was to take place when a knock came at her window. And it was him, it was William. He was outside the window on horseback and he asked her to come with him. 'Let's go away somewhere where they won't bother us,' he said. She didn't need asking twice. Out she came through the window and onto the back of the horse and off they went, galloping across the fields. It was a bright night, the moon was shining, and she was as happy as could be.

Then her mother turns and catches sight of Polly.

'That's not the end, is it?' Polly asks.

'I forget how it ends,' says her mother. 'It's just old rubbish …' She is embarrassed at being caught out. 'I do it to pass the time. I used to hear those old things when I was a child and I thought I'd forgotten them.'

'I'd like to know how it ends,' says Polly.

'They were buried in my head somewhere, and when I told one, the others came back, one after the other. Funny, isn't it?' She stops talking and stares out the window. Then she adds, 'Usually I just watch the television. Most things are subtitled.'

Polly's picture of Paddy's mother was completely inaccurate, as she discovered just days later when she saw her. This was at Paddy's funeral. He was drowned at the beginning of August, while out fishing. The weather had not broken, there was no storm or sudden calamitous change to explain what had happened. But his boat had got into difficulties, for no apparent reason. The rest of the crew were saved, but Paddy was not. 'He was knocked overboard by a freak wave', was the explanation circulating in the community. 'He was swept against the Red Cliff.' Drownings occurred every few years in this area, and the Red Cliff was notoriously dangerous. 'His number was up,' a fisherman said, shrugging casually, in Polly's hearing. More people said, 'The good die young.' They had a proverb or cliché for every occasion, and dozens of them for the occasion of death.

The entire school population of the peninsula turned out at the funeral, which was attended by hundreds and hundreds of people. Polly's friends hugged her and squeezed her, trying to sympathise, horrified at the idea of what had happened to Paddy and to Polly but unable to grasp the enormity of it. Polly's parents were not at the funeral.

They knew about Paddy now. When he had died and become a celebrity, someone had revealed the secret. But they did not take it seriously.

'I believe you were friendly with the young man who drowned, Lord have mercy on him,' said her mother.

'Yes,' said Polly. She was paralysed. She could not believe that Paddy would not be there, at the spot where they met, if she took the bus and walked along the hill road. He was linked with the place, he could not move from it, in her imagination. She had seen his coffin, carried by six boys from the football team through a guard of honour, to the graveyard across the road. She had seen his coffin descend into the earth, and heard the clay fall on it. But she could not believe he was gone for good. How could he be, so quickly? This was four days after they had sat on the hillside discussing his mother's clothes. In that time he had changed from being a goalkeeper, a lover, a fisherman, to this: a corpse in the ground.

'It's a great tragedy for his family,' her mother then said, pursing her lips and tut-tutting. She turned her attention to the tablecloth she was embroidering with pink roses. Polly said nothing, but left the room.

She purses her lips again, in just that way, when Polly tries to tell her about her living arrangements; shows her photos of the house, of Karl. Her mother asks if she is married and Polly shakes her head. In Denmark there is no major legal disadvantage to this, and she and Karl have been together for twenty years. They do not think of themselves as unconnected or likely to part, and getting married is not something Karl believes in. 'I am an old fox,' he says. That's what they say in

Denmark, 'fox' not 'dog'. You can't teach an old fox new tricks. He looks like a fox, though. Polly is reminded when he says this. He has reddish hair, still, and a sharp face. He's a schoolteacher, like her father, but the principal of a large secondary school in one of Copenhagen's best suburbs. They live in a house in the grounds, a privilege for the headmaster. Polly is telling her mother this – she can lip-read, a bit. She is trying to tell her something about Copenhagen, mentioning Tivoli, which is, as a rule, the one thing people have heard of. She talks about the fishing boats at Dragør, how she goes there sometimes to buy flatfish from the fishermen on the quay, how you can get huge flounders for a few crowns. 'They are still alive when you buy them,' Polly says. 'Huge flounders, fat halibut, dancing around in the basket.'

'They don't have the euro in Denmark,' her mother breaks in. She hasn't heard a thing. 'They have more sense, I suppose.'

When Polly found out that she was pregnant, just before the Leaving results came out, she felt not as dismayed as she should have, although she knew it was in any practical sense a hopeless, insuperable tragedy. She had Paddy's baby. It was as if fate had awarded her some compensation for losing him. But it was not great compensation, in the circumstances.

'Tell your mother,' Eileen said. 'You'll have to. I mean, what are you going to do?'

'How can I tell her? She'll die,' said Polly.

Eileen shrugged. 'Sometimes things like that are easier than you think. When you do them.' This advice sounded good. Eileen saw the lift in Polly's expression and pressed her advantage. 'Things are usually easier than you think they'll be,' she reiterated. 'They're always easier, when they happen.'

She convinced Polly. Anyway, she had to tell her parents, as Eileen said. The best thing that could happen would be that they would understand, and help, although at that moment Polly's mind could not wrap itself around the reality of what that help should consist of. A ménage of herself, her child and her parents was not imaginable, even as a dream.

She confronted her mother the next day, in the kitchen. They had been to the beach together. Polly had swum in the breakers, finding the cold shock of water comforting; it demanded so much immediate attention that it diminished her problems. Her mother did not swim but sat, in her full cotton sundress, on a folding chair on the beach, reading the newspaper, *Inniu*. Afterwards, they had lunch together, salad and tea, and now Polly was smoking a cigarette, something her mother did not disapprove of, although she did not smoke herself. It seemed like a good moment to break the news.

Her reaction could not have been more surprising, but it was not surprising in the way Eileen had anticipated. Instead, it surprised, shocked, terrified Polly that her mother was capable of such anger. She screamed abuse and insults. She hit Polly with her fists and seemed to want to flog her in some ritualistic punishment of humiliation, degradation. But her father would have to administer this treatment, and fortunately for himself and Polly he was not available, having gone to the city for the day to buy new textbooks for school. Polly was to be locked in her room until he returned. She was to be starved. When all this was over, it was not clear what her mother's plans for her were, but they did not involve bringing up her grandchild in a normal family environment. *Homes, adoption, hiding*, were words that occurred, in a medley of Irish and English, a macaronic stream of abusive language that had never emanated from Polly's mother before. It seemed that one language did not contain enough invective to express the full depth and range of her anger. Clearly, this was the nadir of her existence. Nothing as tragic, as evil, as shameful, as her only child's pregnancy had ever befallen her.

Afterwards, Polly had simply left the house; as it happened, there were no locks on any of the room doors. She ran away without even a toothbrush, catching the afternoon bus to town and going on to Dublin on the train. She had some money; it was not so difficult. Her Leaving result she got from Eileen a month or so later. Eileen came to Dublin to visit her, to Polly's gratification and surprise, and tried to persuade Polly to go to college, as she had planned: she would have some money from her scholarships; if she padded it out, she would get by. Polly tried it, and her parents were unable, or did not bother, to prevent her. But she had Conor in April, just before the first-year examinations. She missed them and no quarter was given, no special provision could be made. She lost her scholarship and left college. She got a job in a bank, lived in a bedsitter, and kept the baby, although Eileen tried to persuade her to be sensible and give him over for adoption. She could not part with him, although she soon found out that keeping him was quite astonishingly difficult, in every possible way. There was no money, there was no time, nobody even wanted to rent her a place to live; single mothers with babies were blacklisted by most landlords in Dublin. Everyone colluded in making her life as hard as it could be – her parents, the state, the system. Eileen, who was in Dublin herself, studying to be a nurse, continued to help, finding flats in her own name and installing Polly and Conor when the lease was signed.

When Conor was three, Polly got a chance to move to Copenhagen with the bank, and she took it. As she had hoped, nobody cared whether you were a single mother or not in Denmark. In fact, it seemed that most mothers were single, at least the ones she came across; it was almost something to brag about. They had grimly bobbed hair, dressed in corduroy pants and big green parkas, and smoked cigars. Some of them had jobs in the bank, but usually they were doing degrees in impractical subjects. Women's studies or ethnology or Greek and Roman Civilisation. The state paid for their education, and paid them social welfare and child welfare while they were in college. All the talk was of feminism and women's rights and the country was packed with crèches and kindergartens, where children were looked after free, by students and nurses and women from Turkey, in what looked like luxurious surroundings. After a while, Polly left the bank and went to college at last, like all the other single mothers. She chose film studies, and eventually became a scriptwriter, writing soaps for the Danish television channel, then documentaries, which brought her all over the world: Faroes, Shetland, Greenland, Iceland. In Greenland she met Karl, who was hiking around the old Norse settlements, taking photos, and did not mind that she had Conor, although he had no intention of having any children himself, as Polly found out soon enough. By then Conor was twelve. He grew up, became a scientist, a marine biologist. After working for a few years in Denmark, he went on a round-the-world trip, and ended up in Australia, and got a visa and a temporary post at a university doing research on the breeding habits of pilot whales. He is still there.

Polly sits at her window, in her own bungalow, and listens to the fire whispering in the grate, to the wind whispering outside, whistling around the eaves. She has been here for longer than she had planned to stay, and has decided to stay for one more week. She is going to begin work here, sketching the basis for a programme of some kind about the region: the Gaeltachts of Ireland, maybe, a topic she is well suited to covering but has always avoided. The house is warm and cosy, and now the valley seems to hold her, too. People she runs into in the shop nod to her and say hello, do not avoid her, as she thought they were doing initially. A few have recognised her and chatted to her about old times. Nobody mentions Paddy Mullins, or asks about the baby, but when Polly mentions that she has a grown-up son, they do not seem surprised. Eileen probably spilled the beans, or Katherine. It doesn't matter, they are interested in him, too, they want to hear about Australia and the whales. Lots of the local young people do round-the-world trips as a matter of course in their gap year; half the population of twenty-somethings seem to be in Thailand or New South Wales. Nobody cares about what used to be called unmarried mothers now, either. There are heaps of them, even in the Gaeltacht. Still, nobody mentions Paddy Mullins. Maybe they forget he existed.

Polly tries to tell her mother about Conor, since she has told almost everyone else. 'I have a child,' she says. Her mother cocks her head, and smiles uncomprehendingly. Her ability to lip-read is most erratic. 'He's Paddy's child,' Polly continues. 'Paddy Mullins, the boy who drowned. Do you remember?'

'Would you like a cup of tea?' asks her mother. It is the first time she has offered Polly any refreshment. She gets up and walks across the kitchen to the range.

'I was in love with Paddy Mullins,' Polly says.

Her mother smiles and says, 'I was thinking of baking an apple tart.

*

She finds the end of her mother's story.

> When they had gone a few miles, William said, 'I've a terrible
> headache, love.'
> 'Stop,' she said. 'Stop and have a rest. What hurry is on you?'
> 'I can't stop,' he said. 'There is a long journey ahead of us. I'm
> taking you home.'
> So all she could do was take out her handkerchief and she tied
> it around his forehead and she gave him a kiss. His head was as
> cold as ice and she felt frightened when she touched it. But she
> said nothing. And he galloped on until they were passing her own
> father's house. And she shouted and asked him to stop.
> 'Why would you want to stop?' he asked.
> 'The moon shines clear
> The horseman's here.
> Are you afraid, my darling?'
> And he spurred on the horse.
> But the horse would not move an inch. The horse stopped at
> her father's gate and refused to move. He spurred and he whipped
> but it didn't matter. The horse had a mind of its own.
> So – 'Go on inside,' he said, 'and sleep in your own bed tonight.
> And I'll be here waiting for you first thing in the morning. I'll
> sleep in the stable, myself and the horse.'
> She kissed him goodnight and did as he told her.
> And when she went inside, her father was there and he was
> surprised to see her. But she took courage and told him what had
> happened. She said William had come for her, and she could not
> live with anyone else.
> Her father turned pale. 'William?' he said.
> 'Yes,' said she. 'He's outside, asleep in the stable.'
> 'That's impossible,' said her father. 'William died a year ago.'
> She didn't believe him. How could she, the poor girl? So
> her father took her out. He had to do it. He took her to the
> graveyard and he took a shovel and he dug and dug. And there
> was William, in his coffin, dead and decayed. And around his
> poor head her handkerchief was tied, the handkerchief she'd tied
> around his forehead only the night before. Yes. And it was stained
> with blood. So she had to believe him then.

The story is in a collection of German ballads, which she finds
in one of the bedrooms. So how did her mother learn that? Had

she read the book or were the stories flying around in the air like migratory birds, landing wherever they found suitable weather conditions, a good supply of food? What a gloomy story! Polly shivers and shuts the book firmly, feeling the dead hand of William like ice on her forehead.

That night Polly rings Conor and tells him she is here. She hopes he will say he will come over, but since he lives in Brisbane, he is not likely to come today or tomorrow. It is nice to talk to him, though, and to tell him what she is doing. She does not tell the truth, that her mother will not listen to her story. He listens, with appreciation, although it is early morning in Australia, and he has just woken up to a summer's day. He appreciates the drama of her news, Polly can tell that, and suggests that she go and visit Muriel, if she is still alive. Muriel, his paternal grandmother. Maybe Muriel is not deaf? Polly finds herself saying, yes, she will do that, and then she rings Karl to tell him she will stay on in Ireland for another week or perhaps two.

Something happens in the valley now, that takes Polly by surprise.

The Christmas lights go on.

All the little houses come alive.

Coloured lights fill every window, are strung along the edge of the roof, are draped in the hedges. Santa Clauses climb up fairy ladders to chimneys, reindeers glow in the bare gardens. Red and green and blue lights flash and twinkle in the deep dark winter valley; some of the bungalows seem to be jumping, they flash so much.

In the old days there was one candle, lit on Christmas Eve, in every house. When you walked through the valley to Midnight Mass, you saw these candles flickering in every window, the stars flickering overhead. Now the houses are flashing and jumping in a myriad colours glowing against the black sea and sky and mountain, brash and, it seems to Polly, beautiful. 'We're here!' the lights seem to proclaim. 'We've survived, we're not going away!'

She finds Muriel easily. She lives in the house she lived in thirty years ago, Paddy's house. It is, as Polly expected, decorated, though not as extravagantly as some of the other houses. There are coloured lights on a hedge by the gate, and another string around the door.

Muriel is watching TV when Polly calls. She's alone. Polly guesses, correctly, that Paddy's father is dead. It strikes her that the valley is full of widows. Muriel is wearing jeans and a jumper, and she is still small and thin. To Polly's surprise she speaks Irish, but with a north Dublin accent. 'Of course I speak Irish,' she says. 'I've been here for fifty years. I'd have been out of the loop altogether if I hadn't learnt it, wouldn't I?' Her manner is chirpy, friendly, but with an underlying toughness, an urban edge that is different from anything you get around here. She offers tea and biscuits straight away; she turns down the TV but she does not turn it off. Polly opens her mouth and starts to explain why she is here. Muriel listens, half-smiling, her eyes thoughtful rather than sad. Then she takes Polly in her arms and holds her for a minute, against her woolly jumper, her thin body. Polly, of course, cries. She cries and Muriel pats her hand and says, 'Yes, love, yes.'

They drink the tea.

Muriel talks about herself, about Paddy. He was a very quiet boy, but always good-humoured, she could talk to him more easily than she could ever talk to anyone, much more easily than she could talk to his father. His father is dead now, too. He – Paddy – had a depth of understanding. He was more like a daughter than a son. On the night he drowned, he had kissed her goodbye, which was unusual, but she only remarked on it afterwards. It was a calm night, he had been out in much rougher weather and returned home unscathed. The truth about his death would not be known, but she had heard there had been a row on board, another young man had attacked Paddy; Paddy got thrown overboard and hit his head on a rock. The real story would never be told; the other man was the son of the owner of the boat; Paddy was dead, anyway, and the fishermen would never inform on one of their own. The whole story about going aground was made up, a sham. Fiction.

There are no tears from her. She tells the story calmly, pausing occasionally for dramatic effect or to let a shocking point sink in. It is a story she has told before, many times, in spite of her protestations that it is confidential, a secret. Probably, she told it to Paddy's father, and who else? Her best friends, her close relations? The story is polished. What is true is its terrible core, that Paddy, the son she could talk to, is dead. And even this no longer disturbs her. But of course it all happened so long ago. Paddy drowned thirty years ago. How could she cry? Tears do not last that long. Paddy has been transmogrified into a hero: a brave, strongly drawn character in a story that she has half-remembered, half-invented.

So Polly tells her story of Paddy, and for her it is a fresh story, it is the first time she has told it to anyone, and so her tale is not as polished, not as well paced, not as neatly composed as Muriel's. Still, it takes on a certain formality: Polly has to decide, as she sits on the fireside chair, keeping her eyes off the silent TV screen, where to start. The bus, the pier, the park? School? She decides, or memory decides, or Muriel, or the pressures of the moment, the pressure to relate, the pressure to sympathise, the pressure to attract compassion, the pressure to confess, the pressure to create, what to leave in, what to exclude.

The fact is, no matter what she decided, Muriel would be fascinated by this story of her son, which she had not heard before, not at all, although of course people had let her know of Polly's existence, had hinted at the reason for her sudden departure from the valley. But those were rumours, snippets of gossip, that had the power to disturb but not to enthral, console, nourish. So now she listens intently, her whole body still, concentrated on listening. For this story she is the perfect audience, and the story is shaped by her listening as much as by Polly's telling: Paddy's story belongs to the two of them. And why did Polly not understand that until Conor pointed it out?

When the story is finished, Muriel and Polly sit in silence. The coloured lights on the fuchsia bush twinkle against the black sea and the black mountain and the black sky. They sit in silence. They let the story settle. And for minutes it is as if he is here again, on this earth. Alive, seventeen. He is not on the pier or in the park or on the mountainside, but on the bus. He is sitting on the bus, silently staring out the window, motionless as a seagull on rock, lost in a boy's dream.

Red-hot poker

The day after Frank died I went to the bank, withdrew half our savings, and put all the money in a suitcase in the attic (wrapped up in a pair of used pants – I was banking on a burglar balking at rummaging through smelly knickers). There were several reasons why I did this – one, Frank and I had talked about not having all our eggs in one basket, but, typically, hadn't got around to doing anything about finding another receptacle for any of them. And two, last week Martha, in the book club, said the banks were good for a year at the most. And when they'd go bust, you'd get no warning, was what she said. You'd turn on the news one morning and that would be it. (This was when we were having the wine and snacks, after we'd discussed the novel for half an hour, saying how much we hated it, which is the most common reaction in our book club to most of the novels we read.) The book club spent a good bit of time wondering where you could put your money for safe-keeping, if you had any, that is. Some said the post office. The post office is backed by a German bank and Germany is in a better state economically than us. Others said, spend it. Under the mattress, said Clara, who is inclined to be cynical.

In the bank, they wouldn't give me all our money, and it was not easy getting my hands on even half of it. They tried to persuade me to transfer to a different kind of account with better interest rates. Then they started to give me stick. Why did I need so much cash? the girl – Georgina, they're nearly all called something like that – asked, with a smile as warm as a carving knife. When I told them Frank had dropped dead of a heart attack while climbing a hill in Wicklow yesterday and I needed money for funeral expenses, Georgina shut up and handed it over. Her little mask of a face was pale. I should be kinder to these people. She was probably too young to know that it was much more than anyone needs for a funeral (not that death is by any means cheap).

There's a photograph of me beside the hearse, smiling, with all the wreaths in the background heaped up like a bright bank of chrysanthemums at a debs' ball. I, in my dark green winter coat, have one gloved hand on the coffin. I must have felt I was still holding hands with Frank. I knew he was dead and about to be buried, but I must have felt that contact of a sort was still possible. At least his body was still close to me. I was putting my hand on the coffin the way you put your hand on your partner's knee, as you both drive along in the car on a long journey – to reassure him. I'm still here, I love you, thanks for doing all this boring driving and please go right on doing it. Or the way you put your hand on his forehead, in bed, when you wake up in the early hours of the morning, to reassure yourself that he's still breathing. Thanks for staying alive.

Only now he wasn't.

But that's the thing I didn't take in for quite a while. Not really. For a month – at least – I kept thinking that he had just gone away on a trip, or just to work or the shop, and that he'd be home at any moment. Then the recollection that he was dead would assault me, like a robber jumping out of a bush and knocking me on the head. It's often like that, I've heard, from other women whose partners have died. It takes a while for you to realise what death actually means. Which is, that he's not coming back. Ever. When this dawned on me – 'dawn' is the wrong word, it sank in, heavily and slowly like a stone burrowing its way down into the earth over hundreds of years – I also thought that it was all harder for me because I'm an atheist. I was probably wrong about this. I'm sure it's awful for everyone, even ardent believers. For me, though, *never* really does mean *never*. Also, I know that he can't hear what I say or see what I do, which I think is a very comforting aspect of the afterlife belief – the sense that the dead are with you all the time. (In fact, if you believe the whole shebang, nobody is ever dead; it's just that you can't see them while you're still in the land of the living, but they're around all the same, hidden behind a curtain that's going to roll back the minute you die yourself and take your place on their side of it, to strut your stuff in the play that goes on for all eternity.) Atheism is tough on the emotions, which is no doubt why most people don't go in for it. The fact that someone you loved and lived with for thirty-five years no longer exists in any way whatsoever, just as he didn't exist before he was born, is almost impossible to tolerate. (Although it's very easy to accept that he didn't exist before he was born. Eternity has a starting line for individuals, apparently, but not a finishing one.)

When you begin to reach towards the realisation that he's completely gone is the moment you're in the deepest trouble. Then you're in the dark water, and there you'll very likely stay, floundering around, for quite a while.

You need your family at a time like this. But Jamie, our son – well, I can't even think about him. Somebody told him about what had happened but he wasn't at the funeral, not he.

All I had were my neighbours and a few friends.

And they're no replacement for your husband. They're like a few crumbs when you're starving to death. They're deeply inadequate and their company and the diversions they provide are deeply disappointing. They know this.

They also know that they are better than nothing.

The first week after Frank's death, my sister telephoned me every night to ask how I was, and my brother phoned a few times a week. Even my niece, who is twenty-six and engaged to be married and making a film about horses, phoned. Twice. Two of my friends from the book club and three from the office where I used to work called, too, and of course I got a heap of emails. One old colleague, who lives not too far away, actually dropped in, unannounced, just to say hello and have a chat. I almost cried then, I was so grateful. Such a small thing, but nobody calls by any more these days without phoning. Not where I live anyway, out in the suburbs. That visit brought me back to my childhood, when dropping in on a friend, a neighbour, was the most normal thing in the world. Though of course then most people didn't have a phone, let alone email, so they had to come in person if they wanted to have a chat, which is, I notice, an aspect of the neighbourliness thing most people conveniently forget when they're bemoaning the loss of the good old days. They had to be neighbourly because they didn't have a phone, much less Facebook or whatever.

The only people who call in to me casually on a fairly regular basis are Tressa and Denis, who live two doors down. (The person who lives next door I never talk to. Never. She's peculiar – didn't even come to the funeral. Suffers from the depression, I'd say, though she just comes across as a nasty piece of work. Audrey, she's called.)

Tressa and Denis are about ten years younger than me. They have no children. I don't know if that's got anything to do with it, but Tressa is one of those women who makes everyone feel happy. I try to put my finger on what it is she's got – it's not just that she's encouraging and positive, although that's part of it. It's never enough on its own, though. I've tried it, and I know I come across as insincere. Which I am – because I'm seldom more interested in anyone else than I am in myself. That's what it is, I suppose. Tressa is genuinely interested in other people, not altruistic merely, but genuinely, profoundly curious, in the nicest possible way. She makes you believe you are an interesting person and that your stories are worth listening to, whereas the majority of us do the opposite. Also, she looks very nice without being too attractive, which is part of the package – she has the sort of looks you'd describe as 'pleasant'. A roly-poly, no waist, with bright blond hair sticking up on her head like hedgehog prickles, big saucer blue eyes, skin like vanilla ice cream, the soft kind. She likes to wear biscuit and pink tracksuits when she's at home, and navy blue trouser suits when she's at work. Sort of androgynous clothes, though she's enormously feminine-looking. Motherly. (I'm more androgynous myself, muscular and dark, with my big nose and bony face. If it wasn't for my long hair and skirts, I'd pass for a little old man.)

Denis is nice, too. Not motherly. Not fatherly. Boyish. Very funny. He'd make a cat laugh. He'd make a widow laugh and that's what he did, the day of the funeral. That's how funny he is, and clever. A natural comedian.

You'll wonder what the joke was, maybe. But I'm not going to tell you, because jokes never work when I retell them, and this one involved mimicking, of gestures. He was mimicking teenage girls walking on the high heels they wear when they go out. There, I've told some of it, anyway, and it doesn't work but it was hilarious the way he told it. It was the mimicking of the mincing steps that made me giggle. The contrast between Denis, a fifty-year-old, not too tall, slightly chubby and balding man, and the sixteen-year-old bombshells he was imitating, made the joke. Not the contrast. The miracle. The unlikely miracle of the fifty-year-old Denis becoming a sixteen-year-old twit of a girl, which is what he could do, for a minute. That's what he could do. Transform himself into anything, for the sake of a joke.

It never occurred to me then or at any other time that I liked Denis in any sexual way. He wasn't sexy. Funny men aren't. They're the men I like but I don't feel attracted to them – it takes something else, some gravity, to get me hooked. (Frank couldn't tell jokes. He did tell them – well everyone does, occasionally. But usually they weren't very funny, or they fell flat and he'd insist on explaining them laboriously, unable to believe that his audience had understood the point but not laughed.) Not that I was feeling attracted to anyone on the day of my husband's funeral, and hadn't, either, for years before that. Not very often, anyway, or for long, or to any effect. (Not even to Frank, but that's normal, I suppose.)

Tressa often asked me into their house for dinner in the weeks following the death, and I always went in. Dinner, I was finding, was the toughest time. I could get through the day. *Getting through*, the phrase says it all. But getting through satisfied me for the moment. Although I couldn't see light at the end of a tunnel, I believed intellectually, if not emotionally, that it was there, perhaps a few years away. Everyone told me it was, anyway. I believed that in the end I'd feel a bit better, that I'd not be getting through the days, that I'd enjoy the days again, as I'd always enjoyed them before, ever since I met Frank and married and stopped worrying about being a lonely singleton – an anxiety that had spoiled my youth, actually, which I regret, deeply, because of course my youth is dead and buried, too. (Wouldn't it be great if it were there? The younger you, waiting for you to slip back into its lovely skin when you passed over?

193

Now that's an afterlife I could fancy, an afterlife that let me have another go at life and make it work right this time.)

After the first month, when I stopped imagining that Frank had gone on a trip somewhere and would turn up for dinner, I had a short breakdown for about a week. Stayed in bed. Moped.

Then I got bored. The days are very long when you stay in bed, moping. And it all gets so hot and sticky and stale, and you can't sleep at night because you've been half-asleep all day. So I forced myself to get up and began to pull myself together.

This was four months after Frank died.

For a start, I asked Denis and Tressa into my house for dinner.

Tressa hugged me when I issued the invitation, which is a very strange way of saying I stood at the garden wall and said, 'Why don't you come in to me for dinner this evening, then, for a change?' She had to step over the wall, which is only about two feet high, to hug me. But she did that.

I dressed up, for the first time since the death. I'd got used to pulling on the same pair of jeans every day, and sticking on a black T-shirt or jumper. But I selected one of my old favourite hippyish skirts from the wardrobe, and a white Victorian blouse, and I did my face and pinned up my hair nicely. It wasn't easy to do all this tarting up – it felt pointless, and my body seemed stiff and almost paralysed as I rubbed in the foundation cream, mascara-ed my eyelashes. It was as if I was performing these tasks underwater, in a kind of jelly that resisted my every move. But I did it and in the end when I looked at my reflection I felt pleased enough.

But I couldn't muster up the energy to cook. This is the thing: I had always loved cooking. But I couldn't bring myself to do it. Not real cooking. The details of making a complex dish dismayed me. Herbs, garlic-chopping, caramelising onions, the steps you have to take … they struck me as disgustingly trivial. Like playing at having a tea party with doll's cups and saucers, when you are four or five. (Which means, I see now, that my heart was understanding death and what time means. Because when the heart is forgetting it, it takes joy in playing at tea parties, and chopping parsley and doing trivial things. Real life, at its best and most enjoyable, is trivial. It's only death that's serious.)

I roasted a chicken. That's all. Added a few things I'd bought – potato salad, coleslaw, olives, in plastic boxes from the shop. It was OK. And of course we drank more wine than usual – usually we had one bottle between the three of us, on an ordinary evening, when they'd be going to work next day. But this evening, which was special, we had more. And that helped. Talking, joking, Denis was funny as always.

You might think, she cried, she wept, because of the wine. But I didn't. I laughed because of it. That's the effect wine has always had on me and I was very glad to see that it still had.

In the spring, a few days after I had recovered from my bout of depression, Denis dropped in to see me, alone. I'd just come back from my morning walk and was still in my coat when he knocked. It was midday.

'I walk every day now,' I said. 'Rain or shine. Just to get the endomorphins going.'

'Endorphins,' he said kindly. 'An end to all orphans.'

'Yeah yeah, I always get that wrong.' I hung up my coat and asked him why he wasn't at work. He's a civil servant, high enough up.

'Day in lieu,' he said casually. In loo. 'Would you like a cup of coffee, Linda? I'll make it. Sit yourself down at the fire.'

I always lit the fire first thing in the morning, so I'd have something to cheer me up when I got in from my walk.

We had the coffee and chatted and then he asked me if there was anything I needed. He stared at me as he said this and I had this strange thought: Denis is making a pass at me. But I dismissed it as soon as it came into my mind. Of course he wasn't. As if to prove that I was wrong, he said quickly, 'I could cut the grass for you.'

For example.

So that's what he meant.

'No no,' I said hastily. 'I can do that. Anyway, it hasn't even started growing yet.'

'I meant it metaphorically,' he said drily.

A metaphor for what? I wondered.

Actually, there was something I needed. The bolt on the back door had come loose and I'm terrible with screwdrivers. So I showed him that and he said, no problem. I fetched the toolbox from the garage and he fixed it in a jiffy, and then went off, calling, 'See you later.'

I assumed he meant he'd see me for dinner – I was with them almost every second evening at this stage. But Tressa didn't call over to ask me that evening.

That got me thinking that I had misunderstood the meaning of Denis's visit – my first, instinctive, reaction was correct, I thought, he was up to something and somehow Tressa knew or guessed, or he confessed to her. And now they were avoiding me.

I felt dreadful. I ate some bread and cheese for dinner, watched TV – I never had the energy, or the will, to do anything more active; when I read, the words slipped away from me like leaves in the wind, and I couldn't be bothered raking them back. I lay awake for ages; then, when I saw it was 2 a.m. and I'd been awake for three hours, I took two sleeping pills.

No invitation the next evening, either. That was three in a row; I hadn't seen Tressa for three days. By far the longest stretch of not seeing her since the death.

The fourth day was Friday. I was considering frying a rasher and sausage for my dinner and then watching *The Late Late Show*, or else going upstairs and committing suicide by taking an overdose of the sleeping pills, when the doorbell rang.

'What's up?' Tressa asked. 'Are you OK?'

'Yes.' I looked at her questioningly. She looked as usual – cheery, in her work clothes, a navy suit with a pink-and-white striped blouse.

'I was in London – I suppose Denis told you? I asked him to look in on you. I hope he did.'

I hugged her.

And everything was normal again.

A week later Denis dropped by again.

'Hi,' he said. He wasn't wearing a coat, although it was raining. 'Just thought I'd drop in to cheer you up.'

Up went my antennae. But I shoved them back down.

I asked him in.

'Is Tressa away?' I asked, although the minute I did, I realised it was the wrong thing to say.

'Oh, no, no,' he said. 'She's gone up to see her mother, that's all.'

So she was away, for a few hours, anyway.

Denis went into the sitting room, without being asked, and sat down by the fire, also without being asked.

'You're looking well' – he nodded approvingly at me – 'it's great the way you keep it all up.'

'Stiff upper lip,' I said, continuing the 'up' theme. Three ups in less than a minute.

'You've great courage,' he said. 'No, no, I really mean it. I don't know how you do it. You just keep going.'

Then I started to cry.

The tears just jerked out of me, without my volition, as if he had turned on a tap.

(I know now what it was. Sympathy. Nobody had really said anything so sympathetic, so encouraging, to me in ages. Nobody had praised me for surviving and putting on a brave face. Acknowledgement of the effort I was making was what he gave me, and it opened the floodgates.)

He put his arm around me. He held me for a minute or two. The heat from another person's body, especially a man's body, is precious when you haven't felt it for months. It felt so natural, and warm, and necessary, as it seeped into me, through the thick cotton fleece and the T-shirt I had on under that, right into me. An electric current … I don't know what. It seeped in. Then he started to stroke my hair just the way I rub down the cat. She likes it, too.

I don't think it was a ruse. More an opportunity seized, by both of us. An understanding that this was what I really needed, and the friendly, decent thing to do was give it to me.

Of course, I felt guilty when I thought of Tressa. But not very. I somehow convinced myself that she wouldn't mind if she knew, she'd understand, being so understanding about everything. And so generous. And at the same time I assured myself that what she didn't know wouldn't worry her. And at the same time, too, I knew that the last thing in the world I wanted was for her to know, and that if she found out, I'd feel like jumping into the sea and drowning.

And at the same time I felt pleased, fulfilled, delighted, the way I always felt after sex. It cheered me up – like jokes. Sex and jokes made me happy, but sex was better than jokes.

It didn't happen very often. Denis called over when he could, when he had the time and when she was away, because of course we didn't want to upset her. We didn't discuss the details of the thing – never mentioned Tressa, in fact, although we talked about everything else. Denis was a great listener, much better than Frank ever had been. You could – I could – tell him anything. I began to see it as something good, and beneficial, that was doing me a lot of good and wasn't really doing her any harm, as long as nobody else knew what was going on, and as long as she didn't.

The dinners continued, too, but not as frequently, since I was getting stronger, and going out more myself, anyway. Not with men, of course – there was no question of that; if I hadn't sex with Denis, I wouldn't be having it with anyone; it would have to be with a man I trusted completely, a very good friend. No, it was my women friends I was going out with. Still, we three had dinner about twice a week, alternating houses now. The tripartite relationship didn't change. We joked and laughed and discussed the news and the books we were reading – I was reading again. Tressa didn't seem to suspect a thing and we gave her absolutely no reason to.

I looked better. I knew it. Sex is a good cosmetic and I was seeing Denis once a week or so – he was good in bed, as I suppose these womanisers are. (I had no illusions about him. He didn't say, but I guessed I wasn't the first woman he had had outside the marital bed. I hoped I'd be the last because I didn't want this to stop, it was too delicious, too charming, too good … too handy. He was a friend as well as a lover. My neighbour. And still not a husband, not boring. Much better in bed than Frank ever had been, too. He knew things about my body, and wasn't afraid to try new tricks. We trusted each other, in bed, and reaped rewards.)

He never came over when Tressa was home. Audrey saw him, though, coming in and out to me – she often stood at her window upstairs, looking down at the road and seeing what was going on. I didn't think she suspected anything – Denis and Tressa had always been coming and going to my house, so why would she? But one afternoon – this was in May – when Denis was walking back, she was in her front garden, watering some bearded irises (magnificent) she had growing along her dividing wall. I was watching from my window. I always watched Denis as he went back, I never wanted him to leave. There she was, in her black jeans, a jumper and orange anorak, her hands in big white gardening gloves. Denis walked past and nodded – he hated her, too. She accidentally on purpose sprayed him with water from her hose. 'Hey!' he said. 'Watch it.' She didn't seem to say sorry. Or anything. Just turned the hose back on the irises, spraying them for dear life.

After that, he stopped coming over. And the summer went by and autumn came.

Months later I was in the kitchen, where I spend most of my time. It was a cold enough day in October, about eleven thirty in the morning. I hadn't gone for my usual walk because it was raining. For exercise, I was scrubbing the floor. Two birds with one mop.

I heard a strange sound, from the door.

A sort of humming sound.

Before I could investigate, I saw what it was from where I stood. A saw. Someone was sawing around the bolt on the kitchen door.

Someone was trying to break into my house. Anyone who observed me knew I was always out of the house at this time of day.

My first impulse was to get out of it as fast as I could, by the front door. I didn't want to confront a burglar. And I could call the Gardaí from the front.

But I had a better idea.

I was inspired. And I can only guess that this clear headedness – as it seemed to me – came about because Denis had called in the day before, after quite an absence, and I was feeling empowered, as the word has it. Empowered to think, to plan, rather than freeze and flee. (This is the key to survival, I've read somewhere, even in a situation of extreme danger like a plane crash. Most people freeze and die. Some people behave rationally, think and take action, and they have a chance of survival.)

The fire was lit. I watched the saw making a little track around the lock on the door. The robber had sawn three-quarters way around it now. In a few minutes, he would be in.

I went into the front room and plunged the poker into the flames.

I let it stay there for a full minute, until it was red hot.

Then I tiptoed to the kitchen door and waited.

Waited.

Seconds passed, slowly – time is so strange.

Slowly, each second like an hour.

I worried that the poker would cool down. Disastrous. But I didn't dare go back to the fire for fear he'd get in.

Then the piece of wood fell out, onto the floor near my feet. And a hand came through the hole.

Covered in one of those white plastic gloves doctors wear.

The hand was smallish – probably some young thug; there are lots of them in Lourdes Gardens over at the other side of the railway.

I had a momentary qualm. What if it were a child? But no child would do what that hand was doing. Such a deliberate, clever break-in.

Down went the poker onto the hand. Hard.

A scream rose into the air outside. The smell of melted plastic and scorched flesh rushed into the kitchen – how quickly smell travels, the house was full of that smell in no time.

I didn't even hear the robber running away, as I went back and replaced the poker on its stand, and sat down, completely winded by the adventure.

I drank a glass of water. Then I went up to the attic and checked the suitcase where I'd stashed away my money. That didn't make sense – since the robber hadn't got in, how could he have stolen my money? But I checked, anyway. It was there, all of it. Of course nobody had found it.

I was exhilarated and frightened and sick, all at once.

I needed to talk to someone.

Saturday. Tressa and Denis would probably be home – I hoped just Denis.

So I ran to their house to tell them what was happening – I

assumed nobody else would try to break in that day, although the kitchen lock was now exposed.

Their door was open, oddly enough, so I walked in without ringing.

And in the hall the smell assailed me.

The scorched flesh, the melted plastic.

Tressa sobbing.

'It'll be OK.' That was Denis. 'Just hold the ice to it. Just hold the ice.'

I don't think I ever told him about the money. I told him a great deal, but hardly that. So I don't understand what Tressa was after. I never did anything about the attempted break-in. Did not go to the guards, did not mention it. But I did bring my money to the post office and deposited it there. Nowhere is safe but what can you do?

Some days later a 'For Sale' sign went up on Denis and Tressa's house.

'They've moved,' said Audrey. The first time she'd spoken to me in years. She was foostering around in her jungle of a garden.

'But it's just gone on the market,' I said, looking at the sign as if it could tell me something.

'Rented an apartment. Can't wait to get out of here, apparently,' she said. Her voice was nonchalant. But she smiled, as if she had said something funny. 'They're looking for a million,' she went on.

'Hm.' I felt nothing at all. 'Well, let's hope they get that,' I said.

'They won't get anything near it,' she said with satisfaction. 'They'll be lucky to get half. Or to sell it at all, the way things are going.'

I didn't feel shocked, or sad, or anything. I went on my walk, to keep the endorphins up.

And when I came home, and was sitting by the fire drinking my morning coffee, it came to me, like the giant waves they talk about, or like a ghost from the other side bearing a true but bad message. That, no matter how lucky you seem to be, in the end there is nobody taking care of you. No god, no friend, no husband, no lover.

No neighbour.

In the end you're on your own.

Bikes I have lost

THE BUILDINERS

My mother, whom my father calls the Tiger and we call Mammy, is marching purposefully into the Buildins. She's wearing her khaki raincoat, which has a military look to it, and her striped scarf, black and orange. She's on the warpath. Or, more accurately, on an intelligence mission: we are searching for my missing bike. It vanished from our road, where I was out playing this morning. I left it outside when I ran into the house to do a number one. (I told my mother I'd parked it at our garden gate but actually I'd left it standing on the middle of the road several doors down.) I'd spent the previous two hours cycling up and down, up and down, on my pride and joy, my blue Raleigh bike, my three-wheeler. I never called it a tricycle; I don't think that word was known on our road. My granny and granda, who gave me my most precious presents (my big plastic baby doll, Barbara, with the red and white frock, also plastic; my electric train), had given me this three-wheeler for my fourth birthday (they were put to the pin of their collar to pay for it, my mother said). It was by far the best bike on our road, and I was in no way shy about pointing this out to my pals – Annette, the smug owner of two dozen jigsaws; Janet, a frail only child whose mother took a nap in the afternoons (cue for half the neighbourhood, Janet's 'friends', to run wild in

203

her house); Deirdre, whose claim to fame was that her mother was a Protestant; and Miriam May, with hair the colour of straw, curled into corkscrew ringlets, which framed her tiny, pale face like a judge's wig. I would give them a go on my bike in exchange for a favour I judged to be of exactly equivalent value. It might be a long session with the shiny, sweet-smelling, animal jigsaws in Annette's house up the lane, which itself had a provocative look, on account of having no windows on the street side. Or two goes on Miriam's yellow scooter. A 'lend' of one of Deirdre's *Noddy* books – she had half a dozen. Swapping, bartering, exchanging was a way of life with us. We were as good at calculating value and risk as any actuary by the time we were four.

The Buildins were the dark side of our absorbing world. In them lurked the enemy: the children who were rough. Mammy the Tiger kept us from them. Or tried to. The Buildiners wore raggedy clothes, and they were visibly dirty – at a time when none of us had a bath more than once a week and hair-washing was a laborious task that took half the day, and was avoided by everyone, washers and washees, as much as possible. The Buildiners, of course, were said to have nits in their hair, and they spoke a different version of Dublinese from ours, which sounded like a foreign language – but one we could understand all too well. You kept your ears open as you sneaked past the Buildins, stepping around sleeping dogs, black and slimy, who would bite you if you looked at them the wrong way, and carefully avoiding looking at the children, especially the older boys, who had pointy shoes, tight trousers, and flick knives. Looking was the big taboo. 'Hey, young wan,' a Buildiner might call, if she caught you engaging in that nefarious activity. All girls of whatever age were called young wan by them. I thought it was a bad word, like feck, and the sound of it scared me. 'What are ye gawkin' at, young wan?' they'd shout out, and I'd scurry on, scared to death. I didn't know what they would do to me, if they got me, but it would not be nice and would involve knives.

Buildiners usually kept off our cul-de-sac, apparently having as little wish to be in our territory as we had to be in theirs. And we weren't allowed go into the Buildins on our own, except on Saturday afternoons, when we crossed the main yard to

Miss Fontane's flat. Miss Fontane was a dancing teacher and, puzzlingly, she was very nice, in spite of living in the Buildins. Her flat was spacious and attractive, a good deal cosier, with its thick red carpet and potted ferns, its walnut piano and oak gramophone, than our house. I didn't know how to reconcile Miss Fontane and her long, black hair, her red lipstick, and fluttering feet in their minute black 'poms', with the image I had of the Buildins in general. I didn't know how someone like her could live there, and how inside the grim brick walls so much comfort and warmth, so much music and cheer, could hide. I supposed she was the exception that proved the rule.

Which was: keep out.

But now we're in the enemy heartland because, naturally, the Buildiners were the prime suspects when the three-wheeler was found to be missing.

'God help us, Helen! They must've sneaked down the road when nobody was looking,' my mother said, in thoughtful dismay. 'You couldn't be up to them, the so-and-sos, could you?'

Now she's leading us across the main yard of the Buildins – a big concrete ground surrounded on three sides by the stern, red-brick faces of the flats. To call it an atrium or courtyard would give the wrong impression. It hasn't a trace of the greenery, the elegance, that those words suggest. Not a tree, a shrub or a blade of grass relieve its rawness. It's the colour of stainless steel saucepans, or gun metal, and looks like the exercise yard of a very large prison, or some planet that is incapable of supporting organic life. The only living things in it are the Buildiners themselves and their skinny dogs; and the only inanimate thing that is not as bare and functional as a prison yard is a handball alley blocking off the sky. Even that has a penitential look. Nobody plays handball there, ever, although boys are always playing soccer down at that end of the yard. We can see them doing that right now, kicking a battered old ball and shouting as we cross the main yard, ears and eyes alert for ambushes. Good, the enemy is preoccupied. We make it across the first bastion.

But there's no sign of the bike.

On we go, round the corner, into the back lane of the Buildins. This is the very worst part, where the dogs are slimier and the children cheekier and the flick knives sharper than anywhere else. The lane is too narrow to admit any sunshine, and the gutters are so thick with litter you'd think rubbish was growing in them, like some sort of depraved, evil flowers. The entryways to the flats – which are open to the weather – give off a sour smell, the smell, we think, of profligacy, of wanton laziness. (Now, I know, the smell of poverty.) The windows on the ground floor at this side of the Buildins have iron bars on them.

And in there, in one of those dark, foul entries, we see my three-wheeler.

Two young fellas are with it, one sitting on the bike, the other just standing there. One is wearing a cap, pulled down tightly over his head almost to his eyes, even though it's quite a warm day. It's not a cap, actually, but a leather helmet, the kind Biggles wears. These helmets look tough and aggressive. Buildiner boys often have them; ordinary respectable boys wear school caps, made of soft cloth, blue or wine or bottle green. Under their tough helmets these two boys have the hard faces that a lot of the boys in the Buildins have – they're cynical and weary, desperate, by the time they're seven. Already by then they know nobody is on their side – especially not the teachers, or the priests, or the mothers like my mother, who hate their guts. They are constantly on guard.

'Give me that bicycle,' says my mother, in a rough voice, roughened by anger and something else.

'I will not,' the boy on the bike says. He's about eight. There's a bead of green snot at the end of his nose and the skin all around it is red and raw, although otherwise he's very washy, even for a Buildiner.

'Indeed and you will,' says my mother. 'For two pins I'll put the guards on you and yez'll be off to Artane before you know what hit yez.'

'It's my bike,' he says, without conviction. He stays sitting on the saddle, clutching the handlebars. His knuckles are blue.

'Now, where would the like of you get a bike like that?' my mother says, smiling. She sees a funny side to it now.

The three-wheeler stands there, in the dark and filthy porch. With its royal blue paint, its white mudguards, shining chrome handlebars, it gleams like a messenger from some other world. Not the world of our road, which is just a few steps up the social ladder from this one, but the world in the stories my mother reads to us at bedtime, that paradise where children roam carefree and pampered in snow white socks and Mary Anne shoes, to experience great adventures or solve difficult mysteries, then return home to their lovely houses. It's a world to which she wants us to belong. These boys would not know such a world exists.

The boy with the Biggles helmet remains on the bike. The expression on his face changes slightly. His eyes lose that hard, but dead, look they had, and begin to sparkle with anger. His friend, too, stiffens, and scowls at us. He puts a hand in the pocket of his shorts.

I wait for my mother to react, to say something else. But her face has changed, too. It's rigid, with something that might be disbelief, or fear. She looks helpless.

We all stand there, as if we were turned to stone. We are like statues in the life-size crib at Christmas, gathered around the baby Jesus in the stable. Except we're in the Buildins, and we're gathered around my three-wheeler. I keep an eye on the hand in the pocket.

'Davy!' A loud Buildiner woman's voice shouts from somewhere upstairs.

All of us jump, startled out of our paralysis.

'Come up here, your tea's on the table!'

The voice is loud, but also soft and kind. It's not what you'd expect to hear in a place like this. Not at all what you'd expect.

'Come on up now, love, don't be lettin' it get cold on you.'

The two Buildiners exchange glances. The one who is standing with his hand in his pocket shrugs. The one with the helmet – Davy; he has a name, an ordinary name – sighs deeply. He climbs down from the bike. He stands and looks at it for a minute, and then at my mother and me. Then, suddenly, he spits, not at us or even at the bike, but at the ground. And the spit comes slowly from his mouth, like dribbles from a leaky tap, rather than the angry liquid bullet you might expect. My mother looks surprised, but not annoyed. I look at the little puddle of spittle on the ground just beside the back wheel of the bike. The boy looks at it, too. It's the same colour as the snot at the end of his nose, with a dark red trace in it. He snuffles and takes a long look at the bike. His eyes aren't angry any more. He looks tired. The two of them turn and walk away, up the dark stone stairs to wherever they go when they're not out and about, breaking windows and robbing things.

'Well,' my mother says, taking hold of the bike. 'That's that.'

She looks tired, too. She starts to push my three-wheeler down the lane towards our own road. It doesn't occur to me to ride it, here in the Buildins. At this stage in my life and for a long time to come I'm only allowed to ride my bike on my own road, where it is safe to be.

LEARNING TO RIDE

Riding a three-wheeler is child's play, in every sense of the word. The tricycle is rooted to the ground, by the force of gravity, like a bed or a table. It just happens to be on wheels. All you have to learn is how to turn the pedals and you're in motion.

A two-wheeler is obviously different, seeming to defy some physical law of nature. How do they do it? that is what I wondered, watching them: the older children, and grown-up cyclists.

The man next door, for instance. Tony. Every morning he went to work on a high black bike. He just swung his long leg over the bar and off he sped, light as a bird in the air. (My father had an old black bike, too, but it had lain unused in the garden shed ever since he got the car – an ancient Morris Eight. He used to go everywhere on his bike, and now he went everywhere in his car. He never walked, except inside the house.)

Imelda Fogarty, ten years old, had a two-wheeler. A lady's bike. It was a good bit smaller than Tony's and I could easily mount it. But when I tried to move, I fell off immediately. Why? Imelda laughed and said, 'It's cinchy!' But she couldn't tell me how to do it. 'It's easy-peasy,' she said. 'You just do it!' And up she'd hop and fly down the road. Even though she was silly, and had her ears pierced, she could perform this miracle. She could even cycle without putting her hands on the handlebar for several yards at a stretch.

It was very frustrating.

*

When I was seven, I woke up on Christmas morning at about 4 a.m.

At the end of the bed I shared with my sister was a biscuit-faced doll with blue eyes and yellow hair and a pale yellow nylon dress with lace trimmings. There was a heap of other presents on the bed, and two grey socks hanging on the bedposts, lumpy and dumpy and stuffed to the gills with sweets and oranges and amazing little wind-up toys all the way from China.

And just inside the door, something light and elegant and perfect: a bicycle. A two-wheeler.

My heart leaped. I hadn't even asked for a two-wheeler, but Santy had brought me one, anyway! How clever of him!

We ran into our parents' bedroom to tell them the good news.

'No, no, Helen,' my mother said sleepily. 'The two-wheeler is for Orla.'

My sister.

Orla smiled smugly, although she didn't even want a two-wheeler.

The doll in the yellow frock was also hers.

I wondered if there was some mistake? It didn't make sense. And how did my mother know what Santy had intended?

She insisted that she did know, and enumerated the presents I'd got, which were many, but none of them was anything as desirable as the two-wheeler.

The bike was quite small – considerably smaller than Imelda Fogarty's Raleigh. It was a little small for me, in fact. But I wouldn't admit that, even to myself, and persisted in believing Santy had intended it for me, and that my mother was mistaken.

The bicycle didn't even look like a bicycle, but like a motorbike, the sort of motorbike a soldier might have, since it was painted the same grey-green colour as a jeep. Even though it was clearly second-hand, even though it didn't look like any bike I was familiar with, it was the most lovely thing I had ever seen.

I had three books, and two jigsaws, and a dress-up cardboard doll with dozens of paper dresses to be cut out and affixed to her flat body with tabs. Also, a small Irish colleen doll and a pair of leopard-skin gloves. All things I craved and had at some stage, coming up to Christmas, asked for. A good haul. But not half as good as Orla's, it seemed to me now.

There wasn't time to dwell on the problem, though, once we all rose and the great day got under way. We had to get dressed up in our Christmas clothes and go to Mass, and then eat the big Christmas breakfast of grapefruit and sausages and rashers and pudding. Tony and his wife, Marcella, called in from next door and had a glass of sherry with my mother and father. Then there was the huge preparation for dinner, and then dinner itself, which lasted for hours.

The washing-up.

At about five, when the day was slipping away, dismayingly, unbelievably fast, as it did every year, we retired to the dining room. Like everything else, this was part of our ritual. We would sit by the fire there and play one of the board games one of us had got from Santy. This year the game was Cluedo.

Cluedo was a very good game, which I enjoyed tremendously. The interesting characters, Miss Scarlett and Colonel Mustard, the locations – the Library, the Conservatory and the Ballroom – and, above all, the tiny, realistically modelled weapons, elevated it to a different plane from other, less personable board games: it approached the condition of theatre, something we all adored. But after two games, my mother and father wanted to take a break – he fell asleep in his armchair and my mother played some baby game with our little brother who was getting cranky. Orla, who had tried out her bike before dinner and abandoned it in the front room, wanted to have a go of my paper doll. Reluctantly – because once you cut out the dresses, the joy of the paper doll is much diminished – I decided to let her. I instructed her not to cut out more than three outfits, leaving ten for me.

As soon as she started snipping I slipped out.

There were fires in several rooms of the house for Christmas Day – the dining room, the bedrooms. In the kitchen we always had the Aga. But the front room wasn't heated, nor was the hall. It was freezing out there. It felt colder than it would out of doors.

Never mind.

I got the bike out of the front room, wheeled it to the end of the hall, and sat on the saddle.

Down I fell, just the way I fell off Imelda Fogarty's bike.

But it was a small bike and there wasn't far to fall. Also, I fell on the linoleum of our hall, not the rough surface of the road outside.

I tried again immediately.

Again.

Again.

I'd no idea how you did it. And nobody had ever explained how. You just do it, they would say. You just do it.

You have to find out for yourself.

I tried, I tried, I kept falling off.

On what must have been the twentieth attempt, I leaned sideways and started moving. I stayed on for about four cycles of the wheels, for a few yards.

The hall was one of those narrow, long halls you get in the Victorian houses. (It seemed long to me, anyway.) It wasn't a bad place to learn to cycle; it looked like a shiny brown road, but it was indoors and had walls close by to grab onto, so that gave one confidence. I kept at it and after about an hour – it could have been five; it could have been weeks because I was in a zone where time stood still, even as I concentrated fiercely on learning to move – I could cycle the length of the hall.

At about eight o'clock, time for our Christmas tea, my mother came out, yawning, to go down to the kitchen and put the mince pies in the oven.

'What are you doing out here in the cold, alannah?' she said. She didn't give out to me for being on the bike.

'I can ride a two-wheeler!' I might have been declaring that I'd landed on the moon.

I gave a demonstration. By now I could go the full length of the hall, turn around and come back again. Actually, as I knew, I could go anywhere. I could cycle.

They all came out then, to see if it was true.

'It's not her bike,' Orla said. But she was tired and sated with Christmas, and she didn't really care. She preferred the doll to the bike, anyway.

My father had woken up. He laughed and said, 'She can do it, all right.' He seemed to appreciate my sense of triumph more than my mother or Orla did.

He asked me to demonstrate again, which I did, gladly. Then he opened the hall door.

Outside it was dark, but the street lamp on the other side of the road glowed, and there were lights in most of the windows. Janet's window was lit up magically by her Christmas tree, the only one on the street; they were just coming into fashion. Snow was falling. Big flakes drifted down through the black air like petals, and melted as they touched the ground.

My father jerked his head in a gesture that meant, have a go outside.

'She'll catch her death a' cold,' my mother said. She was still standing in the door of the dining room, catching a bit of the heat from the fire in there.

I went out before she could prevent me, not stopping to put on a coat. It wasn't much colder outside than in the hall, anyway. Up I hopped on the two-wheeler that was like a motorbike and down the road I sailed, like a seagull in the foam of the ocean, or an eagle in the sky on a summer's day, the soft white snow falling on my bare head and Christmas frock.

It's easy to ride a bike, everyone says. And that is true. It's a knack, like swimming – or like standing erect on your two legs and walking on the face of this earth. All a question of confidence, and trust. Trust in yourself, and trust in the way the physical world works. You have to know that you can keep your balance, and you have to be certain of that from the second you mount the bicycle and lean forward and start pedalling. He who hesitates falls off.

'Once you learn, you never forget,' my father said.

That's true, too.

My sister asked me how to do it. I couldn't explain. 'You just do it,' I said, as Imelda Fogarty had said to me. 'It's cinchy.' She learned anyway, of course, but I never noticed when. Maybe you never do notice these milestones, which are among the more important in the greater scheme of life, except when you pass them yourself.

*

As a reward for getting the Corporation scholarship (which wasn't all that hard to get, if you were poor, because it was means tested), my mother bought me a real two-wheeler. It was not new. We bought it from our cousin Bernadette, who had used the bike to get from her bedsitter to the box factory in Rathmines, where she worked in the office, doing the books. Bernadette didn't need a bike any more because she'd just got married. Her husband was head foreman in the factory. 'She'll soon be driving her own car, wait and see,' my mother said. She was pleased, because she liked Bernadette and was glad she'd done well for herself. It was my mother the Tiger's ambition that all her younger relatives should end up richer and hence happier than all her older relatives. Her own mother had been a dairymaid who died of tuberculosis of the spine four years after her marriage. Her grandparents had been farm hands who could neither read nor write. My mother was planning that I and my sister should get the Leaving, and everything else, she believed, would follow on from that: new cars, semi-detached houses in the suburbs, pensions. Husbands, she didn't seem so interested in, but if they came with the prerequisite house and car, which Bernadette's did, they were to be welcomed.

The bike was pretty – red with white mudguards, a wicker basket in front, and, on the handlebar, a gleaming silver bell engraved with a schooner in full rig. The saddle was a padded white one, soft on the bum. I would need the basket, because I planned to cycle to school.

I was going to secondary in Ballsbridge, Marymount, an ordinary sort of school, whereas nearly everyone from my primary was going to St Bridget's, a famous all-Irish school on the north side of town. And why was I going to Marymount? Because it was nearer home, because the fees were lower, and because I had a half-scholarship there, as well as the Corporation scholarship, so we'd have a bit of money left over from that for extras, of which there were an enormous number. The uniform alone had cost a fortune, coming from Brown Thomas, a shop we'd never set foot in before. (We seldom even went down Grafton Street. Our shopping was done on Camden Street and South Great Georges Street, which were much less posh.) And then there were lots of little things. A divided skirt for gym, hockey boots, a hockey stick, a tennis racquet – all the things girls in those days needed for school, a long list of very expensive and mostly ugly things to wear and hit balls with.

Now I had the bike I would save money on bus fares, I pointed out to my mother. Somehow she did not seem to understand what a great saving would be involved. But it was eight pence a day at least – thruppence to and from school, and tuppence for the return journey at lunch time, when the fare for schoolchildren going home for their lunch was a penny. 'That's more than half-a-crown a week we'll save,' I said. I chatted a lot to my mother, about everything. 'That's really quite good, isn't it?'

'Yes, alannah,' she said. She looked and sounded drained, and I knew that the whole secondary school project was becoming too much for her before I'd even started. Nobody had ever gone to secondary school in our family before. I mean, not in my immediate family, where I was the eldest, and naturally the first to go, but in the entire family going back to the beginnings of time. They'd all finished school at fourteen, the ones who went at all – which were, my grandparents, born around 1890, and their parents, born around 1865, but not their parents born around the time of the Famine, before there were any schools in Ireland. (You wonder what children actually did all day, when normal children go to school. Just played around until they were old enough to work. Hard to imagine.) Anyway, all this meant that going to secondary was a big step. A small step for me and a giant leap for my family, a jump into, as my mother would have hoped, a new socio-economic milieu. She wanted me to get a good job and be well off, not like her, who had to scrimp and save all her life. Education was the way to riches. And that was the point of it. But the path to riches was proving too costly and impoverishing. And as with all investments, there was risk involved. She knew, I guess, that interest rates could fall as well as rise, and that if the worst came to the worst, even her capital would go. (Though she must have known there wasn't much fear of that, given my general record as a studious and docile child.)

I didn't cycle to school the first day. Togged out in my stiff navy tunic and snowy blouse, my tie and blue blazer and matching beret, I took the number 18 bus from the stop under the chestnut trees around the corner from our road. I went up the stairs at the back of the bus, planning to sit at the very front, but there were three girls in the blue blazers and berets there already. Naturally, I sat as far away from them as I could, even though there was nothing I longed for more than their friendship. There was another girl, from the next road to ours, on the bus, too. I knew her by name and to see. Yvette.

Yvette was one of those girls who was so beautiful, even as a tiny child, that she had acquired a special status, not exactly a celebrity status, but the status of a precious object, maybe like an icon or a work of art, in the neighbourhood. Nobody expected anything of her. She didn't need to be well behaved, or clever, or to help around the house. (Though she was perfectly competent at all these things.) It was enough for her simply to exist. The only child of a widow, who had an office job, her hair was perfectly blond, at a time when 'fair' meant a sort of light brown. (Mine was black, which I did not appreciate one bit. Later, I got to referring to it as chestnut.) She had the face of a big china doll, the kind of doll that we all coveted before Sindy and Barbie came along. Usually, Yvette was dressed in pastel frocks, pink or mint or pale lemon, so it was a shock to see her in the navy tunic and blazer of a peculiar shade of blue, neither light nor dark. She looked lovely in it, of course. The stern design – pleated skirt, narrow waistband, baggy V-necked bodice designed to accommodate a bust in a state of gradual and inexorable expansion – looked chic on her. The beret nestled in her blond curls like a bluebird in a golden nest. Still, it was a shock to see her in the same uniform that I was wearing (hers fitted properly, which helped; it's not easy to look chic in a uniform that is four sizes too big, like mine and most people's). It was awe-inspiring to think that she was embarking on the self-same adventure. I wondered if I would actually get to know her. It would be like becoming acquainted with Shirley Temple.

But getting to know her wouldn't be easy, because the next day I didn't take the bus, but started going to school on my new bicycle.

My mother, it turned out, was worried about that. Her Tiger ambition deserted her. Faced with saying goodbye to me as I set off on my bike, she became an ordinary fussy pussy-cat of a mother.

'Be very careful now,' she said anxiously, as she did my plaits for me. I still couldn't do them properly myself. Her fingers flicked them into shape swiftly and expertly, the way they did everything. There was literally not a hair out of place when she snapped the elastic bands around the ends of the braids, and there wouldn't be, until she released them again next morning. In fact, I could have kept my hair in my mother's plaits for my whole life without bothering to redo them, so perfect and tight was her handiwork. 'Watch out at the traffic lights and when you're turning corners. Make sure to look over your shoulder.'

'Yeah, yeah, yeah, yeah,' I said, tossing my horsewhip hair into her face.

My mother had been fostered out as a child to an old aunt and uncle in Wexford. They were not even her blood relatives, but the brother and sister of her stepmother. Her mother had died when she was three, and after a few years, her father married again. Annie. Granny. My mother loved her. Granny had been a cook for a Big House and could cook delicious puddings and bake a perfect apple pie, a rich fruit cake. In all her ways she was ladylike and meticulous. We had her wedding photograph, a big one that had been doctored to resemble an oil painting, over our dining-room table. But even though she loved her, Granny sent my mother down to Wexford to be company for these old people. Ben and Bea.

But my mother loved life there, too. They lived in a small cottage – maybe it was a council cottage – but there was plenty of room for the three of them. And also for hens and turkeys, a cow, a pig, a garden, where they grew potatoes and cabbage and onions and lettuce. Blackcurrants for jam, strawberries for cream, apple trees for tarts and pies. On Saturdays, Ben and Bea and my mother, whose name was Gretta, drove to the nearest town, in the pony and trap, for the messages. My mother – I imagined her with curls, which she had always had in my experience, though that was because her hair was permed, like all grown-up women's – sat up in front and drove, with

Ben beside her and Bea in the back. That was on the way into town. On the way home, she sat in the back, too, on the leather side-seat, and ate biscuits. Strawberry Creams were her favourite, followed by Custard Creams, and she was given a pound of them in a brown paper bag every Saturday. The horse was called Brock, a big placid chestnut.

She went to the local school, where she was a success. It was a mile and a half away, along the tree-lined road, and when she was twelve, Bea bought her a bicycle. This was a proper lady's bike, black and big.

'That was the happiest day of my life,' my mother told me. 'I couldn't believe I was getting this bike. I'd never owned anything, to tell the God's truth, in me life till then.'

She kept that bike, the same one, until she got married.

The schoolteacher wanted her to go on to the secondary school. My mother was very good at arithmetic and history and English. Auntie Bea and Uncle Ben would have supported her. (She didn't mention a scholarship. Maybe she didn't apply for it – you had to fill in a form, and sit a special examination at Easter to be in with a chance; they mightn't have known about that down there.) And she could have gone to school in town on her bike – it was six miles away, but she could have done that.

'I said no,' she said, without rancour or sentiment. 'I wanted to go home, to be with my father and brother. I didn't see the point.'

I wondered why she wanted to go home, if she was having such a good time in Wexford. And I sighed for her failure, her lack of ambition, and started a daydream about what her alternative life would have been. The life she would have had if she'd stayed with Ben and Bea, and gone to secondary, and moved on from there. She might have become a teacher, and learned to drive, and got her own car. A nice new house with a big window in a suburb, instead of the old brick house with narrow windows we had, near town, where nobody wanted to live any more. Maybe, if she'd gone to secondary, she wouldn't have married my father? Maybe she wouldn't have had me? Maybe I wouldn't exist?

What actually happened was that she got a job in a grocery shop and met her best friend, Teasy, there. They cycled all over Dublin, all over the county. On their day off they'd go out to Enniskerry and have tea in the tea shop there; they'd go to Sandymount, and Dún Laoghaire, and Blackrock. There is a photo of them, in their gabardine coats and headscarves, standing beside their black, practical-looking bikes, laughing. They were terrible gigglers.

'So what happened to your bike?' I asked.

'Och, alannah, I don't know what happened to it,' my mother said, with a certain air she had for moments like this, an air of nostalgia, sentimentality, which I found embarrassing. 'I suppose I left it in some shed after we were married.' She meant, in some shed at the back of the first house they lived in when they married, after she had met my father on the beach at Sandymount one scorching Sunday in July, where she and Teasy had cycled with some other pals for a picnic. He had got talking to Teasy's fiancé, Christy, who was of the party, playing rounders on the sand – they loved rounders. 'I didn't have much use for it after Daddy got the car.' She never learned to drive. Daddy drove her everywhere she wanted to go at weekends, and on weekdays she walked. We could walk most places we needed to get to from our house.

I could have walked to Marymount but it would have taken more than half an hour – too long, in the morning. It was about two miles away. I could cycle it in less than twenty minutes. Down, down, I felt I was going – and the gradient was, subtly, downhill, since the school was nearer the coast then we were, though not on the coast. Down Charleston Road, down Appian Way, which was too narrow for all the traffic it had to support, even then, then down the wide, elegant Waterloo Road, and finally the best part – a quiet, perfect, traffic-free road, called by what seemed to be the elegant and lovely name of Marymount Road.

Charleston Road, Waterloo Road, and Marymount Road were lined all along their edges with trees. Great chestnut trees when I started school in the autumn. Once or twice a ripe chestnut got me on the head. Cycling along these roads was magical. I soared, as on wings. I tried tricks – after a while I could cycle for most of the way without putting my hands on the handlebars, and it gave me a great sense of achievement to do this. I wanted to show off, to boast about it at home, but (wisely) I didn't.

The school was fine. Although I knew nobody when I started, I got to know plenty of people soon enough. Those girls on the bus, the girl who sat beside me in class. Others. I didn't, though, make a best friend. Everyone seemed to have one already – most of them had arrived in the school with a best friend in tow, it was unusual to go to secondary school on your own. My old best friends were far away, living another life in St Bridget's. I hardly ever saw any of them.

Yvette, the only girl in the school from my immediate neighbourhood, was in another class.

The teaching in Marymount was excellent. I realised that when I was there, and even more so now. When I hear people saying they don't remember anything they learned at school, I have to admit, to myself, that I remember a good many things, and most of them I learned during that first year in Marymount. Big chunks of the Gospel According to Saint Luke, which we learned off by heart. Many passages from *The Merchant of Venice*, ditto, and also from *A Midsummer Night's Dream*, which the seniors put on at Easter. We second years were in the choir, singing 'Trip away; make no stay; Meet me all by break of day', and other songs. 'So we grew together like to a double cherry,' I can hear the girl from fifth year who played Helena saying – she was a tall, poignant-looking girl, and the play was so sad, the parting of the friends. *Seeming parted, but yet an union in partition.* I was cycling every morning under the cherry blossom, quoting these lines, wishing I could play Helena.

The menu of subjects lived up to its promise. It was a Christmas stocking of Hector Grey novelties – Latin verbs and French pronunciation, Shakespeare plays and experiments in science. *Bully one, bully two, bully three* on the hockey pitch in Sandymount, fragrant with churned-up turf, cut grass.

But the lack of a best friend – which didn't worry me while I was there – was going to be a problem.

In March or so, I was invited to a birthday party, at the house of my best friend in primary, Deirdre. By now she was settled in and had new companions in St Bridget's, and I had to put up with that. They were at the party, but so were plenty of my old classmates. One of them, a small girl called Mandy, whom I knew from my very earliest days in primary, had changed. She used to be a teacher's pet, cherished because she was exceptionally small (the sort of girl who grows to be less than five foot, as an adult – petite). As a little girl, she was doll-like, though she did not have the fairytale good looks of, say, Yvette. She was famous for never missing a day – she got a prize for this on the last day of school, a silver cup – and for never turning up without her uniform on.

She had grown a bit taller, and was beginning to plump out. Something else had happened to her that happens to girls as they turn into women. She had learned to talk a lot.

Yakety-yak for the whole party.

Her subject was school. St Bridget's. (She called it Biddy's, without explaining what it was. Like people who talk too much, she took it for granted that everyone was familiar with the locations, the connections, the entire context of her life. Or maybe they just have so many stories to tell that they haven't time for boring explanations and trust the audience to fill in the gaps.)

Mandy was a brilliant storyteller. Half the party guests were at her feet, literally, gathered round her in a circle, riveted to her words. Her tales were character-based, and the characters were all teachers with names like Muggins and Bertie and Smutty and Pug. Muggins was an old nun who was crazy, just crazy, and Pug was the Irish teacher who gave the class Cadbury's chocolate every Friday if they did their homework and Pug was getting married in June and came to school one day with two odd shoes on, that was the day after her fiancé had proposed to her – can you imagine? – one shoe a brown moccasin teacher-kind of shoe and the other black patent with a little bow on it, we were in absolute stitches, we were breaking our sides, we just couldn't stop ….

It was this sort of stuff. Nothing much when you thought about it afterwards. But she created a vivid dramatic picture. And the picture was of a school that was not so much like the schools I read about in the Enid Blyton books, as a school that was even better than them. More full of life and laughs and fun. More replete with eccentric teachers. A school where the nuns and teachers were a constant source of amusement, like an ongoing circus, and where the girls never stopped breaking their sides laughing.

My Christmas exams went well. I was now considering becoming a scientist, like Marie Curie, whose biography I had read in a children's series. I imagined myself sitting under a pine tree, fondling the fragrant needles and discovering radiation. In English, I was doing well, too. Our teacher, Miss Burns, had a contact in the radio station, and got us, the class, to put together a complete half-hour programme. We wrote poems and essays and plays, and members of the class got to recite them, present them, on the radio. We did auditions. Presenting was what everyone wanted to do, to be 'on the radio'!

I didn't make the cut.

'I don't know what it is. Your voice is a little nasal,' said Miss Burns.

I didn't know what that meant, to have a voice that was nasal. I did not like my nose, the shape of it, and wondered if, apart from looking funny, it also affected my voice.

'But you can console yourself with the knowledge that you've written most of the programme,' she added.

It was true. I had surpassed myself. Poems, songs, funny anecdotes. A play. I'd written them all, in an orgy of writing. I liked Miss Burns and the topics she suggested, and when I heard the word 'radio', I took off. It didn't surprise me that I'd written most of the programme. I'd done more work than anyone else and I loved writing essays and anything else I was asked to write.

So I thought, if I don't become Marie Curie, I might like to become a writer. Like Frances Hodgson Burnett, whose books Miss Burns had recommended. Or G.K. Chesterton, whom I had discovered myself and liked.

The hockey, I liked too. And in spring we played tennis in Herbert Park.

I loved, above all, the cycling. Four times a day, I flew along those roads. Like a goddess.

*

221

I did not take to the headmistress.

I don't take to heads of institutions much – that's something I know now. Maybe they are often not very nice people. But it is more likely that I am afraid of them, for one thing, and for another, I resent anyone who has any power over me.

Sister Borromeo hadn't given me any cause to dislike her. She had given me a scholarship (but that put me in her power). She told me I was a good girl whenever she ran into me on the corridor. She commended me for wearing the full uniform. I didn't want to be commended. I wore the full uniform because I loved it. I loved the blazer and the tie, and even the beret, which you were supposed to despise. There was an ongoing battle in the school between Sister Borromeo and all the pupils about the wearing of this beret. She would make announcements over the loud-speaker system they had, the Tannoy – a little box in the middle of the every ceiling.

Crackle, it would go, *crackle crackle*. And then Sister Borromeo's voice would come through, like a voice on the radio.

'I want to remind you all that according to the rules of Marymount, you are supposed to wear your full school uniform on the way to and from school. This includes the beret.'

This announcement would usually raise a laugh in the class. Even the teacher, whose work had been interrupted by the Tannoy, would allow herself a smile and a helpless shrug.

Hardly anybody wore the beret. (It flattened the hair, for one thing. This didn't bother me, since I still had my plaits. The hair on top was tightly pulled by my mother's efficient hands, and flat as a ballerina's.)

'Good girl, wearing your beret!' she said, beaming, one morning when she met me on the stairs.

I said nothing.

'Good girl, I said.' She sounded sharper and her smile was gone. 'It's so nice to see the beret on. It suits you so well.'

I smirked then and mumbled something. And as soon as she was out of sight I whipped the beret off and stuffed it into my schoolbag, where it stayed for evermore.

*

The first week of term I had met Sister Borromeo in town.

I was traipsing around hunting for schoolbooks. The way they handled it was that you got lists of texts from the teachers during the first week of school – not one list, nothing as organised as that. Each teacher would write the titles of the books required for her class on the blackboard; the pupils transcribed the list in their jotters or copybooks. Then we'd go into town and go from bookshop to bookshop in search of the books. Every schoolchild in Dublin was doing the same thing for a week or two at the beginning of the first term. Long queues would form outside the bookshops as the children stood in line, waiting to get in. When you got to the counter, the tired and harassed assistants – students doing holiday jobs – would snatch your list and tell you what they had. 'Out of stock' was a phrase you learned quickly. 'Out of print' was another.

It was a tedious way of acquiring books, labour intensive, especially for the children. But it had its advantages: half-days for the first week, putting off the real start of school for at least that length of time. Standing in queues in the hot September sun wasn't all that diverting, but moving around the city, from Greene's on Clare Street to Fallon's on Talbot Street, stopping off at several shops in between, had a certain excitement to offer.

On my third day in school, I was making my way down Talbot Street to Fallon's, and another shop, The Educational Company. I didn't like Talbot Street. It is very long and the shops on it are slightly seedy. The light on it is harsh, somehow, and it's altogether a disheartening, messy kind of street – stretching from too busy O'Connell Street to the bleakness of Amiens Street Station, near the North Strand, which was bombed during the war and which still looked as if a bomb had hit it twenty-odd years later. By the time I had got to Talbot Street, having been up and down to Clare Street, which was lovely and green and mysterious, to the smart, encouraging shops on Dawson Street, and trudged across the Liffey to the north side, I was tired.

Sister Borromeo and another nun, Sister Assumption, were bobbing along up Talbot Street. There were a lot of religious shops on that street, selling holy statues, religious books, nun's habits, for all I know (they must have bought them somewhere).

'Hello, Helen,' said Sister Borromeo brightly.

Sister Assumption, who was good-humoured and mischievous, smiled and, unbelievably, winked.

'Hello, Sister,' I said. I still liked her at this stage.

That was all. They walked on.

This happened in September, just after school had started. The episode of the beret occurred months later, well into the second term, just before Easter, when we were deeply engrossed in rehearsing *A Midsummer Night's Dream*. The pretence of classwork had been dispensed with. We spent the entire schoolday in the hall, singing our songs, and waiting for our cues. By now we knew the play off by heart.

Some of the teachers expressed impatience. Miss Burns was open about it. 'When are we supposed to get our work done?' she asked. She had got engaged to be married and wore her hair, which used to be any old way, a sort of limp bob, in a new style: up, with elaborate ringlets held by a clasp at the back of her head. She wore a white bouclé suit and patent shoes under her black gown. She looked imperious.

'It will soon be over,' we consoled her. She had become our ally, almost our equal, since the radio project.

'Oh well!' she smiled.

A few days after Deirdre's party, which was the day before the play was due to go on, Sister Borromeo called me to the office.

I was terrified. I could think of no reason for this call.

She was sitting behind a huge wooden desk, with a telephone on it and a few files. It was a type of desk I would see often again, in the future, but this was the first time I'd seen one. The desk of a managing director. Her room, too, the office, was spacious and polished, like an important director's. The only difference was that instead of some expensive-looking, inoffensive piece of art on the wall, she had a big statue of the Blessed Virgin in the corner.

'Sit down,' she said.

I sat down on a slippery leather chair.

'Your studies are going well,' she said. She seemed to have my school report opened in front of her. I wondered if this had something to do with the half-scholarship. 'But you are getting to be a little insolent,' she said. 'I have had some bad reports from a few of your teachers.'

This was a lie, I knew. I was never insolent.

'You do not wear your full uniform,' she went on.

This was also unfair. I didn't wear the beret. Now. But I was never without my tie, or anything else. I was more compliant than anyone else as far as the uniform was concerned.

'What I am really worried about is that you have mitched from school.' She stared at me from under her big wimple: the nuns in this school wore very wide wimples. They took the form of two big squares of the stiff white stuff, like plastic, that wimples are made from, on either side of their faces. They were like a sort of small tent with an open front – the kind of tent you see at farmers' markets. Her face was inside the tent, in the space where the stall would be, with its wares, the jars of pickles, the jams, the farm cheeses.

I was so startled I said something natural.

I said, 'What?'

Because I had never in my life mitched from school. For one thing, I didn't particularly want to. And for another, I didn't have the courage it takes to leave home in the morning, in your uniform and with your bag on your back, and head off to the beach, or into town, or wherever mitching kids go.

'I remember meeting you in town one day. Myself and Sister Assumption met you.'

'But that was during the school book week. We had a half-day,' I said.

'I don't think so,' she said firmly.

There was nothing to say to that. I moved into a zone of disbelief, a zone where I knew I was helpless to rescue myself. Because how can you help yourself if you are faced with a liar in a powerful place?

'Mitching is something we take very seriously in Marymount.' Her voice was precise and ladylike, like a little ivory paper knife with a sharp edge. 'You are a scholarship girl and we expect a certain standard of behaviour.'

I had stopped feeling startled, or frightened. I gained composure from my disbelief.

'We don't like to use the strap, Helen,' she said.

Now I was startled again, back into emotion. Strap?

'But we do if we are forced to,' she said.

I looked at her wimple-like a tent, and her black habit, and her black beads and the big black strap around her waist. The acre of polished desk, separating me from her. The slippery chair. The prinking statue of Our Lady. There were lilies in a silver vase in front of her, calla lilies, with their pointy yellow tongues sticking out of their wimple mouths. Like snakes' tongues.

She said she would let me off this time, but that I had better watch out.

She put it more elegantly, of course, but that was what she meant.

That night, I started my campaign to get out of Marymount.

I told my mother I really missed all my old friends. I told her I missed Irish, which was the language we had spoken in my primary school, and was the language of St Bridget's. I told her I had made no new pals, which was a lie – but I didn't have the sort of friend whom I could not betray, the sort of friend who would bind me to the school.

My mother didn't want me to move. It would mean buying a new uniform (which was no small expense). The fees in St Bridget's were higher, too (surprisingly, given its plebeian-sounding name). And there I would have no half-scholarship.

I kept at her.

Orla was going to start secondary in September, and she was going to St Bridget's – she was not like me, experimental. She knew where her friends were going and she was not going to make the mistake of going elsewhere.

Then something happened. Something that would go down in Irish history, and would incidentally change the course of my life. The Minister for Education, Donagh O'Malley, announced that he was introducing free education for secondary schools. From now on there would be no fees. That is, there would be no fees in schools that made the decision to opt in to the free scheme, but fees would continue in schools that decided to opt out, and preserve their exclusive, upper-class tone by keeping out poor children.

Both Marymount and St Bridget's opted into the scheme.

Nobody would have to pay fees in those schools. Ever again.

'Well, I suppose it will just be the uniform,' said my mother. 'If you're really not content in that school, I'll see if you can change.' (Contented in that school, she would have said. Not content.)

So I did.

My mother wrote the necessary letters.

This all happened at the beginning of May.

The weather was glorious, as it often is in Dublin at that time of year. All along the roads on the way to school the cherry blossoms were in bloom. Morning and evening I cycled under the generous branches, flung like long arms out of the gardens over the road, spilling their benison of pink popcorn petals over the road, over me.

And suddenly, in the midst of all this miraculous flowering, I got what had been lacking all year. A special friend. One morning I whizzed around my corner and there was Yvette, turning from her cul-de-sac onto the main road. How like her to start now that the weather was warm and lovely, I thought. I supposed she hadn't wanted to cycle in the bad weather, not being made of such stern stuff as I. But I did her an injustice. In fact, she had just been given the bicycle, for her birthday, a few days ago – she'd asked for it because she'd noticed me, cycling along, and thought it looked like so much fun.

Yvette had copy-catted me. Wonders would never cease.

Immediately, we became cycling companions. She waited for me at her corner in the mornings, and instead of zipping along alone, amusing myself by removing my hands from the bars, I cycled slowly, with Yvette beside me, chatting. It turned out that she wasn't stuck-up or precious or spoiled at all. That she looked exquisite didn't concern her in the least – she did not seem to even realise it, although she was fond of nice frocks (but then, so was I; so were almost all girls). Nor was she especially unusual, in spite of looking it. Our conversation was about teachers, and other girls, and what we had for homework, and where we would go for our holidays (she would go to Liverpool to visit her aunty; I would go to West Cork where my mother had rented a bungalow for a fortnight in August). We talked about sport. Yvette was very good at tennis, a game that suited her, of course, what with the white skirts and sunny courts, but she was even better at hockey, which isn't so glamorous.

After about a week of this cycling companionship, Yvette asked me to come around to her house for tea on Friday.

This was the first time any girl in the school had issued such an invitation.

So I got to see Yvette's house. It was the same type of house as my own, slightly smaller, with smaller gardens. And although it was pleasant enough, it was not as cosy or feminine or beautiful as I had anticipated. True, the favoured colour for floors was red, whereas my mother liked fawn or brown, and the wallpapers were white with red roses in the hall, blue cornflowers in the kitchen, which created a cheerful effect. But when I visited, the hall floor was covered with newspapers, because her mother had just washed it, and a clotheshorse, hung with sheets and underwear, dominated the kitchen and gave off their warm, damp, rather embarrassing, smell. Work went on in Yvette's house, just as in mine, and it wasn't all that different in other respects. The food was chips and fried eggs, for instance, with tinned pears and condensed milk for sweet. Yvette and I watched television afterwards in their dining room, while her mother did the ironing down in the kitchen.

It was an ordinary enough visit. And yet it was momentous. I had got inside her house. She liked me enough to invite me in. We were, in short, en route to being best friends.

Too late. The letters were in the post. Within a week, everything was settled, and although I felt, if not regretful, certainly ambivalent, I was too cowardly to pull back and change my mind again.

So I left Marymount – nobody ever found out why – and I went across town to St Bridget's. It was not half as good a school as Marymount. The teachers were a mixed bunch, but they never used the strap there (or threatened to). And the headmistress was nice. A little mad – she advised me to go to Trinity College when the time came to leave, and then to come back and be a nun. This was at a time when there was a ban on Catholics in the archdiocese of Dublin going to Trinity. The headmistress of St Bridget's was the kind of person who would like to have a pupil flouting that ban. I couldn't imagine Sister Borromeo recommending anyone to ignore an episcopal regulation.

I couldn't cycle to St Bridget's, which was three miles away on the other side of the city. A long enough bus journey – one that we did, all the same, four times a day, usually.

I did not entirely lose contact with Yvette. She lived just around the corner, after all. I invited her back to my house for tea just before school ended; that's when I told her I was changing schools. She was surprised but not devastated; she had plenty of friends. We saw each other from time to time afterwards, but of course our lives moved off in different directions. I was wearing a different uniform from hers now, and I wasn't cycling to school any more.

My bike lay in the garden shed – our garden was full of sheds. For a while after I changed school, I'd take it out and have a spin at weekends. I planned to go on long cycles, to the countryside, to the beach. Once or twice I did actually ride down to Sandymount, cycled along the seafront and then came back again. In my plans, I would go on a cycling holiday with girls from school. (I never made a very close friend in the new school – my old pals were in different classes from me and had regrouped by the time I got there. I had a few girls to whom I was close, but they lived far away and were not the type to cycle.) In my fantasy, we – me and this group of cheerful and enterprising girls – would cycle all over the country, camping in woodlands or fields at night, or staying in country inns. I would have pannier bags, and shorts, and a smile on my freckled face. The bee would suck in the cowslip's bell.

Of course, none of this happened.

I did use my bike again, though.

The year I did the Leaving I got a job in a bookshop. Greene's Bookshop. I was taken on in the summer to sell the schoolbooks, to be there in September when the school book rush was in full swing and they needed a lot of extra hands. It seemed like the perfect job. In practice it wasn't all that wonderful. It was a bit like being in the army during a big war, training and polishing your gun, waiting for the signal to launch an attack.

For two months there was very little to do; boredom was the main problem for me and the other half-dozen students who had been taken on for the summer. Then came D-Day, the first of September. The school book rush. From then on, it was mayhem. There was not one second to draw a breath, from nine to five thirty, nine to one on Saturdays.

Greene's was not far from home. I took out my bike again and got the tyres changed with some of the money I was earning. I could fly down to the shop in the summer mornings in about ten minutes.

Usually, I parked it in the hall – they had a hall door that was not part of the shop proper, at the side. I'd drag it in there. I'd lost the key of the lock and for some reason hadn't bought a new one – I'd had to lash out on the tyres, I didn't feel like spending more money on my bike the minute I started working. I put it off till later. On my third Saturday, the door to the hall was locked, so I left the bike outside the shop at the side of one of the tables they had out there on the footpath, like *bouquinistes* in France. When I came out, the bike was gone.

You couldn't leave an unlocked bike unattended in Dublin in those days. It wasn't like Amsterdam or Copenhagen, those legendary cities, paradises for cyclists, where everyone is honest and most people ride a bike. In Dublin any unlocked bike was robbed while the saddle was still warm. So they said.

CHARIOT OF FIRE

The day my red bicycle was stolen from Greene's Bookshop, I met my first great love.

He came into the shop looking for a copy of a novel and came to the schoolbook counter by mistake. (Later he told me that he had walked into the shop, looked to the left, where Eddie was sitting on his stool among the stands of paperbacks, and then to the right, where four beautiful girls were chatting together in front of a stack of textbooks. Naturally, he chose to turn right.) As always, when a customer came in and broke up our chattering, we all looked guilty (though there was nothing to do but chat, in these early weeks) and rushed to serve. I got there first.

The novel he wanted was *Nausea*. That's what he asked for. Just the title.

I was used to people just knowing the title – for the textbooks, of course, that was what you would need to know. Nobody knew or cared who wrote them. But I already knew that somebody could come looking for a novel called *The Sun Also Rises*, or *Wise Blood*, and say they'd forgotten the name of the author. Sometimes someone would not even know the title – they'd tell you what the book was about. It's about a girl whose sister has married a rich man and who isn't sure if she wants to get married herself or not. They're in London. It's got a bird on the cover.

It was a great thrill for us if we could identify the book for these customers.

'Oh yeah,' I smiled. 'Jean-Paul Sartre.'

He knew that, of course. He was just testing. Teasing.

'It might be over there in the paperback section,' I said. Then, because I could see that this looked like bad service, I added. 'Just hold on a second, I'll see if we have it.'

I went over to the other side of the shop and he followed. So I passed him on to Eddie (who had the Penguin edition).

'Eight hundred and fifty-five,' Andrea, one of my colleagues, said thoughtfully, as we watched him go out the door with his orange paper bag in one hand and his red and white helmet in the other.

The boys – all the summer staff were eighteen or nineteen – had a silly joke. They gave all young women who came into the shop marks out of a thousand for looks. Top marks were for Helen of Troy, the face that launched a thousand ships. Great-looking girls got nine hundred. They were capable of awarding fifteen, or two, to women they didn't like the look of. For a while we girls did the same thing for men. We did it for a few days and then stopped, bored with the exercise. Nobody had played the game for about two weeks at this stage, so Andrea had to add, 'Ships, featherhead', before I copped on.

Seán was chunky, with curly brown hair, and a confident, cheeky smile. He hadn't struck me as especially attractive on the Helen of Troy scale. But he did seem like the kind of person I'd want to know. (Any man who bought *Nausea*, if he was reasonably attractive and friendly, would have seemed like the kind of person I'd want to know. I believed people who read serious books were bound to be interesting.)

Two days later Seán came back.

I recognised him immediately – he was carrying his helmet. Not many customers had them. His big motorbiker's leather jacket also made him distinctive.

He sauntered up to the counter – the schoolbook counter, my counter.

'Hi there,' he said. 'How are you?'

'Oh, hi!' I had no experience of courtship rituals. I'd never met a boy anywhere other than at a dance, and it did not occur to me that you could meet a potential date anywhere else. But, out of politeness, I batted the ball back to him. 'Are you enjoying *Nausea*?'

He smiled. 'I don't think anyone could possibly enjoy it.' I must have looked snubbed. 'It's sort of bleak. Have you read it?'

I shook my head. 'I'm going to do philosophy next year,' I said. 'When I go to college.' I had no doubt but that I would get the Leaving, get the marks I needed for a grant, and go to college. Even though I hadn't worked very hard at some subjects, I was confident. But, knowing it was best to appear modest, I added, 'That's if I get the Leaving, of course.'

The next night we went out, to the cinema.

I met him under Clery's clock. We were to meet at half past seven and go to a film that started at eight, in the Carlton. *Love Story*. I'd dashed home at half past five – it took half an hour, now that I had no bike. Washed and changed into suitable clothes for a date – my first. And it turned out that I didn't have anything, not a single garment that was right, for the occasion. I pulled all the clothes out of my wardrobe and got panicky, trying on one thing, then the other, as the clock ticked inexorably onwards. In the end I wore a pale green blouse and dark green maxi skirt, which looked, I imagined, a bit like a riding habit, one that might have been worn by a nineteenth-century heroine, by Catherine Earnshaw perhaps. Or Lorna Doone (I hadn't read *Lorna Doone* but I loved her name). My aim was to look like a romantic, dreamy girl, but so far none of the clothes I had matched up to my image of what they should be, what I needed to achieve my vision. (My legs were too fat, and that is one reason why I liked the floaty, long, romantic skirts that were just coming into fashion, after the tyranny of the mini.)

By the time I reached Clery's I was nervous and drained, after the ordeal of dressing. It was twenty-five to eight already and I worried that I had kept him waiting. Many people were standing around in the vicinity of the clock, and crowds of young people thronged the pavement, on their way to picture houses, or theatres, to other places of entertainment. But there was no sign of Seán. I waited for five minutes, at a slight distance from the clock, where I could see its big black hands jerkily making their way around its white moon face. I could also see Clery's windows and alternated glancing at the clock with examining the outfits on display. Miniskirts, tiny silk shifts in startling colours and patterns – orange and purple psychedelic blotches. Or black-and-white geometric patterns. So boring. There was nothing that I would want in the window. None of the clothes were designed for a girl who wanted to be called Lorna Doone and who was about to read *Nausea* and embark on a philosophy course in the autumn. Such clothes existed, and not only in my imagination. I saw the clothes I wanted sometimes, on girls who had spent the summer in Copenhagen or Paris or San Francisco. Indian smocks and gypsy skirts. Espadrilles, soft straw baskets. You could not get such things in Dublin then. You had to travel for them – which is what made them so desirable, and so sexy.

By a quarter to eight I had stopped worrying about espadrilles. I had other things on my mind. Where was Seán? It had never occurred to me that he wouldn't come and it still didn't. I had heard the term 'stood up', but usually from girls in my class, the advanced kind of girl who would not be doing philosophy in the autumn but probably doing a shorthand and typing course at a commercial college. Those girls, whose eyes above the school uniform were framed in thick black make-up, would talk about how they had stood a boy up. 'I had to stand him up,' they'd say. It didn't seem very important. They had to stand a boy up because they'd changed their mind about him, after making a date at a dance. Or because they had to wash their hair, or help a friend to manicure her nails. It was easier not to turn up than to phone and make an excuse, and not everyone had a phone, anyway. I'd never considered what it felt like to be that boy. To be waiting for a girl who just didn't show up. Our feeling was that the boy would just shrug and go home. We didn't attribute much sensitivity to them. We didn't believe they had feelings, not in the way we had.

At first I didn't fear that Seán had stood me up, because why would he have bothered coming to the shop and asking to see me if he wasn't going to keep the date?

But as the hands on the big clock jerked on, I began to get anxious. How long should I wait? I played the game you play in these situations. I said to myself, I will wait for five more minutes and then I'll leave. And then when the five minutes had passed, I said that again.

Other people kept meeting one another, in the vicinity of the clock. Mainly couples. The person who had been waiting would see the other one coming, and rush out of their niche to join the partner – they were like magnets, one would move out and the other would run in, and they'd join, kiss maybe, and then walk off hand in hand as often as not, laughing and talking.

Lucky, happy, people!

As eight o'clock drew nearer, I was almost the only person left under the clock, still waiting. The evening was growing colder. A big grey cloud scudded across the sun. The green double-deckers roared along the street, belching out grey fumes.

I was sure that everyone, on the buses, in the cars, was looking out the window at me, thinking, Look at your one, still waiting.

At eight o'clock he came.

He was not on his motorbike, and I hardly recognised him without his leather jacket and helmet under his arm.

'Listen, I'm really sorry …'

He was pink and panting, wearing just a shirt, a pale blue shirt, no tie. His hair was tousled and much more abundant than it had been before (on account of not being flattened by the helmet). He smelt mildly of a mixture of fresh sweat and flowery soap.

'It's OK,' I said, without giving the slightest indication that I'd been upset. And I didn't feel annoyed or angry, as I would have done if it had been anyone else who had kept me waiting.

My main feeling was not even of relief, but of pleasure. All the waiting time was blotted out of my memory as if it had never existed.

We ran across the street, just where the pillar used to be, and up to the Carlton. There was a long queue, already moving, and we joined it.

'God, hope we get in now,' he said.

I didn't care. Already I was happy just to be with him, standing beside him in a queue. I wouldn't have said to myself that I was in love, but I had never really felt like this before. I had never felt happy just being with a person – always there had to be something else. Something to eat, something to do, something to talk about. Even being with my mother, when I was small, had not been like this. I needed to be with my mother, to feel happy, but she was just a background against which my other desires would be fulfilled. She was like, say, the light that fills a room where you want to read, or play a game, or she was like the sunshine that is a background to the fun you have at the beach. Essential, but not by any means an end in herself.

I knew I'd enjoy this film (I loved most films I'd ever seen, which had been precious few). But being with this person, the guy on the motorbike, was the main thing. (I did not think of him as a 'man', nor did I think of him as a 'boy'. He was just himself.) The film was going to be the background to the pleasure of being with him.

I wouldn't have formulated it like that then, or formulated it at all. All I knew, standing there, on the shadowy side of the street, was that I felt at ease, and pleased in a way I had not felt before in my life until then.

One Saturday about three weeks after this he collected me from the bookshop when we closed at one o'clock. This time he had the motorbike – it was parked just around the corner from the shop on Merrion Square.

He wondered if I'd like to go for a walk in the mountains.

I would.

He looked at me thoughtfully. 'That's a very nice skirt,' he said. And after a few seconds, added, 'You look lovely.'

I was wearing a calf-length, black skirt and a high-necked Victorian blouse that I'd bought the day before at lunch time, using more than half my pay packet for the week. The skirt had a very high waist. 'Hm,' Eddie in paperbacks said when he saw it. He was admiring it. Everyone was. 'What would you call that? A cummerbund, I think, that's what it is.' I didn't like the sound of the word 'cummerbund' much, but I was pleased that my outfit impressed people. I'd got it because it was a bit like one of the outfits Ali MacGraw wore in the movie.

For the pillion of a motorbike it was far from ideal.

'Slacks would be easier,' Seán said. 'But I hate slacks.'

I was glad I hadn't worn mine, although I had a new pair of Levis, of which I had been inordinately proud until that moment. (Ali had worn jeans, once or twice, in the movie. But Seán had been less enthusiastic than I about the film. In fact, when I asked him if he'd enjoyed it, as we made our way to my bus stop, he had used a comment of a kind he had plenty of, as I would find out in due course: 'No comment!')

He insisted I wear his helmet.

I didn't think a helmet would suit me, and it didn't go with my high-necked lacy blouse. But I enjoyed putting it on all the same. It was like dressing up to play a game. I felt like an astronaut: an astronaut on top and Ali MacGraw underneath.

Driving – if it was driving – moving, whizzing, racing – along the streets, then along the Bray Road and up the winding ways to the mountains, felt like flying. Cycling had felt like that, sometimes, but this was different. On a bicycle I had felt like a bird. Being on the Honda was more like being on a small plane. Faster and easier.

And there was the joy of being a pillion passenger.

There was a small strap in the middle of the saddle, which perhaps the passenger was supposed to hold on to. But on this model of bike you really had to grab the driver around the waist, to keep your balance. That's what I did. I put my two arms around Seán's waist, and held on tight, as we sped through Dublin and up into the mountains.

My skirt wasn't a problem. There was so much of it that it spread easily over the saddle and covered my legs. In fact, the blouse caused me more difficulty. Even though it was a very fine, sunny afternoon, I felt cold as we drove higher into the foothills and could have done with a jumper, if not a big anorak. Clinging to Seán became more and more necessary.

Somewhere past a pitch-and-putt course called Puck's Castle, we stopped.

In a carpark. There were just two cars in it, though, and it was a mountain carpark, with big evergreen trees embracing it and soft, spicy pine needles carpeting the ground. The air was glaucous – a lovely, delicate greyish-green.

You don't have to hop off a motorbike the second it stops, it's not like a bicycle. There's a stand to keep it steady on the ground. Seán put down the stand and climbed down first. I remained seated, not sure what to do. Truth to tell, I felt stiff and a bit winded from the ride. And I was freezing.

He took my hand and helped me down.

Then he removed the helmet, as if I were a child.

'Are you OK?' he asked. He looked very serious, stern almost, and very gentle at the same time.

I shook my head, ever so slightly.

The smell of the pines mixed with some other smell – the sweet, herby smell of clover. The trees whispered. Other than that, there was absolute silence.

The world was holding its breath.

He put his hand to my cheek and stroked it softly. 'You're cold,' he said. His voice trembled. 'You're cold.'

A bird sang, two notes, somewhere in the forest.

He put his arms around me then and we kissed.

The first time. But we went on and on for ages.

It's easier to learn to kiss than to learn to ride a bicycle, in some ways. But in some ways it's much harder to judge the moment correctly, to seize hold of your confidence, to take the plunge.

And falling in love is not like learning to ride a bicycle. It's more like falling off one.

As time goes on, though, you need to learn to turn into the wind and keep your balance.

That is what we could not do.

The summer was paradise. That's not an exaggeration. The motorbike, the trees in the forest, the salty walks on the beach, mixed together to create heaven on earth. Young love can fuse with nature if it gets a chance – it can become part of the fertile blend. Fish, flesh, fowl commended us all summer long, caught in the sensual music of the birds and the waves and the trees of our own endlessly fascinating story. A country for young men and women it was, especially if they had a means of transport, if they had a motorbike. Up the mountains and to the beaches and all over Dublin we went. We made love in woods and by the sea and on the banks of lakes and rivers – not made love properly, of course, we were far too timid and cautious and puritanical for that. We cuddled and pressed and kissed, for all we were worth, in the midst of nature.

Our examination results were very good when they came through. A further bond. I got an entrance scholarship, and he got a prize for coming first in his year. We felt like a special couple, lucky people, clever people. Obviously, we were made for one another.

Work kept us apart for half the time. We didn't question that limitation much, nor did we appreciate it. Seán would be at the shop door at half past five to collect me on the bike, and we would be together until midnight, or later, when he would leave me home.

When the summer jobs ended and college started, however, we were not constrained by the rigid timetables of jobs. We were not constrained by anything.

That should have been a huge excitement in itself. But it wasn't. That was the first problem. Seán had told me so much about what went on in college that I felt I had been there already. There was a sense of staleness about it, then, where there should have been novelty. And that was not the worst thing. The worst thing was that the most significant thing about the university was that Seán was in it.

My first day, for instance, focused on meeting Seán for lunch. So when I was walking up the avenue, finding my way around the warren of dark corridors, figuring out where Theatre R was, and the library, and greeting schoolfriends I had not seen since June, I was thinking, At half past twelve. Half past twelve. I'll meet him for lunch.

The canteen was thronged with thousands of students. Seán kept greeting people – girls and boys – he knew from last year.

He'd kept his head down in first year, studying obsessively, to earn the high honours he wanted to achieve. But he had got to know people all the same. And now they nodded to him, with a certain deference, because he had come top of the class.

We ate lunch and then Seán suggested we go into town. He needed to get some books.

The suggestion surprised me. It was my first day, I didn't want to leave. And I had a lecture after lunch.

'Go if you want to,' he said. 'But you'll be missing nothing if you don't. He's a terrible lecturer. Just read the text.'

I would have liked to go, anyway. After all, I had only been to two lectures in my life so far, and I did not think they were boring.

But.

'OK,' I said, looking around the canteen and the crowds of young people, talking and laughing. They looked carefree to me, like children playing a game, and I felt set apart, burdened with the heavy weight of my love.

I went into town with Seán, on the bike.

We walked around the bookshops and had coffee in Bewley's.

He told me about lecturers and professors I would have, and about the content of some of the courses. He spoke interestingly, vividly, of these things, as he was vivid and entertaining about everything. But I felt I was missing something. And I was not sharp enough, ruthless enough, to give a name to what that was.

Seán also talked about people in his own class, which was some special sub-group of high-powered students. Camilla and Olwyn and Rebecca – the girls had romantic, posh names, and even the sound of them sent pangs of jealousy pricking at my heart.

'Camilla is the most attractive girl in college,' he said then. This was when we were eating cherry buns. He went on to talk about some lecturer who fancied her, and laughed. 'They're all smitten! They're gas!' he said.

I picked a cherry from the bun, then left the yellow cake on my plate.

*

I neglected about a third of my lectures in the first term, and half in the second and third.

Seán missed much more. By the final term, he wasn't attending anything. Caught in something – a sensual confusion, or some other sort of confusion for which we had no name – he neglected everything. It was as if he had said goodbye to his old life of study and concentration, and jumped off a cliff, bringing me with him.

Instead of studying or attending classes, we sat in the canteen, drinking coffee, or we walked around the campus, finding secret places where we could sit and kiss and press our bodies together. In the cold weather we found secret places indoors, too, even though that was taking a risk.

This was all appalling. But it happened gradually and, anyway, did not seem quite so appalling then. It was not very unusual for students to skip classes and lectures. With this observation, I tried to console myself. There were lots who did that, for no reason at all, and perhaps there still are. I had friends who didn't bother, quite often, going to class. They had no reason for that, no reason as compelling as mine (which was that Seán wanted me to stay with him). Not being an attender was one way of getting through college in those days. What was strange and discomfiting was that I didn't see myself as that type of student. I saw myself as the other kind, who was studious and careful, and who went to everything, and then to the library to work for hours. What were they doing there? Those students who sat for eight hours, reading, and taking notes? I couldn't even imagine what they were up to. That's how far I had gone. I had always loved reading but on the rare occasions when I managed to get to the library the words danced before my eyes.

A strange thing happens to students who don't attend lectures. They lose track of what is going on, at a superficial level and also at a deep level. The problem is not that they miss the content of what the lecturer is saying, which is often not all that important, anyway, at least not in Arts. The problem is more that they lose the thread of the course. They lose the plot.

They lose their balance.

They tumble off the wheel and they get completely lost.

*

We got fed up of the life we were leading, naturally. But it affected us in different ways. Seán got fed up of me, while I clung more and more to him, in ever-increasing desperation. I was afraid if I lost my grip on him, I'd tumble into some even deeper abyss and be totally lost and destroyed. I feared this, although I hated the chaos we were in. (I was in love with him. That was the only thing I was sure of.)

At the end of the year, Seán failed his examinations and I scraped through mine. We struggled on through the summer – he was studying for repeats; I was back working in the bookshop. It rained all the time. I ate chocolate and missed Seán when I was at work. In the evenings and at weekends he was often busy – he had to study hard to cover the entire syllabus in two months, so that he would pass the repeats.

He passed, and we were both back in college in October.

But the relationship was over. During the summer he'd fallen in love with a girl in his class, one of those with the names. Not Camilla, the belle of Belfield. Rebecca. Rebecca hadn't failed her exams, but she'd been in college during the summer, anyway; she had some sort of summer job in the examinations office. (Also, wavy, fair hair, a small pert face, and a motherly demeanour. She wore a pale blue blouse, often, and a knee-length navy skirt, and had big round glasses. She looked like a cute little owl.)

I cut my hair and stopped wearing the flowing, hippy clothes Seán liked. Now I wore jeans and a denim jacket, or a miniskirt and high leather boots. I'd gone on a diet and lost a great deal of weight, so those clothes suited me now. People told me I looked great. Girls often told me they wished they had my figure, and boys, young-looking skinny boys, asked me on dates, which I sometimes accepted, though usually I did not enjoy them, since those boys could not measure up to Seán. Who could? I was very pleased with my new body, however – when I stopped menstruating, I wasn't worried in the slightest. No more mess.

Once, I got a shock. I became blind. I had walked from home to college, about half an hour's walk. When I came into the main hall, I felt my vision begin to fade from my eyes, slowly, like a light dimming. For a quarter of an hour I was in the dark. And then the sight returned, as slowly as it had disappeared, with bright spots and flashes and darts like lightning bolts. A bad headache. I guessed this temporary blindness was related to my dieting in some way, just like the loss of my periods was. But I told nobody about it. I thought they wouldn't believe me, anyway, and say it was my imagination. Nobody knew about anorexia in those days in Dublin. In that field I was a pioneer.

I didn't do well in my second-year examinations, either, even though I had attended everything. You can't really do well in exams if you're starving to death. I had realised that, after an academic year on my self-imposed fast, but the low marks I was getting on the weighing scales meant more to me than high marks on an examination transcript. One figure sank in tandem with the other. I was lucky to pass, just as I was lucky to be alive and healthy, to all intents and purposes. My brain and my body seemed to have a great capacity for survival. My heart was the trouble-spot. It was unreasonable and pathetic, but even after almost a whole year, I was still pining. I hardly knew why then, and I do not now. That sort of heartbreak is difficult to understand. If you're not enduring it, it seems ridiculous. It is ridiculous. But it's horrible, and real, and can be fatal.

When summer came around once more, I attempted to find a cure for love in the time-honoured way: foreign travel. A change of scene might obliterate the memory, patch up my broken heart. Adventure, excitement, something more exotic than the bookshop was prescribed, by myself, as the most likely panacea for my woe.

The miracle cure was to be this: a job in a hotel on the Isle of Wight. I was to be a still-room waitress. I didn't know what that was, but it sounded all right. Stillness was something I was fond of, and there is a touch of glamour to the word 'waitress'. The Isle of Wight, obviously, had a nice summery ring to it. I had always been a sucker for Isles. And working in a hotel would force me to be sociable, bring me out of myself (which was where I'd spent nearly the whole year, deep inside that spot at the back of my eyes where I hid from the dangerous world outside). I'd meet people – the people who took their holidays in the Green Gables Boarding House in Sandown.

Finally, one definite advantage the Isle of Wight had over Dublin was that Seán and Rebecca were most unlikely to be there. Although I spent my days and nights longing to be with Seán, the very worst moments had been those when I had actually seen him, walking around arm in arm with Rebecca, or zipping through the campus on his motorbike, with her stuck to him like a human rucksack. In college I had developed elaborate ruses for avoiding encounters with them, hiding out in the ladies' reading room, for instance, where he wasn't allowed and where Rebecca would never come, either, since she was always glued to Seán. I had spent most of the year finding ways to make myself invisible, but somehow hoping that that would blot him out, too. But it hadn't. I am sure he didn't enjoy seeing me, but he didn't seem to make serious efforts to avoid that eventuality. He had Rebecca, after all, to cheer him up if the sight of the abandoned waif pricked his conscience.

I headed off to the Isle of Wight with Orla. Neither of us had ever been out of Ireland before and were delighted to be getting away from the place. The sound of the ship's siren when the anchor was lifted was a blast of some heavenly trumpet to my ears. The sound reverberated through me; it was a siren call heralding freedom, adventure, mysterious and unimaginable delights.

The Holyhead ferry was full of students from Dublin, going over to England, like us, for summer jobs – on building sites, in hotels and shops. A good few of them were going to pick fruit in Norfolk. 'For the jam factories,' as somebody explained, with some impatience, when I asked. 'That's where the money is. Doesn't every fool know that?'

Nobody else was going to the Isle of Wight.

It was a bright evening, post-exam-time, midsummer. The ferry bobbed out of the harbour, with seagulls screaming in great excitement around the stern. Up on deck I stayed, watching Ireland recede, delighted with the view of the coastline as we moved away across that mythical water, the Irish Sea. How different Dún Laoghaire looked from out here! Its stacked rooftops, its steeples rising into the peachy evening sky, the dusky purple hills behind all that, gave it a fairytale appearance that it didn't have at all when you were in it. It seemed that the further away you got from Ireland, the more beautiful it became.

When it finally disappeared, I sighed with joy and went below deck, my sister with me.

The crossing to Wales lasts three and a half hours. You could hire a berth but it's not worth it, so we sat up in the plastic Pullman seats in a big lounge. A musician was playing folk songs in the adjoining pub, to the great pleasure of the hundreds of young people on board. He was a star at the time, and he was a good musician. There was plenty of singing, and drinking of beer, and a certain amount of vomiting over the gunwale or simply straight onto the deck.

We didn't drink alcohol then, and we weren't 'into' music (well, I wasn't into anything much), so we didn't join them. Just sat in our big chairs, reading. (I had a Margaret Drabble novel; I suppose you could say I was into her.) According to a well-considered plan, at eleven, halfway through the voyage, we treated ourselves to a snack. There was a canteen place at the end of the lounge, and I went there to get the tea and sandwiches. (When it came to the crunch, I just got one sandwich, for my sister. I could not bring myself to eat one. I didn't feel hungry. I never did.)

In the queue at the counter I met a girl who had been in my tutorial in first year. Iseult. I hadn't known her well – I knew no one well in first year because I was so busy with Seán.

'Hi!' She was a cheery girl with an electric mop of black hair, wiry glasses. A wide, generous smile. She looked like an American but she was from Clonskeagh or Stillorgan or somewhere like that.

She was going to Chester to work in an inn there, as a barmaid. She would make a terrific barmaid.

'Hey,' she said, after we had exchanged information about our summer jobs. 'That was terrible, what happened to Seán Smyth.'

I turned to jelly. Whenever I heard his name, this happened to me – a mountain of panic and shame avalanched on top of me.

'What?' I could hardly squeeze the word out.

'Don't you know?' Concern darkened her lively face. 'You used to be friendly with him, I thought.'

Friendly.

'Well, I haven't seen him for a while,' I said. Even saying the pronoun 'him' was a struggle.

'OK.' She looked at me carefully.

Could it be that she did not know about me and Seán? Could it be that there were people in the world who did not know the whole sorry, shameful story?

'He was in an accident,' she said. 'Just a few days ago. It was in the paper.'

I must have reacted strongly because she put her hand on my elbow and guided me to a seat.

'Sorry,' she said. She held my hand. Hers was very hot and mine was very cold. 'I gave you a shock. I'm sorry, I thought everyone knew.' She paused again. Then, quietly, she told me he was dead. He came off his motorbike. 'Remember, he used to go everywhere on a Honda?'

I remembered.

My strength was beginning to return to me – the way my sight had returned that time I lost it last term, or the way the blood goes back to your head after you faint. Your balance is restored.

'I hadn't heard,' I said. I could hear that my voice was steadier and louder.

The holiday in England changed me again, body and soul. I stopped being anorexic. The work as a still-room waitress, which means washing up, combined with making beds and chambermaiding, was so hard that you couldn't do it on the tiny rations I was accustomed to. I had to eat. And I got to like the food; the chef, who owned the hotel, was very good, and the menu of a seaside boarding house seemed tasty enough to me. Roast beef on Sunday, steak-and-kidney pie on Monday. Curried eggs on Friday – that was my favourite. Enormous salads with ham and grated cheddar cheese and beetroot, Everests of potato salad. I learned how to drink, too – lager and lime in pubs, and strawberry wine at barn dances. At one of those dances I met a chap from Liverpool, who looked like Ringo, with a long fringe of black hair, a black polo neck, jeans. Steve. He liked football and *Top of the Pops* and worked as a lifeguard on the beach at Sandown. And he had a car – a red sports car. In the evenings after work he would drive me around the island – to Cowes, Ventnor, Shanklin Chine. To the Downs. How I loved that name, the Downs! So summery, so English, so Isle of Wight!

I couldn't love Steve, though, and when we kissed in the car, I felt nothing much, but I went along with it. I knew he liked me more than I liked him, and I felt sorry for him because of that. But I assumed that is how it would be for me from now on. I wasn't all that sorry.

(That wasn't true, as it turned out. But it was never like the Seán summer again.)

Seán didn't break it off with me in the normal way. There is a normal way, even if it's not easy. Have a serious, sad talk. Write a note. Even make a phone call. But he didn't do any of these things. He never actually told me he had another girlfriend. I found out about Rebecca when I saw her on the back of his bike on the first day of my second year in college. The writing had been on the wall for months and I hadn't read it, but when I saw her, with his helmet on her long, fair hair, glued to him like a limpet, I knew I had lost him forever. I didn't need the confirmation I got all too soon of seeing them arm in arm, walking down the main concourse of Belfield.

But I wanted to hear him say something. I wanted to hear his voice.

On the second day of term I saw him – and Rebecca – eating lunch in the canteen. (I was still eating lunches then myself.) So, with my legs trembling, everything trembling, I approached him.

'Hi, can I talk to you?' I glanced at the girl and she looked at me distastefully, as if I were milk that had turned sour.

'No,' he said bluntly, and attended to his chips and burger.

I didn't say another word. I walked out of the crowded canteen. I ran away.

In my memory I replayed this scene very often during the year after he had left me. I relived the horror of it, and the embarrassment, both of which were acute. It was not, though, until about thirty years later that I rewrote my script. I realised then, suddenly, that I could have handled it in a different way. I could have made a scene. I could have shamed him, there, in front of Rebecca, in front of the whole college. 'What is the meaning of this?' I could have roared. (Or I could have asked in a calm, deadly voice – there was more than one version of the episode.) 'You were kissing me in the mountains last week. Why haven't you contacted me since then?'

I wouldn't have got him back. But I could have made plenty of trouble for him. I could have made trouble for Rebecca and there might have been some satisfaction for me in that, some salvation of pride, some pleasure in revenge.

But it didn't occur to me that I could fight back, or ask for anything, even a word. The only thing I wanted to do was disappear, try to become invisible, and fade off the face of the earth.

When I got back to Dublin, I was tanned and filled out. Everyone said I looked wonderful, although I could read behind their eyes and see that some of them were thinking, My, hasn't she put on weight. (I hadn't put on much. A stone. I didn't care. I liked my brown skin and my short hair and my tanned legs, and I'd bought lots of sassy, dolly bird clothes in London on the way home, to show myself off.)

I asked my father to teach me to drive. He said yes, and on Sundays he brought me to the carpark in college – a place unofficially designated as a weekend driving school by the residents of the local suburbs – and gave me lessons in the car he had then – an Anglia, with a strange inverted back window, fourteen years old and rusting.

There was no question of putting me on his insurance policy. He would never have dreamt of sharing his car with anyone; he would as soon have shared his underpants or toothbrush. He didn't particularly relish me taking the wheel for the supervised lessons, either, but that sacrifice he was willing to make, because he believed that everyone should have their own means of locomotion (he believed in private transport more than he believed in education, or perhaps in anything).

By Christmas I could drive from college to home and back again (uninsured, too). Then my mother, who was thrilled that I ate food again and had stopped moping about Seán – we never mentioned his death – had a bright idea. She went to a garage in town – it was over on the north side, a big Ford dealer – and bought a Cortina, huge and shiny, silver blue. It was not brand new, it had been a showroom model, but it was the newest and best car we'd ever had. She didn't tell my father about it until she'd paid for it. Then he had to go over there on the bus and drive it home; she didn't drive herself.

The Cortina was for him – and her, he continued to drive her everywhere. (It was fine, it seemed, not to drive if you had a husband to chauffeur you around, but my father was preparing me for a single life, just in case.) I got the ancient Anglia as my Christmas present.

Hardly any students had their own cars then, especially if they were girls.

During second year, one of the things I did to try to get over Seán was join the drama society. I auditioned and got a part in a production of *Medea*. It wasn't a real part – it was in the Chorus. I was so preoccupied with my problems that I hardly understood what was going on in the play, and I mimed many of the lines I was supposed to chant, with a large choir of women. (I think everyone who auditioned was given a part in the Chorus, so it didn't matter that I wasn't pulling my weight.) Medea was played by a girl with an aquiline nose and black frizzy hair, and she was made up to look like a real witch. I had no sympathy with her, as she stood centre stage, ranting and screaming her head off in a stream of invective that I couldn't take in. If I'd listened more carefully, I might have gained something from the play, catharsis even, but I was too hungry to focus on it.

The only scene that impressed me was the most horrible scene in all of drama – where Medea sends the gift of the poisoned dress and crown to Creon's daughter, using her own two children as go-betweens, and Creon's daughter tries them on, prinking before the mirror, and then burns to death in agony. With her, I sympathised – who could not? I could feel the strange poisonous burning on my own skin.

We had no children in our production. We were all students – we had no access to children, or interest in having anything to do with them. (You would think, to hear us discuss the problem of the children, that we hardly knew what a child was.) The director of the play asked me to step out from the Chorus and carry the gift from Medea to Creon's daughter – they had someone playing her part, behind a muslin curtain. I was happy to do something that was so effortless. I glided out, like a wraith, and took the dress and crown from the black-haired Medea, and walked to the curtain where Creon's daughter waited, also thin as a wraith in a white nightdress. She had fair hair, softly curly, and was as dainty and translucent as a glass doll. (This scene is supposed to happen offstage. But our director, like many others, couldn't resist dramatising it.)

Creon's daughter has no name in the play, and no speaking part. But some sources say that she was called Glauce. That sounds ugly, but it has a nice meaning. Owl. The noun 'glaucoma', a disease of the eye, derives from it, I think, as does the adjective glaucous, which I always thought meant 'green', but means 'greyish-green', the colour of army tanks, and certain lichens.

The Blind

Father Braygy of the Blind was one of those men whose charm makes them look more handsome than they really are. Once a year he would come, *tap tap tap*, on the thick oak door of our classroom, and when the teacher said, 'Come in', he would hop into the room and skip along the aisle between the ancient oak desks, his face collapsing in rings of laughter. And we would all start laughing, too. He laughed so much that you didn't notice that his round green eyes bulged and that his hair was like slimy riverweed, slicked over his shiny head.

Our teacher, Mrs Doyle, who had worn the same blue blouse with a droopy bow every day for seven years, melted quickly under the smiles, the irresistible warmth, of Father Braygy. Although his skin looked like cold rubber, affection and enthusiasm poured out of him like cocoa and the minute he hopped through the door the air in our room changed; happiness, always bubbling just below the surface of the imprisoning schoolday, leapt out to meet him. I thought of the fountain in the Green, the water squirting out of the funny sort of pine cone thing in the middle, shooting up in the air and sparkling in the sunshine. He made our hearts sparkle like that, just by coming in and talking.

We were extraordinary girls! So clever and good and so neat. And so good-looking. Do you know what, he'd never seen a classful of such beautiful girls! Mrs Doyle was a marvellous teacher, exceptional, and he knew what he was talking about because he visited all the schools in Ballanar. And we'd collected so much money that nobody could believe it. Our school was the all-Ireland champ of Ballanar when it came to collecting money.

For St Lucia's School for the Blind, he meant. That's really why Father Braygy visited us, to get us to take flag boxes and collect money for the school he taught in.

'Last year, do you know how much money we collected, girls?' His green eyes changed colour and glowed blue as the sea at the very thought of it.

'No, Father,' we chorused.

'Go on. Take a guess. How much do you think? All the schools in the city of Ballanar?'

We looked at Mrs Doyle for help. How many schools were there in Ballanar? We hadn't a clue; it wasn't a thing we'd ever thought about. We had no idea how many flag boxes Father Braygy distributed. Mrs Doyle did not meet the sea of eager eyes that begged her for help. She hadn't a clue, either, but she would never admit ignorance in front of a class, or a priest.

'You'll never believe it. But we collected more than five thousand pounds, girls. That's what you and all the other boys and girls did for St Lucia's last year.'

He was silent for a second to let the enormity of the communication sink in. Five thousand pounds. My friend, Margaretta, and I, let out a big, loud gasp to let him know we were impressed, even though we didn't know the difference between five thousand pounds and five hundred, or five million.

'And the boys in St Lucia's are so grateful for that money. They pray for you every day, because you've done so much for them. The money means that our building fund is getting so big that soon we'll be able to build a new wing with lovely new classrooms and a swimming pool.'

Now our eyes glowed, too. Five thousand pounds meant nothing to us but a swimming pool did. There were no swimming pools in Ballanar that I was allowed use. Mountpleasant Baths were too rough and the Blue Pool at Blackrock too cold and far away. Those blind boys would get a pool in their own school! It would almost be worth it, being blind.

If we could collect even more money in the boxes this year, the day of the swimming pool would draw closer. For them.

And for us who were not blind there was another incentive.

The party.

'When the collection is done, we'll have our big, big party. If you collect more than two pounds, you'll get your own personal invitation.'

Two pounds. Four hundred and eighty pennies. Margaretta and I looked at each other and shook our heads.

'Girls, this is the best party in Ireland. We have loads of cakes and biscuits and sweets and lemonade, and singing and games and fun. Everyone who comes to the party says they have the time of their life. I'll write a letter to Mrs Doyle and tell her all about it after the flag day, and tell you how to get there.'

The collection boxes arrived at the school ten days before the Easter holidays. They were about the size of a tin of beans, covered with yellow paper. 'St Lucia's School for the Blind' was printed on them in thick black letters around the middle, and there was a little black man, a blind person, underneath. With the boxes came cartons of the small, yellow, paper flags and packets of pins. We prepared for the collecting by sticking a pin into each little flag. Then these were pinned around the rim of the box in a frill. At first it was fun to stick a pin in the little stiff flags, but after about forty of them, it got boring, and your fingers were pricked and sore. However, I'd have to get rid of about four hundred flags to be in with a chance, so I went on sticking pins in flags for hours and hours.

Saturday, the Saturday before Palm Sunday, was a chilly day, but I was up before anyone in my house, getting ready to set off into town. Margaretta was going to go collecting, too, and we had arranged to meet outside Pim's at noon. My mother said, 'Wrap up well now or you'll get your death a' cold', and gave me fourpence for the bus fare to and from town. But as soon as I turned the corner of our road, I put the pennies in my flag box to make it rattle, and walked down town.

There was nobody about on the streets near my home. All stuffed up in their beds, the lazy bones, sleeping it out. But in the English Market there were plenty of early birds scrutinising the stalls for the best bargains in the way of fruit and vegetables. I could, I should, rattle my box at them and start collecting now. But it wasn't as easy as I'd thought to beg for money, even for a good cause like the Blind.

I went and stood outside Driscoll's, the poultry shop; dead chickens, partly feathered, were hung by the feet from hooks outside the shop, their white skin loose and goose-pimpled, their long, scrawny necks swinging, their beady eyes horrified. There was a long queue of women buying their chickens for Sunday dinner, and the week's supply of eggs.

I shut my eyes. I said: do it.

Then I rattled my box under the nose of the next woman who came out of the shop, the flabby, cherry red comb of a bird's head dangling over the edge of her straw basket.

'Please help the Blind,' I sang, in a mantra, like the woman on the stalls. 'Help St Lucy's School for the Blind.'

It was easier to say 'St Lucy's' than 'St Lucia's' when you were chanting – I found that out just as I was saying it.

Rattle rattle rattle went a few pennies in the bottom of the box.

'Oh thank you,' I said, and jabbed the flag into the brown lapel of her coat.

'You're welcome, love,' she said.

After that it was easy.

A lot of women just looked away and hurried on with their bags of shopping. But a few stopped, looked worried, rooted in their bags and found a penny. One said:

'Aren't you the good girl?'

Some said:

'I gave already.'

Another said:

'Mother of God, youse are all over the place.'

At about half past eleven I left my post outside the poultry shop and walked down to Donegall Street. It was cold and it would have been nice to have a cup of tea or something to eat, but I had no money to buy anything. I met several other children with collection boxes as I made my way down past

Tesky's biscuit factory, where the smell of baking was so hot and thick you could almost believe you were eating it, but not quite, because it was a smell that made you hungrier than ever.

'I'm starving,' I said to Margaretta, who came, a bit late, as was her style, to meet me outside Pim's.

She rattled my box, then shook her head.

'You didn't get much!'

I thought I'd got quite a lot, so I pouted, but she didn't pay any attention to me.

'Women are stingy', is what she said. 'We need to get some men.'

We looked up and down the street. Women everywhere. Young and old, in shabby, belted gabardines, lugging big brown shopping bags, or in smart pastel woollen coats, tiny pill box hats perched on glossy curls, swinging the smart cardboard bags with the names of the fashion shops on them. Shaw's. Switzer's. Brown Thomas.

No men.

Where are they? The men?

At work.

Most people still worked then, on Saturdays. Most men. That's what we had forgotten.

'Tomorrow will be good,' she said. 'There'll be men to get after Mass tomorrow.' She clamped her lips together and stared hard at the collection box. 'You know what I'm going to do? Put on my dancing costume. When we had the flag day for our dancing school, I got loads of money.'

I was dubious. I, too, had collected for my dancing school, the Lily O'Brien School of Irish Dancing, and it was true that the costumes attracted attention. An American tourist had even taken my picture, on the corner of North Mall, and given me half-a-crown.

'But we're not collecting for the dancing, we're collecting for the Blind.'

Margaretta screwed up her eyes again and thought hard. 'We've got to do something.'

She rattled her box vehemently and from the loud, clear rattle you could tell it was still nearly empty.

'Empty vessels make most noise!' she said, and we started to giggle, because that was something Mrs Doyle said at least three times a day, before she slapped us for talking.

Next morning, instead of putting on my ordinary Sunday outfit, which was my Confirmation suit from last year – a pale blue tweed suit, white straw hat – I dressed in my dancing costume.

'What in the name of God are you doing in that rig-out?' my mother asked.

'I'll sell more flags for the Blind in this. People will see me.'

'They'll see you all right!' she said, and rolled her eyes up to heaven.

But she let me wear it, because she could see there would be a sulk if she didn't.

My dancing costume was not all that nice. In Lily O' Brien's, boys and girls wore more or less the same outfit: a saffron kilt, a black jacket, and a green shawl slung down the back, not like any real shawl or scarf – it was just to get something green into the outfit, green, white and gold, the colours of the Irish flag. The only lovely thing was the white blouse, starched and nicely stiff, with a wide Peter Pan collar and tiny black buttons down the front. It fitted snugly to the body. (The boys wore an ordinary white shirt.) And you could pull up the kilt to make it short, like a miniskirt, which is what I did, revealing my fat, white knees. We had no black tights – we wore white knee socks, and our dancing shoes, the soft poms for the reels and the patent, hard-soled sailor shoes with the shining silver buckle for the hornpipe. I put on my hornpipe shoes and grabbed my box and bag of flags – I had three hundred left – and went off to the chapel.

Clip clip, I went. *Clip clop*. I pretended to be a horse, and tried to beat out a pattern as I clopped along the stone pavement.

I met Margaretta outside her house on Malone Avenue.

She went to the Rory Murphy School of Irish Dancing and her costume was gorgeous. It was a white báinín dress, fitted to the waist and with a nice swirl to the skirt. It was heavily embroidered with Celtic spirals, red and pink and green, and was much closer to the dresses you see nowadays, the cartoon Celtic dresses in fluorescent colours, with the wigs of red ringlets. Margaretta even wore black tights, and her hornpipe shoes were neat and girlish, with a simple black strap, not like something from *The Pirates of Penzance*. Of course, she didn't have a wig – nobody had then – but her own long, black hair was curly and nearly as nice as one of those wigs.

In other words, she looked stunning. She looked *Riverdance*. I didn't know either of those words but I felt them. I was like something made of tin that you'd get in a Christmas stocking and could wind up and send waddling across the floor, to crash into the leg of the chair. And she was a Barbie doll in a Mystical Mythical Celt costume, as graceful as a ballerina.

'Good!' she said, approving of my outfit. 'And now for the finishing touch!'

From behind a hedge in her front garden she took a bamboo stick, which she said was used to support sweet peas. (I knew there was another use for those bamboo canes: you could use them to cane children on their hands, or even on the bare bum. I wondered if Margaretta's mother or father did that to her. She would never have admitted it; no self-respecting child would.)

Margaretta opened her Confirmation handbag – on outings we always carried our handbags, which were identical, made of shiny white plastic, with big fake gold clasps. We loved them. She pulled out a pair of sunglasses. Put them on.

'See! I'm blind!' she said, tapping the bamboo stick on the path.

'Oh Margaretta!'

Could she be serious? The stick wasn't even white. It looked like a stick that had supported sweet peas in a garden. And her sunglasses were silly-looking toy glasses. No grown-ups wore sunglasses then, and the children's ones were made of soft plastic that wouldn't hook behind your ears and were always falling off. Margaretta's were pink, the colour of bubble gum.

'You're leading me,' she said. 'That's all you have to do. You don't have to be blind.'

'What am I supposed to say? Help my poor blind friend?'

'Say nothing. If anyone asks, "Is she blind?" just nod your big head.'

I nodded my big head and said nothing.

We took the bus across the river to Shandon on the other side of the city where nobody would know us. Just outside the chapel gate we stood, next to the newspaper stand. There were two other people there with flag boxes, two boys in grey shorts and blazers. They looked at us in amusement.

'Why is she wearing sunglasses?' one of them asked, pointing his finger at Margaretta.

I nodded and said nothing.

They waited expectantly and after I while I managed to stutter, 'She's blind.'

'Janey Mack!'

'Why are yez wearing dancing costumes?' the other one asked.

'Why shouldn't we?' said Margaretta, tossing her head so that the sunglasses wobbled and nearly fell off. 'It's a free country.'

They were shocked and so was I. We didn't expect a blind person to talk.

'Can you dance?' the first boy asked Margaretta. He had blond curly hair and nice shiny brown shoes, Clarks.

'Of course I can.'

'How do you learn the steps?' He was genuinely curious.

Margaretta paused for a few seconds.

'There are ways and means', was what she came up with. It wasn't a great answer, but it satisfied them. They moved to the other gatepost to start their collecting.

At about eleven the ten o'clock Mass – the endless Mass of Palm Sunday – was over and the congregation streamed out of the chapel and through the gate. We started to rattle our boxes under their noses, concentrating on the men. 'Help the Blind, help the Blind,' we chanted. The coins poured in, a silver stream.

Only two people asked if Margaretta was blind, and I nodded.

When someone dared to ask Margaretta directly, though, she adjusted her pink glasses, which were sliding down her nose, and said, 'Partially sighted.'

One woman, who had a dead fox hanging around her neck, asked, 'How did it happen, love?'

Again Margaretta had to pause and think.

'The blindness,' I whispered.

Why hadn't we thought of all this beforehand?

'I had an accident when I was four,' she said. Her lips were

257

pressed together so tightly that there was hardly any mouth at all. 'I stepped on a garden rake and it blinded me in both eyes.'

'Glory be to God,' said the old woman, opening her black handbag. 'I do always think that's the worst kind of blindness, because you know what you're missing.'

She pulled a big brown purse out of her bag.

'And tell me, love, do you remember anything?'

'What?'

Margaretta played for time.

'From the time before you were blinded. When you could see. Colours?'

'I remember a lot.'

She paused.

'My dolls.'

She paused again and added slowly, 'I remember my mammy's face.'

'Ah!' said the woman, digging in her purse and pulling out a shillingy bit. She looked at the shilling, put it back in her purse, and put a yellow thrupenny bit in the box instead.

Margaretta remembered to let her take the flag off the box herself, although sometimes she forgot this and pinned a flag on the lapel of a man's coat, very expertly – for a partially sighted person – finding exactly the right spot. Luckily the men never noticed, since they were busy staring at her thick dark hair, and her legs in their black stockings.

By half past twelve our boxes were heavy. Mine made a dull thud when I rattled it, and Margaretta's was completely silent. Because it was stuffed full of money.

When the time came, we got invitations to the party.

It was held on the second last Friday in June, just a week to the summer holidays. Father Braygy sent a letter to Mrs Doyle, with the names of the girls who had merited an invitation, and ten cloakroom tickets. Ten of us had made it. We lived in different places and planned to meet at the party, at St Lucia's for the Blind, which was far away, up on Hollywood Heights.

But Margaretta and I went out there together, taking the

number 7 bus from town. We dressed in our newest clothes. Mine were tartan slacks with little bands under the feet to hold them down – there must have been some fear that girls' slacks would ride up the legs, unlike men's or boys'. With these, I wore a white blouse and a nice red cardigan. Margaretta had a denim skirt – the very latest thing. With it, she had a stripy T-shirt with long sleeves, blue and white, which meant she didn't have to wear a jumper or a cardigan. We both carried our Confirmation handbags, of course. Margaretta had hidden her latest treasure, a charm bracelet that her father had given her for her eleventh birthday, in her bag. She wasn't allowed to wear it outside the house because it was, she said, made of solid gold. But on the bus she pulled it out and fastened it carefully onto her wrist. There were only two charms on it: a tiny doll and a tiny beach ball. The doll was plain gold and the ball was gold with red stripes.

'I'm just starting to collect them,' she explained. 'I'll have dozens by the time I'm getting married. They bring you luck.'

I spent ages examining the bracelet, and the charms, which seemed to be the most desirable things on earth at that moment. The little beach ball was especially lovely, more intricate than the doll, the stripes made of some hard red stuff like marble – enamel probably. Collecting charms – that's what I wanted to do, more than anything, and somehow I knew that each charm would transform me, bringing me luck, whatever that was, and something else I couldn't put my finger on, something without a name that I longed for.

We got off the bus in Hollywood Heights village and walked up the hill. But we had difficulty in finding the School for the Blind. It was in a big manor house in grounds behind a high stone wall, Mrs Doyle had read from Father Braygy's letter, but Hollywood Heights was all manor houses behind high stone walls, miles and miles of them, snaking up the hill like the ramparts of some medieval fortress. We walked on and on, trying to find the right wall, the right gate. The party was on from four o'clock but it was almost six when we finally found the brass plaque that told us St Lucia's School for the Blind lay behind that particular wall.

I had had a vision of the party as I had a vision of everything in those days. Father Braygy would be in the hall of the school, standing under a big oil portrait, or a stuffed stag's head, to greet us and to congratulate us on doing so well in the collection. He would introduce us to other people and point us out as exemplary collectors – we would get some sort of recognition, a certificate, maybe a silver medal. Then we would go into a long, elegant dining hall, sit at tables covered with white cloths and set with china. Plates of cream slices, chocolate éclairs, triangular sandwiches, egg and cress and ham and cheese and beef, would be there, fruit cake, apple tart. Jugs of lemonade and orange juice. Afterwards, there would be a funfair in the grounds – swings and merry-go-rounds, a big wheel. In my vision fairylights dangled from the summer trees, and the grounds of the school smelt of jasmine, roses, sweet peas – anything that smelled good.

This was the best party in Ireland.

Nobody had ever had a better time.

Behind the grey wall there was no merry-go-round or big wheel, not even a swing, in sight. But there was a big tent, a marquee – marquees are always promising. Inside it, long trestle tables stood like biers – not covered with even a paper cloth. Lots of empty paper plates and cups, rubbish scattered on the table and the ground. A few children were raking over what was left on the table, but most people had gone home. There was no sign of Father Braygy.

Margaretta sighed, 'We musta missed it.'

I examined a piece of barm brack, from which someone had taken a bite, and considered eating it.

You could tell it hadn't been much of a party. The debris told its own story. Brack, packets of Tayto, red lemonade.

We found an unopened packet of crisps and two fig rolls that hadn't been bitten and didn't look as if anyone had licked them, and split them between us. Then we left and had a look around the grounds, partly out of curiosity and partly in the hopes of seeing someone we knew. By which we meant Father Braygy.

In a brick wall near the tent was a small gate on which there was a sign: 'Private. Keep Out'.

It opened when Margaretta pushed it and we went through.

Inside was another garden. Long green lawns, dotted with circular beds of roses, pink, yellow, red, and rectangular beds of lavender. Copses of trees, their leaves the light, shining green of

June, with woodland paths winding sweetly under them, like paths in a storybook. Carpets of bluebells.

'We should leave,' I said.

This garden was so beautiful that children would obviously be barred from it. It must have been a special garden for teachers, or priests.

But we were tired and dreamy after our exertions, and enchanted by the garden, too lazy to make a decision and go back. The sun was still high in the June sky and we kept walking on and on, through paths that wound this way and that, through dappled mazes of light and leaves, perfumed flowers and rippling purple shadows.

In a clearing a small fountain spouted from the willies of five fat cupids and splashed dancing sprays of water into a circular pond. Sitting on its crumbling old walls, we bathed our hands in the green water. Musically, the drops splashed into the pond; roses and lavender perfumed the air and behind the distant lilac mountains the sun shone still warm and summery, caressing our skin like the breath of calves or some soft sweet animal.

In and out goes Dusty Bluebells
In and out goes Dusty Bluebells.

I started to sing a rhyme we used to sing when we were four or five and playing on the street. Margaretta sang along, too; she had a nice soprano voice. The dusty words floated into the warm evening air and over the bluebell patch and the green copses.

In and out goes Dusty Bluebells,
Who will be my Master?

Then Margaretta yelped. Yelped violently, as if she'd been stung by a bee or bitten by an animal.

I was cross, startled out of my dreamy singing.

Her bracelet. The charm bracelet with the doll and the golden ball had disappeared.

'Did you drop it in the pond?'

She might have. Or maybe she dropped it on the path, or on the grass, or into the bluebells. Or on the floor of the tent. Or on the bus – though she was pretty sure she'd had it when she came to St Lucia's School for the Blind.

I reached as far as I could into the pond. It looked shallow but the water was almost opaque and I couldn't reach the bottom. Slimy green weeds rubbed against my arm, disgustingly, and I wondered if there were fish in the murky water, or eels, that would nibble my fingers to the bone. Margaretta tried, too, leaning over so that her skirt rose right up and you could see her frilly pants sticking up in the summer air like the tail of a fat, white turkey.

'Hello girls!'

Father Braygy.

We jumped down from the edge of the pond, guiltily, Margaretta smoothing down her skirt.

'Is something the matter?'

His green eyes popped. He's like a frog, I thought, but it didn't bother me. I knew that now everything would be all right.

'Margaretta lost her charm bracelet.'

Margaretta gave me a puck in the ribs.

'Oh, that's a terrible state of affairs!' he said, but he was laughing, as always. 'Where did she lose it? Sure, I suppose if you knew the answer, it wouldn't be lost, says you?'

He laughed louder and we did, too, to keep him company.

'It might be in the pond.' I jerked my head towards the fountain.

'Oh well then …'

He rolled up his sleeve, dipped his arm into the green water and fiddled around. His arm, it was surprising to see, was an ordinary man's arm, strong, with a thick coat of black hair, like my own father's arm.

'Would this be it?'

Aloft, the golden bracelet glittered in the sun.

His hand was not like my father's, which was thick and broad as a bear's paw. This was a soft white hand.

'Ah!' Margaretta was delighted. She reached for the bracelet.

He snatched it away and put it behind his back, chuckling.

'Not so quick!' he said. 'Not so quick!'

We smiled politely. Another not really funny joke.

'I'll give it to you if you tell me all about the party!'

We looked at one another and shrugged. He beckoned and

we had to follow him along the dappled pathway through the beds of roses and purple lavender. Nimble as always, he moved easily and quickly with a hop and a skip. Into the greeny woods we went. Bluebells spread underfoot, dark blue, purple now, as the sun reddened and prepared to sink behind the mountains.

A park bench appeared, under a spreading oak tree. An ordinary green bench under an ordinary green tree.

'Sit yourselves down beside me now and tell me everything.'

I sat beside him. So did Margaretta. What was going to happen now?

This:

He picked her up as if she were a doll and sat her on his lap.

I shook my head but Margaretta did not respond. She sat on his lap as if it were the most normal place in the world to be.

'Look what I have here!'

Laughter.

Two big sixpenny bars of Cadbury's Dairy Milk, in the pocket of his soutane. He handed a bar to each of us, and I peeled off the purple paper and the golden foil, and broke off two squares. The chocolate was beastly soft from being so close to his skin but beggars can't be choosers. As soon as it melted honey gentle chocolaty on my tongue I realised I was starving.

We were supposed to tell him about the party (though how could we do that, since we'd missed it?), but actually we didn't have to, because, as we sat and ate the chocolate, me on the bench and Margaretta on his knee, Father Braygy started to talk himself, as he always did. *Yap yap yap*, he went, just as in the classroom. *Yap yap yap*, and nobody else gets to say a word and doesn't want to because it's the cheerful priest that's talking, so who'd want to listen to a little girl? The pools of light grew paler and paler in the greenwood and the fragrant air cooled and the songbirds ceased their singing and Father Braygy yapped on and on and I sang under my breath:

> *Clap a clap a clap trap*
> *On her shoulder*
> *Clap a clap a clap trap*
> *On her shoulder*
> *Clap a clap a clap trap*
> *On her shoulder*
> *He will be her Master.*

The blue shadows shivered around us like ghosts and we ate the chocolate, and we got more chocolate, oh he had a lot of chocolate in that deep, dark soutane pocket, and he kept talking, for a long time.

I was getting impatient. But at last he said 'Ah!', as if he had just remembered that we were with him. 'Here!' He handed Margaretta her bracelet. She shoved it into her white Confirmation bag. Snapped it shut with the golden clasp.

As the bus wound down the hill towards home, swaying on the narrow road in the dying light of evening, I asked her if she minded sitting on the priest's lap.

She tossed her head and said it was a free country.

'I got my bracelet back, didn't I? If I'd lost it, my father would've murdered me.'

In an office in Dublin where I worked years later there was a switchboard operator who was sight impaired. His official title, the name of his grade, was 'Blind Telephonist' and that is what we called him. I was walking down the street with him one evening, towards his bus stop. It was the Friday of the June bank holiday. I was working in an office, though I had hoped to travel the world and do exciting things, and I still hoped that, and believed that my job (which was permanent and pensionable and interesting enough and well paid) was temporary, that soon I would be embarking on my real life of adventure and exploration. I was twenty-five.

He was a past pupil of St Lucia's. The blind telephonist was. This he told me between Leinster House and Nassau Street.

'Oh, yes.' It came back to me in a rush. 'Did you know Father Braygy?'

'Yes.'

'He used to come to our school.'

I told him briefly about the flag days. We were standing at the traffic lights at the corner. It was five o'clock and the traffic was heavy, the air smoky with fumes. But it was sunny and the city had that fizzy, light-hearted mood it has at the beginning of a long summer weekend.

The blind man was silent for a while and then he said, 'He was a lovely man.'

He fixed me with his blank look.

'A heart of gold.'

The lights changed and I helped him across to the other side, where his bus stop was, outside the dark green railings of Trinity College.

SHORTLISTED FOR THE ORANGE PRIZE FOR FICTION

the
dancers,
dancing

éilís ní dhuibhne

EXCLUSIVE BOOKENDS SECTION WITH A NEW ESSAY BY DECLAN KIBERD

'Ní Dhuibhne's writing is marvellous, building layers
of impression until a complex, vital and true-false picture
of liberation is revealed.'
IRISH TIMES

Paperback

ISBN 978-0-85640-806-9
£7.99

Also available as an eBook

EPUB ISBN 978-0-85640-874-8
KINDLE ISBN 978-0-85640-875-5
£5.99

www.blackstaffpress.com

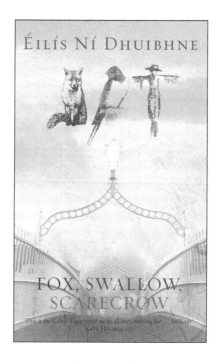

ÉILÍS NÍ DHUIBHNE

FOX, SWALLOW, SCARECROW

'This is the Celtic Tiger novel we've all been waiting for ... Brilliant'
KATE HOLMQUIST

'Thank goodness for Éilís Ní Dhuibhne and her novel –
a warm, sardonic, unflinchingly and horribly accurate
examination of the world of Irish letters.'

CARLO GÉBLER

Available as an eBook

EPUB ISBN 978-0-85640-030-8
KINDLE ISBN 978-0-85640-037-7
£6.99

www.blackstaffpress.com

.